# MOON BOUND

STEPHANIE JULIAN

# ONE

She ran, blood pounding in her ears, lungs straining, at their limit.

The rough sound of his breath pushed her to go faster. The huge trunks of pine and oak trees provided cover...just not enough, considering his sense of smell. But she was fast and she had a head start.

She'd veered off the path immediately, her bare feet cut and bleeding from the forest underbrush. She needed a place to hide, somewhere he couldn't find her.

A slim beam of pale gold sunlight caught the tip of a nearby pine. Midsummer air in the southeastern Pennsylvania forest smelled of heat, heavy and wet.

Spotting a large trunk ahead, she pulled in close, stopped to catch her breath and listen, eliminating noises one by one—birds singing in the branches, deer rustling in the brush, the sound of cars on the nearest highway at least ten miles away.

She didn't hear him. She'd run while he'd been turned, gaining the advantage. If he caught her...

No, she couldn't think about that. She had to get back to the house, had to—

The grey wolf jumped out from behind her, sharp teeth bared, awful growling echoing in her ears. Unable to help herself, she screamed, the high-pitched screech reverberating through the trees. Turning, she ran, though she knew she couldn't outrun him.

Sure enough, his jaws clamped around her ankle, careful not to break the skin but not letting go, either. Scrambling backward, she grabbed a broken branch and raised it above her head.

With a snarl, the beast released her and backed away, hazel eyes narrowed, watching her. Then he lifted his snout and howled in pain as his body began to contort. Her eyes widened as his limbs lengthened, the fur rippled and disappeared as the wolf transformed into a chestnut-haired teen boy.

"That was *cheating*, Cole." She threw the stick at her older brother, though not close enough to hit him, and followed it with his backpack. She'd stolen it from his hiding place in the woods, intending to stash it somewhere as a gag. But he'd caught her and the chase had been on. "You're not allowed to change. That's not fair."

Panting as he pulled on his jeans, the lanky seventeen-year-old stood, stretching the kinks out of his back.

"And you know Dad'll tell you everything's fair in love and war, brat." Cole smiled the smart-ass grin that never failed to get him out of trouble. "You didn't know I was there, did you?"

She hadn't, but she wasn't about to admit it. She stuck out her tongue at him instead. "And Dad'll tell you not to use me as prey."

Cole snorted. "Oh, come on. You're almost fifteen. It's not like you don't know how to take care of yourself."

With a huff, she turned away to walk back to the house. "Then why do you and Cal still treat me like a kid?"

" 'Cause we're your older brothers. That's what we're supposed to do." He fell into step beside her. "You'll have your change soon, brat. Girls usually have their first change before they're fifteen. Soon, you'll be—"

Cole cut off and Bella turned to find her brother frozen, hazel eyes wide, nostrils flared as he scented the air. "Cole? What's wrong?"

He lifted a hand to silence her and his eyes narrowed. "Gunsmoke. Blood."

It wasn't hunting season. Goosebumps broke out over her skin. "Where?"

"*Shit*. Home."

Cole took off like a shot, Bella on his heels, fear close behind.

Her brother pulled ahead and lost her in seconds. She ran flat out, concentrating on breathing as she tried to catch up to Cole. A half mile from the house, she heard her brother cry out, something in his voice she'd never heard before—fear.

She ran faster.

She'd almost caught up to Cole when she saw a flash of tanned skin through the trees.

"Cole. Bella. Stop!"

Her oldest brother, Cal, leaped out of the bushes in front of her and grabbed her around the waist, taking her off her feet. Cole stopped and turned frightened eyes on their brother.

"Take Bella into the forest and hide," Cal snapped at Cole. "I'll go to the house."

"Where's Mom and Dad?" she asked.

Cal shook his head, not meeting her gaze. "Take her, hide her." He growled the words. "Now. Right now."

She didn't understand. Why did Cal want her to hide? Where were her parents?

"Let me go, Cal." She started to struggle, but she couldn't break away from his strong arms. With a snarl, Cole grabbed her, threw her over his shoulder and took off.

"No! Cole, let go! What's going on?"

"Quiet!" was all Cole said, his tone a nearly silent hiss, dread pouring from him in waves. She shut up and held on.

He ran flat out and she tried not to let her stomach revolt from hanging upside down as she thumped along on his shoulder.

She didn't know how long they ran, but when he stopped, gasping for air, she saw the mound of the cold cellar hidden in the deep woods. He practically threw her on the ground then fell to tear at the leaves and brush hiding the door.

Sensing Cole's fear and urgency, terror began to build in her chest, nearly choking her.

"What's happening?" She tried to keep the whimper out of her voice but didn't succeed.

Cole wouldn't look at her, just shook his head. "I'm not sure."

"Are you going to the house?"

"Yes."

"Why can't I come with you?"

Cole shook his head again and this time he did meet her eyes. "You need to stay here. Don't leave until one of us comes for you."

She could barely force the words out of her mouth. "What if no one comes?"

"Someone will come." With a grunt, he pulled the old wooden door away to reveal the high-tech steel beneath. Keying in the access code, he flipped the hatch open.

She could barely breathe out the words. "Don't leave me, Cole."

"I have to. Cal needs me."

No way was she going in that dark hole by herself. "Then take me with—"

Cole slashed a hand through the air. "You can't protect

yourself yet. We can't look out for you and deal with...whatever's going on. Get in, Bella. Now."

Her teenage brother's face hardened and she had a glimpse of the man he'd become.

She went into the shelter.

---

BELLA SAT on the cool earth floor, the lantern in the corner providing enough light to see the entire space, which wasn't much more than three solid concrete walls and ceiling, the dirt floor and that cold steel door.

The batteries in the clock on the wall had corroded so she had no idea what time it was. She had enough fresh batteries for the lantern to last a few days, but she wouldn't wait that long. She *couldn't* wait that long.

She had to get out of here. Soon. Her skin tingled, like bugs had crawled under it, and her stomach hurt, though she didn't feel sick. She realized she was panting and took a deep breath—in through her nose and out through her mouth like her dad had taught her. She couldn't afford to let the fear to overtake her.

But, Blessed Goddess, her skin *itched*.

She tried to keep her mind off what was going on outside by singing songs, playing tic-tac-toe on the floor.

But after what seemed like forever, she settled into a corner, arms wrapped around her legs, and watched the door for any sign of movement, ears straining for the slightest sound.

She willed the door to open, prayed to the Great Goddess Uni for her mom to step through and wrap her in her arms, to tell her everything was okay.

Nothing happened.

What was going on out there?

The first intense pain took her by surprise, making her legs twitch as if she'd been hit by an electric shock. She screamed and grabbed her calves, felt the muscles contort like rubber bands being manipulated by a two-year-old.

*No, no, no. Goddess, please, not now.*

The second agonizing jolt made it perfectly clear the Goddess wasn't going to answer her prayer.

It wasn't supposed to happen like this. Alone. Afraid. Her mother was supposed to be here, helping her through this first time. Her dad needed to teach her how to run on four legs.

She howled, the sound a guttural cry of agony as her shoulders and backbone began their transformation. Cartilage twisted and bones reshaped, making her body hunch.

Now her stomach began to heave as the change took her to all fours in the dirt. Brown fur began to sprout from her skin, an agonizing itch she couldn't scratch. Her clothes shredded as her body reformed, seams bursting and buttons flying.

Terror wanted to consume her but she knew she had to keep it under control. She was all alone. If something went wrong—

No, she couldn't think about that. Pushing those thoughts to the back of her mind, she concentrated instead on riding out the pain, on not letting it overpower her. She was hyperventilating and she knew it, so she made an effort to rein it in, taking long, deep breaths even as the bones in her face reconfigured in terrifying ways.

*No, not terrifying. Get a grip, Arabella. You've seen your family do this a hundred times.*

She clung to the thought like it was a lifeline and she was drowning as her ribs restructured and the joints in her arms bent backwards.

She had no sense of time as her body made its first change, just that the agony never seemed to end.

Until finally, it did.

For several minutes, she lay on the ground, just breathing.

When she thought she'd be able to stand, she rose on her paws, unsteady in her new form. Her joints ached, her bones hurt— her snout, especially.

She wanted her mother. Whining, she made her way to the door, stumbling on wobbly legs. She sniffed the air around the door, her sense of smell ten times more powerful in this form than in her human body.

She caught Cole's scent, Cal's, and, beyond that, her parents. She began to claw at the door, though it hurt her still-tender paws. She had to get out. She was trapped in here and she couldn't stand— No, the wolf couldn't stand it. Cover was good but not without an exit, an escape.

Suddenly, she caught a scent she didn't recognize, a human. But not human. Someone with power, though it was different from hers. It came from within, instead of being drawn from nature.

He was running, fast, straight for her, until he was right outside. Backing into the corner farthest from the door, she bared her teeth, trying to look fearsome though she shook like a leaf in the wind.

It seemed to take forever for the door to open and when it did, she growled, surprised that she still sounded vaguely like herself.

She didn't expect a boy to open the door, a dark-haired teenager who looked to be Cole's age.

He drew in a deep breath at the sight of her and froze, though she didn't smell fear. Confusion, doubt, then shocked realization crossed his expression and he slowly lowered himself onto his knees, one hand outstretched.

"Arabella, I'm Steven Castiglione. I'm here to help. You have to come with me now."

She growled again. Who was this boy to tell her what she

had to do? Cole had said he would come for her. Or Cal or her parents. She wasn't going anywhere with this stranger.

As if he'd read her mind, Steven grimaced and his eyes shadowed. "Your parents can't come for you, Arabella. You must come with me. I won't hurt you."

He backed away until he stood outside the shelter, far enough away from the door that she had enough room to escape. Sniffing, she didn't smell anyone else. He'd come alone.

She growled, unable to speak in this form. She needed to speak, needed to ask questions. But how was she supposed to change back?

She tried to think even as she snapped at the boy, who continued to talk to her. What had her mom told her when she'd asked how you changed back? How had she explained it?

*Concentrate on reshaping the body, on calling back the pelt and the snout and the paws.*

Blessed Goddess, she didn't know if she could do this, not with the uncertainty and the fear and the realization that something was very wrong.

No. No, she could do this. She *had* to do this.

Pushing everything out of her mind, she found the strength of will to call back the animal, to conquer nature and return to human form. It wasn't as painful this way. Her bones and muscles knew the wolf was only a temporary state, that this was her true form.

It took her longer than it should have, but it would get easier. Her mom had told her that, too.

When she recovered, drained and naked on the ground that had absorbed her energy back into it, she raised her head to find the boy standing with his back to her.

When he turned and moved toward her, his expression held an overwhelming sadness that chilled her to the bone. He towered over her, his too-long hair shadowing a lean face. Then he pulled his t-shirt over his head and kneeled beside her. He helped her sit, helped her into his shirt, averting his eyes as if embarrassed by her nudity.

*Must not be* versipellis.

The random thought flitted through her mind. He didn't smell like one, either, though his blood carried *arus*, the magic inherent in all descendents of the Etruscan magical races.

"I'm sorry, Arabella, but we have to go."

She shook her head. "Where's my mom and dad?"

His mouth firmed but he looked her straight in the eyes. "They can't help you now. You have to come with me."

No. She refused to hear what he wasn't saying. With a burst of strength, she broke away from the startled teen and ran out the door.

Through the forest, her legs still wobbly, her stomach knotted tight in fear, she ran toward the house. She could smell blood and, though it made her want to curl into a tight little ball and cry, she forced herself to run faster.

Steven followed, but she outdistanced him in seconds, fear giving her wings. Vaguely, she felt some power call to her, something that wanted her to slow, to calm, to wait.

She was too far gone to wait. She barely felt the underbrush tear at her legs as she raced home.

It didn't take her long to reach the house by the edge of the woods. An unfamiliar, battered Jeep sat in the dirt driveway.

Her heart leapt to see her brother sitting on its tailgate, head in his hands.

"Cole!"

Her scream made him lift his head and she saw tears streaming down his face.

"Are you okay?" She skidded to a stop by his side and threw her arms around his shoulders. "What's going on? Where's Mom and Dad?"

Cole's arms wrapped around her waist and crushed her against him, as if he needed the comfort.

And that terrified her.

"Cole?"

"I'm sorry, Bella. I'm so sorry. I couldn't help...they were already gone."

That's when she saw them. Or rather, their bodies.

Cal, her mother, her father. Lying next to the house while a stranger stood over them, hands outstretched, chanting.

"No!"

She tore away from Cole and ran for them, for her mom, but another pair of arms came around her from behind and lifted her off her feet.

Kicking and crying, she fought to get away.

Steven held her, crooning something she didn't fully understand in her ear. The words helped to calm her but the grief continued to build.

"Let her go, Steven. It's alright."

"Dad, I don't think—"

"She needs to see. Come here, Arabella."

The man who'd been standing over her parents and brother stood and held out his hand. She ignored him and ran for her family, dropping to her knees beside them.

Cal had a wound on his chest. Mom did, too. There was a blanket over her dad's face. Instinctively, she reached for it, but the man who'd called to her grabbed her hand.

She turned. He looked somewhat like the boy, though he was older and his dark hair was laced with gray.

"You don't want to do that." The man's voice held a gentle note despite his hard expression. "They shot him first. They had to, or he could have beaten them. Your mother and brother fought well, but the cowards shot them both in the back."

Her chest hurt so bad, she didn't know if she could breathe. Gone. Her parents were gone. And Cal, too.

She sobbed, laying her head on her mom's stomach and cried even harder at the stillness of the body.

———

STEVEN WATCHED the girl pour out her agony with her tears, his own sense of failure weighing on his shoulders.

They'd been too late. His dad, a legendary Etruscan *grigorio* with magical powers to rival the gods, had gotten the call only an hour ago that the *lucani* royal family was under attack. They'd raced up here from Chester County but the four *Malandante* assassins had killed Cole and Bella's parents and older brother before his dad had killed them.

In one swoop, the *Mal* had killed the king and queen of the Etruscan *lucani* and their oldest heir. As one of the last royal *versipelli* families in the world, their deaths would rock the foundation of the magical Etruscan society in America.

The question was, why now? The *lucani* hadn't made any aggressive moves on the *Mal* in years. More like centuries. The Luporeales had been more interested in keeping the *lucani* from splintering into factions.

Why the hell had the *Mal* killed them?

And broken this girl's heart?

After a while, Arabella's sobs finally faded but her expression was so desolate, his heart hurt for her. The boy, Cole, was just as devastated. His dad was talking to Cole now, his voice strong and solid as Cole cried too.

Leaving Steven with Arabella.

Kneeling next to the girl, remembering the absolute sorrow he'd felt when his mom had died, he laid his hand on her shoulder.

After several minutes, she finally calmed enough to look up at him, her pretty face red and blotchy. He wanted to take away all her fear, all her sorrow. He wanted to make this better.

He knew he couldn't.

"We need to go." He held out his hand and watched as she stared at it for several seconds. Finally, she took it and let him draw her to her feet. Then he picked her up in his arms and held her against his chest. She couldn't weigh more than eighty pounds.

"We can't leave them." Her voice, barely a whisper, reverberated against his chest.

"We won't." He kept his voice soft, not wanting to make her cry again. "We'll bury them first."

Her lower lip trembled and she bit into it until she drew blood. "Where are we going? Where's Cole?"

"Cole's right here. He's coming with us, too. You'll live with us now. I'll take care of you, Arabella."

# TWO

*Present Day*

Bella stared at the envelope in her hand, chest tight as she traced his name with her finger.

Would he come? Hell, would he even open the damn thing when he realized it was from her?

Damn him to the depths of Aitás and the not-so-loving embrace of a *tukhulkha* demon. She was *so* sick of this situation.

Her nose wrinkled and she sighed. Okay, maybe the demon was a little much. She didn't want him injured. At least, not permanently.

She needed him. And he needed her.

Last week had proved it.

The blasted man either didn't have a clue what was going on in his narrow little world or he didn't care and was lost to her forever.

Sudden, agonizing pain burned in her chest, like acid on skin. Her lungs contracted and tears gathered in her eyes.

*Damn him.*

He'd been gone three years. Three, torturous years and she'd had enough.

He would come back.

Whether he wanted to or not.

---

I NEED YOU. *Please come.*

The note wasn't signed but Steven Carter would recognize that handwriting anywhere.

He didn't know if he was more shocked by the letter's arrival or by Bella's use of the word "please."

Then shock gave way to something else, something dark and forbidden. Something he'd worked hard to eradicate from his life these past three years.

Fierce, hot desire.

His body wanted to wallow in it, to let it rise up and devour him whole. He wanted to go to her, run to her and—

*And what? What has changed?*

Not a damn thing.

With an effort, Steven submerged those feelings and the fierce rush of anger that came with them. He couldn't afford the emotion.

Rising, he tossed the note on the desk and walked to the wall of windows overlooking Tampa Bay. Strong summer sunshine beat on the glass but behind it, here on the top floor, he was cool.

He'd worked hard the past three years to get here, to this office. To forget that the name his coworkers called him was as much a cover as the expensive clothes he wore. To forget the life he'd left behind. To forget her.

The contract on his desk, a will for one of the richest men in the state, showed just how far he'd come.

Garrison Laveau trusted Steven to write a will that would screw his family six ways to Sunday. Laveau was a twisted son-of-a-bitch with more power and money than any man should have. And he'd chosen Steven to do his dirty work.

Bella had chosen him once. From the moment they'd met, eleven years ago, they'd been inseparable.

Until it had all fallen apart three years ago.

Why had she contacted him now?

"Steven."

The woman's voice caught him off guard and he took a brief second to compose his expression before he turned to face Tiffani Jones.

The dark wood of the door trim framed her blonde beauty perfectly, her aristocratic features the very definition of haughty. Smart, spoiled and supremely self-absorbed, Tiff wanted for nothing and what she couldn't get for herself, her father— Steven's mentor and a senior partner at Case and Jones —gave her.

Unfortunately, she'd set her sights on Steven.

He'd tried to disabuse her of the notion but she clung to the thought like a terrier with a bone.

He didn't have to force a smile with that thought rolling around his head. Good thing she couldn't read his mind. "Hello, Tiffani. What's up?"

She waved a piece of paper in his direction. "The museum gala is next Friday. We need to RSVP today."

He stifled a sigh at her possessive tone and forced an appropriately apologetic smile. "I'd love to but I've got too much on my plate at the moment. And I may have to take a trip."

*May* being the operative word.

Tiff pouted full lips, designed by the best plastic surgeon money could buy. Steven couldn't help compare them to another woman's more beautiful mouth. Bella never pouted. She snarled or beamed, scowled or grinned. Nothing as tame as a pout.

Damn, now he had Bella on the brain. And that was dangerous.

"Then dinner tonight." Tiff's eyebrows lifted. "Daddy said I should bring you along and not take no for an answer."

And that, he knew, was a royal command. Still...

He glanced at the note on his desk. What was he going to do?

"Steven? Tonight? What time should I expect you?"

He looked into Tiff's contact-enhanced blue eyes, saw her knowledge that she had him by the balls and liked it.

*Fuck. That.*

His chin lifted. "I'm afraid I have to decline. I'm taking a few days off. I've got business in Pennsylvania. I'll be back Tuesday."

Tiff's lips parted in shock and Steven had a short-lived victory that quickly turned to realization of what he'd agreed to.

He was going home, which had more to do with where *she* was than a geographical area.

Tiff recovered quickly, a shrewd look in her eyes. "I thought your dad died a few years ago."

"He did." Three years and three months ago to be exact. One more loss. "One of my dad's wards needs...help."

"I'm sure it can wait until tomorrow."

The arrogance in Tiff's voice put his back up and he had to rein in the urge to use just a tiny bit of power and redirect her misguided affections. But that would be like a reformed crack addict thinking he could have just one more fix.

Power was dangerous. Magic, off limits.

And Bella...forbidden.

Still, he couldn't ignore her plea. She never asked. She always demanded.

This was different. Something was wrong.

Steven looked Tiffani in the eyes again and smiled, pouring

on the charm he'd become known for instead of the power he fought back every day. "Ask your father if dinner when I get back could be arranged. I'll see you when I return."

---

REMO PAGANELLI STARED out the window of his home in The Majestic on Central Park West.

Central Park was a sea of green at the moment but not for long. Fall was nearly here and the leaves would turn brown and blow away like so much dirt.

Good thing he'd never have to worry about shriveling up and dying like those leaves. His father had taken care of that little problem with mortality five hundred years ago.

And all it'd cost was the death of Fabrizio Paganelli's beloved youngest son, Christo.

Who'd been a complete waste of space as far as Remo was concerned.

Still, Christo's death had been Remo's gain so Remo figured he should be thankful to his little brother for dying of cancer and throwing their father into a black pit of despair.

Who would've thought their father, a member of the *Malandante*, an ancient and powerful cult of Etruscan magic users, would have been able to convince Veive, the Etruscan God of Revenge, to lay a curse on the heads of the *streghe*, Etruscan witches who'd failed to save his son?

And who could have expected Fabrizio to screw it up so wonderfully and not only curse the *streghe* to everlasting life but have that curse rebound on his three remaining sons?

That had just been pure good luck.

Staring out on the expanse of his adopted hometown, most of which he could see from these windows, Remo spared a moment to wonder at the whereabouts of his spineless younger brothers, Dario and Parente. Immortality had been wasted on them. They'd whined and bitched and wrung their hands like women, crying about being taken out of the natural order of life.

Not Remo. Only he'd been smart enough to see the beauty and advantage of eternity. He'd embraced it, thrived on it.

Never wanted it to end.

Dario... Remo sneered thinking about his youngest remaining brother. For centuries Dario had hunted the *streghe*, believing that when he'd burned all of their bodies to ash, the curse would be broken.

In five-hundred years, the fool had only managed to kill three of the thirteen women.

Remo shook his head. Christ, how inept did you have to be to manage to kill only three women in *five hundred* years?

Damn good thing Dario would never come to him for a job. Even though they were family, Remo didn't need another screw-up on his staff. He had enough of those already.

What he didn't have was powerful magic.

Parente had inherited the lion's share of their father's gift, leaving only crumbs for Remo and Dario.

How the hell was he supposed to become a god among men if he didn't have the power to back it up?

For five hundred years, Remo had built an empire. Five hundred years to amass a fortune, manipulate world leaders, gather information. Five hundred years leading the *Malandante* from behind the scenes.

But what good was all that if he was unable to wield true power himself?

Remo felt his *arus* rise, like warm cognac flowing through his body. Lifting his fingers, he directed a stream of power down into the street below.

And smiled when a taxi crashed into the Benz in front of it. The driver of the Benz jumped out of the car, arms waving, red-faced. The taxi driver barely paid him any attention as he reached for his phone.

Damn, no blood.

That was the problem. He wanted blood.

He wanted the power to control the elements. He knew only one man who could.

And Remo had decided he wanted that power. He was sick of waiting for the man to agree to work for him.

He would take what he wanted.

Even if that meant he had to enlist the aid of a real god.

———

STEVEN'S CELL rang as he tossed clothes in a duffel bag, enough for the weekend.

The digital display read Private Caller. He answered on the off-chance it was her.

"Bella?"

"Where the hell is she?"

Steven knew that deep growl, though they hadn't spoken for three years. "Cole! *Dio*, Cole—"

"Where is she? Is she with you? You bastard, you promised you'd stay away from her."

Pain slashed into his chest like sharp claws but he kept his voice steady. "She's not here."

There was a pause and Steven heard the man he loved like a brother take a deep breath, trying to control the temper that could overwhelm him if he wasn't careful. And Cole had learned to be very careful.

"Then where the hell is she?" Cole spoke each word carefully, as if they were trying to get away from him.

Shit, Cole didn't know where she was either.

*Not good.*

When he'd first read the note, his immediate reaction had been to call his best friend. For eight years after the death of Cole's parents, they'd shared a room, their secrets, their lives. And then everything had gone to shit.

*Three fucking years.*

Anger started to creep into his spine. "I got a note in the mail today. 'I need you. Please come.' What the hell does that mean? What's going on?"

Cole sighed and Steven heard a wealth of frustration in the sound. "*Baciami il culo.* I don't know. She dropped off the radar a week ago and I haven't heard from her since. I've tried to call her but I haven't been able to get through to her cell and if she's at the house, she's not answering the phone. You were my last call."

Hurt sideswiped him even as fear took a bite out of his lungs. Three years ago, he would've been the first person Cole called.

Of course, he hadn't picked up the phone to call Cole in all that time either, so...

*Focus. No time for past bullshit now.* "What do you mean, she disappeared?"

"I mean, she hasn't called and I haven't been able to reach her. Why the *hell* would she get in touch with you? *I'm* her brother."

Steven's back straightened at Cole's tone. "I know that. You never let me forget."

Cole sighed again. "Shit. *Shit.* That's not— *Fuck.* Where the *hell* is she, Steven?"

Fear had started to seep into Cole's voice and Steven tried not to let it crank up his own anxiety. They'd find her. They had to. "The note didn't say where she was, just that she needed me. I'm assuming she's at your parents' house because she knows that's the first place I'd look for her. I'm getting ready to go there now."

*Does she still need me?*

And if she did, what would he do about it? What *could* he do about it? Nothing had changed.

"Why the hell did she send for you and not me?" Cole asked.

*Good question.* "Are you two fighting again?"

Cole huffed. "We're always fighting about something, you know that. We talked two weeks ago. She was in Philly, getting ready to go to work. She didn't mention anything out of the ordinary. We don't talk as much as we used to so I only called her three days ago and haven't been able to reach her." Cole took an unsteady breath. "What if the *Mal* caught up with her? What if—"

"Jesus, Cole. Chill. You sound like a fucking old woman. Pull it together." There would be time to fall apart later. "The letter was postmarked two day ago."

"Two days." Now Steven heard anger in Cole's voice. The guy's mood swings were almost as bad as his had been. "*Vaffan-culo.* I'm gonna strangle her. Steven, I can't lose—"

"No. Just shut up." He didn't want to hear the words, didn't need a reminder of the past. And he knew telling Cole to do anything usually made the man do the exact opposite. "You know Bella. She's probably gotten out of whatever fix she got herself into but I booked a flight out tonight. It leaves in two hours. I should be at the house by one a.m. Where are you?"

Cole took a few seconds to answer. "New Orleans. I'll take the next flight out."

"What are you doing in New Orleans?"

Cole paused again. "*Congress.*"

Shit. Something was going down.

As king of the *lucani*, the position he'd inherited when his father and older brother had been killed, Cole had never held *congress*, a meeting of the leaders of the American *versipelli*. It was too dangerous for them all to be in the same place at the same time.

Why now?

*No. Not my business. Not anymore.*

"Can you take the time?" he asked Cole.

"No. *Congress* is in less than a week and it's *fucking* hard to hide five-hundred *fucking* shapeshifters in this *fucking* city!"

Steven had to laugh. In the world he lived in now, it was a ludicrous statement. Sometimes he wondered—

No. He couldn't afford to think about what could have been. "I'll find her, Cole."

What the hell he'd do with her afterward was something different. Because nothing had changed.

Cole sighed. "Steven..."

There it was again, that tone in Cole's voice. The one that made pain ooze from every pore of Steven's body.

*Vaffanculo*, he missed Cole. And Bella.

Cole sighed again. "I thought you two weren't talking. Hell, I specifically told you *not* to talk to her."

Yeah, he had. And Steven had listened.

*Idiot.*

"When was the last time I listened to you?"

Cole's snort sounded slightly amused. "Yeah, fuck you, *ceffo*. You never listen to me. Just... Shit, don't screw with her head. Find her, bring her to me. She needs to be with family."

That dig cut him off at the balls. "I *am* family."

The silence from the other end of the phone was deafening. "I know that. Damn it, Steven. Don't..." Cole sighed one more time. In resignation. "Just find her. And put her on the first fucking plane down here. And Steven...you be on that damn plane, too."

FOUR HOURS after he talked to Cole, Steven walked out of Philadelphia International Airport, picked up a rental car and headed northwest.

Rush-hour traffic on the Schuylkill Expressway hadn't changed since he'd been here years ago. The bumper-to-bumper crawl made it difficult for him to concentrate on anything but driving.

Which was probably a good thing because if he had too much time to think about what he was doing, he might turn tail and run.

Damn it, he didn't have a tail.

But Bella did. Occasionally.

She was a beautiful wolf, her coat sleek and silver, nothing as ordinary as grey.

Gods be damned, he hadn't seen her in three years. What the hell would he say—

*Idiot. You sound like you're going on a first date.*

This was no date.

By the time he reached the Pennsylvania Turnpike, where finally he could put his foot to the floor and cover some miles, his temples pounded and his stomach roiled.

He needed to stop and get some food and something for his headache before he drove to the Luporeale family house in northern Berks County. Bella and Cole owned the property where they'd grown up...before moving in with him and his father in Chester County after the death of their parents and brother. But the place held too many memories for her to stay there for any length of time.

Hell, maybe she wasn't even there.

Instead of spending another forty minutes in the car— after the two and a half hours on the plane and now the nearly two hours behind the wheel—he decided to stop in Reading first.

If Bella was in the area, Harry would know. Of course, the guy might refuse to talk to him.

By the time he pulled up outside The Spyder Club, it was nearly midnight and his headache threatened to make his eyes bleed.

He parked down the street from the club then sat in the car for a few seconds, staring at the once-grand building that housed one of the best-kept secrets in the state.

Built in the early 1800s, the three-story brick structure presented itself to the *eteri* world as a strip club. What the human world didn't know— Well, it was probably better they never found out.

When he finally forced himself out of the car and walked to the door, he didn't recognize the suspicious bouncer. The guy made no bones about finding his scent disturbing but waved him through into the dark, cool hall when Steven told him he was there to talk to Harry.

The temperature drop might've helped his headache if not for the throbbing music. His eyes nearly popped out of his head with pain.

And the power...

He swallowed hard. Hell, this better not take long. The *arus* in his blood simmered, threatening his hard-won control. And his gut clenched as he sensed something else.

Damn it. Bella was *here*. He felt her.

Anger, hot and biting, rose from his gut into his throat. She knew, better than anyone, why he shouldn't be here. She also knew him well enough to know he'd check here for her.

He stalked into the main room, ready to rip someone's head off. Scaninng the dingy surroundings, he saw a dozen or so *eteri* at tables on the floor, eyes glued to the lone stripper working a pole on the catwalk.

The blonde wore a black leather thong and nothing else and had to be at least six foot.

Definitely not Bella.

At the long bar to the left of the stage, Steven nodded to the young guy behind the bar, his ears curiously pointed beneath long dark hair. The guy stared at him, a sneer on his lips and a hint of fear in his eyes.

Steven didn't bother to acknowledge either. "Where's Harry?"

"In the back. What do you want, *stregone?*"

Steven didn't bother to correct him. The designation was mostly correct. He was a witch. It just didn't have any bearing on his life now.

"Nothing you can help me with. Just get Harry."

The *linchetto*—with those ears, he was definitely an Etruscan night elf—smirked. "Maybe you want to rethink the 'tude, buddy, or Harry'll have your balls for a snack."

Steven opened his mouth to tell the kid where he could stick his threats but a section of the wall behind the bar opened and Harry walked out.

Short, dark-haired and sharp-featured, Harry had owned this club longer than anyone could remember. No one knew his last name. Or his age. He wasn't *versipellis* of any flavor. And he wasn't *stregone*, although he was of Etruscan descent. He admitted to that much. No one bothered to ask him any other questions, because he wouldn't answer.

Harry didn't seem surprised to see him, even though Steven had broken his ties with his old life years ago. Still, he shook his head and waved Steven through. "In the back."

Steven followed Harry into an office not much bigger than a

walk-in closet. Steven didn't bother to sit on one of the two wood chairs. He wouldn't be here that long. Harry sat on the edge of the battered wooden desk and looked him straight in the eyes.

"Sorry to hear about your father. He was a good man."

Grief sideswiped Steven, the pain so unexpected and sharp, he had to breathe through it. Damn Harry for going directly for the jugular.

He managed to nod in acknowledgement but he'd been knocked sideways by the true respect in the other man's voice.

"So," Harry continued, "what'dya want?"

Steven took a breath, pushing the pain aside. "I'm looking for Arabella."

Harry nodded. "Heard you're down in Florida now. Working for a firm called Case and Jones."

Why the hell would Harry know that? Or care? "Arabella. Is she here?"

Harry just stared. "Yeah, she is, Castiglione. Or should I call you Carter?"

His blood pressure started to rise. "Either is fine. She sent for me."

Harry sat silently for several seconds before jerking his head at the wall behind him. "It's full. Just a warning." Then he turned and pushed on the back wall until it slid away. "Try not to get yourself killed, *stregone*."

A long hall appeared, the floor dirt, the walls stone. The throb emanating from the end of the hall reminded Steven of large machinery. The engines of hell.

*Idiot. You know what's down there.*

Yeah, he did. Bella.

His feet started moving, carrying him down the long hall even as his brain kept trying to talk him out this.

By the time he reached the door at the other end, the

increasing noise level had inflamed his formerly receding headache. His eyes narrowed against the pain.

*Christ.* Emo-pop. And it sounded like the band had a few extra players tonight.

Forcing his eyes open, he pushed through the door into the gloom of DownBelow.

Carved into the bedrock beneath Harry's club and several other buildings on the block, the amphitheater had been here for centuries. And had remained secret just as long.

Dim light illuminated the space from above, though there were no visible light fixtures in the entire space. Hell, there were no visible means of electricity at all.

Any *eteri* who got into DownBelow wouldn't think twice about that fact. Then again, no *eteri* were allowed into DownBelow. You had to have Etruscan blood to gain entrance. Which meant the *Mal* could get in, as well, though violence was forbidden. Harry's domain was a sanctuary. No fighting. No weapons. No use of magic for violent purposes.

Wards covered every centimeter of the place, blocking any sound from leaking beyond the perimeter.

Free of cigarette smoke, the air instead was glazed with magical power that fueled the wards. Gemma, the band's *strega*, had already woven the basis of what would be one hell of a powerful euphoria spell.

Christ, this was going to be pure torture.

His *arus* rose again, dark and seductive, followed by the almost overpowering urge to let it consume him. To burn him into infinity and forever rip him from the world in which he'd been raised.

Then sanity returned.

He glanced at Harry, who'd followed behind. The other man stared back, sympathy in his dark eyes.

Steven's back stiffened. He didn't want sympathy. Didn't need it. And fuck Harry for thinking he did.

He walked into the steamy mix of the crowded club, a prayer to the Great Mother Goddess for the strength to continue on his lips.

---

BELLA SENSED A DOOR OPENING, felt the fine hair on her nape rise.

*Steven.* He was here.

Her heart kicked into a painful rhythm. After three long years, it took everything she had not to run to him and leap into his arms. She wasn't sure he'd still catch her.

He was probably pissed that she'd sent him a deliberately vague note and lured him out of hiding in Florida.

Dancing in a dark corner of the room with a group of local *lucani*, friends she hadn't seen in years, Bella slid a glance over her shoulder and found him searching the room with his eyes only. The dark hid more than the runes carved into the walls from that navy-blue gaze she knew so well. If he wouldn't use his magic, he'd never find her if she didn't want to be found.

Steven was nothing if not stubborn. But he was leaving himself open to attack. Already, a few of the younger males, foolish boys who couldn't sense the power he submerged so well, eyed him like a side of beef.

Of course, the women did, too, but for completely different reasons.

The long-haired teen who'd come to her rescue a decade ago had matured into a man with a fondness for custom-made Italian suits and hundred-dollar haircuts.

The look fit.

*Damn him.*

But so did worn jeans that molded strong thighs and t-shirts that clung to the taut muscles of his chest. For years, that had been his wardrobe. No longer.

While the other club patrons were practically naked, what little clothing they wore black to better absorb the magic, Steven stood out in more ways than being overdressed. He was taller than almost everyone else and, if challenged, he wouldn't be able to defend himself from attack. At least, not with the claws the *versipelli* here could grow.

Of course, if he used his *arus*... He could kill them all.

But he wouldn't. She knew that.

Damn him, he needed her, belonged with her, and the Blessed Goddess spite him if he didn't finally admit it. She was sick of waiting.

Bella started around the room, keeping close to the wall as she circled toward him. He knew she was here. His eyes narrowed to slits and his fists clenched at his side. But she kept one step ahead of his searching gaze.

The band had kicked into high gear, Dilby's clear vocals overlaying Caeles' shredding guitar in a dead-on version of Bullet For My Valentine's "Tears Don't Fall." The raw emotion of the song raked nails down her spine.

Her body still moving to the beat of the music, she drew in a deep breath and picked out his scent, the mix of musk and male and magic that was uniquely Steven. It took her back, back to when he'd been her world. Back to when she'd believed he loved her enough to stay with her forever. No matter what.

A man grabbed her around the waist and ground her hips into his, moving in a primal rhythm that elevated her blood pressure. The stranger was handsome, young and strong, everything she should want. She disentangled herself from him without a second thought and continued.

Steven's eyes narrowed even more as she slipped behind

him, several people still between them. Maybe he hadn't submerged all his abilities, after all.

Maybe there was a chance—

Kerri Donato approached him, white-blond hair to her waist, wearing black leather shorts and a shredded white tank top that barely covered pendulous breasts. She oozed sexuality in an invitation Steven couldn't miss. Or ignore.

The woman rubbed herself against him, her front to his back. He didn't move. He knew better. When Kerri slinked around to his front, he looked down at her, his gaze taking in all she wanted him to see. His nostrils flared and his gaze arrowed down between her breasts. He was a man, after all.

Then he dismissed her with a slight shake of his head.

Kerri's expression turned incredulous as Bella's own smile widened. The other woman wasn't used to being brushed off. When Steven continued his search for her, Kerri huffed off, drawing just enough unwanted attention to Steven that Bella began to get concerned.

Someone would realize soon enough what he was. Then they would tear him to shreds.

*Stupid Arabella. Still thinking only of yourself. Again.*

Still behind him, she moved to within inches, inhaling his scent and letting it seep through her body, into her chest, where he lived in her heart. Blessed Goddess, she'd missed him.

Steven tensed a split second before she whispered in his ear.

"You're in danger."

He didn't turn, didn't acknowledge her at all, except for the clenching of his hands at his sides.

"The only danger I'm in, you put me in, Arabella." He didn't bother to turn. He knew she would hear him.

She huffed but he was right, to a point. She had to get him out of here now. She saw Kerri jawing to her friends on the other side of the stage about the jerk who'd offended her.

"Then I supposed it's up to me to save your ass this time. Come on."

He turned and the anger in his eyes knocked her back a step. Anger directed at her. In all the years she'd known him, even the last time she'd seen him, his anger had never been directed at her. It made her heart shrink to realize just how pissed off he was.

*Your fault. All your fault.*

Turning, she headed for the door through which he'd entered, knowing he'd follow. Steven wasn't stupid. He knew if he stayed any longer, one of the men would challenge him.

Neither of them needed that. Steven wouldn't use his magic to defend himself, and she was still shaken by what had happened last week.

Instead of heading through Harry's office, Bella turned left into another hall. She didn't need light to see the way. And even though Steven couldn't see as well as she could, he should be able to follow her with his senses only. If the stubborn fool would use them.

*Serve him right if he walks into a wall.*

The brat who lived in her head, the voice she'd tried to control, to smother, for the past three years piped up. Bitchy, spoiled rotten.

That wasn't her anymore.

The brat snorted.

Bella wanted to slap her.

At the end of the hall, the metal door needed only a push on the right spot to open. They stepped into the alley behind the club, the space so narrow a car couldn't fit through.

Her nose twitched at the musty odor, but the scent of the man behind her made her thighs ache to wrap around his waist while he buried himself deep inside her. She remembered warm summer nights, making love under the stars at the Castigliones' house in

Chester County. She tilted her head to look up at the sky. Bruised and swollen clouds obscured the nearly full moon and stars.

Her skin itched, just as it had her first time. She wanted to howl. The wolf wanted out.

She had control of her change now.

She just couldn't control him.

She turned to face Steven, his gorgeous lips set in a straight line as he glared at her.

Fine, she'd break the ice.

Her back straightened and she settled her hands on her waist. "Someone tried to kidnap me last week. They wanted me to get to you."

RAGE AND FEAR fell into Steven's stomach like acid.

Rage that she'd made him come after her, forced him back to the world he'd left behind three years ago.

But the fear... The fear sunk hooks deep into his stomach.

His gaze flew over her. He didn't see any outward bruises but she wasn't lying. He knew Bella. She was spoiled, willful, uncontrollable, passionate. But a liar? It wasn't in her.

He took a deep breath, forcing down both emotions before they overwhelmed him to the point that he couldn't think. "What happened?"

She stared up at him, her brown eyes wary. She'd expected him to doubt her.

His stomach clenched with regret. What did that say about their relationship?

*What relationship?*

That clench became pain.

Her eyes narrowed as she drew in a breath. "After work Tuesday a week ago, I was walking to my car and two men nearly ran me over. They said it was an accident then they tried to get me into their car, said they'd give me a ride to the hospital. But I could smell the lie on them. I turned and ran."

She paused and his gaze narrowed. None of this remotely related to him. Yes, it sounded as if the men had tried to abduct her but...she lived in Philadelphia. It was frightening but not out of the realm of possibility in the big city.

"And how does this have anything to do with me?"

She paused and bit her lip. "Because when I doubled back, I heard them say your name."

He shook his head. "You had to be mista—"

"They worked for Charles Jones."

No. Absolutely not. He prepared to find the flaw in her reasoning. "Why do you think that?"

She sighed. "Because they called your boss after they lost me."

*No.* He shook his head again. "There is no way Charles would be connected in any way with an attempt to kidnap you. He knows nothing about you. I've never mentioned you."

She flinched. He barely caught her slight motion but he felt it like a blow to his chest. Damn it. When was he going to stop hurting her?

Then she straightened, her mouth settled in grim lines. "I know what I heard, Steven. Those men told Charles Jones that they were unable to 'detain' me."

"You must have heard wrong. Why would Charles want to kidnap you?"

"Maybe you don't know the man as well as you think."

"No—"

The door to the club opened and they both turned to look at the lanky, blond man who walked out.

"Quinn!" Bella practically squealed, drawing Steven's gaze

back to see the bright smile that had broken out on her face. "I didn't know you were in town. How are you?"

"Hey, babe." His hands on her hips, Quinn lifted Bella against him and smacked a kiss on her lips. "How's it going?"

Steven's hands clenched into fists at the easy familiarity between them while Bella's laugh made the bottom drop out of his stomach. Jealousy curled around his lungs like a vise, depriving his brain of much-needed oxygen. He wanted to pound the man for touching her. Maybe more so for making her laugh.

"Fine. I'm fine. What are you doing here?"

"Seeing a friend in town."

With another smile, Quinn set Bella on her feet and turned to Steven, his arm still around her waist, his smile disappearing.

Steven had expected Quinn to ignore him but was shocked when the man held out his hand. "Castiglione. Been a while."

Steven took his hand. "Kennett."

As Cole's *tribunus*, Quinn was second in command of the *lucani* army, which Cole led by birthright. He was one of Cole's most trusted advisors, but Steven had only met him a few times before Cole had cut Steven out of his life. And Bella's.

"So my brother sent you here to check on me, didn't he?" Bella broke the awkward silence that fell as Steven released Quinn's hand.

Quinn dismissed Steven completely when he turned to smile at Bella. "What've you gotten yourself into now, babe?" Lifting his hand, Quinn ran his fingers through her sleek brown hair. It was shorter than it had been the last time he'd seen her, exposing her neck. He wanted to cut off Quinn's hand. "Your brother called a few hours ago, asked me to check here for you." He held up one hand to stop Bella's immediate outburst. "And, since I was in the area, I figured I'd stop and say hi. Cole's worried about you, babe. You should give him a call."

Anger and something that felt a lot like betrayal burned through Steven. Damn it. He should have known Cole wouldn't let him be alone with Bella for any length of time.

Bella shook her head. "I didn't want to worry him. And I don't want this getting back to him, not now. Not with *congress* in less than a week." She paused to take a breath. "Someone tried to snatch me last week."

# THREE

There was an art to dealing with a god.

Remo dropped to one knee when Veive walked into his private office. He made sure no one saw him do it, though. Wouldn't be good to have the peons catch him in this subservient position. Might give them ideas.

"Lord of the Avenging Arrow. Welcome—"

"Yeah, whatever." The dark-haired man waved one large, tanned hand in the air, which Remo took to mean he could get off his knees. "Cut to the chase, *Mal*."

The Etruscan God of Revenge stood in the middle of Remo's multimillion-dollar square footage, a bored expression on his handsome face. But his dark gaze roamed the expansive room, taking in every piece of antique wood trim, the carved detail on the ceiling and the view of the city.

Remo had rehearsed this speech until he knew it backward and forward. He'd made sure he'd spelled out exactly what he wanted before he'd performed the summoning ritual. He'd been a little rusty. For five centuries, he hadn't needed the help of the Etruscan deities to create his empire.

Other Etruscans continued to pay homage to the gods and

goddesses in hidden temples, particularly in Reading, Pennsylvania, where much of the Etruscan race had settled when they emigrated from Italy.

The *Mal* weren't welcome there. Hell, they weren't welcome anywhere the rest of the Etruscans gathered. They were afraid of the *Mal*. And with good reason, considering the *Mal* had kicked their asses during the Purge of 1758. He'd had only been testing the waters then.

He was planning some serious fun now.

"I have a deal to offer you, Lord," he started. "One I believe you'll be interested in."

Veive didn't even bother to look at him. "I don't believe you have anything to offer me."

*Then why'd you come?*

Remo tried to bury the thought before Veive picked up on it. The deities had lost some of their powers over the millennia of their existence, but not all. So there was a good chance Veive could read his mind if he wanted too.

Still, his unspoken question remained a valid one. Why had he come?

The god turned his gaze on Remo. Pain shot through his gut, nearly taking him to his knees. Remo gritted his teeth and locked his knees. He refused to go down.

"Maybe I just like to keep up on current events, Paganelli." The god's lips lifted in a cruel twist. "Or maybe I just like to fuck with the *humans* every now and then."

The god his father had called on to curse the *streghe* five hundred years ago wanted to play with him. Well, Remo would let him have his fun. For a while.

"I request your aid." He managed to speak through his gritted teeth. "And for it, I can deliver the *lucani* king to you on a platter. If you agree to grant my request."

Veive's expression remained bored but his eyes flickered

with interest and the pain receded. For the most part. "And why would I want the *lucani* king?"

That would be a legitimate question...if Remo didn't know just how badly Veive hated Tivr, God of the Moon, who kept close ties with the *lucani*.

The Etruscans deities could hold a grudge a damn long time.

"Because it will be sure to piss off Tivr."

---

"GABE'S out of town so we have the place to ourselves."

Several blocks from the club, Quinn opened a concealed panel on the front door of a nondescript row home and entered several numbers into the state-of-the-art security system.

Bella scented magic surrounding the building. The wards were strong and the air literally moved aside when Quinn muttered the spells to let them enter.

Steven stiffened beside her and she knew he felt it, too, though he'd never admit it.

*Stubborn fool.*

Stifling a sigh, she followed Quinn through a sparse living room into a seventies' era kitchen. Waving them into chairs at the breakfast bar, he pulled coffee out of the fridge as if he owned the place. After setting up the coffeemaker, he leaned against the counter and snagged Bella's gaze.

"So, are you going to tell me what happened or do I pull rank on you?"

And he'd do it, too. Quinn might act like an easy-going guy but he had a streak of steel that made him perfect as Cole's *tribunus*.

And even though she was a princess of the Luporeale ruling

family, her title held no meaning to the legion. Only Cole's title as *legatus* did.

She took a deep breath and shot a quick glance at Steven. He hadn't said a word on the way over here. She knew he was sifting through information, trying to find the flaws. He didn't want to believe her.

Screw that. Quinn would know she wasn't lying.

"Last week, two men tried to run me down. They told me it was an accident, but they were lying. They deliberately tried to hit me then tried to get me in their car. Said they wanted to take me to the hospital which was complete bullshit. I ran. They followed but I lost them after a few blocks. When I doubled back, I heard them mention Steven's boss's name."

"Then you were mistaken." Steven's calm voice was in direct opposition to the furious look in his eyes.

That look made her stomach clench in on itself. He didn't believe her. Or...he just didn't want to believe her.

"Are you sure that's what you heard, Bella?" Quinn's sharp green gaze held hers. "Could they have known you were listening and tried to frame this guy... What's his name?"

"Charles Jones." Steven's voice sounded strangled. "He's the senior partner in the law firm I work for in Florida. Charles could have nothing to do with this."

Quinn looked at Stephen with raised eyebrows. "And you know this how?"

"Because I checked him out before I went to work for him. He has no ties to the Etruscans, no ties to the *Mal*, no magic of his own."

Quinn cocked his head, considering. "So your boss has no idea what you are?"

Steven flinched like Quinn had hit him. "No. And I don't think he'd believe me if I told him. He's a rational man."

"And we're all crazy, right?"

Quinn's tone was light, but she could tell Steven was starting to piss him off. And it took a hell of a lot to piss off Quinn.

Steven wouldn't back down. "Sometimes I'd rather believe that than the truth."

Her stomach rolled at the flat statement of fact of Steven's voice. Damn him. The man had already broken her heart once. Why was she giving him another chance?

She must have made some sound because both men turned toward her—Quinn's expression sympathetic, Steven stone-faced. But his eyes...those beautiful blue eyes burned.

"When did you become a coward, Steven?" she asked.

His gaze narrowed. Good, that barb stuck.

"I'm not a coward." His voice held a too-rational edge that went through her like nails on a chalkboard. "I'm a realist. The earth's magic is fading. The Old Gods are long gone and those who are left don't give a shit about our people."

Her hands immediately went to her hips as they assumed well-worn fighting stances. "So we should forget about our culture? Our way of life? Forget all the wonderful things we can do and become like the *eteri*? Deaf and blind to magic?"

Her anger rose, consuming her in thick heat, and she went for his most vulnerable point. "Your dad would be ashamed of you. When he died, you tied all your emotions into a neat little package and stuck them away somewhere no one could touch them."

He inhaled, eyes narrowing even more. "My father was *murdered*. And I left because I couldn't bear to lose anyone else."

Her hands flew into the air, as if she could brush aside his words. "But you did anyway! You lost us, lost *me*—"

"With good fucking reason!"

There, now he was riled. Though his hands were still

clenched at his sides, he'd started to swear and that mean he was losing his control. Good.

"Gods-be-damned, Bella—"

"How can you say that?" She poked a finger into his chest, only peripherally aware that they still had an audience. "What good reason? There is no good reason to deny your heritage. To deny me or Cole. As if you're ashamed of us. Ashamed of me."

Her voice broke on that last word and she shut her mouth with a snap. Damn it. She hadn't meant for that to slip out. She wanted to take the words back as soon as they left her mouth. She sucked her top lip between her teeth to hold back anything else. But tears still formed in the corners of her eyes.

*I will not cry. Not now. I won't give him that satisfaction.*

Dragging in a deep breath, she bit her tongue until they receded, watching with satisfaction when Steven recoiled as if she'd slapped him.

Finally, emotion. Just not the emotion she'd wanted.

*Stupid, stupid, stupid.*

"Arabella."

Quinn's calm voice slid between them, cutting off whatever Steven might have said.

With an effort, she turned to Quinn. His sympathetic expression made tears rise again but she refused to let them fall.

"I'm no mediator. I'm a soldier. If you want me to kill someone..." he slid a quick glance at Steven and bared his teeth, "I can do that. But this... I can't fix this. This is something you two have to figure it out." He rose, wrote a few numbers on the notepad in the center of the table. "Those are the codes to lock the house when you leave. Burn them when you're done. Don't bother with the wards. I'll fix them later."

Stepping between her and Steven, with his back to the other man, Quinn smiled down into her eyes. She'd never seen Quinn upset. Had never heard him raise his voice or get angry. Not once.

"If you need me, you know how to find me. I'll call Cole, let him know you're okay. I'll get him to give you an hour before he starts to bombard your cell which you damn well will turn on." He dropped a kiss on her lips, gave it a little more enthusiasm than your average goodbye kiss. Then he winked before he turned to Steven. "Hey, man. A little unwanted advice. Don't waste your time fighting. You don't have as much as you think you do."

Quinn didn't wait for Steven to reply. He walked away, closing the door behind him.

Steven never took his eyes off of her. His chest rose and fell as if he'd just run a five-minute mile but his expression had gone blank.

She didn't know what to say, what he was thinking. There had been a time when she could read his every expression. Now she wouldn't want to guess.

After several tense moments, he finally shook his head. "You think I'm ashamed of you?"

She inhaled to replace the stale air she'd been holding. "Yes. I think you're ashamed of me. You think I'd taint the perfect world you've created for yourself in Florida. Away from the world you've tried so hard to forget."

He looked away and she couldn't tell if she'd hit on the truth or angered him again.

"My world is far from perfect, Bella. How can it be when the one thing I want, I can never have."


AS BELLA'S eyes widened in shock, Steven turned and walked out the front door, not quite sure where he was going. Not caring.

He had to walk away. He couldn't stand there and continue to hurt the woman he loved. Would always love.

Could never have.

Hands in his pants pockets, he walked past neglected brownstones with boarded windows.

There had to be a reason for Bella's attempted kidnapping. A rational explanation.

One that didn't include Charles Jones.

After his dad's death and the aftermath, he'd changed his name, left behind everything that mattered to him, and moved to Florida to finish his law degree.

Charles had recruited him out of the Florida State University Law School. He'd been free with his praise of Steven's skill and even more frank about his shortcomings. And the man had been honest. Steven had used the tiniest bit of forbidden magic to make sure.

For the past three years, they'd worked side-by-side and Steven had noticed nothing out of the ordinary. Charles could be ruthless when he had to be but he was a damn good lawyer. Steven had fit into the firm as if it'd been born to it.

Had it all been a set-up?

And if it was, how would Charles know Bella was the key to controlling Steven?

*Shit.* He stopped, the urge to hit something nearly overwhelming. Then he realized where he was. Marelli's Trattoria on South Sixth Street.

This late at night, the restaurant was closed but Uni's Temple, concealed in the back of the building, was open all hours.

From the outside, the brick building looked like all the others on the block. Three stories separated by only three or four feet. In the early part of the century until the late seventies, most of the neighborhood south of Penn Street had been populated by Italian immigrants and their families.

The barbers, grocers and doctors had names like Cambria, Puccini and Damato. Holy Rosary Church at Third and Franklin served that community and every Sunday morning after church, the parishioners stopped at ATV Bakery next door for bread for Sunday dinner.

The Etruscans lived among their fellow Italians, blended into the *eteri* society. Some even attended church to keep up appearances.

Today, the landscape hadn't changed much but the demographics had. The Latin population had eclipsed the Italian, but the heart of the Etruscan religious community beat here, in the back of a century-old Italian restaurant.

The Temple of the Great Goddess Uni had an open door policy. Not only was its doors never locked to those of Etruscan descent, but anyone of Etruscan descent could enter. Including the *Mal*.

Slipping into the dark walkway to the left of the restaurant's front door, he walked to past the kitchen entrance to the very end of the building. Steven finally stopped at an iron door disguised as an emergency exit. This door would only open for an Etruscan with *arus* in his blood.

Taking the skeleton key that always hung around his neck, the one his mom had given him when he was five, he inserted it into the lock and let the wards surrounding the building sense his *arus*, though he was careful not to let it rise. In this state, he could easily lose control.

The door opened silently. Steven took a deep breath as he slid the key back into his shirt and stepped into the hallway that led to the main sanctuary. It'd been years since he'd been here. Years that seemed like centuries.

He tried to dismiss the immediate lift in his spirits when he stepped over the threshold. But he couldn't, not completely.

Like DownBelow, any *eteri* stumbling in would think he'd time traveled to ancient Rome because this truly was the domain of an ancient goddess.

The temple was open to the top of the three-story building, pure white marble walls reaching to the vaulted ceiling. Three columns on each side of a center aisle led to the wooden altar decorated with gold leaf.

Wooden benches lined the sides of the temple, leaving the floor mosaic uncovered. A skilled artist had created a Tuscan forest populated by the various members of the *Fata* and *Enu*.

A half-hided *salbinelli* chased after a winged *folletta*. A mass of tiny human-shaped *candelas* glowing like fireflies danced around a tree stump as a *linchetti* couple, their pointed ears prominently displayed, lay entwined on a moonlit patch of grass.

A pack of *lucani* howled at the bright moon while a *strega* bent over a moon bowl and her male companion held an athame in his hands. The conical hat on his head signified his status as a *netsvis*, a priest of the gods and goddesses.

That one picture, the *netsvis*, had always drawn him for some reason. Maybe because the young man resembled him. The artist had created him with the same dark hair and blue eyes, the same body shape.

Steven had known, even before his parents had told him, that there was something different about him. Something that made his parents live apart from the rest of Etruscan society. Something in the way people looked at him when they went to temple.

When his power had manifested when he turned thirteen, his parents had told him the truth of what he was. How, because of a fluke of birth, he'd been born *Mal*.

Not that his parents had accepted that. They'd taught him to submerge his power. To live without it. To bury the emotions that made it harder for him to control the power.

It'd worked.

Until he'd met Bella.

Then everything had gone to shit.

He lifted his gaze to the statue of the Mother Goddess Uni behind the altar. She looked so damn serene. And he felt all the bitter anger he thought he'd gotten rid of rise up.

Why the hell was he here? Uni had never heard his prayer before. What made him think this time...this time, maybe she'd listen, maybe she'd—

A velvet-soft snout nudged the hand hanging at his side.

In a motion as natural as breathing, he lifted his hand and ran it along her sleek pelt, beginning between the pointed ears and following the line of her spine.

"Sorry. I just...needed to walk."

She rubbed against his side, drawing his gaze away from the statue and down to her.

He'd never seen a more beautiful animal. Her silver fur sparkled and she stared up at him with brown, human eyes. She must have followed him, had probably watched over him as he walked blindly through the city. She wouldn't allow anything to happen to him.

If she'd been hurt last week...

Would he have been able to live with himself?

His hand tightened in her fur and he forced himself to let go before he hurt her.

*Don't think you can more than you already have.*

She bumped his hand again and shook her head, her jeweled collar jangling in her mouth.

"Yeah, I know. I left the rental at Harry's. We need to get it."

He bent to take the collar and leash. Bella hated those strips of leather, hated to put her control in someone else's hands. She'd only ever allowed him to put a collar on her. Not Cole, not his father, not anyone.

She'd been right to bring it. They were in a city where unleashed dogs were taken to the pound. Or, in a shifter's case, shot for its intimidating size.

He slipped the collar around her neck like he was fastening a string of pearls, stroking her soft fur at the same time.

"I guess I should be glad you're not biting my hand right about now, huh?"

He knew she never would, at least not while she wore her pelt. The bite of a *versipellis* in animal form could result in that person becoming *versipellis*. If they lived through the transformation process.

Bella cocked her head to the side and stared at him with a look so haughty, he couldn't help but smile. He left the collar loose so it wouldn't bind then clipped the leash to it.

As she led him out of the temple, Steven held the leash loosely. They walked back to the club and his car without speaking. When they reached the car, Bella hopped in the back seat and tilted her head so he could remove the collar. Then she sat on her haunches, her face turned toward the window. She would never stick her head out the window. Too pedestrian. Still, he lowered the glass so she could feel the wind on her face.

They headed north out of the city, past the overdevelopment of Muhlenberg Township and into the relative peace of Alsace Township. By the time they got to Bella's family house in Rockland Township, it was nearly three in the morning. The moon had set and tiny pinpricks of stars dotted the black velvet sky.

He turned off the main road and onto a side road that curved into gentle hills. The countryside here still held a patchwork of farms and woodland, although more housing developments encroached every year.

Cole and Bella owned nearly a thousand acres out here, the deeds to the property distributed between various dummy corporations his father had set up. They leased some of the outlying land to area farmers, but most of it remained forest. As it had since Bella's grandfather had brought the property in the early 1900s when he'd first arrived from Sicily.

As Steven pulled into the lane that led to the two-hundred-year-old farmhouse, Bella whined. He stopped in front of the house and got out to open the back door. As soon as she could, Bella leaped out of the back seat and dashed for the small field to the west of the house. On all sides, old-growth forest surrounded them, cool and dark.

Sliding onto the warm hood of the car, he watched her run, a pale blur in the night. The grass had been mown recently and she tore through the stubble, startling a couple of rabbits and a family of quail. She gave chase but she wouldn't hunt. Not while he watched.

He drew in a deep breath of crisp, clean air, not tainted with the stench of city. Just a faint hint of cow manure, so different and so much more alive than the salty breezes in Florida that could turn rancid in seconds.

He loved Florida, loved living in a place where nine months out of the year you didn't have to worry about the temperature dropping below sixty. Still, he missed the fields, the woods, the hills of Pennsylvania. You could drive for miles in Florida and never find more than a bump in the road.

He turned his gaze to the woods that flanked the field. The trees had barely started their autumn show, the brilliant leaf colors muted in the dark.

He'd lost sight of her, though he knew she wouldn't go far. From the trees, he traced the line of the creek at the woods' edge. She'd stop there for a drink eventually. At least a mile up the hill in the woods, the creek bubbled out of an underground spring and ran through the woods, cutting across the middle of the field and passing within a few hundred yards of the house.

Out here, the land still retained some of its wildness. That wildness called to him.

He couldn't let it.

He should leave now, before he found himself slipping into old ways he'd fought to suppress. He should get back in the car and drive away. She wouldn't be stranded. There was a car in the garage and a closet full of clothes. The pantry and freezer in the basement were stocked, always ready for unexpected visitors. Or fugitives.

Leaving now made sense—

He saw her then, standing in the creek. The water had to be cold but she had returned to her own beautiful skin.

She stared straight at him, and he couldn't remember why he'd wanted to leave only seconds ago. When she started toward him, collar in her hand, he let his gaze take in every inch of her perfection.

It'd been three years since he'd seen her. It could be forty and he'd still be blown away by her.

Her chestnut-brown hair fell in a mass of curls to just below her ears and her dark eyes stared into his, wide and unyielding. Her delicate features were almost too pointed to be pretty. Still, he'd never known anyone more beautiful.

When his gaze dipped to trace the curves of her breasts, he saw she wasn't unaffected. He wanted to reach out and grab her hips, press his throbbing erection against the slight swell of her stomach. Force his knees between her strong thighs and spread them so he could run his fingers through the darker curls of her mound.

He lifted his gaze to hers, trying to control the rate of his own tortured breathing. Sliding off the hood to stand, he straightened until he towered over her. She waited until he'd met her gaze before she let hers drop to wander over him. When she'd gone from head to toe, and everywhere in between, he knew he'd lost the battle.

Would always lose this fight. But couldn't bear to win, either.

Wrapping one arm around her waist, he pulled her against him. She had her mouth tilted at the exact perfect angle for him to cover it with his and he sank into the kiss with a groan of surrender.

Arm curled around her, he lifted her until she could wrap her legs around his waist, pressing her breasts and her mound against him. His free hand sank into the curls at the back of her head and held her steady for his outpouring of raging emotions.

Her mouth opened and she tasted exactly as he remembered, exactly as he'd tried so fucking hard to forget. Hot and sweet and so familiar he nearly couldn't stand it.

When he slid his tongue between her lips, hers glided around his as she arched into him. Groaning, he drew back to draw in a deep breath and walked to the front door, digging his keys out of his front pocket. Bella didn't speak as he walked, her head resting on his shoulder, arms warm around his neck.

How many times had he carried her like this? How many times had they made love? Too many times to count. And he swore he remembered every single time.

The door swung open without a sound and he made sure to lock it behind him before taking the stairs to the second floor.

He didn't need light to see where he was going. He knew this house as well as he knew the house he'd grown up in.

And he knew this woman like he knew no one else in the world.

Goddess, was he crazy?

He stopped at the open doorway to her childhood bedroom. He *was* crazy. He shouldn't be here.

"Steven." Bella's voice wrapped around him like silk threads, binding him to her. "Please."

Her hand lifted to his cheek and caressed him, causing his eyelids to drop.

"We shouldn't." He should set her on her feet and move away. Hell, he should run. He couldn't get his arms to release her.

"Yes, we should." Her voice, so calm and rational, dragged against his libido. "Put me down."

He did, wondering if she was going to be the one to pull away this time. Instead, she took his hand and pulled him into the room.

Fool that he was, he let her.

When they reached the bed, she tugged on his polo shirt. And he lifted his arms so she could pull it over his head.

Cool air brushed against his skin but heat shot to his groin as her fingers unbuttoned his jeans, slid down the zipper then pushed them off his hips. When she wrapped her warm fingers around his shaft, he had to reach for her shoulders to steady himself.

"Bella—"

She rose on her toes to seal her mouth over his, cutting off any protest he might have had. After a few seconds of her tongue dueling with his, he couldn't remember what he'd been going to say.

Not with her hand stroking him in the exact way guaranteed to make him lose every ounce of his hard-won control.

It shouldn't be this damn hard to say no but it'd been so long. It'd been three years since he'd held her like this, since his father—

He broke away, drawing in a breath that felt like glass shards in his lungs.

Bella knew exactly what he was thinking. And set out to totally obliterate his control by dropping to her knees and taking his cock in her mouth.

His groan echoed in the room as her lips engulfed the head, licking the sensitive skin on the underside then using her teeth to scrape as she took him deeper.

"Bella, please." He was begging but—oh, Christ—he couldn't stop.

*Push her away*, the rational part of his brain said.

Instead, his hands lowered to cup her head as her mouth blew his mind.

It'd been so long, too long, and there'd never been anyone but her.

She took him right to the edge, ready to explode. Then she withdrew, releasing his shaft with an audible pop, nearly louder than his deep groan.

Now was the time to stop, to get the hell off this runaway train that had only one possible destination.

*Yeah, right.*

When she rose to her feet and gave him a tiny push with her index finger, he dropped back onto the bed. And when she crawled onto the bed and over him, he grabbed her hips to help her.

Three years without her. He hadn't seen her, hadn't held her in his arms, hadn't been inside her. She was everything he considered home and he'd missed her so fucking much.

On her hands and knees, she crawled over his body until his cock brushed the soft, trimmed curls between her legs and the even softer skin of her thighs. His lungs strained with the effort to breathe.

When she wrapped her hand around his cock and pulled it

away from his stomach, he bit his tongue so hard he tasted blood. For three years, the only release he'd achieved had been through his own hand. He didn't want to come in hers when he would be in her body in seconds.

"Steven, open your eyes."

No, if he opened his eyes, it'd be all over.

"Steven, please."

The plea in her voice helped him back from the edge and he cracked his lids, enough to see her above him.

*Beautiful.* Goddess, she was beautiful. Her olive-toned skin glowed in the dark, her expression rapt, her dark eyes trained on his.

Releasing the sheets, he palmed her hips and guided her down. The head of his cock pierced her and he felt warm moisture coat his flesh, easing his way, sealing them together as she slid further. When she'd engulfed him completely, she stilled, fingers on his chest kneading like a cat, nails biting into his skin.

Perfect. It was perfect. Exactly where they were both meant to be. Goddess, he was an idiot—

Then she moved and sensation shot through his nervous system like a hit from a lightning bolt, searing every synapse.

Torturously slowly, she lifted and lowered herself onto him, gaze locked on his. The drag of flesh against flesh long denied made his balls tighten in an agony of delay. He was going to come any second.

One of his hands slid from her hip and arrowed straight to her clit, knowing exactly what she liked. It wouldn't take him long to get her off and then he could come, too.

His thumb flicked over that nub, rubbed soft then hard, falling into her rhythm. He needed her to come, needed to hear her scream his name when she did.

Her breath started to fall from her mouth in soft moans and her hips started to pick up speed until she rode him mercilessly.

Damn, he couldn't...couldn't take it. He pressed his thumb hard and ground her against him. She broke, collapsing onto his chest and crying his name, her body convulsing on his as he released his control and pumped into her.

*Shit. No condom.*

*Doesn't matter. She's mine.*

Eyes closed now, he wrapped his arms around her, holding her as if she was trying to get away.

Tomorrow. They'd talk tomorrow.

# FOUR

Menrva's Nails.

Remo shook his head, still trying to wrap his brain around the concept.

The legend of the nails had been ancient even at the time of his birth, five hundred years ago. A curious piece of history from the time before the Romans assimilated the Etruscans. Long before the advent of Christianity.

Remo had never given much thought to the legend of the nails. The stories were just that...stories about an ancient tradition that had been abandoned more than two millennia ago.

Legend said Menrva had crafted the nails herself and had given them to her priestesses as a gift. They were to be hammered into the walls of her temple by Nortia, Goddess of Fate, at the end of each year, cutting the threads of destiny so they could begin the new year fresh, unencumbered by mistakes of the past.

They were said to hold a powerful magic.

Remo had never suspected the nails could be real.

Or that they could be used to wield the kind of power he wanted.

For a price—a pretty damn high price—Veive had told Remo he needed at least four of the nails to make the spell work.

Of course, all twelve would be better.

With twelve nails in his possession, Veive had assured Remo he would be able to pretty much do whatever he wanted, including absorb the life force of another person.

Remo knew exactly whose powers he wanted to start with.

With his still-aching fingers, he pressed the intercom button on his phone. "Patricia, come in here."

Seconds later, the door to his office opened and his aide walked into the room. Patricia Gigliotti stood five-two in heels, wore her hair in a mass of loose black curls that complimented her overtly Italian features and never failed to remind him of his long-departed Aunt Aurelia.

His father's sister had run his father's villa with an iron fist and a branch from a willow tree. She was the only woman who had ever given Remo a beating. Just one, though. She'd learned her lesson after that.

Patricia—never Patty or Trish—had been born *Mal*, which automatically put her at the top of the list when he'd been searching for a replacement for his former aide. He would have preferred a man, but she'd served her purpose well, so far.

"I need to talk to Charles. Tell him I'll call him this afternoon around four. And find me a sharpshooter."

---

STEVEN'S EYES opened and he stared at a familiar ceiling he hadn't seen in years.

Memories flooded in, all starring Bella. Some from years ago, some from last night. Some he wasn't sure he wanted to remember. Others he knew he'd never forget.

He let his mind linger on the latter because she wasn't here. The bed beside him was cold.

Turning his head, he found a piece of paper on the next pillow.

*I've gone to Cole. I'm sorry I took advantage. Have a good life. All my love.*

Tension tightened his muscles until he thought he'd snap. He took a deep breath, trying to get it to release its stranglehold on him.

She was gone.

He sat up, threw off the sheets and headed for the bathroom down the hall.

Good. This was good. Exactly the result he'd wanted when he'd decided to fly up here. She would be safe with Cole.

*She'd left without saying goodbye.*

The paper-cup holder on sink flew across the room and smashed into the wall. He didn't know if he'd hit it with his hand or if his power had gotten away from him.

*Damn it.* He would *not* be pissed off about this. He should be relieved. It kept them from saying things they might regret later, things they'd kept to themselves for years.

Yeah, maybe if he kept telling himself that, he'd believe it someday.

Looking into the mirror, he saw tears in his eyes.

———

STEVEN COULDN'T GET a seat on a plane to Tampa until three in the afternoon but he was back in Florida before six.

He hailed a taxi to Case and Jones' sleek new building on East Kennedy Boulevard and took the elevator to the ninth floor, not surprised to find the glass doors to the office locked. It was Friday. Everyone was gone by five if not before.

Good thing he had his keys because the night guard wasn't at the front desk. Probably on rounds.

Transferring to the private elevator for Case and Jones employees on the ninth floor, he hit the button for the tenth.

When the door opened without a sound, he heard voices coming from Charles' office at the end of the hall.

Bella's accusations replayed in his head. He didn't— No, he *couldn't* believe Charles had had anything to do with Bella's attempted kidnapping.

He'd managed not to think about anything since leaving the house this morning. Not Cole or Bella or his own...problems.

Still, that kernel of doubt had been planted.

He walked down the hall, not making a sound. He hadn't forgotten everything his dad had taught him. The voices became clearer as he drew closer. Charles and Tiffani—talking. And then another voice, on the speaker phone.

He began to make out words, sentences.

Ice crept into his veins when their words started to make sense.

"Until now, Steven hasn't suspected. It's time to bring him up to speed."

He stopped several feet from the half-open door, breath catching in his chest.

"We'll make sure he's turned in a few days," Charles added. "The boy is stubborn but I'm sure Tiffani will be able to handle him. Power like his, even though he's submerged it, won't be buried forever."

"We need to step this up." The voice on the speaker. "I need him now."

*No, no, no.*

Steven's blood froze, as if it'd crystallized in his veins. This wasn't happening.

"Once the heirs are gone," Tiffani's tone held a sneer, "Steven will be mine."

"No, he'll be mine," said the unknown speaker. "I need him here within the week. Once I know he's on board then we'll discuss options, Tiffani. Until then, remember your job."

The unknown speaker hung up so loudly, Steven heard it even though the blood had drained from his head, making him dizzy. He feared he might actually pass out.

Using his right hand, he grabbed his left arm and squeezed until he felt bone. The pain forced him to clear his head.

Just in time for him to hear Charles say, "Don't worry, baby. He'll be yours. We'll find a way to get rid of his little bitch."

*Vaffanculo.* Bella had been right. His stomach flipped and he swallowed down the urge to vomit.

*They're* Mal.

If this was a movie, the ominous music would start now. Instead, all he heard was a high-pitched whistle that reminded him of a hurricane blowing through. That whistle was in his head, threatening to bring him to his knees.

How had he missed it? How could he have missed the fact that the two people he'd spent the most time with in the past three years were exactly what he'd tried so hard to stay away from? And how had they known about him?

He shook his head. He couldn't think about that now. He had to get out before they realized he was here. Had to leave and never come back.

*Need to find Bella and keep her safe. Need to tell Cole.*

Shit. They knew about Cole's *congress.*

He closed his eyes for a brief second and swallowed a groan of despair.

He hadn't believed her. If anything happened to her, he'd never forgive himself. Bella had been right. They'd wanted to use against him then kill her so Tiffani would have no rivals for her affections. But someone else wanted him, too. Someone who wanted him to give in to the darkness that ate up a part of his soul.

From infancy, his parents had told him horror stories of the *Mal*, had taught him to fear what he'd been born to become. His mother had shown him how to submerge his magic, to only use pieces of that great, black well of power. But then he'd turned fifteen and they'd come for him...

And his mother had died protecting him.

He'd made her a promise before she'd died. He'd promised never to go willingly. That he'd fight until he couldn't.

He'd lost so much. And walked straight into a trap.

How could he have been so stupid?

"According to Dietrich," Tiffani continued, "Steven took the bitch back to her house and stayed the night."

His stomach heaved. He'd been followed.

"Dietrich said she's got a flight out of Philadelphia to New Orleans late tonight, around one a.m. Steven hadn't left the last time I talked to him."

So they didn't know he was back in Tampa. He had to leave, now, before they realized. And he needed to warn Cole, needed to make sure Bella was safe.

The sound of a vacuum cleaner jolted him into action. He backed toward the elevator so he could watch Charles's office, throwing glances over his shoulder to keep an eye out for the cleaning woman. He'd almost reached the elevator when he realized the night watchman had probably returned to his post by now. The elevator released directly in front of the reception desk. He'd have to take the stairs. They would take him all the way to the bottom floor.

Still, there were cameras in the stairwell. Heart pounding, hyperventilation a real possibility, he took a deep breath and forced down the fear.

And reached deeper still for his magic, praying he could control it.

———

BELLA LET her gaze roam over the people waiting in the gate area of the Philadelphia airport.

She'd been sitting here for at least an hour. And she still had another hour before her plane left for New Orleans.

But she hadn't been able to sit in her apartment on Bainbridge Street and mope any more.

*Alright, at least be honest with yourself. You don't want to cry anymore.*

That's all she'd done since she'd left Steven this morning.

She'd hoped—prayed—that Steven would follow her back to her apartment, beg her to let him back in her life.

Damn him for crushing her dreams. Again.

Well, shit. Her eyes were flooded. Again.

Wiping them, she took a deep breath and forced herself to continue people watching. It was a favorite pastime—watching the *eteri*.

There were a few families with young children, several businessmen in suits carrying briefcases and a whole crowd of seniors dressed in polo shirts and casual slacks. And white sneakers. Every single one of them. Smiling, she wondered if there was a shop that only sold white sneakers to seniors. Must have a booming business.

She closed her eyes and took a breath, sorting through the smells to pick out a few people with magic, none strong enough to worry about.

Wait. What was that? She'd caught a hint of something... different. Her eyes shot open.

Power, strong and nearly feral. Drawn from the same source as hers but more inherent, more a fiber of his being.

A *grigorio*.

Rising and slinging her duffle bag over her shoulder, she wandered toward the news stand farther up the concourse, discreetly sniffing.

She turned right when she came to the hallway that led back to the security metal detectors and ended up in front of the small snack bar serving muffins, sandwiches and other finger foods.

"Hello, Princess. Took you long enough. Must be slacking off."

---

WATCHING CHARLES' door for the slightest movement, Steven began chanting, a bare whisper of sound. His skills were rusty, but he performed the spell without screwing it up, testing for wards of protection around the building.

He found what he was looking for then thanked the Blessed Goddess Charles relied more on technology than he did magic. He still had no idea how Charles had hidden his *Mal* background from Steven. It didn't seem possible. He must have a shitload of power.

The words were coming back to him now, his Etruscan gaining momentum as he began the spell that would make him invisible to the cameras.

Even with just these simple spells, he could feel the darker magic trying to consume his will. Whispering to him, trying to seduce him with possibilities.

Battling back, he spoke the last word as Tiffani stepped into the hall, followed by her father. Steven froze, but they never glanced his way.

"I think I'm going to stop at Steven's, maybe hang out until he gets home," Tiffani said as she pressed the button for the elevator. "A naked woman in his bed might finally break down his reserve."

Charles winced but chuckled. "I'm sure you'll find a way, dear. But I don't need to know details."

The elevator dinged and the doors slid back silently. Charles and Tiffani entered and disappeared while Steven stood there.

It took him several minutes to unfreeze his muscles, to make sure his power wasn't leaking out of him and affecting the environment around him.

A buzz sounded in his ears and his muscles twitched with the sparks of magic.

Gods-be-damned, it felt good. Wonderful. Fucking amazing.

And he couldn't let it.

As if he was tearing pieces of his flesh from his body, he forced the magic back into that black hole inside his chest. Where it brooded and sulked and grew.

Then he walked down the stairs to the first floor.

---

"DIEGO!"

Bella swung around and leaped at the dark-haired man, throwing her arms around him for a hug, knowing it would exasperate the quiet *grigorio*. "What are you doing here?"

She pulled back and looked at the gorgeous man her brother had hoped she'd marry some day. Never gonna happen, but...oh, my.

Diego shook his head, brown waves falling to his shoulders. Those copper-colored eyes held amusement but his unsmiling mouth and handsome face with all those broad Latin planes looked tense.

"Your brother asked me to keep an eye on you. I was going to New Orleans for *congress* anyway, so I agreed."

She liked Diego, she really did. He didn't believe in giving you a line of crap. Her brother, however... She was going to kill him.

Her eyes narrowed. "So, Cole asked you to babysit, too? Quinn had his turn in Reading."

He shrugged. "I guess you can look at it that way. I look at it as companionship."

She glared at Diego for several seconds until he lifted one perfectly dark eyebrow. "You gonna sulk the entire flight or do you want to get a drink?"

They got drinks at the bar next door—a ginger ale for Diego and a whiskey sour for her.

Diego turned a deceptively lazy gaze her way. "Something you want to talk about?"

She shook her head then sighed and nodded. "Can we wait until I get some alcohol in me for the answer to that question?"

He nodded. "Sounds like a plan."

"Yeah, well, I got a lot of those but they never seem to work out for me."

The bartender brought their drinks and she downed half of hers in one gulp, appreciating the burn on the way down. Not that the buzz would last long. *Lucani* metabolism burned alcohol out of the system faster than an *eteri*.

As Diego sipped his soda, she turned back to him, her head tilted. "Do you think I'm spoiled?"

Both of Diego's brows rose this time. "Is that a trick question?"

She frowned. "What do you mean?"

He snorted. "You've been spoiled by every man in your life. You've got to know that."

A grimace twisted her mouth, but she couldn't really dispute his statement. "Alright, let me ask you this. Do you think I manipulate events and people for my own benefit?"

"Don't we all?"

She sighed. "Diego, please. You're the only person I know who'll give me a straight answer. And if you don't, I'm going to start calling you, 'Your Highness.'"

He winced. "Let's not get nasty. Help me out, Arabella. What're you talking about?"

Chin on hand, she stared into Diego's beautiful eyes, wondering why she hadn't fallen in love with him. Damn Steven, maybe it was time she tried.

As heirs of two of the oldest *versipelli* families in the world, she and Diego should have been made for each other. It didn't matter that he was an Iberian lynx and she was a grey wolf. If they had children, they would be either wolf or lynx. Or have the ability to shift between both forms.

While the old European families hadn't intermingled much, the influx of immigrants to the United States had meant more mixed unions, something the elders had looked on with horror. They'd predicted dire consequences—contaminated blood, the end of the *versipelli*, the end of the world.

Of course, it hadn't happened.

However, the hereditary families were dying off and mixed unions with humans only rarely produced children with magic.

Diego had been born from a *versipellis* father, king of the Falcus family of Galicia, Spain, and a *strega* mother, a direct descendent of the legendary *boschetta* of thirteen Etruscan witches cursed to immortality.

Diego had been double-whammied, born *versipellis* and

*grigorio* and that combination made for one mean, fighting machine.

"Hey, Bella. You zoned out on me. What happened?"

She sighed. "Do you believe in soul mates, Diego? One love for your entire life?"

He didn't answer right away but seemed to give it some real thought. "Yeah, I do. But I also believe we can be happy without our soul mates in our life."

"Do you know who your mate is? Have you met her?"

He shook his head. "Don't know that I want to, either."

Feeling tears well, she blinked them back and gulped more of her drink. "I'd rather not know mine. He's a bastard, pig-scum, lying sonofabitch."

Diego snorted. "So tell me how you really feel."

"Like I've had my heart ripped out of my chest."

"Tell me the word and I'll kill him for you. Then you can get on with your life."

The thought of Diego disemboweling Steven gave her a warm, fuzzy feeling, even though she knew she'd never let anyone truly hurt him.

"Maybe I'll just let you maim him a little."

Diego nodded. "Better to be by yourself."

"Is that why you don't talk to anyone? Live with anyone, date anyone, associate with anyone? Are you a virgin? Gay?"

In the process of drinking his soda, Diego nearly spewed it across the bar. "*What?*"

She shrugged, as if she hadn't just accused one of the most masculine men she knew of being gay. Of course, that didn't mean he wasn't. "You heard me. No one's ever seen you with a woman. You skulk around like a wraith, you have no friends. No one knows where you live. Where do you live, anyway?"

His gaze narrowed. "If I told you, I'd have to kill you. Why the sudden interest in my life?"

"Because I've decided it's time to move on and you're the lucky guy."

If she hadn't inhaled her drink, she would've been able to think fast enough to figure out the expression that crossed Diego's face. But by the time she got her thoughts together, he spoke.

"Luck's not a word I'm acquainted with, though, for you, I'd make an exception."

Bella signaled the bartender for another drink but Diego waved him off.

She flashed Diego a look that would have made a lesser man cower in fear. "*You* are not my brother. Or my keeper. If I want another drink, I'm going to have one."

He shook his head. "Right now, I need you sober."

She huffed. "Alright, no more alcohol for me."

"Come on," he said. "Let's get out of here."

Diego helped her to her feet and she felt the room swing, reminding her that she was a lightweight when it came to alcohol, even if the buzz wouldn't last long.

"I've gotta go to the rest room."

She swayed on her feet and took a moment to steady herself, taking a deep breath and heading for the bathroom across the hall. She had to cut through a crowd of what looked like Japanese tourists to get there, the smell of humanity almost overpowering her with its blood and tension and sweat.

In the bathroom, she used the toilet, trying to shut off her olfactory glands as she did. The amount of chemicals they used in this place was going to make her sick.

Breathing heavily through her mouth, she stepped to the sink to wash her hands, trying not to look at her reflection in the mirror. She knew she must look like crap. Grief and lack of sleep would not be kind to her complexion.

She needed—

A slight movement behind her caught her attention.

She looked into the mirror and saw a woman behind her raise a hypodermic needle.

---

DIEGO WATCHED BELLA WALK AWAY, shaking his head at her unsteady gait.

He'd always had a soft spot for her, had actually considered taking her for his mate, something her brother had pushed for long and hard. But he knew he'd never have her heart. She'd given that away long ago.

To a man unworthy of her attention, much less her heart. A man who turned his back on his loved ones was a man Diego did not want by his side in a fight.

As she disappeared into the bathroom, he scanned the crowd, always alert to a threat.

He didn't sense one now.

Until he saw Bella fly out of the bathroom seconds later, her expression pissed off as she hurried toward him.

"Someone jumped me in the bathroom," she hissed. "Female. Wasn't expecting it. Stupid, stupid."

Diego grabbed her arm and started pulling her toward the escalators, tightening his grip when she tried to pull away. "Let's get the hell out of here before we start laying blame. Do you know her?"

Bella glanced behind her as they hurried toward the bank of escalators that would take them to the first-floor exit. "No, but here she comes."

They made it to the escalators and Diego looked over his shoulder to see a blonde nursing a split lip leave the bathroom at a run.

When her eyes lit on Bella, they narrowed and Diego could

easily imagine flames erupting from her ears. He didn't wait around to see her light anything on fire. He started down the escalator. Disgruntled travelers sniped as he barreled through, dragging Bella with him. He ignored them.

"Diego," Bella said.

He turned, saw the blonde closing in and jumped the last five steps to the bottom. Bella stumbled but didn't fall and they ran for the exit.

"We can't get to my car without her catching us," he said. "We need to lose her first."

"Diego." Bella stumbled again as they dodged traffic to get across the street to the parking garage.

"What?" he asked over his shoulder.

"She...she injected me with something. I'm not feeling too good."

He spared a look at Bella. Shit, she didn't look good. "What do you mean? Injected you with what?"

She stumbled and went to her knees before he could catch her. He pulled her to her feet, threw his arm around her waist, tangling momentarily with her small backpack, and made for the stairs.

He tried to calculate where they were in relation to where his car was. His car was parked in C-lot and they were in E.

"She had a hypo, got at least half of it in me before I got away. I don't know what it was, but it's making me sleepy."

They began to climb, Bella leaning more heavily on him with each passing minute. Diego wanted to stop and deal with the other woman but he had to get Bella somewhere safe first. "Come on. Stay with me a little longer."

"Sorry, Diego. Wasn't expecting it."

"It's alright. I shouldn't have let you go alone."

"Can take care of myself...you big oaf."

"Yeah, and you're doing such a great job of it right now."

He knew that one would hit its mark and, sure enough, she took a deep breath and put forth a little more effort as they ran.

But the blonde was gaining on them. He was going to have to take her out, but he'd have to put Bella down to get the knives in his boots.

He needed to find an alcove. He could put Bella there and—

Something whizzed by his head. Something small and sharp. Not a bullet, something with...a tail?

Tranquilizer darts. A shiver raced up his spine. Damn, he hated needles.

Who the hell *was* this bitch?

His gaze raked the area. There, a stairwell, straight ahead.

"Come on, babe. Just a little further."

He heard Bella's breathing get slower with each second.

"Trying. Sorry. Stupid."

"Just stay with me."

Another dart raced by his ear as they ran into the stairwell. Then a thick pane of glass stood between them and their tail, who stopped in the middle of the parking garage and stared at them.

The woman couldn't be more than five-foot-two and probably wouldn't crack a hundred on a scale. But the intent blazing from her pale eyes gave her delicate features weight and purpose.

She looked like the all-American girl-next-door. Her pixie-short blond hair wisped around a heart-shaped face with a button nose, full lips and big eyes. Not beautiful but pretty.

Especially when she smiled.

Like she did right now.

Except that smile held a wealth of ill will.

What the hell had Bella done to this woman?

And what the hell was she smiling about?

The blow to the back of his head answered that one.

# FIVE

"I'm on my way back to Philly."

Steven didn't bother to identify himself. He knew Cole would realize who it was immediately.

"What? What the hell's going on?" Cole asked, his voice breaking slightly over a bad connection. "Are you okay? Where's Bella?"

"She's still there. Something's happened. Something I can't talk about over the phone. I'll explain when I get there but the *Mal* know about your *congress*."

"*Shit*. How the hell did they find out?" Cole's voice took on a low growl. "I do *not* need this now. And what the hell happened with you and Bella last night? She left me a message at the hotel this morning so she wouldn't have to talk to me and now she's not answering her cell. She told me she was on her way out here and she'd see me early tomorrow. What'd you do to my sister, you bastard?"

Steven blamed himself for the frustration and anger in Cole's voice. "I screwed up. But I'll fix this. I'll make sure Bella gets out there then I'll take care of my problem."

"Problem? What problem?" Cole's tone changed immediately. "Damn it, are you okay?"

Steven took a deep breath, wondering the same thing. "Yeah, I'm fine."

"Then don't worry about Bella. I've got Diego Falco looking after her."

Jealousy reared its ugly head and he had to take a deep breath before he spoke again. "I'm already on my way. And you know Bella will walk all over him."

Cole laughed. "Bites you in the ass, doesn't it? That there might be another man for her?"

"*Vaffanculo.* You're a prick, Cole."

"Yeah, but I'm your best friend."

The bald statement hit Steven like a punch in the gut. After all they'd been through, Cole still thought that. "Just goes to show I have awful taste in friends." And employers.

"Take care, Steven." Cole's voice turned serious. "I expect to see you here with Bella."

After he got Bella's flight information from Cole, Steven took the next flight back to Philadelphia, which, as luck would have it, left in half an hour.

He ordered a rum and Coke from the flight attendant, gave her a healthy tip to make up for his lack of geniality, but he was pretty sure he'd scared the guy sitting next to him into ignoring him for the rest of the flight.

Clear skies and a good tail wind should make the flight only two hours and fifteen minutes. He wouldn't have to go through baggage claim when they landed because he hadn't checked a bag in Florida. Where his ever-growing rage had been born. He was having a hard time controlling that anger right now.

And it was leaking past his guards.

"Ladies and gentlemen, the captain has asked that you please return your seats to their upright position and fasten your seatbelts," the flight attendant's disembodied voice came over the loudspeaker. "We are experiencing some clear-air turbulence, but we should be through it in just a few minutes."

*Shit.* He had to calm down. If he couldn't control himself, turbulence would be the least of their worries.

*Fulminifex* was the proper Latin term for what he was. Creator of lightning, though storm-maker was also correct.

He had a special affinity for weather, for manipulating it. Even when he didn't want to. Like now.

Closing his eyes, he forced the magic inside him back into its hole. Where it didn't want to go. It fought him, fought for control. Sweat dripped down his face, his heart pounding in his chest, as the plane dipped and bumped along the rough air currents until finally he managed to cage that power.

He sat there, grinding his teeth for the last hour of the flight, pretending to sleep until they landed. By the time he left the plane, every muscle in his body hurt as he veered away from the crowd headed toward baggage claim and sought out the gate for Bella's plane.

He knew she'd have to show up sooner or later, so he took a seat and waited, trying to relax his aching muscles.

But as it got closer to departure time and still no Bella, he decided to stretch his legs. Which was when he caught sight of her being dragged down the escalators by Falco.

He started to run but was too far away to get to her before Falco dragged her out of the building. He did his best to keep up, fear urging him faster. It wasn't until they'd reached the first floor that he caught sight of the blonde on their tail.

Steven didn't recognize the woman and he wasn't close enough to see what she took from her pocket when they went into the parking garage across from the terminal.

And then she stopped. Steven dropped behind a car and

peered around the bumper until he could see Bella and Falco in the glass stairwell. Bella looked unconscious.

Gods damn, he would kill Falco if anything happened—

A man stepped into view behind Falco and swung a bat at his head. Falco dropped like a stone, taking Bella with him.

With a growl, Steven rushed the blonde, taking her to the ground and knocking her head against the ground before she knew hit her.

She stayed on the ground, unconscious, while the guy who'd hit Falco took off.

---

BELLA WOKE with a bitch of a headache.

"Don't move around too much. I'm still not sure what you've got in your system."

A shiver ran through her at the sound of that voice. "Steven?"

"Yeah. It's me."

She opened her eyes slowly, afraid he wouldn't be there when she did. Afraid the pain in her head was making her hallucinate. She cracked her eyes but couldn't bring the world into focus. She saw only a dark blob above her.

She reached toward it and someone wrapped his hand around hers.

*Steven. Thank the Blessed Goddess.*

"What happened?" She kept blinking until her eyes focused more fully on him. "Where are we?"

He ran his other, shaking hand through her hair and released a loud sigh. "In a motel somewhere off the Pennsylvania turnpike. And I thought maybe you'd be able to tell me what the hell was going on."

She sat up, her stomach shifting like a rough ocean. Swallowing a few times to make sure she wasn't going to throw up, she finally opened her eyes and let her gaze travel the room. She saw Diego out cold on the bed across the room. "What'd you do to Diego?"

She glanced up in time to see Steven's lips twist. "I didn't do anything to him. Someone whacked him with a baseball bat. Someone working with her."

Steven pointed at the floor, and Bella transferred her gaze to the blonde who'd tried to take her out in the bathroom. Steven had tied her in a fetal position with rope.

"The other guy got away," Steven continued. "I haven't been able to wake this one. But...she's a biter."

She tried to stand, thinking if she got up, she'd feel better. Then her stomach rolled again and she decided maybe she'd just lay here a while longer. "How do you know?"

"She's still got the mark."

Sighing, she tried to think why a biter would want her but the only question running through her mind was, "What are you doing here?"

Something crossed Steven's expression. Something bitter and raw. He wiped it away but not fast enough for her to miss it. "You were right. Charles is *Mal*. He and his daughter."

Her gut clenched at the pain in his voice. "Oh, shit. Oh, Steven, I'm sorry."

"Sorry you were right?"

The bite was back in his tone but she knew it wasn't directed at her. Her hand clenched to stop from reaching for him because she didn't think he'd appreciate her comfort right now. "No. Sorry you were wrong. Do you know what they want from you?"

He shrugged. "They know about Cole's *congress*. And what do they always want from me? Same shit, different day."

He was lying. There was more. She could smell it on him, but she didn't push. Not now.

"What are you going to do?"

With a sigh, he sat on the bed next to her. She waited for him to touch her, needed him to touch her so she could comfort him. He didn't. So she couldn't.

"I don't know," he said. "First I'm going to get you to Cole then I'll take care of my own problems. Right now, your safety is my first priority. Cole will have my ass if anything happens to you. And it doesn't look like pretty boy over there is any good."

"Diego is one of the best—"

"You don't need to stick up for me." Diego sat up on the other bed, one hand rubbing the back of his head while he glared at Steven. "You're the reason Bella is in trouble, Castiglione. She wasn't thinking clearly."

Steven whipped around to look at Diego. "That still doesn't explain how you nearly let her get snatched."

Steven's low tone held a distinct menace and Diego's expression got downright nasty.

She sighed. "Boys, boys. Give me a break, will you? I'm still not feeling good enough to deal with your pissy little games."

They stared at each other for a few more seconds before Steven turned back to her. "How are you feeling? Any better?"

Not really but she didn't want to freak Steven out more than he already was. "Maybe a little food will help. My vision's still not clear, my stomach's upset and my legs feel like lead bricks. Let's wake up this little Barbie doll and find out what the hell she gave me."

Diego walked over to the girl on the floor and kneeled beside her.

"Time to wake up and face the music, little girl," he said, in a tone that would have made Bella wake up swinging.

But the Barbie doll only fluttered her eyelids and groaned.

"Let's go," Diego continued. "I don't have all day and you really don't want to piss me off more than I already am."

There, that made her eyes finally open.

Whoa. The girl had gorgeous pale blue eyes. Husky eyes.

She blinked them a couple of times until they were saucer-sized and locked onto Diego's.

"Tell me what's going on," Diego said. "Or I'll start tearing pieces out of your flesh."

---

AMY JO BAUER'S head throbbed like someone was picking away at her brain with a jackhammer.

It hurt to open her eyes. It hurt to move her head, though probably not as much as it should, considering someone had jumped her from behind and slammed her into the ground.

Well, that plan hadn't worked out too well.

And now the gorgeous guy sitting next to her wanted to flay her like a rainbow trout.

She swallowed heavily and broke away from his hypnotic gaze long enough to take notice of the two other people in the room.

Another gorgeous guy and one very pissed-off Princess. Not sure whether she should get up and bow—which she couldn't do because she seemed to be trussed like a branded steer—or keep her mouth shut and hope they killed her quick, she decided on the latter.

"We promise we won't hurt you...unless you make us." That came from the Princess and Amy Jo didn't think that was any more encouraging than what the first guy had said.

"Steven." The almost-too-pretty guy with the gorgeous long hair kneeling next to her spoke to the other gorgeous guy with the short, dark hair. It might have been a banner day in Amy Jo's life. If it wasn't her last. "Why don't you take Bella out of the room? I work better alone."

Oh, now, that wasn't good. Amy Jo needed the Princess. Desperately.

"No, please," she blurted out. "I'll talk. But only to the Princess."

There, that got their attention. The man named Steven leaned a little closer to her, his dark blue eyes nearly hypnotizing in their intensity.

"What do you need with Arabella?"

Amy Jo took a deep breath. "I need her to save me."

The man's gaze narrowed.

"Save you from what?"

The Princess and Steven had spoken in stereo, which brought out Amy Jo's weak smile.

"I guess, 'from the bad guys' wouldn't be enough of an explanation, huh?"

"No, it wouldn't. What's your name?" Pretty Boy asked.

Now, that was a question she could answer without prevarication. "Amy Jo Bauer. I'm twenty-six and I was born and raised in the Blue Ridge Mountains. Transylvania County, North Carolina. And I'm not making that up. There really is a Transylvania in the States."

The Princess and Pretty Boy flashed each other a look and she hurried on before they decided they didn't want to hear any more and gagged her. Or something.

"You know, I lived all my life reading about werewolves and vampires. I love that kinda stuff but I never really believed in them. I mean, who would, right? Well, except for you all, of course." The Princess raised her eyebrows and Amy Joy figured she better move on. "Anyway, I was in New York City for a librarian conference three months ago. At the New York Public Library. I'd never been to New York and I thought this conference would be a great way to see the city and get some credits.

"So one night after a lecture left out early, I got a cab to Central Park just to take a walk. I know you're not supposed to walk alone in Central Park after dark but it wasn't dark when I went in. And then I just started to walk. It's beautiful and so amazing that the park is right there in the center of that big city. But then it got dark. I started to get a little scared but I figured I'd have to come out somewhere, right? Or there'd be a cop walking around and he could tell me how to get out. Only...they found me first."

She stopped to take a breath and Bella said, "Who found you?"

A chill ran up her spine just thinking about this part but in for a penny, in for a pound. She looked straight at the princess, trying to ignore the two men sitting there as well. "I don't know who they were. I don't know how many there were. I do know there were at least three."

Amy Jo swore the air stopped moving in the room, it got so very still. But that could just be her. She'd never spoken about this part aloud. Not to anyone.

"I didn't expect there to be werewolves in Central Park. Stupid me, huh? Caught by werewolves on the night of a full moon."

Pretty Boy drew in a sharp breath and muttered something in a foreign language under his breath. But she couldn't look at him. Not him or Steven. The pity she saw on Arabella's face was enough to make it hard for her to breathe. But Amy Jo forged ahead because she hadn't even gotten to the important stuff yet. After a long, slow breath and a mental skip over the next few hours—it *had* been a full moon—she continued.

"I lost consciousness sometime before dawn and I'm pretty sure they didn't mean to leave me alive. I think they got scared, maybe heard a cop. I don't know. Anyway, they never took my wallet so I don't think they even knew my name. Maybe they thought I was close to death after...after what happened, but obviously they don't know me all that well. My momma made sure I could take care of myself. She made sure I could fight. And I'm damn sure not a quitter. When the sun came up, I walked until I found my way out."

Luckily, the dress she'd been wearing hadn't been too badly damaged. The cab driver hadn't even given her a second look. "I got a cab back to my hotel and took, like, a few showers." Try ten. "Then I started researching. That's what I do. I'm a research librarian. Mostly I work on the Internet, so I knew where I had to look to find the answers. I am so sorry about the hypo, but I calculated everything out precisely, 'though I had to guess at your weight. But you can't weigh more than a hundred and ten, Princess."

Then she turned to Pretty Boy, still watching her with such intense copper eyes, she almost couldn't hold his gaze. "And I'm so sorry about that bump on the back of your head. I told James not to hurt anyone, but he's a little slow on the uptake. I really didn't want to hurt anyone. I just need you to save me."

There. That was everything. She took another deep breath, waiting for someone to answer her but they just kept looking at her.

"Well?" she asked.

The Princess looked at Steven, who shrugged his shoulders and looked at Pretty Boy. Pretty Boy never took his eyes off of her. "Save you from what?" he finally said.

"From the curse."

Pretty Boy's eyes narrowed even further. "What curse?"

She huffed and would have stamped her feet if she wasn't all tied up. "Weren't you listening to anything I said? Why, from being a werewolf, dummy."

# SIX

Bella had thought she'd heard it all.

Not only had Amy Jo been bitten on the night of a full moon, when *lucani* had been known to lose themselves to the call of the wild, but she thought she was cursed.

And she thought Bella could un-curse her.

Even better, she'd called Diego a dummy.

"Ex*cuse* me?" Diego said, as if Amy Jo had called him a bastard. The look on his face was almost worth the convoluted but amazingly coherent story the girl had told.

Bella jumped in before the girl could go off on another long-winded explanation. She held up one hand and both the girl and Diego turned to her.

"I get the curse part, Amy Jo. Tell me why you think I can lift it."

"Okay, so here's the deal." The woman shifted as if trying to get comfortable. "Do you think maybe you could sit me up or something? I'm kinda getting a crick in my neck from looking up at y'all."

Diego leaned back and crossed his arms. "Are you really this stupid or do you have to work at it?"

Amy Jo's eyes narrowed down to slits, managing to look down her nose at him even though she had to look up at him.

Bella figured Diego deserved whatever the girl threw at him.

"For your information," Amy Jo said, "I have a master's degree in information and library science from the University of North Carolina, Chapel Hill. I have a level-three security clearance from the United States government and I have worked with the current administration on delicate matters of national security. I have never had so much as a *parking* ticket in my life. Three months ago, I became a werewolf, *which*, I have to tell you, was *not* the worst thing that's ever happened to me. But I will *not* be called stupid by a man who lets his hair grow as long as a *girl's!*"

Diego's mouth actually dropped open but he said nothing as Steven choked back a laugh. But Bella couldn't contain hers. "Untie her, Diego. Right now. Before she says something else and makes the top of your head fly off."

Diego didn't move for at least ten seconds. And for those moments, she thought he might simply refuse. Finally, he whipped out one of his knives with more flourish than normal and made a show of slicing through the rope Steven had tied Amy Jo with.

While he did, Bella started to sift through the myriad pieces of information Amy Jo had related. Curse, uncurse, men in Central Park, full moon, bitten. Had she really been bitten on the night of a full moon?

Bella shivered. She'd heard stories...actually she'd heard horror stories of *eteri* who'd been bitten on a full moon. Stories meant to terrify young *versipelli* away from ever inflicting *eteri* with the *versipelli* spell through their bite.

This woman had to have the heart of a lion to have lived through what she'd described.

And if the look she was giving Diego was any indication, she did.

Amy Jo rose, rubbing her hands over her jean-clad thighs. The woman had curves to rival Marilyn Monroe's and straight, platinum hair that framed her face. Her features were pretty, not beautiful, except for those eyes. They were the most remarkable shade of blue.

"May I sit, Princess?"

Bella grimaced. "Yes, but please, my name's Arabella. I'm not really a princess."

Amy Jo sat on the bed opposite her, as far from Diego as she could get. "Yes, actually, you are. A descendent of the ruling wolves of Sicily, your family came to America in 1905 to control the American legion. You're a veterinarian by training, but I'm assuming you're really considered a doctor."

*Holy hell.* Bella's lips parted but she didn't have a clue what to say. This woman knew a hell of a lot for being *eteri*. Way more than she should. And she'd found it all in the past three months? Hell, was there a website somewhere listing every Etruscan secret for the world?

"And you know all of this how?" Diego asked in a clipped tone. "You're not hereditary."

Amy Jo stuck her nose in the air and gave him that haughty look again, even as he towered over her. "I assume you use that term to identify yourself as being *born* into a werewolf family. Obviously that's correct since I already told you I was only *bitten* a few months ago. I also told you I'm a research librarian. If the information is out there, I can find it."

"But it's not like we have a website where you can go and look this stuff up. Right?" Bella cut in before Diego could say whatever he had on his mind. "How did you discover so much about us? You said the man who bit you left you for dead."

Amy Jo swallowed hard and nodded, returning her gaze to

Bella's. "He did. But that was after they'd...played with me for a while."

Bella felt both men stiffen—and her heart weakened just a little bit more for this woman.

"Do you know who they were?" Diego's fury leaked out of his tone.

Amy Jo shook her head but wouldn't look at him, her gaze now glued to a spot on the bedspread. "No. I haven't been able to find that out. Not yet. But believe me, when I do, I'll take care of them."

Diego's mouth curled in an approximation of a smile. One that would've made his enemies think twice about attacking. Still, he couldn't seem to stop egging Amy Jo on. "Maybe you should leave your revenge to the experts, considering how this little fiasco turned out for you."

The girl stiffened but didn't rise to the bait. And Bella's estimation of her went up just a little more.

"Anyway." Amy Jo snagged her gaze again. "I heard them say your name, Princess, and it gave me a starting point."

"Did they mention any other names? And really, the princess thing's getting old. Call me Bella." She smiled at Amy Jo. "Considering you've shot me up with a hypodermic needle already, we should be on more familiar terms."

Shaking her head, Amy Jo's mouth fell into a frown. "No, I heard no other names. I truly am sorry about that hypo but I really thought it was my only option. Your, ah, reputation made me a little leery about approaching you."

"My reputation?" She frowned. What reputation? "What did you read about me on the Internet, anyway?"

Amy Jo shrugged, her gaze shifting just to the left of Bella's. "Well...you kind of have a reputation for being a bit of a... well, kind of stuck up."

"Kind of?" Diego's amused tone increased her ire. "Guess you *can* believe some of what you read."

Bella ignored him. "I still don't understand what you think I can do for you."

Amy Jo sighed. "The legends say you have the power to reverse the curse."

Bella shook her head. "Do you mean cure you of lycanthropy?"

Now Amy Jo smiled and it lit her entire face. "Yes. That's exactly what I mean."

Okay, now Bella knew the myth Amy Jo was talking about. Knew it well and knew it was just that. A myth.

The other woman stared at her with such hope that Bella felt like a complete and utter failure when she said, "I'm sorry. I don't know how to cure you."

For one brief second, all the life left Amy Jo's face and she looked like she might pass out. Diego actually made a move to catch her as she swayed. But before she toppled over, she caught herself and some of her determination returned.

"Now, I don't mean to be rude, but I've researched this whole thing pretty much top to bottom and I have a ninety-seven-point-nine-percent rate of accuracy. According to my research, your blood, when mixed with mine, should have a negative effect on the virus. Kind of like making it null and void, you see. I know it sounds irrational, but, jeez, six months ago, if you had told me werewolves were going to ra— bite me and turn me into some creature from a horror movie every month, no offense, I would've told you to get your head examined. But I've adapted. I've even been able to curb the impulse to rip out the throat of every living thing I see. But you can't just dismiss my re—"

"Amy Jo."

"—search out of hand. There's got to be a way—"

"I'm sorry," Bella said as gently as she could. "There's no cure that I know of that's ever worked."

Amy Jo's eyelids flickered, as if she'd been slapped. Then she took a deep breath.

"I can see how you might... I mean, I know you might not have ever..." Her eyes filled with tears and lower lip began to tremble. "Really? Never?"

Bella shook her head, her heart twisting painfully in her chest. "No."

"Oh." That one word held a wealth of disappointment. "Okay, then." She paused for so long Bella wondered if she'd finally talked herself out. After at least thirty seconds, Amy Jo said, "So I suppose you'll want to punish me for that hypo, huh? I understand completely. But if you wouldn't mind, could you make it fast? I really don't think—"

Amy Jo started to cry then. Big, heaving sobs that weren't pretty but would have melted the heart of a stone statue. Steven and Diego froze like teenage boys on a first date.

*Idiots.*

Without a word, Bella motioned for the men to leave the room. Steven nodded and headed for the door. He never could handle women's tears. Diego stared at the sobbing woman for several seconds before backing off. She ignored the warning look he sent her before closing the door behind him.

She wasn't afraid of Amy Jo. Hell, she didn't think the woman had enough breath left to crawl away much less overpower her.

Moving to her side, Bella sat next to Amy Jo, put her arm around her shoulder and let her cry.

She'd only heard of two other people, like Amy Jo, who had been bitten during a full moon. They hadn't survived the night. For this woman to do so was somewhat of a miracle.

Never having known another life, Bella couldn't imagine

how a regular human would cope with the physical changes of becoming something else. Something other than human.

This woman seemed to have made the leap without losing her mind. Amy Jo was definitely someone Bella wanted to know.

They sat there for several minutes until Amy Jo pulled herself together and took one final, shuddering breath before wiping her eyes.

"I'm sorry." Amy Jo drew in a deep breath, held it then straightened her shoulders. "I didn't mean to break down like that."

"Sounds like you needed it." Bella put her arm around the girl's still-shaking shoulders. "I've got to tell you, I've never met another person who survived a bite on the full moon. Except for the fact that you attacked me with a hypodermic needle, I'd say you're just about one of the smartest and strongest people I've ever met."

Amy Jo snorted but didn't meet her gaze. "Oh no, I'm a coward. For the past two months, I've locked myself in a cage every full moon. I don't leave my house unless the paper boy misses the front porch. I have my groceries delivered because I'm afraid of what will happen if I get a craving for raw meat at the grocery story. I'm terrified that the men who did this to me will find me."

Bella personally wanted a shot at the men who'd done this. Steven's dad had taught her how to defend herself but Cole had taught her to be ruthless. How to use her claws and her teeth to kill. "And yet, here you are."

"Yeah, here I am." She sniffed, sounding ready to sob again. "But what am I going to do with my life now?"

"Why can't you do what you did before?"

Amy Jo's shoulders moved up and down. "I can. I mean, I have been, from home. But... I'm a werewolf!" she wailed. "Can

I get married? Can I have children or will I have little wolf puppies? Will I want to tear my husband apart every full moon? What do I tell my mom?"

It should have been funny. It wasn't. Bella had never had to worry about these questions. She'd known all her life what she was.

"Well... I wouldn't tell your mother. At least not until you've learned to control your new instincts a little better. The blood lust will pass in about a year. You can get married. You will *not* have puppies." She wasn't about to tell Amy Jo that no biter had ever had children. "You can't pass your change to your offspring since you're not a hereditary *versipellis*." Which was complete conjecture on her part but Bella figured if you couldn't have kids, you weren't going to pass on the spell that made you *versipelli*. "You will learn to control it. I can help with that. I promise."

Amy Jo looked at her with awe. "Even after what I did, you'd be willing to help me?"

Bella thought about all that had been taken from Amy Jo by those malicious animals and vowed those men would pay with their worthless lives. She forced her mouth to produce a smile as she nodded. "We have a system in place for biters who ask for help. They're paired with someone, kind of like AA, but for the furry."

There, that raised a bit of a smile. "I don't think I came across that information during my research."

"Yeah, that's something else we need to talk about. How you found out so much about me. But—" She held up her hand to stop Amy Jo's response, "we can talk about that later. Right now, I need to know more about what the men who did this to you said that night. I know it's going to be hard to remember and I apologize for that."

Amy Jo went stiff as a board. "I never got a clear look at their faces. I was face down in the dirt most of the time."

And that, Bella could tell, was all she'd get out of Amy Jo right now. She didn't have the heart to push the woman any further.

"Well, if you think of anything, anything at all, I'd appreciate it. Any information might help keep safe the people I love."

Amy Jo frowned. "Like Pretty Boy out there? Sister, I hope you're not wrapped up with him. He doesn't seem to have a soft bone in his body." Her eyes widened as Bella began to grin. "Oh, wait. Now that just didn't come out right, but you know what I mean."

"Actually, yeah, I know what you mean, but no, he's not the one. I'm talking about my brother." And Steven. Did those men have anything at all to do with what Steven had overheard in Florida?

The *Mal* had been trying to get Steven to join them by any means possible for years. They'd killed his mother, secretly hired him to work for them and had tried to kidnap her, probably to force him to do what they wanted.

But why had they upped the stakes now? What, if anything, had changed for the *Mal*?

"So," Amy Jo's hesitant tone drew Bella's attention back, "would I have to go somewhere, like a halfway house for new werewolves or what?"

Since the *lucani* didn't have anything like that, that wasn't an option. So what did she do with Amy Jo?

Well, that was a no-brainer, Bella decided. She liked this woman. Liked her a lot. And, though Bella had been trained since childhood not to be taken in by first impressions, this woman smelled like a friend.

"No. You're not going anywhere. You're going to stay with me."

Amy Jo cocked her head to the side. "Like a handmaid or something?"

Bella laughed. "Where are you getting this stuff? Yes, I'm descended from royalty, but honestly, this is twenty-first-century America. We don't live by a feudal system." Well, not feudal though the *lucani* did have a distinctive way of governing themselves. "How about as a traveling partner for now?"

Amy Jo didn't answer right away and Bella couldn't decipher her expression. "With both of those men?"

*Ah.* "I trust those men with my life. They'll never hurt you. I've known Steven since I was fourteen. We met the day my parents and older brother were killed. Diego is a...protector." *Of what* would be a conversation for another time. "He'll give his life for yours if that's what it takes to keep you safe."

Amy Jo's back straightened. "I don't need anyone to save me."

"That's not what you were saying a little while ago."

"I know it sounds stupid now but," Amy Jo grimaced, "at the time, I thought it would work."

Bella tightened her arm around her new friend's shoulders. "It's not stupid. All myths have basis in fact. But you've figured that one out already, haven't you? Look, I know you don't want to talk about what happened that night, but if you ever need someone to listen, I'm here. I can't imagine—"

"No." Amy Jo cut her off with a shake of her head. "You can't. And I'd rather not talk about what they did to me. Not ever."

"Okay, but if you change your mind, I'm here. I *am* going to have to ask you what you heard those men say. I need to know. It could be important to my family." She drew in a deep breath and let it out, watched Amy Jo do the same.

"Okay. I think... I think it's probably better if we do that now. Before I lose my nerve."

Shaking her head, Bella laughed. "I don't think that's a problem you'll ever have."

---

"DO YOU BELIEVE HER STORY?"

Steven broke the silence that had descended when Bella had kicked him and Diego out onto the concrete slab that passed for a porch at this third-rate motel off the Pennsylvania Turnpike.

Diego didn't turn. The *grigorio* looked wound tight enough to snap. "Yes. She's telling the truth."

Steven shook his head, amazed. "Then she's a damn strong woman, to live through that."

Diego nodded. "Those men are animals. We are not animals, though some may think so."

*Son of a bitch.* Steven's hands clenched into fists at his sides as his eyes shut for a few brief seconds. That was the final fucking straw. He swore he heard it break somewhere in his brain.

He opened his eyes to see Diego watching him, calculation in his eyes.

"You know what, asshole?" Steven's hands clenched at his sides. "I've had a fucking shitty day and I'm sick of your attitude. I've known Bella since she was fourteen years old. I was there the day her parents were killed. After my dad died, the only people left in the world that I care about are her and Cole. If anything happens to her..."

No. He couldn't think about that. Not now. "Apparently you and I are going to have to work together. If we can't do that, you're going to have to leave, because I won't. Not this time."

Raising one eyebrow, Diego leaned against the rusted wrought-iron railing that delineated each room and crossed his arms over his chest. "You don't own the woman, Castiglione. And from what I've heard, you cut yourself out of the loop. So what the hell are you doing here? She doesn't need you to screw up her life again. You're no good for her."

Steven's hands curled into fists, itching to slug the arrogant bastard. "You mean not good enough, don't you? And you are? You just want her because she's a purebred. Isn't that right?"

If Diego's expression was any indication, Steven decided he might've finally pushed the other guy far enough. Good. He needed to work off some of this excess energy and a fight would do it. Besides, if this prick dared to lay one hand on Bella, Steven would flay him alive and hang his pelt on his wall. If last night had proven anything, it was that she would always be his. No matter what.

*Come on, bastard. Throw the first punch.*

Diego's eyes narrowed to slits. "You don't want to go there. Not now."

Steven bared his teeth. "Yeah, actually, I do."

"No, you don't." Diego bared his teeth in an approximation of a smile and turned back to stare at the parking lot. "You just want to pound the shit out of someone and I'm handy. What we need to do is talk about what we're going to do now. You know Bella's in there making a new friend. We're going to get stuck taking that crazy woman with us to New Orleans. And we need to figure out what the *Mal* wants with Bella."

Steven knew what the *Mal* wanted with Bella—to use as leverage against him. And from the look Diego gave him, apparently he knew it, too.

Steven turned away. "I'll take care of the *Mal* after we get Bella to Cole."

"You and what army?"

Steven didn't have an answer for that. And he was saved from thinking of one when the door opened.

Bella stood there, her gaze weighing the situation. "Amy Jo's ready to answer some questions. Did you boys play n—"

Steven wrapped his hand around her neck and pulled her flush against his body before she could finish her sentence. He had an instant hard-on as he dropped his lips on hers and kissed her until he felt her yield against him. His tongue pushed past her lips, but she was already opening for him.

His hand moved from her neck to her hair, threading through the strands until she couldn't move without his consent.

She tasted so hot and so damn familiar that the lust he'd tried to keep under wraps exploded, raising his body temperature and threatening the hold on his *arus*.

With a groan, she returned his passion, her lips moving against his in a way that nearly had him ripping off her clothes and pushing her back onto the bed in the room.

Only the knowledge that Amy Jo and Diego were watching forced him to rein in that hunger. When he broke away, he looked into her eyes, searching for something.

He didn't find what he was looking for until she smiled and warmth flooded her gaze.

"It'll be alright, Steven." She lifted a hand to cup his cheek, her skin warm against his.

He wanted to turn his head and press another kiss into the center of her palm. But over Bella's shoulder, he caught Amy Jo staring at them with wide eyes.

He nodded. "We need to find out what she knows about what the *Mal* is planning and how *congress* works into it. Then I need to get you to Cole."

Bella smiled as she shook her head. "I'm not leaving your side, not until we find out what's going on. You need me. I fight better than you do and I know what's been going on the last three years."

She didn't say it, but he knew the rest of that sentence was "since you left me." Since he'd turned his back on his heritage and his family.

But he refused to put her in any more danger.

"This is my problem—"

"No," she cut him off, shaking her head. "It's not. It's *our* problem. I'm not a child anymore, Steven. I'm a grown woman who's been taking care of herself for years. Years you wanted nothing to do with me."

That hit him low in the gut with the force of an Ali punch. He could deny that he hadn't wanted anything to do with her. He'd thought about her every day. Dreamed about her every night.

But he couldn't deny that he wanted to keep her in a safe little box, away from the *Mal*, away from all of his shit.

And he wasn't sure he could concentrate if she was around.

Before he could open his mouth, she continued. "I'm not throwing that in your face to hurt you. Well," she grimaced, "maybe just a little. But it doesn't change the fact that I'm not leaving your side. Get used to it."

With a sigh, Diego said, "Then I suggest we take the rest of this inside. We need a plan."

# SEVEN

"We need you to tell us everything you can remember from that night," Bella said. "Every word, no matter how trivial it might seem. I know this is going to suck big time but we need to hear it."

Bella didn't know the half of it, Amy Jo thought as they sat on the bed while the men stood against the wall. Not too close but in her line of sight. As if they knew she wouldn't want them behind her.

*Smart men.*

She rolled her shoulders, trying to work out the tension, and attempted to control her breathing. She could very easily hyperventilate here and that would be completely embarrassing. Still, the Princess wanted her to talk about something she'd tried desperately to put out of her mind.

Amy Jo shrugged, her gaze downcast. "I don't know that I'll be able to tell you much."

"Anything you can tell us will be more than we know now," Bella urged.

Well, that sounded rational enough. But her heart

continued to flutter like a trapped bird and her throat dried to the consistency of the Sahara.

"Alright, but I'm not completely sure what I heard."

Which was somewhat of a lie. There were parts of that night she would never forget and parts she would never remember.

"I know I heard them say something about a meeting." As she was lying on the ground, forgotten for the moment after a second rape. She had focused on their voices, imprinting them into her brain so she could identify the men later. "They laughed about it, about how they could wipe out all the 'fucking royalty' —their words, not mine—at one time."

Bella's gaze never wavered. "Did they say where this was going to happen?"

"One of them said they were leaving for New Orleans in the morning, to scout."

"Did they talk about what they were planning?"

She shook her head. "No. At least, I don't remember that they said anything about that."

Bella slid her hand over Amy Jo's, resting on her knee, then squeezed lightly. And didn't let go. "Do you know how many men were there?"

Amy Jo's heart tripped like someone had flicked a switch, making it hard for her to breath. "I know...there were four men but there might have been fifth who didn't..."

Sweat broke out in a fine sheen over her entire body. Bella's hand squeezed her knee and she focused on that.

"Do you know if the men mentioned the word 'congress'?"

She shook her head, her hands already starting to tremble. "No. I only remember them saying your name, Princess, and, well, yours." She pointed at Steven, whose expression hardened like quick-drying cement and she quickly looked away. "I don't remember what they said about you, or even if they were talking about you. Just that they said the name Steven."

Bella squeezed her knee again. "And you didn't hear what they wanted Steven to do for them?"

She shook her head, more to dislodge memories than as an answer. "No, nothing like that. They didn't speak English all the time. I think they must have been speaking Italian or Arabic. Some foreign language."

Bella nodded. "It probably was. Can you remember any of those words?"

"Only a few. They used *mal* a lot. I know that means bad. And *bene*, and that means good. But some of the others, I didn't memorize. I was listening more for what their voices sounded like."

"So you could recognize them later." Pretty Boy spoke, not bothering to make his words a question. She looked up to find an expression almost like approval on his face.

Her spine straightened just the tiniest bit. "Yeah, it was... difficult." She shook her head again, blinking away the ugly memory that just popped into her head. "But I'm good at blocking out distractions." That was a good word. Distraction.

"Can you tell me what the men looked like?"

*No. Absolutely not.* "I don't know."

That stopped Bella for a few seconds. "Were you blindfolded?"

Amy Jo shook her head. "I just don't know what they look like. I...blocked it out."

Bella's eyes narrowed. "But I'm sure you remember some-thing. Just generally. Dark hair, light hair, tall, short—"

"Arabella." Diego cut her off. "Stop."

The world had started to spin and darkness tinged Amy Jo's vision on the edges. Snippets of sound were beginning to creep out of her subconscious, things she'd ruthlessly suppressed after that night.

Images, like subliminal photos in advertisements, were there one second and gone the next. Hands, hair, legs. None belonged to any man in particular, but they were all intertwined.

Her chest ached, like someone had grabbed her lungs in a vise and tightened. She started to hyperventilate. And then she felt it, that sense that her body was no longer her own. What she imagined it must feel like to know you have a cancer that was eating you alive from the inside.

It started like goosebumps under the skin, but it went deeper, into her very cells. She moaned, unable to speak, and her eyes closed, blocking out everything but the need to control her body.

Vaguely, she heard yelling. She felt Bella's hand wrap even more tightly around her knee and she tried to hold on. She cried out with loss when she couldn't.

Then she could only think about fighting off the alien that wanted to take over her body.

Even though she knew fighting didn't help. It only made the process that much more difficult. She'd learned that over the past three months, but it was so hard to let go of herself. This wasn't her, this animal. She couldn't concede.

The others continued to yell at each other. Something about a bullet.

Jesus God, were they going to shoot her?

The little piece of her brain that was still thinking rationally said, "Maybe that would be better than this agony."

Just before the fur could dissolve her skin into one ungodly itch, she felt a pinch on her arm then an almost unbearable coldness crept through her veins.

Now this, she decided, was agony. Then everything went black.

AMY JO PASSED out like someone flipped a switch in her head. Diego caught her before she slid off the bed.

"Well, shit." Bella released a shaky breath and tossed the used hypodermic needle into the trash. "This is gonna be a problem. We can't give her a Bullet every time this happens. It could kill her."

Diego lifted the woman against his chest, feeling the slow, steady cadence of her breathing. The Bullet—the drug the *versipelli* had developed to stop their change—had knocked her out. Unconscious, her features were almost plain—pug nose, full cheeks, rosebud lips. His gaze snagged on the freckles scattered across her nose. There weren't many of them. He could probably count them if he tried. He wanted to lick them.

*No way in hell.*

"Diego, I think you can put her down now."

He found Bella watching him with a carefully blank expression.

He laid Amy Jo on the bed and stepped away until he felt the wall against his spine, telling himself with every backward step that he did *not* want to stay by her side.

"What the hell just happened?" Steven asked.

Bella sighed and sank onto the other bed, her gaze still on Amy Jo. "Some biters have more of a problem controlling their change than others. Sometimes stress will trigger it, even if it's not a full moon. They can be damn unpredictable."

"And that's going to be a problem." Diego moved across the room, to let his feet move and get his brain in working order.

*Bullshit. You just want to put more space between you and the girl.*

He wanted to tell himself to shut up. Instead, he said,

"Whatever happened to her, whenever she thinks about it, it could trigger her change.

"*Congress* is in three days," Steven said. "We need to find out what she knows fast. How do we do that?"

Diego looked at Bella and found her staring back.

"Andrea," Bella said.

"One of the *streghe*." Diego sighed and sat on the chair on the far side of the room, running his fingers through the hair Amy Jo seemed to think was girlish.

His gaze kept straying to the bed. His brain wouldn't stop conjuring images of what those animals had done to her. He knew firsthand the depths to which some men fell.

"Yeah," Bella said. "Andrea can read her mind without having to put her through more trauma."

"Where is she now?" Steven asked.

"New Orleans, believe it or not," Bella said. "Damn, we're going to have to rent a charter. We can't risk taking Amy Jo on a commercial flight. And it's going to have to be someone we know, someone who's not going to ask questions."

Steven snorted. "Where the hell are we going to find someone like that one short notice?"

Diego reached for his cell phone. "I know a guy. Flies out of Allentown but I'll have him pick us up at Reading. He owes me one."

Hell, Marco owed him more than one and Diego was about to collect on all of them.

---

"LONG TIME, no see, Brother. Finally found something the bastard's good for, huh?"

Sitting with Amy Jo—still out cold and beginning to worry

her—in the back seat of the windowless rented van, Bella heard the man speaking to Diego but couldn't see him.

It'd been a short trip from the hotel to Reading Regional Airport. Whoever Diego had called had already been in Reading, so they didn't have to wait for him to fly in from Allentown.

And whoever he was, he didn't sound friendly.

"*Vaffanculo,*" Steven muttered under his breath. "Bella, come see this."

Scooting forward into the next row of seats, she peered out the front window.

And gaped at a man who looked so much like Diego it was scary.

"Holy twin brother, Batman."

"Who the hell is that?" Steven whispered the words in her ear, causing awareness to trickle down her spine.

Even with everything else going on, she wanted him. Damn it, she didn't have time for that now.

Shaking her head, she whispered back, "I have no idea."

After Diego had made his phone call, he'd gone to the nearest agency and rented the van. The *Mal* probably had a trace on Steven's credit cards so he wouldn't be able to use them. Same for hers. Nobody was looking for Diego. At least not yet.

The man who could be Diego's short-haired twin stood in front of a hanger containing a small plane.

"I see you haven't lost that chip on your shoulder, Marco. When are you going to stop blaming the world for your problems?"

The guy shrugged. "As soon as you admit that those of us without completely pure blood are not *unworthy* of your attention."

For a second, Bella thought Diego might actually hit the guy. Even though she couldn't see Diego's face, she saw his hands curl into fists at his sides and his back straightened until she thought he might actually break. But after a brief second, his hands loosened.

"As I told you over the phone," Diego continued, his voice carefully neutral, "I need you to transport myself and three others to New Orleans. No questions asked."

The man Diego called Marco grimaced in disgust and ushered Diego into the hanger with the rag he'd been using to wipe his hands. "Your wish is my command. You're lucky the plane's fueled and ready to go. Another half hour and I would've been out of here. I'm sure whatever business the mighty legit heir has, it must be important."

Diego nodded, as if the other man had spoken the truth and not just been trying to get a rise out of him. "It is and if you'd step off your high horse for a few seconds, I just might tell you."

Marco didn't answer and Bella examined his features. The more she looked, the more differences she noted. She could see now that Marco was younger than Diego. Where Diego was dense muscle, Marco was a tiny bit shorter and a few pounds leaner. His hair was a half shade lighter than Diego's dark chestnut and it was straight where Diego's had a slight wave.

Both men, however, were drop-dead gorgeous.

"I think you should probably shut your mouth before it completely unhinges, Bella."

She shot Steven a scowl for his wry dig but made sure she closed her mouth as Diego and Marco disappeared into the hanger.

Steven had the door open as he said, "I'm going to find out what's happening."

As the door closed, Bella heard a muted groan from the backseat.

"Jesus H. Christmas," Amy Jo groaned. "What truck hit me this time?"

Bella turned to find Amy Jo sitting up in the back seat, rubbing her head with her eyes closed tight.

"Don't move around so much." Bella turned so she could address Amy Jo. "It's going to take a few hours for the Bullet to wear off."

Amy Jo slitted one eye open. "Well, I certainly feel like you shot me but I don't think I'm bleeding anywhere."

Reaching over the seat, Bella pressed her hand against Amy Jo's forehead. "Your temperature's coming down. That's good."

"What the hell did you give me?"

Placing her hands on Amy Jo's cheeks, she turned the woman's head to check her eyes. No sign of striation. That was good. "We call it the Bullet. It's a combination of drugs that includes silver nitrate. The silver keeps your body from changing while the other drugs keep you from dying from the silver."

Amy Jo's mouth fell open. "And it works?"

Bella nodded. "It works. But it's hard on the body. Just like any drug, you can O.D. on it."

"But it stops the change?"

The hope in the woman's voice made Bella sigh. "Yes, it stops the change, but it's not a cure. Use too much and your body starts to become accustomed to it and you need higher doses. And higher doses will kill you."

That dulled the hope in Amy Jo's eyes, but not by much. "How often can you use it?"

"Depends on the individual. I've known some who used it three days a month for nine months to get through college. Some people can only use it once or twice a year because they have severe reactions to the silver. Biters can usually use it more often because they don't have the hereditary gene."

Amy Jo paused, blue eyes searching. "Have you used it?"

"Once." Bella couldn't hold her gaze and turned to move

into the middle row of seats, staring out the front window. "I nearly died. Spent a month in the hospital in a coma."

"My gosh, your family must have been worried sick."

"My brother thought I'd tried to commit suicide. Steven thought I did it for attention."

Amy Jo's hand clasped her shoulder. "Did you?"

Bella liked this woman, she really did. She wasn't afraid to ask questions and she seemed to have a genuinely caring heart. "No. But I was a mess at the time. You know my parents and older brother were killed when I was fourteen, right?"

She felt Amy Jo nod. "That must have been awful."

She still couldn't answer that one without breaking down. "What you probably don't know is that Michael, Steven's father, took in my brother and me. He raised us, trained us, sent us to school, kept us safe."

"Sounds like a great guy."

"He was. And when he was killed, I had a really hard time."

"How'd he die?"

"He was a *grigorio*, a protector, like Diego. He was killed defending a young girl from the *Mal*. I was twenty-one, having a hard time adjusting to college and the real world. Then Michael died and Steven told me he was leaving, and he'd never see me again."

Amy Jo's hand tightened. "Well, that certainly sounds like a sucky period of life."

Amy Jo's tone was affronted and sympathetic at the same time and Bella laughed. "Yeah, actually, it was. And when the full moon came, I decided my life was going to change."

"And that meant changing who you are."

Bella nodded. "When I came out of the coma, my brother cried like a baby. Steven passed out cold on the floor. Stress. The next day, my brother told Steven to leave and never come back, so he did."

"Sounds like your brother was hurting and Steven blamed himself for what happened."

Yes, she knew that. Still... "For three years, I didn't see or speak to the man I love. About a week ago, I got sick of waiting for him to come to me and I sent him a note. I told him I needed him and asked him to come to me." Her gaze picked out Steven in the hanger with Diego and Marco. The men were huddled together, their hands going as they discussed their plans. "Someone tried to kidnap me two weeks ago."

"So I'm not the only one."

Bella smiled as she met Amy Jo's gaze. "No, but these men didn't want me. They wanted to use me to get to Steven."

"Were these men from this *Mal* you keep talking about?"

"Yeah. Sorry, I keep forgetting you don't know as much as we think you do. I can't believe the *Mal* never came up in your research."

"I wasn't searching for anything other than you." Amy Jo grimaced. "I was a little fixated."

"The *Malandante* is an ancient secret society descended from the Etruscans. Their magic is the same magic we all possess—even you, now. But there's something in their genetics that causes them to lean to the dark side."

Amy Jo cocked her head and stared straight into her eyes. "So... What? They have a gene that predisposes them to evil, kind of like the gene that makes it more likely you'll get cancer?"

"Yeah, kind of. And, since it's awfully hard to fight genetics, when you're born *Mal*, you stay *Mal*."

"So why do they want Steven?"

"Because he was born *Mal*."

Amy Jo's jaw practically dropped to the floor, shock making her eyes huge. But as shocked as the other woman was, it would never match the gut-crushing despair that hit Bella every time she let herself really think about what it meant.

Steven couldn't change what he was. Just as she couldn't. But where she embraced her nature with open arms, Steven had to fight his every day.

"It's the reason Steven won't stay with me. He's able to control his magic only because he shuts down all emotion. When he lets himself feel, he loses control of his magic. He's afraid he'll be seduced by it, that he'll become what he hates most.

"Steven's parents were able to hide his nature for years, shield him behind their own magic. When a new *Mal* is born, the others can sense him somehow. They're drawn to them, like they're born with a homing beacon. In the old country, they'd come and take the baby. Or the family would leave the child in the woods after its birth. The baby would either die of exposure or be collected by the *Mal*."

Bella heard Amy Jo's shocked gasp but didn't stop. Couldn't stop now.

"His mom tried to teach him how to harness that magic, to fight the evil in it. But when she died, part of him died, too, and he submerged his power, buried it. When his dad died, he buried his heart and cut himself off from everyone he loved."

"Wow," Amy Jo breathed. "This story sucks."

Bella nodded. "Yes, it does."

They sat in silence for several minutes, just staring out the window, until Amy Jo asked, "How did his mom die?"

How did she answer that? "Somehow, the *Mal* found out about him and tracked him down. He used his power to defend himself against the *Mal* and somehow one of the *Mal* deflected it back at him before it killed him. His mom pushed him out of the way but the bolt struck her and she died instantly. Steven believes he killed her."

Amy Jo's hand tightened on her shoulder. "What? Why would he even think that?"

"Because Steven is a *fulminifex*. He can create lightning and draw storms."

Amy Jo paused for several seconds before she said, "Holy crap. You're kidding, right?"

"Wish I was. But Steven's wrong. His dad told me his mom was trying to teach him how to control his power, possibly harness it to use in some other way. Steven believes it will never happen, that it's his fault his mom's dead. Steven won't forgive himself."

"Jesus H. Christmas, this story just never gets better, does it?"

Bella looked over her shoulder, a bitter smile on her lips, and found Amy Jo staring at her with compassion in her pale blue eyes. "Not really."

Amy Jo sighed before changing the subject. "So, what's in New Orleans? You said something about going there before I did my little, um, freak show."

She ignored the comment about the freak show. They'd have time to work on Amy Jo's perception of herself later. "The *versipelli* are having a meeting there and it's also the home of a woman who can help you remember—"

Amy Jo pulled away, her mouth a tight line. "No. No, I don't want to remember. I'm sorry, but I don't want to know what happened that night. Not now. Not ever."

Bella's heart contracted at the pain in Amy Jo's eyes. "I understand, but this woman can see into your mind and extract information. Information you may have and not know. And if you want, she can take those memories and erase them."

Amy Jo shook her head but Bella wasn't sure why. Then the other woman turned to look out the front window. "Looks like we're ready to go."

Following Amy Jo's gaze, Bella saw the men walking toward

the van. None of them looked happy, but then, Diego and Steven never really smiled.

Diego slid open the side door and stuck his head in to speak to Bella. "We can leave in about a half hour. How is she feeling?"

Her eyebrows lifted at Diego's phrasing. His question and the fact that it was aimed at her was guaranteed to piss off Amy Jo. Sure enough, the other woman answered.

"'She' is feeling just fine, thank you very much. Well, maybe not fine, but well enough. And I don't appreciate you talking around me like I'm not here. Where do you get off, mister?"

Diego's mouth twisted into a grimace that he wasn't fast enough to hide. Turning, he faced Amy Jo. "Obviously, we're not getting off on the right foot. Please let me apologize for my behavior. I was only inquiring after your health from Bella because I thought you might still be incapacitated. Please allow me to escort you to the plane."

Bella squelched a smile when Amy Jo's mouth opened but no words came out. Then felt like applauding when the other woman frowned.

"Don't think you're going to get away with this," Amy Jo scolded. "It doesn't matter how pretty you talk, you still have a problem with me. Well, let me tell you—"

Amy Jo broke off, her eyes going blank as she inhaled deeply. Then her mouth trembled. "Oh, God, he's here."

Bella exchanged a glance with Diego, who shook his head.

"Who's here?" they asked.

Amy Jo's gaze flew around the van, as if trying to see all around her. "Oh, no, no, *no*. I've got to get out of here. He can't touch me again. I won't let him. I'll kill myself first."

Bella smelled fear coming off of the other woman in waves.

"Amy Jo, I don't know who you mean. Who's here?"

But Amy Jo never answered. She bolted for the door of the van but Diego caught her before she got far.

"No! Let me go. I've got to get away. He's *here*."

She fought against Diego's hold, but she was no match for the bigger man. Still, Diego had a tough time confining without harming her and took a few flying elbows.

Bella took another deep breath...and caught a whiff of something. Another *versipellis*. Not Marco, but someone else. And, judging from Amy Jo's reaction, someone she knew.

Amy Jo started to sob and fight harder. For a brief second, it looked as if she might win when she kneed Diego in the groin and his arms loosened just enough for her to squirm free.

But before she could get far, Diego cold-cocked her with a right hook. She slumped into his arms, unconscious.

"What the *fuck* is going on?" Diego practically growled as he situated Amy Jo against his chest, staring down at the already swelling bruise on her chin.

"Someone's here." Bella climbed into the front seat and looked around. "Someone she knows. And, from her reaction, someone she doesn't want to see again."

Diego sniffed the air and caught the scent as well. "I don't recognize the scent. Do you?"

She shook her head. "Which means we've got trouble or this is just a shitty coincidence."

"I don't believe in coincidence," Diego said flatly. "Come on, let's get to the hangar. I don't want whoever's out there to see her."

"Wait, throw this over her."

Bella grabbed the blanket lying in the backseat and arranged it over Amy Jo so she was completely covered. Diego moved to the side so Bella could get out of the van but before could, he stepped in front of her again.

Raking her gaze around the area, she saw the runway about

a hundred yards to the left, where a small plane waited for take-off. The nearest hangar door was closed, as were all the others. But a car approached from the road, headed straight for them.

"Marco, who is it?" Diego called.

Marco shook his head slowly, his gaze glued to the dark sedan. "I don't know. Are you sure you weren't followed?"

The look Marco gave Diego spoke volumes, but Diego ignored it. "No, I'm not sure."

Diego set off at a flat run, Amy Jo against his chest. Bella followed at his heels, not questioning his instincts to get the hell out of Dodge as fast as they could.

As they began to run, the car accelerated.

"He's going to cut us off," Diego yelled. "Jump, Bella!"

She leaped over the car hood to the entrance of the hangar, landing hard on the ground. But even as she rolled, she started her change.

Diego couldn't make the jump, not carrying Amy Jo. Instead, he pivoted and ran for the back of the car.

By this time, Bella stood on four paws, snarling and ready to attack. But they'd cut off Diego from the hangar entrance. He started to chant. Casting a protection spell. As a *grigorio*, he'd be able to deflect any bullets they might shoot. But he couldn't ward off a hand-to-hand attack.

She heard Steven yelling at her to get out of the way, but she knew he couldn't defend himself. He wouldn't use his magic and he didn't have a weapon—

Then again, maybe he did. She heard the ping of safeties being released. Marco and Steven had guns trained on the four men who piled out of the car. Men who also carried guns.

"What the hell's going on?" Marco called.

She growled, low and deep, and all four men glanced her way before scoping out the rest of the crowd.

The man who answered smelled like *Mal.* He stood behind

the other three men, using them as shields. Blond, blue-eyed and average height. A woman might think him handsome—if you didn't notice the lack of humanity in his eyes.

"You've got something of ours, something we want back. Give me the girl."

Marco's expression was a carbon copy of Diego's—hard and unmoving. "I don't know what the hell you're talking about, but I suggest you back the hell off."

Bella wanted to tear into them with her teeth and claws. How could they have found her so fast? Had Marco betrayed them?

A quick glance at Diego told her nothing. But one sniff and she could tell Marco was just as confused as they were.

She snarled again and the three *lucani* acting as the *Mal*'s muscle glanced her way. She didn't recognize them and cold fear wanted to consume her.

Who were they and why were they working for the *Mal*? And what the hell were they doing here?

When the *Mal* focused his gaze on Diego, or more specifically, on Amy Jo, Bella started to put two and two together and didn't like her solution.

The man sneered. "We're not here for you. And you don't want to involve yourself in this. We just want the girl."

"Not going to happen." Diego's voice sounded like a growl, guttural and dangerous.

The man's gaze shifted again and, when he looked at Diego this time, recognition lit in his eyes. "Well, well. The famous Diego Falco. It's an honor to meet you." The man bared his teeth in an approximation of a smile and Bella shivered. Evil flowed off of him in waves. "You have something that belongs to us and we want her back."

"Over my dead body," Diego said. "Marco."

One second, Marco stood next to Steven—in the next, he

stood next to the *Mal*, one hand on his throat, the other pressing a gun to his temple.

*Holy hell—*

A shot rang out then something hit her front leg, something that knocked her to the ground but didn't hurt at first. She glanced down, saw blood begin to trickle down her leg.

And then it started to burn like acid.

As she howled in agony, Steven cried out and she heard another shot fired.

Then silence.

She heard her own labored panting and licked at the blood seeping down her leg. The bullet contained a trace of silver—not enough to kill her but enough to immobilize her with pain. She forced herself to look up and find out what was going on.

"—getting on the plane now," Marco said, his gun stuck under the man's chin. One of the other men was on the ground, bleeding from a wound in the stomach. The other two had their guns trained on Diego. "Don't even think about it or I'll blow his head off."

Steven kneeled beside her and lifted her into his arms, gun still clenched in one fist.

She was vaguely aware of Diego, Amy Jo in his arms, backing toward the plane, only turning to climb the few steps into the plane. Then Steven started to move. The pain crept up her leg and she couldn't help the pitiful whine that escaped. Strong arms tightened around her, and one hand sank into the fur of her back in a caress.

Then she gave into the pain and passed out.

# EIGHT

Steven placed an unconscious Bella on the floor near the cockpit as Marco got them on the runway and in the air.

The men who'd ambushed them ran for their car when Marco started the engines and made a run at them, barely missing their dark sedan as he taxied to the runway. Luckily, there was no traffic at the small airport.

"That's right, you bastard," Marco growled. "You better move that car or I'm going to run it right into the ground." Then he turned and yelled over his shoulder. "I'm gonna go straight to the runway and get us in the air. Might be a little shaky but don't worry. The plane's solid. It can take it."

Steven couldn't care less. Bella was bleeding. Shot. And he couldn't do a damn thing to help her.

Diego strapped the still unconscious Amy Jo into a seat then pushed him away from Bella. Steven was too stunned to react. Closing his eyes, Diego stretched out his hands over her body, attempting to use his magic to extract the bullet.

"*Vaffanculo*, those bastards." Diego's guttural words could be heard over the engine noise. "There's silver in the bullet. No wonder she passed out."

Steven's blood froze then threatened to boil over. He was going to hunt down every one of those men and tear them limb from limb—

"Steven, you're going to have to do this."

His gaze locked on Diego's face. "I can't." He had to grit the words out between his teeth.

"You have to." Diego's expression was implacable. "I can't work the bullet out because of the silver. If you must, use a knife and dig it out. But it has to come out. She can't change with the bullet in there."

No. He couldn't do it. But as he stood there, watching the labored rise and fall of her chest, he knew he'd have to. Diego was a powerful *grigorio* but he was also *versipellis*. This was one of those rare instances when one contradicted the other.

*Fuck.*

He might be able to use his magic to remove the bullet. Then again, he might not be able to control it and he could kill them all with a lightning strike out of the clear blue sky.

His gut twisted but he held out his hand. "Give me your knife."

Diego laid it in his palm and Steven took a deep breath, trying to calm the painful pounding of his heart. His father had made sure he'd had medical training, particularly after his mom's death. But this... He didn't know if he could...

No. No, he *could* do this. He had to. Bella needed him.

Calling on the detachment he'd sworn by for the past three years, he slid the knife into the wound, ignoring the dark red blood that streamed out. He sank it in until the blade hit metal with a sickening thud. His stomach rolled and he took a deep breath to calm it, but all he could smell was the metallic scent of her blood.

His chest tightened until he could barely breathe and it hurt to try. *Shit*. This couldn't be happening now. He couldn't let it happen now.

His magic rose like a dark wave that threatened to drown him. He struggled to push it back down but it wouldn't go willingly.

"Steven." Diego's voice cut through the fog in his brain, low and urgent. "Pull it together. She can't take much more blood loss. Do something. Now. Or she's going to die."

Damn it, he knew that. He bit back the angry words that were on the tip of his tongue because Diego was right.

But the magic he'd strangled for so long craved blood and Bella's seeped from her body in steady rivulets. She'd almost died before. The coma after she'd taken the Bullet. He hadn't been able to leave the hospital building where they'd kept her. Her doctor had been ready to confine him to his own room with an IV tranquilizer.

This felt a thousand times worse. His hands started to shake and the knife wobbled, tearing into her flesh even more.

Gritting his teeth, he forced his hands to still. Then he blanked his mind of everything.

---

DIEGO WATCHED the tears drip down Steven's face.

He didn't think Steven knew he was crying as he dug the bullet out of Bella's front haunch. The sheer agony in his expression made Diego's gut clench. Silently he cursed this failing. One of many.

He couldn't do a damn thing for Bella. Not until Steven pulled the bullet out. What good was he as a *grigorio* when he couldn't perform the most basic healing because his *versipellis* nature conflicted?

The Etruscan deities had fucked him over good—

Steven's barely audible sigh as he worked the bullet out of the wound drew him out of his thoughts. When he met Steven's eyes, he knew the other man had reached the end of his rope.

"I've got it from here." Diego spoke slowly, as if to a child. "See if you can wake Amy Jo."

Steven nodded but didn't move, continuing to stare at Bella. "Steven."

"Yeah. Yeah." Finally he stood. "I'll check on the girl." Then he looked into Diego's eyes. "Don't fail."

Diego couldn't respond. The emotion in Steven's words made his throat tighten. He forced himself to nod and Steven finally moved away, toward Amy Jo.

Now it was his turn. He had to do this fast and right. He couldn't fail. It wasn't an option.

Shutting his eyes, he forced himself to focus. He gathered the magic from the place inside where it dwelled and drew it through his body into his hands.

If anyone ever asked how he did it, he wouldn't be able to explain. The power was there, lying in wait until he needed it. He drew it from inside himself but also from the air, the earth, the people around him.

He gathered it together and forced it into his hands. From his hands, he bent it to his will and used it to fix Bella's wound. In his mind, he saw the torn flesh and muscle. The wound was worse than he'd thought.

Sweat broke out along his brow as he realized Steven had hit the major artery in Bella's shoulder. He had to fix that before he could repair the rest of the wound. Damn it, he was much better with human wounds. Bella was the vet, not him, though this wasn't the first time he'd had to tend to a wolf.

Dripping sweat made his eyes burn until he could barely

see. Still, he didn't move his hands. After several minutes, the artery was repaired and he moved onto the wound itself.

By this time, his hands burned so badly it was almost unbearable. Still, he held his hands steady until Bella's wound was healed.

When he finally lowered his hands, they trembled uncontrollably. As did the rest of his body. He tried to stand and found he couldn't get his legs under him. When he raised his head to look around, everything was blurry.

"Here, Diego. Let me give you a hand."

Steven's voice sounded blurry, too, as if Diego's head was wrapped in cotton. He tried to focus on the other man's face but he couldn't make it clear.

"Steven, I'm—"

He passed out.

———

STEVEN CAUGHT Diego before he hit the floor of the plane and pulled him over to the seat next to Amy Jo.

He'd checked on the other woman but whatever Diego had done to her had knocked her out cold. Since she didn't seem to be injured, he left her strapped in. He made sure Diego was strapped in before he moved to Bella's side.

He didn't realize he was holding his breath until he had to draw in another when her eyes opened and she whined at him.

"Bella." He didn't know what else to say.

She smiled that wolf smile, the one that made him think she was considering having him for dinner. He laid a shaking hand on her head but she shook him off and started her change.

He averted his eyes. It wasn't considered polite to stare while a shifter changed skins. It was one of the first things he'd learned living with her and Cole.

When she lay naked, panting, on the cold metal floor of the plane, he grabbed a blanket from a pile near the door and draped it around her.

"Damn it, Bella. You're going to be the death of me."

"I'm the one who took the bullet, Steven."

"And if I ever have to watch that again, I might just shoot myself."

He wanted to cry, felt his eyes well and hated it. Hated how he lost control of his emotions where she was concerned. That had always terrified him. It was part of the reason he'd broken all ties with her. If he couldn't control himself around her, it was a short leap from his hold on his emotions to his hold on his magic. The two were so closely intertwined, especially the darker, more volatile emotions—hate, love, jealousy, fear.

"Steven—"

He held up one hand. "How do you feel?"

It took her a few seconds to answer. "Better than you might think. How's Diego?"

"Passed out."

"And you? How are you?"

He shook his head before he realized he was doing it. "I'm fine. Let's get you off the floor and into some clothes. It's cool in here."

Her gaze finally drifted away from him and took in their surroundings. "Marco got us in the air."

"Yeah." He turned away to look for something, anything she could wear. Her nudity made his hands itch to touch her. "I'm going to go talk to him as soon as I find... Good. Here, put this on."

He held out the beige coverall he found folded on one of the seats. It looked clean but, at this point, he didn't care. He had to get her dressed. He was so damn happy to see her awake and alert. But now shock was setting in and there was no time for it.

He turned to check on Diego and Amy Jo once more while Bella got dressed. If he watched, he'd grab her and take her back to the floor and neither one of them could afford that.

Diego's pulse was strong but he didn't move when Steven shook his shoulder. As soon as he touched Amy Jo's wrist, however, she moaned and her eyelids fluttered open.

Her big blue eyes looked resigned when they focused on him. "Well, what the *hell* happened this time?"

He heard the rasp of a zipper. It threw him off track and it took him a few seconds to process Amy Jo's question. By the time he had, Bella answered.

"You freaked and Diego knocked you out." Bella moved closer and he saw she was covered neck to toe with the jump-suit, which was about three sizes too big for her.

Amy Jo shook her head gingerly and rotated her jaw. "Wow. That's really gonna hurt in a little while—" Her eyes widened as she looked out the window. "Oh, my God. How did we get away? Did he see me? Is he following us?"

"Whoa." Bella moved to the other woman's side and put an arm around her shoulder. "We're fine. We're all fine."

Eyes huge, Amy Jo practically panted with fear. "But he was there, wasn't he?"

"Who was there?" Bella asked.

Steven answered that one. "One of the men who bit you. He was there at the airport, wasn't he?"

Amy Jo slowly nodded. "Yeah, he must have been following me— *Oh, no.*" Her gaze snagged on Diego and she turned, her hands reaching out to cup his chin before she stopped and drew back. "What happened?"

"Bella was shot." It still made him cringe to think of it. "Diego healed her then passed out."

"Healed her how?"

"With his hands."

Amy Jo's eyebrows shot up, her gaze never leaving Diego's face. "He can do that?"

Steven nodded. "The *grigori* all have certain traits in common. The ability to manipulate metal, increased strength, enhanced senses, the ability to work magic. Some can heal. Some have more individualized powers."

Amy Jo shook her head as if that would help put some of the pieces together. But her expression radiated sorrow. "You know, sometimes I think I lost my mind that night I was bitten. That I'm really living in a mental hospital somewhere and this is all some demented dream. Kind of like 'The Matrix,' you know?"

Bella nodded, tightening her grip around Amy Jo's shoulders. "It must have been hell, but I promise to answer any questions you've got. Anything at all. You're not alone anymore."

She said it with such conviction, Steven couldn't help but sigh. "More like out of the frying pan and into the fire."

Both women looked at him. Bella's lips pressed together in a frown but Amy Jo smiled.

"Yeah," Amy Jo nodded, "I guess you could say that. Still, I'm not real sure about this voodoo woman in New Orleans."

Bella started to answer but he jumped in before she could.

"Just give it a shot. See what happens. You can always stop."

Amy Jo slid a look at the still-unconscious Diego then at Bella then back to him. "Alright. If you think I should."

He nodded. "I do. Just—"

"Diego!" Marco called. "Get up here. I need you. Now."

Steven caught the hint of fear in Marco's voice and turned but not before ordering the women to buckle up and stay seated. Surprisingly, neither of them took his head off for the command.

"We've got a problem," Marco said as soon as he leaned into the cockpit. "Where the hell's Diego? I need him."

"Passed out in the back. What's wrong?"

Marco swore under his breath in a language Steven didn't understand. "We took a bullet in the gas tank. We're losing fuel. We're not gonna make it to New Orleans. I don't know how long I can keep us in the air."

Steven couldn't work up the energy to be surprised. "And you just noticed this?"

"Yeah, well, I had my mind on other things. Look, I gotta find somewhere to put us down before the plane goes down by itself and we really don't want that to happen."

It might've been funny if circumstances had been different. As it was... Hell, it fit right in with the rest of the day. "What do you need from me?"

"You have to wake Diego. I need him up here in the copilot's seat. He's got his pilot's license and, if anything happens to me, he can take over. Just get him up here now."

"I don't think he'll be much use to you right now. He's really out of it."

"*Shit.*" Marco's expletive sounded as sharp as broken glass. "*Vaffanculo.* Strap in to the copilot's seat and hang on. Do what I tell you when I tell you. This could get really fucking rough."

---

DIEGO JOLTED awake when the plane wrenched to a stop.

He had a magic hangover he knew would take a while to dissipate. He also knew something was wrong because Marco was a much better pilot than that landing indicated.

Blinking, he tried to get his eyes to focus while he picked apart the voices. Steven calling for Bella. Marco cursing.

"Hey there, Pretty Boy. I suggest you wake up now. We gotta get off the plane and you're a mite too heavy for me to carry."

Amy Jo.

He saw the outline of her face leaning over him and let his blurry gaze connect with her pure blue eyes. He blinked a couple of times trying to bring her into focus.

"What's going on?"

"I'm assuming something happened to the plane," she said. "The pilot landed us then jumped out about a minute ago, cursing up a storm."

His vision became clearer by the second as fear began to settle in. He sat straight up. "Did we crash? Is everyone okay?"

"Whoa, now, just settle down." She laid a hand on his shoulder and warmth seeped through him. "We all seem to be fine, but I think we better get off the plane."

He blinked faster until the blurriness faded and he saw her clearly. She smiled, her blue eyes a little too wide, but she didn't seem injured.

And he really didn't like how much that relieved him.

"Are you okay?"

He reached out to push her disheveled hair from her face so he could check for bruises. She didn't push his hands away and it took him a full minute to realize his fingers had gone from checking for injuries to caressing the fine bones of her face.

"I seem to be in one piece." Her voice sounded huskier than normal and she dropped her gaze.

"I see you're awake."

Diego dropped his hand and turned toward Marco's voice. He found his brother standing in the open hatch on the left side of the plane, watching them with an indecipherable expression.

"What the hell happened?" Diego jumped out his chair at the sight of the blood running down Marco's face. "Are you okay? Do you feel faint? Is your vision blurry?"

He grabbed Marco's chin and turned his face to the side.

The cut looked deep but not life-threatening and Diego let out a relieved sigh.

Marco may hate him but he was Diego's only remaining family and that meant more than Marco would ever know.

"Sorry to disappoint you, but I'm fine. Stop pawing me." Marco drew back, out of reach. "And get the hell off the plane. I don't want to have to explain to Cole why you were still on it if it blows up."

Turning, Marco climbed down the ladder and out of sight.

*Shit.* Marco had needed him and he hadn't been there. Again. Didn't matter that he'd been passed out.

*Shit.*

Diego turned to find Amy Jo staring at him.

She smiled, just a short quirk of her lips. "Family can suck."

Her words held a wealth of compassion and understanding. Then she moved past him and down the stairs, missing the ghost of a smile that curved his lips. Even after everything she'd been through, she still managed to hold it together. Hopping over the last step to the ground, she made straight for Bella and Steven, standing several yards away from the plane.

He caught the flash of her silver-blond hair shining in the sun. Blonde didn't usually do it for him. But that tight little ass in those jeans that only reached her knees made his skin feel too tight for his body. And the bounce of breasts under the blue t-shirt that matched her eyes... His cock hardened, throbbing and insistent.

Fuck it all. It was a bitch of a time to notice the way the woman moved, but he couldn't help it. He wanted her. Wanted to throw her over his shoulder and find somewhere private and screw her brains out.

Which just made him feel like an animal.

Even from this distance, he could see the bruise on her chin where he'd hit her. His fingers throbbed in response. He wanted to put his hands on her and heal her then put his lips there and kiss the spot, slowly moving to her—

"Diego, get the *fuck* down here so we can figure out what the hell to do."

Marco stared up at him from the bottom of the stairs. The wound on his forehead had yet to stop bleeding. But it was the hint of fear in Marco's eyes that got him moving despite the pounding headache threatening to split his head open.

Outside, he took stock of their surroundings. Marco had put them down on what appeared to be the only strip of flat land in sight. Hills ringed the area and a forest covered the hills.

It had taken tremendous skill to do what Marco had done. His little brother was a damn fine pilot. No matter what Marco might think, Diego was proud of him. Except when he wanted to kill him.

Marco had ducked under the plane and now stood on the opposite side from Steven, Bella and Amy Jo. Diego locked gazes with Steven for a brief second, shaking his head just once. Steven nodded in acknowledgement. They'd be left alone.

Diego walked over to Marco. "Let me see your head. I don't want you to bleed to death on me."

Taller and stronger though he was, Diego knew Marco could be on the other side of the plane in two seconds if he wanted. Marco had inherited his *versipellis* nature from their father, but he'd learned how to flash—to move from one point to another in a second—from his half-*linchetta*, half-human mother, Paloma.

Diego took it as a good sign that Marco didn't pull away when he put his hand over the bloody gash.

"What would you care?" Marco didn't bother to put much heat in his words. This was an old fight, one Diego despaired they would ever find a way to end.

Still... He caught and held his brother's gaze, so like their father's. "Grow up, Marco. The only person here with a problem is you. You may not want to believe this but you *are* my family. We may not have had the closest upbringing but I love you more than anything in the world. Now, shut up for two seconds while I fix this. Then we'll try to figure out what to do."

Marco's eyes widened in shock for several seconds before he wiped his expression clear.

Despite how similar they looked, Diego was more than seven years older. Neither had known the other existed until Marco was a young teen and Diego almost twenty-one. They'd met over their father's grave.

Needless to say, it hadn't been a good day.

Their father had a lot to answer for. Too bad he'd died before Diego could kill the son-of-a-bitch for completely screwing up his sons.

"We don't have all day here." Marco's low growl pushed through his memories.

Diego sighed and shook his head. "Shut up, Marco. Just...shut up."

Surprisingly, he did, and Diego forced himself to concentrate on healing his brother's forehead. The blood they shared should have made it easier, but emotion got in the way.

He remembered Marco's fear of him the first time they'd met. His own initial rejection. His mother's quiet sobbing after the funeral. The hatred in Paloma's eyes as Diego took his father's ring from his dead hand before they lowered the casket into the grave.

That ring was his birthright as the oldest son of Gilbert Falco, only son of Vincent. Should anything happen to him, Marco would take the ring.

Of course, as of now, if anything happened to both of them, their line would die. There were less than twenty *versipelli*

Iberian lynx left in the world. He and Marco represented the last hope of their kind.

And neither of them seemed inclined to find wives and produce heirs.

"Diego."

He didn't answer right away. He knew he'd finished healing Marco's injury but hadn't removed his hand. He waited a second before he moved it to Marco's shoulder. Marco shrugged it off and turned to pace.

Damn stubborn fool. Diego wanted to slap his brother's thick head. Wanted to tell him how much of what his mother had ingrained into him had been flat-out lies.

Sighing, he shook his head again. "So, what happened and where are we?"

Marco stopped but didn't turn to face him. Instead, he looked out over the trees.

"We're in the southern Appalachian Mountains, Georgia. The bastards hit one of the gas tanks. I didn't send out an SOS, but I can't be sure no one saw us go down. I hate to leave the plane but we need to get out of here." He paused, appeared to weighing his words. "I thi— We need to split up. Steven and Bella should fly ahead. We take the girl in the car."

Diego didn't say anything right away, watching as Marco stiffened, just waiting for Diego to shoot him down.

So he had to fight back a smile when Marco's jaw dropped as he said, "You're right. Let's go."

---

"SO, Castiglione is with the wolf bitch, the *grigorio*, and three others."

Remo repeated what his enforcer had just told him. Just to make sure he had it correct.

Damien swallowed audibly. "Yes. We believe they're headed for New Orleans."

Of course they were headed for New Orleans. Cole's *congress* was being held there.

The *grigorio* was an unexpected bonus because where there were *grigori*, there were bound to be cursed *streghe*. And Menrva's nails.

How perfectly wonderful for the Etruscans to gather all the pieces together for him in one place. Unknowingly, of course, but that just made it all the better.

Veive wanted Remo to put the *lucani* on notice that they were under attack and vulnerable. The god wanted Cole dead. And since Veive didn't want all-out war with the other Etruscan deities, he'd chosen Remo as his instrument of delivery.

The deities would think nothing of the *Mal* going after the *lucani*. Business as usual.

After Remo had delivered Cole on a plate, Veive would give him the *streghe*. And the nails.

And, of course, he'd have Steven.

First things first, though. Remo kept his gaze on his underling. "And you were doing *what* exactly in Pennsylvania?"

Damien didn't answer right away. Which meant Remo wasn't going to like what he had to say. Still, the man was *Mal*, and pure *Mal* were hard to come by. Remo could build an army of *eteri* willing to do his bidding for the right price, but a pure-blood *Mal* was worth his weight in gold.

Even if he was an occasional idiot.

"Looking for *grigori*, like you told us."

Yes, Remo had told his men to look for *grigori*. If he happened to find a few nails without Veive's help, so much the better.

Still, Remo paused, knowing there was more to the story

than Damien was admitting to. "Is there something I should know?"

Damien didn't hesitate. "It's under control."

Remo wondered for a second if he should push it then decided it didn't matter. All that mattered were finding the nails. "Then get on a plane for New Orleans. I'll meet you there."

# NINE

"So, we're splitting up?"

Amy Jo sat on the bed dressed in new khaki shorts and a blue t-shirt, her hair still damp. Bella had just walked out of the motel bathroom, a towel wrapped around her head, dressed in new clothes, as well.

How the woman could make Walmart denim shorts and a five-dollar tank top sexy confounded Amy Jo. Must be magic. Of course, the woman was a by-god princess.

It hadn't taken them long to find a path that led to a road off the mountain. Though she hadn't liked it, they'd stolen a car at the first house they'd come across then stopped at the first chain department store they'd passed, buying food and clothes and a few things Amy Jo wasn't sure she wanted to know about.

Diego had paid for it all with a credit card that didn't have his name on it.

They'd found a motel no one would look at twice. The boys had one room, the girls the other. Bella had let her shower first, the hot water washing away some of the stress of the past hours. Still, she couldn't help feeling she had a huge target on the back of her head and, sooner or later, someone was going to take her out.

Bella huffed and tossed the towel on the floor in a ball. "Yeah, I'm pretty sure that's what the guys are deciding. They think we don't know they're over there hatching plans. Wouldn't it shock the shit out of them if we decided to leave without them? It's not like we're incapable. Bastards."

"I don't particularly like feeling helpless either, but it's nice to have someone else do the thinking, at least for a little while." Amy Joy couldn't contain her sigh as she fell back on the full-size mattress and closed her eyes. "I feel like I haven't slept in years, I'm so tired."

The bed dipped beside her as Bella sat. "How *are* you feeling? I know the past two days must have seemed surreal to you. Especially on top of everything else."

Amy Jo snorted. "Yeah, you could say that."

"Are you worried about being alone with Diego?" Bella rushed on as if Amy Jo was going to stop her. "He can be hardheaded and close-mouthed. But he really is one of the best *grigori* and he'll keep you safe. I don't know Marco but Diego will keep him in line."

Amy Jo opened her eyes to find Bella staring down at her. "Sounds like you know Diego pretty well."

Bella nodded. "My brother has been pushing me to marry him for a while now. He keeps finding ways to put us together."

Amy Jo felt her mouth drop open. "You're kidding."

The princess' smile was infectious. "Nope. Diego's never expressed an opinion one way or the other, but it'll never happen."

"Because you love Steven."

Bella's smile disappeared. "For all the good it does me."

Amy Jo scooted farther onto the bed and propped herself on

an elbow. Now seemed the perfect time for questions and answers. And she had more than her fair share.

"And your brother wants you to marry Diego because he's a werewolf, too."

"Actually, Diego's an Iberian lynx. And he's from a royal family, too."

"He's a prince *and* a cat?"

Bella smiled. "King, actually. And don't ever call him kitty to his face. There aren't many of them left."

Whoa. Werewolves and now werelynx. And kings and princesses, to boot. "I grew up dirt poor in North Carolina. My daddy left when I was born and my momma had four kids to feed and clothe. We didn't have much time to dream about fairies and elves and stuff. We were too worried about where our next meal was going to come from. So, what else is out there that I don't know about?"

"Like the Tooth Fairy and the Boogeyman?" Bella teased, her smile showing just a hint of her sharp little canines.

At least, Amy Jo hoped she was teasing. "I always hoped there were fairies, pretty little girls with wings who glowed."

"Actually," Bella sighed and her expression sobered, "there are. We call them *folletti*."

"What do you mean, 'we'?"

"I'm a member of the Etruscan race. Our civilization has been intact for more centuries than we can recall. Most of our written history has been lost to us. Some historians believe the Etruscans migrated from northern Europe centuries before the Italian tribes settled in the seven hills area that would become Rome."

Amy Jo cocked her head to the side. "But you don't think so?"

"No. Our oral history tells us we originated there, indigenous to the peninsula. We have always been magical, a race apart from humans. Actually, two races, the *Enu* and the *Fata*. The *Enu* are magical humans. The *Fata* are earth elementals, what you'd call fairies and elves. And then there are our deities who..."

Bella sighed, drawing her top lip between her teeth to chew on it.

"Who...what?" Amy Jo prompted.

"Well, they're..."

Amy Jo caught the undercurrent of what Bella wasn't saying. And started to shake her head. "No. No, that's just— No."

Bella just stared at her before she shrugged. "Okay. You're right. You don't need to know everything all at once."

Yeah. Okay. She could handle this. She could. Deep breaths, in and out. After everything that had happened to her, she couldn't figure out why this was messing with her head. Maybe it was just too much. Fairies and Puck and things called *folletti*. And now gods and goddesses...

She'd managed not to lose her sanity after that night in Central Park. And she'd been damn proud of herself, even on the days she couldn't force herself to get out of bed. She was still here. And now she had people willing to help her.

But the one friend she'd made was about to abandon her to the man who'd managed to reawaken her damaged sex drive.

She didn't know if she could trust herself with Diego. And that truly sucked.

"Amy Jo, are you okay?"

The princess had that look on her face again—part concern, part apologetic understanding.

She shook her head but she wasn't answering the question. She was trying to shake some sense back into her life. Time to change the subject. "So, what can I expect from this voodoo woman?"

Bella's mouth twisted in a quick grin. "Andrea is a *strega*, a witch. She'll be able to see inside your mind and pick out the information you're repressing. If this group is planning to attack during *congress*, your information could save lives."

"So, this *congress*... What does it do?"

"*Congress* is basically a strategy session but Cole has never held one. My father never held one that I know about."

"And what do they do?"

The princess' expression shuttered and Amy Jo knew she'd stepped into forbidden territory. Which just made her all the more curious.

"I can't actually tell you," Bella said. "Partly because I don't know all the details and partly because it's *lucani* army business."

Amy Jo's mouth opened and closed before she got her voice to work. "Did you just say army?"

"Yes, I did. The *lucani* are the Etruscan enforcers. The American legion was pretty out of hand when my grandfather agreed to move here and whip the *lucani* into shape. The Roman legion actually had an entire auxiliary of *lucani* during the height of the empire. When the Etruscans moved to the new world in the 1800s, they went a little wild, nearly wiped themselves out. My grandfather reinstated the legion as a way to keep order."

Damn. Amy Jo had considered herself a pretty open-minded person. Hell, she turned into a wolf three nights out of every month. And she was still having a hard time wrapping her brain around all of this. "I feel like my head should be spinning around in circles."

Bella grinned. "And I can't believe how well you're handling all of this."

"You do know this all sounds like the plot of some Joss Whedon show, right?"

Laughing, Bella fell back on the bed to stare at the ceiling. "Mm, I loved 'Angel,' but I thought the show lost its focus in the third season."

"Oh, God, I *so* agree. They should have left that twit Fred on Pilea."

"*Thank* you." Bella laughed, throwing her hands in the air. "Ooh, please tell me you're a Dr. Who fan?"

"Are you kidding? I would have followed Ten anywhere. And I have to say Eleven's growing on me."

They sighed in unison. Television was so much more fun than real life.

"It's going to be okay." Bella's softly spoken words broke through the fog that had surrounded Amy Jo's brain when reality crashed back in. "Diego would die before he let anything happen to you."

"I do remember some of what they did to me." She could barely get the words out but couldn't hold them back. They soured in the back of her throat. "I lied about that. Are you telling me this woman could erase what happened that night from my mind?"

"If you want."

Did she want that? "I know this sounds crazy, but I don't know if I want to forget. I don't want to forget their scent because one day I'm going to hunt them down and kill them."

"And that's what you want?" Bella's voice was barely audible.

Amy Jo nodded, fierce resolve stiffening her backbone. "Yes. I want to rip out their throats and tear their beating hearts from their bodies. I want them to know I've taken their lives, just as they took mine."

Almost a minute passed before she lifted her gaze to Bella's, almost afraid of what she'd find there. But there was no condemnation. Only understanding.

The knock on the door startled them both.

Bella turned toward the door and drew in a deep breath. "Steven. Are you ready?"

She nodded, not really ready at all.

Bella sat up, grabbed her hand and squeezed. "You'll be fine. Just don't let Diego walk all over you."

Amy Jo's lips curled in a smile. "You don't have to worry about that. I can handle him."

---

"DON'T WORRY. I'll handle her."

Diego remembered saying those exact words to Steven before they'd gone their separate ways. He'd meant them, too.

But an hour later, he wasn't sure he was going to be able to live up to it. And Diego was nothing if not a man of his word.

"I'm assuming you and Marco are brothers. Bella told me you're an Iberian lynx. Does that mean Marco is, too? What do you look like when you're changed? I mean, lynx aren't that big, are they? Not like lions. Do you shrink to average size or what?"

Why the hell had he agreed to Marco's suggestion that they keep the hotel rooms for a few more hours to get some sleep?

Well, that one was simple. Marco had needed the rest. His skin looked ashen beneath his tan and he probably ached all over from the crash. Not that he'd ever admit it.

No, Marco had taken the easy way out and suggested it for Amy Jo's sake. From the bed, the tiny blonde now stared at him, sitting on the chair along the wall.

Cross-legged in khaki shorts that barely covered her ass and a blue t-shirt with no bra, she had huge blue eyes and a growing bruise on her chin. A bruise he'd put there.

"So do you?"

He blinked and tried to focus on her question, settling farther into the chair he'd pulled to the bedside. "Do I what?"

She rolled her eyes and waved her hands in the air for some reason he couldn't decipher. "Do you shrink to normal lynx size? Aren't you listening to a word I say?"

Yeah, he was, but her words and their meaning got lost in the sweet drawl of her voice, the one that wrapped itself around his cock like a fist and squeezed.

Damn, he really didn't need to be thinking like that. "No, I don't shrink. I'm larger than the average lynx."

Her gaze dropped to his shoulders then continued on to his chest and down to his lap. He refused to shift in his seat like a nervous kid, though she'd probably already noticed his growing erection, becoming more painful by the minute.

As was the throbbing in his head. He couldn't shake the headache from healing Bella. Maybe Marco had been right to suggest the rest. Of course, Marco was asleep in the next room and here he sat, captivated by a woman he should have no interest in whatsoever.

All the biters Diego had ever known were unstable. Of course, they had all been men. He'd never known a woman who'd survived the process. Hell, he'd never met a male biter who retained the mental capabilities Amy Jo had. She was one of a kind.

"You should probably get some sleep while you can." He tried not sound as desperate as he was starting to feel. "We'll be on the road for at least seven hours."

Her lips twisted in a grimace. "I can't seem to settle down. Aren't you tired?"

He wondered what she'd say if he told her what he really wanted to do. With her.

He shook his head.

She shrugged. "Me either. I can't seem to shut off and I

know when I get over-stimulated I tend to talk too much. So, about your dad—"

He slashed a hand in front of him, stopping her words. "That subject is not open for discussion. I really think you need to get some sleep."

She fell silent then, her head cocked to the side watching him.

"What about your mom?"

He wondered what she'd do if he pulled out the duct tape he never left home with out and put it over her mouth? Or if he just put his mouth over hers and kissed all the talk out of her?

"Dead. So is our father. Marco's mother is still alive. She hates me."

Her full pink mouth tilted in a sympathetic smile. "So you *are* brothers?"

He sighed, realizing she wasn't going to give up on this. "Look, I'll make you a deal. I'll answer your questions—if you answer mine."

She fell silent and he let himself relax. He knew she'd never—

Then her bruised chin popped up. "Okay, you're on. But I get to ask the first questions." Without taking a breath, she barreled on. "Are you and Marco brothers?"

That was easy. "Yes."

"So—"

"Ah." He held up his hand. "My turn."

Amy Jo huffed and crossed her arms under her breasts, forcing them into plump mounds beneath the top, making his mouth go dry. "Oh, go on then."

She tried to sound offhand but he heard fear in her voice. He knew she thought he was going to ask about that night in Central Park. Part of him did want to know what had happened. What those animals had done to her. He wanted to know so that when he found them, he would know exactly why he was ripping their still-beating hearts out of their chests.

But he didn't want her to fear him. Gods, no. What he wanted he couldn't even put into words in his own head.

"How did you manage to stay sane through the transformation process? I know how hard it can be on a woman."

Her head tilted to the side. "How do you know that?"

"Answer my question first."

"Then mine doesn't count."

She fell silent and he knew she was waiting for him to agree to her terms. He contained his smile. "Fine. Your question doesn't count."

"Okay then." Another deep breath as she turned to stare at the wall. "Honestly, I can't say that I did. Stay sane, I mean. There are moments during the day when I can't be sure if I'm dreaming or if I'm just crazy. I have this incredible sense of smell now. That actually took the longest to get used to. I kind of expected my eyesight to get better as well, but that didn't happen."

She looked at him as if for an answer to her unspoken question, but he wasn't going to make it so easy on her. Truth be told, he wanted her to keep talking.

When he didn't speak, she shrugged. "Anyway, after that first night, when I realized something had happened to me and I couldn't ignore it, I bought the biggest dog cage I could find, locked myself in it in my bedroom on the first night of the next full moon and made sure I could see myself in the mirror. I figured I had two possibilities. One, I was crazy but not because I was actually becoming a wolf on the nights of the full moon. Or two, that I had an even bigger problem."

"You're not married."

He didn't make it a question but she answered it as if he had. "Tying myself to a man isn't high on my to-do list. Where I come from, you get married because you want to get out of your parents' house or you get yourself knocked up. I was a freak because I wanted to go to college." She shrugged, as if what she wanted hadn't been much of a consideration and turned back to meet his gaze. "So I left. What about you, Pretty Boy? Why aren't you married yet?"

"Who says I'm not?"

She smiled, one that light up those blue eyes. "Ah-ah-ah, no answering a question with a question."

He swore his heart skipped a beat. Damn but her smile was addictive. "Let's just say I haven't found the right woman yet."

"And who would that be?"

"Are you volunteering for the job?"

Shit, how the hell had that slipped out? Of course, that didn't mean he didn't want to hear her answer.

Her head tilted to the side again, considering. "Would I fit the role, your highness?"

Yesterday, he would've had no qualms telling her precisely why she would never be able to fill that role. Today...

"From the day I was born, my father drilled into my head the need to continue the bloodline by marrying a woman of noble birth. In our world, that means a member of a ruling family who can trace her lineage back to at least the tenth century. To make sure the blood remained pure." Anger rose as he remembered exactly the words his father had used, words that had had everything to do with control. "My mother was the last-born child of her line, as was my father. They did their duty by producing me."

Amy Jo's blue eyes dimmed considerably. "Sounds cold."

"It was." He'd never admitted that before. Not even to himself. "They lived in the same building but it was like two strangers sharing the space."

"Did they love you?"

He snorted. "They loved what I represented."

Compassion shone in the depths of those blue eyes. "I'm so sorry."

Damn it, this woman should *not* be able to make his heart beat faster and his blood burn like it was lava. "Are you and Marco close?"

Now that was a million-dollar question and one that should've made him shut off his verbal diarrhea. But those eyes... "I would like us to be. I love my brother even though I didn't know he existed until he was fourteen."

She paused and he knew she was picking through words carefully. "How did you find out?"

"We met over my father's grave."

That silenced her for a few seconds. "Gee, you two have some history, don't you?"

He nodded, his gaze still locked on hers. "You could say that."

"My daddy left after my mom had me, so I guess I could have other brothers or sisters out there in addition to the three I already know about. Guess you weren't all that happy to find out that way, huh?"

"It wouldn't have been my first choice, no. But I am happy to have him."

Especially since a bit of the pressure to produce an heir had settled onto Marco's shoulders, as well. He just wished they could find a way past all the rest of the bullshit their father had left them with.

He wondered what Marco would say if he told him how much guilt he felt for the way Marco had been treated by his father. How much he felt he had to atone for.

"You're happy not to be the only one any more, aren't you?"

This woman was much more perceptive than he gave her

credit for. Something else to add to the increasingly delectable puzzle of Amy Jo.

*Maybe a little sex would help them both sleep.*

The idea had been sitting on the back burner of his brain since he'd walked into her room to babysit. He'd tried to ignore it, dismiss it, shame himself into denying just how much he was attracted to her.

But he couldn't deny himself any longer. He leaned forward, her eyes widening as he came closer then ran one finger down her jaw. "Does this hurt?"

He could have sworn she shivered before she leaned away. She wasn't unaware of him, either.

"Like a bitch."

He smiled at her phrasing. "I am sorry about that, but we couldn't give you another Bullet. Do you want me to heal it?"

She didn't answer right away, sucking in her bottom lip to bite on it. "Will you be okay afterward? I mean, I don't want to hurt you like you were after healing Bella. I can live with a bruise."

Gods be damned. The woman might just as well throw him on the bed and jump him. He wanted her. Knew it was just a matter of time. And why not? They were adults and sex was serious stress relief. But was she able to even think about sex, after what those monsters had done to her?

He let his lips lift in an approximation of a smile. "I'll be fine. It won't hurt. It's magic."

Her easy smile answered his. "I bet that's what all the shapeshifters say."

"Amy Jo."

Her eyes widened even more. "Yeah?"

"Shut up."

He reached out to cup her jaw in both hands. Her skin felt

like silk beneath his, her warmth making his fingers itch to caress her.

Holding her gaze, he let his pinky brush the fast-beating artery in her neck, felt her throat contract as she swallowed hard. Her lids slid to half-mast as he drew the heat from her bruise into his hands. The injury wasn't life-threatening, would have healed by itself in a few days. Still, he hated the constant reminder of the violence he'd done to her.

It only took a minute to heal the bruise. And when he was finished, he let his hands rest against her pale skin.

"Diego."

"Yes?"

"Are you finished?"

"Yes."

"Good."

She threw her arms around his neck and pulled him toward her, dragging him onto the bed with her.

Well, drag probably wasn't the right word because he came without a fight. Hell, he'd been waiting for some sign that showed she wasn't terrified of him so he could kiss her.

Better this way that she'd made the first move.

Much better.

Stretching out beside her, he tilted her head so he could kiss her even deeper. Her mouth opened beneath his, her tongue curling around his as he stroked in and out. Moaning, she arched into him, her hands digging into his shoulders, urging him closer.

Hot and sweet, her mouth clung to his with a hint of desperation he understood completely. Heart pounding against his ribs, hands locked on her waist, he felt as if he couldn't get close enough, couldn't get enough of her to satisfy the raging hunger roaring in his head, in his gut.

Her unique flavor sank into his body like a drug and he sank just a little deeper under her influence.

Breaking away, despite her attempts to hold onto him, he strung kisses along her jaw to her ear, nipping at her earlobe, before licking the skin behind it, causing her to shiver and her hands to sink deeper into his shoulders, her nails puncturing his skin through his cotton t-shirt. The slight pain made whatever sanity he might have had vacate the premises. All he had left was sensation.

His hands slid up from her shorts to the soft skin of her waist, stroking, kneading. Her body arched toward him as her head twisted away, baring more of her neck. He took the hint and ran his tongue from her collarbone to ear.

She moaned, bumping her hip into his erection, making it throb and ache. Already hard, his body practically vibrated with desire for her.

His lips covered hers again as his hands continued to tunnel under her shirt until he cupped her breasts in his hand. Firm and sleek as satin, they nestled into his palm, a perfect fit.

Her breath stuttered to a halt and he opened his eyes to find hers fluttering open. Wide and now a deep stormy blue, they gazed into his.

He pulled back, just enough so he could see her, try to gauge her reaction. "Amy Jo. Are you sure?"

After a few, interminable seconds, the corners of her mouth tilted up at the corners and her hands slipped beneath his t-shirt to splay across his back.

"Yes. I'm sure."

*Thank the Gods.*

He smiled as he ran his hands down the length of her body, caressing the lean muscles of her thighs then back up to her hips, past her ribs to her breasts. He kneaded the firm mounds until she squirmed, thrusting her hips into his in an ever-increasing rhythm, each movement rubbing his erection against the seam between her legs.

The vague notion that this was probably a bad idea evaporated the second she put her hand on his cock through his jeans and wrapped her fingers around him.

She moaned as he popped the button on her shorts, dragged down the zipper and slid his hand into her underwear, eliciting an answering groan from him. Short, soft hair covered her mound, and he let his fingers linger over it for one second before he delved farther and rubbed his middle finger against her clit.

Bucking against him, she grabbed his shoulders but not to push him away. She broke their kiss, drawing in a deep breath. With her eyes closed, she bowed away from the bed as he began a slow massage that he increased steadily until she struggled to draw in air.

She was wet, hot and slick between her legs, completely bare but for the short hair on her mound. That turned him on more than he would've thought possible.

Alternating strokes on her clit with increasingly hard thrusts into her sheath, he worked her ruthlessly. And when she came, her cry echoed in his ears, settled in his chest and fired his blood to full boil. He wanted to hear her again.

She didn't move for a few seconds, only breathed. When she finally stopped pulsing around his fingers, he pulled them free reluctantly but left them lying on her mound.

He looked up and found her staring at him. Her mouth barely moved, but he knew she was smiling.

Especially when she moved her hand to the button on his jeans.

Taking her time, she forced the button through the hole, keeping her gaze locked to his. His breath caught in his throat when her fingers moved to the zipper tab. She wouldn't be able to release the zipper, his erection pressed against it too tightly.

Still, he didn't move, wondering what she'd do when she realized that.

He wasn't prepared for her to flip him on his back in one smooth move. Or for her to trap him between her thighs and kneel over him.

Did she think he was going to try to get away?

Two days ago, he wouldn't have believed they'd ever be in this position. He still wasn't quite sure how they'd gotten here. He thought—

With a metallic rasp, she released his zipper and pulled his pants down his hips and Diego stopped thinking. Time enough for that later.

Right now, he'd just enjoy.

As he watched, her gaze slid from his chest to his stomach and finally to his cock, throbbing with lust.

He had no idea what she'd do next and realized he was holding his breath. His lungs released the pent-up air in a harsh sigh when she laid her cool palm across his shaft then let her fingers trail from the already seeping tip to the base. Her fingers combed through the wiry hairs at the base then cupped his tight balls. He bit back a groan as lightning shot from his cock into his stomach then up his spine when she pressed her middle finger in the center of his sac and lightly scraped her fingernail on the perineum.

Heart tripping in his chest, he thought he might have heart failure. She stared down at him and, though his eyes wanted to roll back into his head with pleasure, he forced his gaze to stay connected to hers.

It was important to maintain that connection between them, for her to know exactly who she was in bed with.

Until she ran that fingernail from his ass to his balls to the tip of his cock and sent shivers up his spine. His eyes closed as he bit back a groan and sank his fingers into the bedcover. He wanted to grab her and force her to kiss him, but remembered how she'd come to be in his world. He refused to be labeled among the animals who'd bitten her.

The pressure on his legs lessened as she shifted away from him. Keeping his eyes closed, he struggled to catch his breath.

Shit, she was coming to her senses.

No. No, this was good. He'd been crazy to let it get this far, even though he'd be left with an aching erection that'd require at least half an hour in a freezing cold shower.

When the bed moved again, he prepared himself to get up and let her get some sleep. Maybe she'd be able to now.

He, on the other hand, would be wide awake for hours.

Amy Jo didn't move away from him. She began to move up his body. His eyes flew open and he found himself staring straight into hers, directly above him. Completely unsmiling now, heat flaring in her eyes, she wrapped her hand around his cock and pulled him back. He drew in a deep breath. This time, his hands grabbed her hips to help her move into place over him.

The tip of his cock brushed against her wet labia, parting them just as his fingers had only a minute ago. She rubbed him back and forth, coating the head in her moisture. He could barely breathe when she finally held him steady and began to sink onto him, a centimeter at a time.

That smooth slide seemed to take forever, trailing heat in her wake. He couldn't control the thrust of his hips to seat her completely.

When she gasped, he froze, biting down hard on his lip to control his urge to move.

"Oh, God," she murmured, barely audible. "Don't stop."

That was all he needed to hear. He got a better grip on her hips, determined not to rush her or hurt her, and started a slow, steady pace.

Her eyes closed as she sucked her bottom lip between her

teeth. Her expression hovered somewhere between pleasure and pain but her hands... Hell, her hands enflamed him.

She ran one from her neck to her breasts, cupping and kneading herself until he thought he'd go cross-eyed watching her. Her other hand reached behind her to caress his balls.

She did so until the sensation nearly drove him out of his skin. He had no idea how he kept up any kind of rhythm. Especially when she moved the hand from her breast to her clit and began to rub herself in time to his thrusts. When he lifted her, her fingernail grazed his cock, hastening his climax until he knew he wasn't going to last much longer.

Lowering her again, he said, "Come on, baby. Come for me. Now."

When she did—gasping his name, her sheath contracting around him—he released into her warmth.

She remained upright on his lap until his last spasm then leaned forward until she lay against his chest, her body still clamped around his slowly softening cock.

Silence closed them in, shutting out the no-star hotel room and the rest of the world. He didn't want to move and wouldn't. At least not until she'd fallen asleep.

Which happened in seconds. Her body relaxed into his until she went boneless. He let her rest there for a few minutes, listening to her steady breathing, her head under his chin.

He wanted to fall asleep here with her as his blanket. But... he should check on Marco, make sure no one had followed them. He should set up a ward spell around both rooms to alert him if anyone tried to get in.

With a sigh, he shifted her to the side, only to feel her arms wrap around his neck.

"Don't go," she whispered into his chest, her lips raising goosebumps along his skin.

His own arms tightened around her. "I won't. Just let me take our clothes off."

Her eyes never opened but her lips perked in a drowsy smile. "And you didn't think of that earlier?"

"I was busy earlier." Rolling her onto her back, he skimmed out of his jeans and t-shirt then helped her take off her top.

The second he laid back down, she scooted against him, draping her body over his, as if to stop him from getting away.

He didn't mind. He combed his fingers through her hair then palmed her head to keep her cheek against his chest.

"Go to sleep."

Surprisingly, she had nothing to say to that.

# TEN

"I never did find out who Marco is."

Steven didn't bother to turn away from the window to answer her. "He's Diego's half brother. They share the same father."

Fingers curling into the arm of the airplane seat so she didn't smack him on the back of his rock-hard head, Bella took a deep breath and made a grab for her fast-disappearing patience.

She'd told herself she was going to take the high road, not goad him into speaking to her or start wailing on him with all of her pent-up frustration.

Even though he would totally deserve it if she did.

But, so help her, if he didn't pull his head out of his ass soon, he was going to find himself with a screaming bitch on his hands.

After a short debate about the wisdom of taking a commercial flight, which limited their escape options should they need one, they'd decided to risk it. They needed to get to Cole as soon as possible and figure out what the hell they were going to do about the *congress* crashers. And what the *Mal* wanted with Cole and the *lucani*.

They'd been able to get a nonstop flight out of Atlanta to New Orleans that left only an hour or so after they got to the airport.

Now they were trapped together, surrounded by *eteri*, and she wanted to talk so he would, by-all-the-gods, going to talk.

"I take it they don't have such a great relationship," she said.

Steven shrugged, the motion barely visible in the darkened cabin. "I didn't ask." He sighed, shifting in his seat. "Look, we should probably get some sleep. We don't know what's going to happen when we get to New Orleans."

Anger seethed in her gut as he dropped the final straw that broke the hold she had on her temper.

She knew now was *not* the best time to have this conversation but she was sick of waiting, and frankly, he was a captive audience. They were seated in the last row of first class. The only other occupants were an elderly couple near the front of the plane and a business-suited man asleep two rows in front of them.

Trying to keep her voice level, she said, "No, Steven. I don't want to get any sleep. I want to talk. Right now."

He tensed and she scented his rising anger. Fine. It should match her own in a few minutes.

"Now is not the time—"

"You're wrong." Her voice snapped through his, fighting to keep her voice to a low growl. "Now is the perfect time. We need to get some things settled before we get to Cole."

After a second, he turned to face her. He opened his mouth then closed it without saying a word.

Apparently, she'd said the magic word. Cole.

As screwed-up as their relationship was, his relationship with Cole was possibly even more complicated. They had been as close as brothers. Hell, they'd been closer. They'd shared a room. They'd trained together. For eight years, they'd been each other's sole confidante, bonding over loss and despair.

And it'd only taken one stupid, stupid decision by her to tear them apart.

Her heart hurt to see raw pain flash across his face. It hurt even more to admit she was the cause.

His jaw tensed as he nodded. "Fine."

She waited but he said nothing. So she gave him both barrels.

"I love you, Steven. I can't stand living apart from you any more. We're meant to be together." She grabbed his hand, clenched around the seat's arm between them. "Stop denying yourself and me. Cole offered you a job three years ago, before I...before my accident. I know he'd offer it to you again. Take it. Come back to us—"

"You don't have a clue what you're asking."

Startled by the harsh tone of his voice, she pulled away, her brain trying to formulate a rebuttal. But she couldn't because the raw agony emanating from him stopped her cold, despair making his eyes bleak.

"Do you think it's been easy, living apart from the only people I love in the world?" Every word he spoke held a bite, a sharp jagged edge that tore through her flesh. "Do you think I enjoy having my heart torn out of my chest every time I hear... every time I even *think* your name or Cole's?"

Blessed Goddess, this wasn't what she'd wanted. He sounded as if she had ripped out his heart with her bare hands.

"Steven—"

"*No.*" He slashed a hand in front of her face. "You asked for this. Now you have to listen." His dark gaze fixed on hers with blinding intensity. "I *have* to stay away from you. Don't you understand what will happen if I don't? If I let go and let myself love you the way I want to?"

He leaned closer, as if she couldn't hear every word he said.

"If I release my control over my emotions, over *any* of them, that blackness I've managed to contain until now will worm its way out of the its hole and it'll take me under. I'll lose the part of me you say you love. And I'll become the monster I was born to be. The monster no one wants to talk about."

Tears crept into her eyes as he spoke. Tears of despair and frustration, tears she tried to blink away but couldn't quite. She felt one run down her cheek and watched his eyes track its progress.

"Steven, please—"

"Please what?" His gaze returned to hers and her despair was mirrored in his eyes. "Please love you? Please shut up? Please fuck you? I can do all of those things but they still won't mean anything at the end of the day because I will never be what you want me to be."

He moved to frame her face with hands that shook.

Or was that the plane?

"You know how my magic works, Bella. At least you say you do. It's tied to my emotions. Fear, anger, love. When I'm with you, they're all mixed together in one huge mess that sits in my stomach like a tumor. It festers there, waiting for a trigger. Waiting for me to use the magic.

"Being around you, being around Cole, it's like this huge magnet to that darkness. It's drawn closer to the surface, close enough that I find myself reaching for it before I know I'm doing it."

Fear began to chill her blood. "Steven, stop—"

He shook his head. "Don't you see? I can never stop."

She didn't believe that, *couldn't* believe that because if she did, she'd have to admit that she'd lost him forever. "No. When you were working with your mom—"

"Don't—"

"—you had it under control. You could keep it under control. Why—"

"I killed my mother."

Her heart hurt at the agony in his voice. "No, Steven. You didn't."

But she also knew this was a battle he lived with daily and nothing she said would change his mind.

"When the *Mal* came for me that day, I thought I could use my magic to protect her, to kill them." His voice sounded dry and raspy, like five miles of bad road. "And I did. I killed them, but I couldn't control it. I would have killed myself but she... pushed me out of the way of the bolt of lightning I couldn't control. And it killed her. *I* killed her."

"No. She saved you. Not even your dad believed you killed her."

A rumble of thunder echoed through the plane as a flash of lightning shone through the windows.

"Ladies and gentlemen, please return your seats and trays to their upright position and fasten your seatbelts. We're experiencing some unexpected turbulence..."

The words faded out as she saw tears well in his eyes and another rumble of thunder shook the plane.

A storm had formed out of the seemingly clear blue sky. Thunder vibrated through the plane like a bass echo. In her peripheral vision, she saw dark clouds roiling in the sky and flashes of lightning made the cabin glow for seconds at a time like a strobe light.

This was his doing.

Fear began to build in the pit of her stomach. "Steven, rein it in. You've got stop."

He shook his head, gaze still so intense, his blue eyes glowing in the dark. "Don't you see, Bella? This is what happens when I'm around you and everyone else I love. I can't control it."

"Yes, you can." He had to. "Make it go away, Steven. Now."

She felt the strength in his hands, shaking as they cupped her face.

She covered them with her own. "Look at me. You can do it. You can call it back."

A gust of wind buffeted the plane, making it drop several feet. Several passengers screamed and her stomach rolled but she didn't move her eyes from Steven's. "Let it go, love. Let the anger go and close your eyes."

He shook his head and pulled his hands from under hers. She mourned the contact immediately. "I can't. That darkness is always there, waiting."

"No, it's not. Focus on me." This time, she placed her hands on his cheeks. "Look at me, Steven. I know you don't want anything to happen to me. Release the storm. Breathe with me."

The plane lurched again, not as hard this time and the next roll of thunder sounded farther away than the last.

His gaze bored into hers as he struggled with the part of himself he hated. Sweat beaded on his forehead and he took a deep breath, then another, following her lead.

Another rumble of thunder, this one even farther away.

The plane began to level off and the sky outside began to clear.

Time passed, she didn't know how much. But finally, with a shaky sigh, Steven fell back into his seat, closing his eyes. Shutting her out.

*Blessed Goddess.*

Bella leaned back and closed her eyes as well, trying to catch her breath and stop the shakes.

Tinia's teat. He'd pulled that storm from the air without so much as a ritual spell. His powers had increased over the past three years they'd been apart.

*Or he'd been practicing.*

No. She didn't believe that.

When they got to New Orleans, she'd talk to Cole. Cole would be able to figure something out.

Since the death of her parents, the men in her life had been able to fix whatever she'd screwed up. It had taken her several months to control her animal form without her mom's guiding influence. For those months, Cole had slept by her bed for an entire week on either side of the full moon, when she would wake screaming in terror, fighting her change for fear someone would hunt her down and kill her.

Steven's father, Michael, had held her hand during her family's funeral. When Cole had collapsed and Michael had had to help him away from the gravesite, Steven had lifted her into his arms when she would have sat beside the gravestones until she'd died of starvation.

And when Michael had been killed, it had been Cole and Steven holding her hands, forcing her to eat, forcing her to continue to choose the college courses she would return to in the fall.

But then everything had changed. Her stupidity had led to the rift between Cole and Steven. Her brother still blamed Steven for her near-death, wouldn't forgive the man he loved just as much as he had their brother, Cal.

Because of her.

Her eyes snapped open and she stared at the headrest in front of her.

No, she couldn't rely on Cole to fix this. *She* had to fix this.

But how?

AMY JO WOKE, her head pillowed on Diego's slowly rising and falling chest. Complete darkness covered the room. No hint of daylight showed through the curtains at the windows.

*Shit.* She was in deep shit.

She inhaled, his spicy scent seeping into her brain, causing last night to replay in extreme slow motion. Her heart raced and she struggled to control her breathing for fear of waking him.

*Yeah, right. At least be honest with yourself. You want him to wake so you can have him again.*

Oh, God, did she ever.

She'd never had sex like that in her life. Never had it felt so good or so damn right. They'd screwed like they'd known each other for years instead of days.

But now what?

Diego hadn't exactly pledged his undying love last night. She might have run screaming if he had. Still, he could've said something, anything. Like, "Wow, babe. Great lay." Hell, she would've settled for "Thanks."

Of course, she hadn't said anything either. Although she had asked him to stay, and here he still was.

Sure, he'd listened to that. Now here they were. An awkward situation just waiting to happen.

She sighed and he stirred, making her freeze in place.

"I know you're awake." He spoke directly into her ear. "I can practically hear you thinking."

He shifted beneath her then dim light spilled from the lamp on the bedside table. Steeling her spine, she propped herself up on an elbow and forced herself to look at him. Dark and heavy-lidded, his gaze made the muscles between her legs contract and she dismantled her sigh in mid-formation.

"Good morning." It was the only thing she could think of to say that didn't invoke a lot of questions.

The upward tilt of his gorgeous mouth made it clear he knew what she was doing. "Good morning. Did you sleep well?"

A blush began to burn her cheeks but she forced an answer. "Yes, I did. Thank you."

She wasn't exactly positive what she was thanking him for—the good night's sleep or the sex.

Diego's mouth twisted just a little bit into a grimace and she thought he might have winced, as well. But he didn't look away. "I'm glad."

He held her gaze for another few seconds then turned to look at the digital clock beside the light. It read 8:08 a.m. "We should probably get up and get going. Marco's—" He stopped and an expression that looked suspiciously like pain crossed his face.

What? He didn't want to face his brother after spending the night with her? Why? Was he ashamed he'd succumbed and lowered his standards to sleep with her?

She took an involuntary gulp of air and his gaze arrowed back to her.

"Are you okay?"

She shrugged, trying for nonchalant, and probably only achieved pathetic. "I'm fine."

Sitting up, she ran shaking hands through her tangled hair. God, she must look like something the cat dragged in. Whereas he looked good enough to eat for breakfast with his hair rumpled and sexy.

"You're right," she continued. "We should probably get going. I know you wanted to get on the road as soon as we could, so I'm just going to take a quick shower." She started to get up but realized she was naked. And he was watching every move she made. She pulled the sheet more tightly around her and looked anywhere but at him. "Then again, maybe you want to get in first? You go right ahead. I'll just, um, wait 'til you're finished."

His sigh filled the dead space left when she stopped talking.

"Amy Jo. Look at me."

"You know, we really should get a-move-on. You just go on—"

He cupped her chin, turned her toward him and kissed her.

Actually, he kissed the shit out of her. She was too stunned to move. And then she realized she didn't want to move. Releasing her death grip on the sheet, she threw her arms around his neck. She would have deepened the kiss but he drew back and cupped her face in both hands.

"You have a beautiful body." He looked straight into her eyes, his voice a husky rasp. "Your breasts are gorgeous and your legs are a work of art. The perfect curve of your lips makes my mouth water. You talk too damn much, you're too smart for your own good and I want to kill the men who—" He stopped, shook his head and drew in a deep breath. "Drop the sheet then get in the damn shower so I can talk to Marco before we leave. He's been pacing in the next room for the past half hour."

She heard something in his voice, something that might have been regret, might have been anger. She couldn't tell and she didn't care. His words rang in her head, made her stomach clench in arousal.

*Please take me. Please take me. Please...*

He groaned low in his throat before he closed his eyes. Shaking his head, he got off the bed and grabbed his jeans. "If you continue to look at me like that, I'm not going to be able to leave this room without having you again and we do need get moving."

Satisfaction warmed her blood and her mouth curved in a smile. She liked knowing she had the same effect on him. Emboldened by his words, she took her time sliding off the bed then walked to the bathroom, knowing he watched every step she made. When she reached the door, she stopped and turned to look at him.

"Just so you know, I *am* grateful for the full night's sleep." She let her smile bloom and watched his expression go taut with desire. "And I expect there to be more in my future. Don't run scared on me, Diego."

Then she closed the door behind her and leaned against it, heart racing.

Jesus H. Christmas. What in holy hell had possessed her to say that? Not that she hadn't meant every word. It was just, she'd never been much of a tease. Hadn't seen much reason for it, when men either wanted you or they didn't. Some of them would take you whether you wanted them or not. She'd seen too many girls tease a man to the point that he thought you were giving him the go-ahead when you weren't.

But there was something about Diego that made her push. Something about his ingrained honor that made her feel safe enough to tease him. And after what had happened, it was a major step forward for her.

Still, if whatever this voodoo woman in New Orleans was going to do to her worked, and he found out exactly what those other men had done to her, would he still want her?

Would he be sickened by it, or God forbid, pity her? She didn't want anyone's pity. Hell, she didn't know what she wanted, but she knew it wasn't pity.

Moving to the shower, she turned the taps and waited until the water hit lukewarm before she stepped in.

For months, her only reason for living had been to find a cure. Now, knowing that was a lost cause, she had to reevaluate her plan.

Like it or not, she was going to have to learn how to deal with this new life of hers, as freaky as it may seem. But there were others. Bella had promised to help her. Diego... Well, that would have to wait.

First things first. New Orleans.

And if she lived through that... Maybe she could think about other, more enjoyable things.

# ELEVEN

Bella woke to the sound of the landing gear lowering as the plane descended toward New Orleans.

She'd slept funny and her neck hurt. When she twisted her head to get rid of the kink, she caught Steven's gaze. He looked wide awake but there was a hint of wildness in his eyes.

They said nothing as the plane landed and they disembarked. By the time they reached the terminal, she thought her head might explode from the tension.

Since they had no luggage, they headed straight for the lobby, where Cole had told her he'd meet them. Her gaze darted around the space until she caught sight of a familiar head of perfectly cut chestnut-brown hair.

Cole, flanked by his three *centuriones* and his ever-present *praetorian*. Joy skipped through her heart and she felt sixteen again, desperate to see her beloved big brother who'd been away at college for months.

Cole had been a wiry teen but he'd grown into a tall, solid wall of muscle who drew the eye of every woman wherever he went. He was broader than Steven and heavier, though not by much. And his brown and green hazel eyes never failed to calm her.

He looked like an intensely masculine version of their mother, his nose and cheeks razor straight, his mouth a gorgeous bow—that looked ready to crack, it was so stiff. He looked like he was going to curse or break down and sob.

"Cole!"

Her happy cry cracked his lips into a smile as she ran through the crowd and launched herself into his arms from several feet away.

She didn't care that they were making a scene, that *eteri* were staring at them. She only wanted the comfort of her brother's arms.

"Hey, brat." He grabbed her out of the air into a hug that would have crushed another woman's ribs. "Damn, Bella. You scared the living shit out of me."

She nodded, her chin bumping his shoulder, as she clung, just for a few seconds. Well, maybe more than a few seconds.

She didn't know how long he held her, arms tight, her feet dangling off the ground, before he set her down to look at her. "Are you really okay?"

Her smile made an appearance then. "I'm fine, Cole. Really." She leaned in to give him another hug, whispering in his ear as she did. "I'm not the one you should be worried about."

"I'll always worry about you, baby."

Yeah, he would, though he should know she could take care of herself. He'd taught her how himself.

Of course, since the moment of her birth, their parents had ingrained in him his duty to keep her safe. Before Cal had died, it had been his job to look after Cole and Bella. Now, it was just the two of them.

And Steven.

Cole's gaze transferred to the man standing several feet behind her.

She turned as well and tried to look at Steven through the eyes of the best friend he hadn't seen in three years.

He'd lost weight and his hair was longer. But the wild, almost feral look he'd had in his eyes the night Cole sent him away had returned.

That look made Cole grimace in pain.

Steven might have had a tight rein on his emotions but he looked ready to snap at any moment. She wanted so badly to make this easier for them, but she didn't know how. They had to figure that out for themselves, even if Steven broke and brought the wrath of the heavens down on them.

When Cole glanced at her, she nodded her encouragement and watched with baited breath as Cole stepped around her toward Steven.

Steven's chin lifted as if gearing up to take a punch. Instead, Cole walked right up to him, wrapped his arms around Steven and hugged him just as hard as he'd hugged her. It took a second for Steven to respond, a second in which she was sure Steven was going to push Cole away. But then Steven hugged him back.

Somcone else might have mistaken them for lovers, they held onto each other for so long.

Neither man said a word. Too many people around.

When they parted—reluctantly, she knew—she saw some of Steven's wildness had calmed. And most of the stiffness had left Cole's expression

Cole inclined his head in a silent question and Steven nodded once.

A long-suffering sigh came from behind Bella. "As touching as this is, we need to get a move on. Sir."

Cole's back stiffened at the implied insult in that last little word and Bella had to work to stifle her grin. If Dorian Pelligrini hadn't been such a damn good *praetorian*, Cole would've found a way to get rid of his personal bodyguard years ago.

At thirty-eight, Dorian was still considered young to be Cole's *praetorian*. Her short dark hair, somewhere between black and brown, held no trace of gray and her five-foot-eight body was still as slim and toned as a twenty-year-old's. She was pretty in a way that belied her training, possibly making her more deadly than a man who looked like he could kill you with one hand tied behind his back.

Dorian had been trained almost from birth for the position, though she'd been meant for Cal, their older brother. When Cole had decided to go to college at nineteen, Dorian's father, who'd been their father's most trusted advisor, had assigned Dorian to him as *praetorian*.

Cole had raged and demanded she be un-assigned but their father's three *centuriones* had insisted, no matter that he was now *legatus* and outranked them. They'd told him they weren't going to lose another king and he either kept her close or learned to live under lock and key.

He and Steven had kicked almost a case of beer between them that night and never got to bed. In the morning, Cole had agreed and he and Dorian had enrolled at Penn State's main campus where they shared a two-bedroom apartment. To say they tolerated each other was an overstatement.

They barely spoke, though in terms of his safety, whatever Dorian said was law.

As Dorian herded them toward the exit, Bella and Cole made careful small talk, Steven silent and watchful behind them. A limousine drove up the second they stepped out of the doors.

Cole, Steven, Bella and Dorian got in the back, while one *centuriones* got into the front with the driver and the other two headed for the parking lot for the other car.

"Princess, I hope all is well with you."

Dorian's formality had Bella straightening in her seat.

"Very well, thank you." Bella smiled, hoping for an answering one from Dorian. She'd always looked up to this strong woman. "And you, *Praetorian*? And your family? They're all well?"

Dorian's mouth actually curved into something resembling a smile. "Yes. My parents are in Mexico at the moment, lying on a beach. My brothers look after the shop and my sister..." She paused and shook her head, her smile becoming more pronounced, "well, let's just say Kaley's still trying to find herself. But she's fine, thank you."

Bella hadn't seen Kaley in years. She remembered a skinny kid with braces and blond hair, a few years younger than herself, with a snorting laugh that could stop traffic. Kaley had laughed a lot.

"I'm glad to hear it."

"And I'm glad to hear you're unharmed after your recent troubles. But, Princess, we need to revisit the subject of a full-time guard. I know you've refused in the past—"

"Dorian, I'm not—"

"—but this last episode proves my point. You need someone to watch your back at all times."

Bella tried not to sigh but this was an old fight, one she'd known would be reopened following this last incident. She just hadn't expected it so soon. She turned to her brother. "Cole, I don't want someone shadowing my every move twenty-four hours a day. I just don't think it's necessary. Until this incident, no one has hassled me. You know how I feel about this."

Cole nodded. "Yeah, I do and I know how Dorian feels about it and I know how I feel about it." Cole looked at Steven. "What do you think?"

Steven blinked, his shock at Cole's question plain on his face. It took him a few seconds to formulate an answer.

Then the old Steven reappeared. The Steven who knew Cole better than anyone, even his sister. Who had been his confidante, his best friend. He relaxed further into the leather seat.

"You know what I think. She should've had one years ago."

Curses leapt to the tip of her tongue but she bit them back. "Don't you think we have more important things to worry about right now than finding me a babysitter?"

The men exchanged a glance then said, "No," in perfect unison.

Oh, sure, now they decide join forces.

As Bella opened her mouth to respond, Dorian raised her hand. "Once we have this settled, we can move on to the next problem. But let's take them one at a time. And you're first on the agenda."

She took a deep breath as she counted to ten. Time seemed to have reversed itself and she was eighteen again, fighting with Michael, Steven's dad, about the need for a bodyguard. He'd caved to her pleading—begging, actually—that she not be assigned a jailer. She wasn't king. She knew how to take care of herself. He had trained her well. And she'd draw more attention to herself if she had an entourage.

Besides, the *Mal* believed her to be dead. Michael had managed to make her disappear after the death of her parents. While the *lucani* had needed to know that Cole still lived to lead them, Bella had been extraneous.

Sometimes, she believed that was part of her problem.

Three pairs of eyes continued to stare at her, all with varying degrees of raised eyebrows. She wasn't going to win this one.

Taking a deep breath, she nodded, knowing that the sooner

they got this out of their system, the sooner they could discuss the situation at hand. Besides, she wasn't stupid. She knew Cole would worry about her if she didn't cooperate. And he didn't need to worry about her now.

"Fine, I'll agree to a *temporary* guard. One, and only one. Now can we discuss what's going on?"

Victory swept across Dorian's expression before she wiped it away and leaned forward, hands on her knees, ready to listen. "Start at the beginning. Tell me everything you heard that night. I want to know every detail."

So she told the tale again. How she had been walking home from dinner—

"With who?" Steven demanded.

She turned to give him a cool look. "With a group of friends, which I would have explained if you'd let me finish."

"Do you go out with that same group at the same time every week?" Dorian asked.

She shook her head. "No, this was a spur-of-the-moment thing. One of the receptionists is getting married and—"

"Do you mean one of the workers at the veterinary clinic?" Dorian interrupted.

"Yes, her wedding's in two weeks and we decided to take her out to dinner."

"So this was totally unexpected?" Dorian asked.

"Well, no, a bunch of us had been planning to take her out for drinks after work one night and this just happened to work out."

"And you're sure no one at the clinic knows your real name?"

Bella sighed. This was another old fight. When she'd decided to take the job at the Philadelphia veterinary clinic run by *eteri*, both Cole and Dorian had had a fit. If she was going to work, they'd argued, why couldn't she at least take a job with an

Etruscan, preferably one of the *lucani* doctors working in Berks County. It had probably been one of the only times Cole and Dorian had ever been in agreement.

But she hadn't wanted to work for an Etruscan. She'd wanted to cut herself off completely from the society that had cost her the love of her life.

When she'd refused, Cole had threatened to lock her away somewhere safe. Possibly in his basement. Dorian had actually left Cole's side to visit her at school in Philadelphia and try to talk her out of it.

Bella had threatened to leave and never return. She didn't want to be stuck in Berks County, she'd told him. She'd wanted to live in a big city. She'd actually considered New York City, but knew her brother would've had a heart attack. So she'd decided to stay in Philadelphia. It was close to Reading and southeastern Berks County, where the legion owned thousands of acres not far from her parents' property.

She had laid out her plan and stuck to it. She'd made it through college and veterinary school without anyone learning her real identity. A job wouldn't be much different. Not many people outside of the *lucani* community knew what she looked like. Those who did knew better than to identify her when there were others around who weren't *lucani*.

"I'm positive," she answered. "No one at the clinic knows who I am. And the night out was not planned. I had to hang out for a while after work, didn't feel like running back to my apartment then heading back right away to meet up with everyone."

Dorian's eyes narrowed. "And they tried to grab you after you left the bar, so they either followed you there or they got lucky and saw your car parked on the street."

Hmm. Which meant these guys had been watching her, following her. Both creeped her out.

"Either way," Dorian continued, "the bad guys knew exactly what you looked like and where to find you."

Well, when Dorian put it that way, it sounded much more...calculated.

She glanced at her brother and Steven just as they were exchanging *that* look. She remembered that look from her teen years. It meant she'd screwed up again and wasn't that a shock.

Well, screw them. She wasn't taking the rap for this one. She'd done everything she could—well, except for the bodyguard part—and someone had almost gotten to her.

With a huff, she held up one hand, partly in surrender. She wasn't going to argue that point. Mostly because she couldn't. "Yeah, they did. But I think we're missing the bigger problem here. Jones knew I was the way to get to Steven. How?"

Now all eyes turned toward Steven.

Who never shifted his gaze from hers.

"I know I'm to blame for this." His voice barely shook. "*I'll* take care of it. But that—"

"No way," Cole said. "Don't even think about—"

"That's definitely not the way to handle this—" Dorian said.

"—doesn't change the fact that Bella needs a guard, preferably *grigorio* or *praetorian*," Steven finished.

Bella couldn't help but roll her eyes as they all talked over one another. And since none of them wanted to listen to her, she didn't bother to interrupt again. She'd learned at an early age to let everyone else make plans and when they finished, she'd do what she wanted.

"Steven, there's no way I'm gonna let you do this on your own." Cole shook his head. "You think I want to lose anyone else—"

"Oh hell." Steven sounded brusque but she could see he was touched. "Don't be melodramatic. I've been taking care of myself for years."

Cole snorted, his mouth twisting in a snarl. "Yeah, and look how well that turned out. You're working for the fucking enemy and you didn't even know it."

She gasped as Steven's face paled and even Dorian raised her eyebrows and stared at Cole in disbelief.

"*Shit*." Cole bit out the curse, slamming his hands on his knees. "That didn't come out right. *Vaffanculo*. I've been so fucking worried about you for so many years. You're so damn stubborn, I don't know—"

"Stubborn? I'm *stubborn?*" Steven's voice sounded incredulous. "You told me to stay away. You *ordered* me to stay away."

Uh oh. They'd started to gesture with their hands. When they'd been kids, that usually meant blows would follow.

"I was angry and you knew it." Cole's index finger came dangerously close to Steven's chest. "You should have come back, you bastard."

"Why the hell didn't you ask me to?" Steven bit off each word.

"Because you broke her heart and she nearly killed herself!"

And that was her cue to put a stop to this. Leaning forward, she set one hand on either man's chest and pushed them back into their seats. "That's enough!"

They didn't even glance at her.

"I was trying to protect her," Steven shouted. "Do you think I wanted her to die? Don't you know I would give my life for her? Or for you, you fucking idiot."

Okay, that was nice but the choked sound of Steven's voice ripped at her heart. "Steven! Cole!" She shoved at them again. "That's it. Stop it. Right now. Or I'm heading back to Philly on the next plane."

Ah, now she had their attention. Their faces held almost identical expressions of anger tinged with fear as they turned to look at her.

"You are going nowhere—"

"You're not going anywhere—"

She whipped one hand in front of each man like a traffic cop. "I'll go if I want to and neither of you will have a damn thing to say about it."

That shut them up.

"You." She pointed to Cole. "My accident wasn't Steven's fault. If you had listened to me when I talked to you afterward, you would've known that." She turned to Steven. "And you... you should have known better than to think Cole wanted you gone. You should've stuck by us."

Steven's jaw clenched. She could tell he wanted to say something but wasn't sure it wouldn't dig him in deeper.

She took a deep breath. "Now, if you two are done, we've got things to discuss."

Cole turned to Dorian. "I want Matt."

*Shit.* Cole had immediately returned to her situation about a bodyguard. And there was no *freaking* way she would put up with *grigorio* Matt Tedaldi. Not for all the chocolate in the world. She opened her mouth to protest but Dorian answered first. "He won't come. He's dealing with some family issues. It'll have to be someone else."

"Who's closest?" Stephen asked.

Dorian's brows rose. "Luca. He came with me."

Bella tried to hide her smile but couldn't. "I can live with Luca."

"Oh, no way in hell," Cole said. "She'll walk all over him. Shit, Dori, you know how he is."

Just as she'd hoped, Dorian went to bat for her younger cousin. "He's been training for this his whole life, Cole. Don't you dare say anything—"

"Oh, please, you know what I'm talking about. Don't twist this—"

"—about my cousin being unable to take care—"

"—into something it's not."

"—of his charges. He knows what he's doing."

While Dorian and Cole continued to face off across the car, Bella caught Steven staring at her, shaking his head, his expression grave.

"I'll stay," he said.

Elation lit her smile though she tried to hide it.

"Don't say it if you don't mean it, Steven. I don't want you here if you don't want to be here."

And she meant that. She wanted him to want to be here. Wanted him to want to stay with her. She could manipulate him into staying, work on his guilt until he cried uncle and gave in. But it wouldn't mean a damn thing if he didn't *want* to be here.

His expression solemn, he gazed into her eyes. "You know damn well I'm exactly where I want to be and why this is the place I should be farthest from." He held up his hand when she would have protested. "Don't. Just don't. I'll stay. For now. And you'll still have Luca stuck to you like glue. Got it?"

She nodded, her smile fading. "Thank you."

---

THE ATMOSPHERE in the car was so loaded with tension, Amy Jo swore she could feel it crawling over her skin like ants.

She sat in the front with Diego, needed to sit in the front because she got violently ill if she sat in the back. Motion sickness sucked.

Marco hadn't given her a fight, had simply climbed into the backseat and turned his head to look out the window. Neither brother had said a word to the other since they'd left the hotel.

After an hour of trying to draw one or the other into conversation, she gave up and tried to take a nap.

That lasted all of about an hour, leaving another five hours of driving time, according to Diego's calculations.

They could've cut down on that time if they'd flown, but of course, they couldn't risk a commercial flight with her.

She sighed. Life sucked.

Although...last night certainly hadn't.

She slid a look at Diego then couldn't force herself to look away. The man seemed to have gotten more gorgeous in the hours between last night and right now.

Of course, the great sex might've had something to do with that.

"Amy Jo."

Oh, hell, she even liked the way he said her name. His voice was husky and hinted at dark secrets.

"Amy Jo."

"Yeah?"

"You're staring."

"So?"

His eyebrows rose into arches, so different from their normal straight slash. "Why?"

Her mouth tilted into a smile. She'd learned a little bit about this man in the past hours, enough to know he didn't like to be the center of attention. He liked to be the one who watched. "Why shouldn't I?"

He sighed and shook his head. "Why don't you get some sleep?"

She shrugged. "Tried that already. I'm too wound."

"Then find something else to stare at."

"Y'know, you really are too masculine to be pretty, but I gotta say, your hair is much prettier than mine. Do you curl it or is it just natural?"

In the backseat, Marco snorted, exposing his sleep as a fraud. Diego shot her a look that was part embarrassment, part bemusement.

Lucky for her, she'd gotten used to that as one of the only kids in her high school who'd actually enjoyed learning and had been determined to go to college. All the others just wanted to get a job or find a man.

"No, I don't curl my hair. Do you say everything that comes into your head?"

She nodded. "Yeah, mostly. Bad habit I've picked up since I gained fangs and a new fur coat."

That sent the mood in the car plummeting again as Diego stiffened, his knuckles going white as he clenched the steering wheel, and Marco drew in a short, sharp breath.

Damn, she should've kept her mouth shut. Again. When the hell was she going to learn?

"Turning furry every month is a shock to the system, especially for those who don't ask for it," Marco said from the backseat. "Don't beat yourself up over what you can't control."

She turned her head as much as she dared—the motion sickness was a real bitch—to look at Marco.

"I try not to, but it's hard, ya know?"

Marco actually cracked a smile. "Yeah, I know."

Amy Jo's lips curved and she felt a short sharp tug in her middle that felt a hell of a lot like attraction.

Wow. Was it just because he looked so much like Diego?

Although, the more she time she spent with the brothers, the more different they looked.

Both were wildly attractive. So much so, Amy Jo found it hard to breathe.

She'd never been attracted to two men at the same time, especially not brothers. God, she could just imagine the mess that would make.

She'd slept with Diego last night, for Christ's sake. How stupid was she to smile at Marco this morning?

Dropping her gaze, she turned around, catching Diego's thoughtful expression.

Did he know what she was thinking? He'd probably be furious with her if he did. Marco and Diego had a rocky enough relationship without a woman getting in the middle of them.

Although, what woman wouldn't want to be in the middle of those two—

Jesus, what the hell was wrong with her? Had she become a sex maniac in addition to a werewolf?

Blinking, she turned to stare out the front window. She vaguely heard Diego say something to her and forced herself to ask him to repeat.

"I'm amazed you managed to come through those first months with your mind intact," Diego said. "How did you learn to handle it?"

She shrugged, almost ashamed to admit that part of it had been sheer stubbornness. "I immersed myself in research. Anything and everything I could get my hands on about werewolves. There's a lot of superstition out there but a lot of truth is hidden in all those old tales. Besides, I knew I didn't want to slit my wrists, so I had to find a cure."

Diego paused. "And now that you know there is no cure?"

His softly spoken words gave her goosebumps but it was his hand, which he'd slid across the seat to squeeze her knee, that made her stomach twist in on itself. She wanted him to leave it there, wanted him to put his arm around her shoulders and draw her against him.

When he withdrew, the warmth remained for a few seconds.

"I...haven't really thought about it." Which was true, but now that he mentioned it, she knew she wouldn't be able to let go. There *had* to be a cure. She couldn't live like this for the rest of her life—

"Do you have any questions you want to ask us, questions you weren't able to find answers to?" Marco asked.

Try hundreds. "Actually, I do."

"Then ask," Diego said.

"Yeah, we've got nothing else to do for the next four-and-a-half hours," Marco agreed. "Shoot."

She had so many, she didn't know where to start. So she asked the one uppermost in her mind. "Is it really magic?"

Diego grinned and she snuck a peek at Marco and found the same expression on his face. She went hot all over and her sex ached. Man, she really needed to get her hormones under control.

"You turn into a wolf three nights out of every month and you still don't believe in magic?" Diego said.

Okay, she sounded pretty damn naïve when he put it that way. "But how does it *work*?" she continued. "There has to be some mechanism involved, something you can explain."

"Magic just is." Diego said. "Energy exists in every living thing on earth. Some of us can channel that energy, that magic, and bend it to our will. My parents weren't...receptive to questioning and my tutors were even less so, so maybe Marco can tell you more about the mechanics."

"You didn't go to school?"

Diego shook his head, staring straight ahead. "I lived on an estate in West Chester County, New York, as a child. I was not allowed to leave the grounds without an armed guard. I had a tutor for academics and another for *grigori* studies."

His cold words held a world of hurt that Amy Jo knew had to be eating him alive.

"You didn't have any friends?"

"Not allowed. I occasionally met other children when my parents entertained hereditary families, but that wasn't often."

"Is that how you met Bella?"

"Yes, we met before her parents were killed."

"Sounds like a lonely way to grow up."

He shrugged then stiffened at Marco's editorial snort from the back seat. "Though you might not believe it," Diego directed this over his shoulder, "you had the easier time of it, Marco. Our father could be a vicious bastard."

"That's your story and you're sticking to it, aren't you?" Marco's voice was a low growl. "I don't know why you continue to shit on his name—"

"He was a master manipulator, Marco. He never did anything without a reason. He was never going to legitimize you. Never. It wasn't in his plan."

"That's bullshit and you know it." Marco's voice started to get louder. "He died before he could."

"Then why the hell did he wait so long? Control, Marco. He could control you, but he was never going to legitimize you because of your mother. She was—"

"Don't go there, Diego—"

" –a wonderful woman, but Father always said she was nothing more than a piece on the side and you were little more than a toy."

The flat tone of Diego's words held the weight of truth and Amy Jo wanted to disappear into the seat. The emotion in the car had risen along with the men's voices. Diego's complexion darkened and his hands clenched around the steering wheel. She was afraid to look back at Marco. The two men seemed to be screaming in pain, though they did it with words.

"You bastard." Marco growled.

"Damn it, Marco. When are you going to realize our father was a prick and stop worshiping the asshole?"

Silence fell. And it was worse than the fighting.

She heard both men breathing as if they'd just run a marathon. Diego's intense gaze focused on the road as if he were trying to burn a hole through the windshield. She snuck a peek in the rearview but could only see the side of Marco's face, his jaw clenched tight.

She didn't know how long they drove like that but suddenly Diego swore under his breath and yanked the wheel to the right.

# TWELVE

"I've got a meeting, Bella" Cole said. "And I want you there."

Bella rolled her eyes and flopped down on the bed in her room at the Hotel *Nuit sans Lune*. Steven had the room next to hers. Cole was across the hall as was Dorian. Steven had gone to take a shower and that's what she'd intended as well, until Cole had followed her into the room and closed the door behind him.

"Cole, you know I hate meeting with your council."

Cole shook his head. "This isn't a meeting with the council. This is something else. Something you're going to want to hear."

Sitting up on her elbows, she watched her brother pace. Cole only paced when something bothered him. Not that he didn't have enough on his plate with *congress*. And Steven.

But this was something else.

"Who are you meeting with?"

"I think it's probably better if you just...go into the meeting with an open mind. I want you to give me your opinion afterward."

"You want my opinion on your meeting?"

Her incredulous tone made Cole grimace, something he seemed to be doing a lot of lately. Cole rarely asked for her opinion. Probably because she'd never expressed much of an interest in the legion. Which made her a pretty shitty sister.

And an even more shitty royal wolf.

What would her parents have thought?

"Of course I want your opinion." He stopped pacing to stand at the bottom of the bed and gave her his serious face. "You're good with people, Bella. You pick up on things other people miss. You're smarter than you give yourself credit for."

Praise from her brother made her heart swell and she smiled, forcing back tears that would have made Cole shake his head. But the fact that he wanted her opinion meant the world to her. "Okay. Let's go."

Cole nodded and held out his hand to help her off the bed. "Come on, then. We're meeting downstairs."

In the hall, Cole knocked on Dorian's door and waited for her to join them. As they passed Steven's door, Cole paused for a brief second before continuing.

In the lobby, a few people lounged in the seating area. Bella recognized most of the faces, all of them *versipelli*. She didn't know all their names.

And she should.

Just another way in which she'd shirked her duties as a royal daughter. As her parents' daughter.

Her parents would have known every name. Cole knew all their names.

She'd let the men in her life—

No, that wasn't fair. It wasn't Cole's or Steven's or Michael's fault. She'd allowed herself to fall out of the loop, to withdraw from her society.

Her family—Steven, Cole and her—had fallen apart and she'd allowed it.

Damn it. No more.

Following Cole, Bella thought they'd head for the meeting

rooms she'd noticed to the left of the registration desk. Instead Cole turned left and pushed through a door marked Employees Only.

Several doors lined a hallway and Cole pushed through the second on the right. Bella stopped short when she saw three women sitting at the board table. They all looked up with polite smiles when she walked in. She smiled back, nodded then smacked a kiss on the cheek of the lanky blonde standing behind the women.

"Hey, Quinn."

Her brother's second-in-command ruffled her hair, knowing she hated it. "Hey, babe. Heard you had some excitement since the last time I saw you."

"Just a little."

Quinn smiled. "Well, hold onto your hat, because you're about to get your mind blown. Let me introduce you."

He gestured to the woman at the table. "Arabella Luporeale meet Serena."

Why did that name sound fami—

Bella's eyes widen even as she felt the odd impulse to curtsey. This was one of the fabled cursed *streghe*, the thirteen women who had lived for five-hundred years, cursed to immortality by Fabrizio Paganelli in his grief over is youngest son's death.

Bella had been born in the modern world but raised in a community where magic was commonplace. Where *streghe* and winged *folletti* and half-hided *salbinelli* lived, not to mention deities who occasionally showed up in temple to lead the rituals for Uni and Tinia.

Serena had been born in the late 1400s and lived for 500 years under the constant threat of discovery and torture by the *Mal*.

"I'm honored to meet you, ma'am."

The beautiful woman smiled and held out her hand to shake Bella's. "Please, call me Serena. I feel I know you already. I've heard much about you from Quinn."

Bella slid a wry glance at Quinn, who had lost his ever-present smile. "I certainly hope some of it was good."

Serena shook her head, her lips curved in solemn amusement, dark hair falling around her shoulders in long waves. The woman was a beauty, with strong Etruscan features visible to those who knew what they were looking for. Anyone else would only guess that she was Italian, possibly Greek.

"Actually, all of it was. He thinks very highly of you. And your brother."

"Well, Cole is the true brains in the family."

"Don't sell yourself short." Serena paused and she bit her lip as if she was going to say something else but finally she merely smiled and turned to the two teens seated next to her. "Arabella, these are my daughters, Furia and Madrona."

The fraternal twin girls, who Bella knew had been cursed at the age of sixteen, also shook her hand. They looked so young but their eyes...looked haunted. They all had the same whiskey gold eyes, which made sense considering they were related.

But those eyes—

Blessed Goddess. Their *eyes*. The legends all said the cursed *streghe* had eyes that resembled shattered glass.

Her gaze swung first to Quinn then to her brother before flying back to Serena's, who nodded.

"Yes. The curse was broken."

Bella's mouth dropped open as she slid into the nearest chair. "Holy shit. Seriously?"

The second the words were out, Bella wanted to smack herself but Serena's laughter filled through the room, echoed by her daughters'.

"I'm so sorry that—"

"Was a totally appropriate response," Madrona completed Bella's sentence. "Seriously. Don't stress yourself. That's exactly how we feel some days."

"Our lives have become...even more interesting in the past year." Serena paused and, behind her, Quinn stiffened. "But we're not here to discuss the curse."

"How well do you know Etruscan history?" Madrona asked.

Bella stared at the 500-year-old woman who looked like a teenager. "Which part?"

"The part about Menrva's nails," Furia spoke up for the first time.

"I know they were hammered into Menrva's temple at the end of each year by the Goddess Nortia to cut the threads of fate for the past year, allowing our people to begin the year without the problems of the past following us."

Madrona smiled as if Bella were a star pupil, which was a little freaky considering the other woman looked young enough to be in junior high school. "Do you believe in the nails, Arabella?"

Her nose wrinkled as she frowned. "I guess so. I mean, I believe our ancestors performed a ritual that involved nails and a hammer. Do I believe *the* nails actually exist?" She paused, looking around the table. "Should I?"

In answer, Madrona hooked a finger in the silver chain around her neck and drew it from beneath her Skelanimals t-shirt. An iron key hung at the end.

Many Etruscans wore a key just like it from the time they were children. The key was a talisman, a ward of protection and used in some magical rituals and spells.

Though she didn't wear hers, Bella had received one from her parents when she was five. Cole wore his at all times on a leather thong around his neck.

As Bella watched, Madrona closed her hand around the key.

When she spread her fingers again, a thick, rough-hewn nail lay there.

Bella's mouth dropped open. *Holy shit.*

"Through the years, we've lost our seer and two other *streghe*," Serena said. "My *boschetta* has been scattered for centuries. We've shirked our duties as Menrva's priestesses. We've *hidden*." Serena said the word like it was a obscenity. "But recently, Furia has been having...well, visions, for lack of a better word."

The redhead who'd been silent until now snorted. "More like nightmares. I dismissed them at first. Chalked them up to stress. But they didn't go away and then they got worse. Then one of them actually came true."

Bella waited for Furia to elaborate but Serena took over again. "Needless to say, we've had to rethink our first impression. We believe the visions are trying to tell us it's time."

"Time for what?" Bella frowned.

Serena's gaze bored into hers. "For the *boschetta* to resume its duties. For us to become a functioning part of the Etruscan community again.

"There's a war coming, Bella. We don't know with whom. The *Mal* would be the easy answer but nothing's ever easy, is it? This conflict is going to be bloody and it's going to require sacrifice. We need to be ready."

Ice coated her spine and Bella shivered. Serena's expression and her tone frankly scared the crap out of her. The woman utterly believed. But why Serena felt the need to tell Bella this in a private meeting, she didn't know. "And what does that have to do with me?"

Serena gaze skipped to Furia for a brief second. "As you know, we are missing three members. Two of them held nails. We're here to talk about your future."

DIEGO COULDN'T TAKE this anymore.

He and Marco had to settle this old fight before their poison affected Amy Jo. They had been living with it for years, but Diego didn't want her caught in the middle.

He aimed for the shoulder of the road then turned into the first break in the trees he found. A rutted lane led to a long-neglected picnic area, a moldy-looking table and benches sitting in a small clearing overgrown with weeds.

Slamming on the breaks, he threw out one arm to stop Amy Jo's forward motion then pushed out of the car. Marco slammed the back door at almost the same moment.

Diego let Marco spin him around and get in the first punch. His brother had a hell of a strong arm and Diego rocked back on his heels with the force of it. He figured he owed Marco at least that much.

Then he put up his fists. "You want to go a few rounds with me, Marco? Fine. It doesn't change the fact that our father was an arrogant asshole!"

Marco's expression pulled into a savage grimace as he threw a roundhouse at Diego's head that would have flattened him if he hadn't dodged it. Diego followed with a jab in Marco's ribs. Diego didn't want to hurt his brother but he wasn't going to take a beating just because Marco needed to punch something.

Marco feinted to the left and caught him with an uppercut in the jaw that rattled his teeth. Adrenaline flooded his system until he felt it zinging through his veins. Diego battled back his anger, barely restraining the urge to throw another punch.

"You didn't really know our father, Marco. You weren't the one he'd starve for days because you failed to address an elder by his proper name. You weren't the one he beat if your mother dared speak her mind in front of him. You weren't the one he set the guard dogs on to help with his so-called training."

His father had been a mean son of a bitch who had treated his wife like a possession and his son —at least one of his sons— like a slave.

Marco's eyes narrowed but he didn't lower his fists. "That's not the man I knew."

"The man you knew was a lie. He had a purpose for everything he did. You were his way of controlling me after his death. Why the hell do you think he never told us about each other?"

"Because he knew you'd try to poison my mind—"

"Fucking hell, Marco. Get a grip. You were just another tool in my education. Call it Family 101."

Diego's fists clenched so hard, his knuckles cracked. He wanted to shake some sense into his thick-headed brother but refused to stoop to his father's level and beat the shit out of Marco. Their father had used his fists to beat a backbone into Diego.

He was not his father, the bastard who had aligned brothers against one another.

"What the fuck are you talking about?" Marco demanded.

"You were my final lesson, Marco. He spoiled you. He told you he loved you, that you were his favorite. And he knew, when we met, that I'd see that. And hate it. Because I spent years wanting him to love *me*."

Marco's mouth parted in shock and his fists lowered several inches. "What—"

"But by the time I was ten, I knew it would never happen. He was a sadistic prick who considered emotion a weakness no leader could afford. He assumed I'd be jealous when I found out he had another son, a son who thought he walked on water. Well, he fucked up. Because when I saw you, Marco, I saw *family*. And I knew I could never follow his will and cut you and your mother off completely."

He heard Amy Jo's quiet gasp behind him but it was the shock in Marco's eyes that held his gaze. "That's bullshit. We never—"

"—went without a goddamn thing," Diego finished for him. "At the will reading, I watched your mother's face across the table as the lawyer told her my father hadn't left her or you anything. She looked like she'd been gut-shot. Our bastard father had told her she'd be taken care of. That you would finally be acknowledged as a legitimate heir. Instead, you were left with nothing and I was forbidden to help you in any way."

Diego shook his head, his mouth firm but his eyes... "No."

"Yes. He made it part of the damn will that I wasn't allowed to help you or your mother in any way or I would forfeit everything and you would get it. He wanted me to be as ruthless and cruel as he was and he wanted everyone else to know it."

Diego started to see the cracks in Marco's façade. His eyes looked bleak, desolate. Diego didn't want this but Marco had to know. Diego couldn't keep it to himself anymore.

"Yes, I agreed to the terms of the will. I let everyone believe I cut you off." Diego shook his head. "But I never would've let you and your mother starve. Paloma was...unprepared." Which was the nicest way of saying she was clueless as Diego could manage. The woman hated him. Always would. "She'd believed that bastard, too. She thought our father would take care of her."

Marco started to shake his head but Diego pushed on.

"I tried to talk to her after the funeral but she refused to listen. She saw me exactly the way our father taught her to see me. As his clone. But that's not me."

"Bullshit. You never gave us—"

"Gods *damn* it, Marco. Shut the *fuck* up and listen." Diego's anger started to bubble like hot tar because this was the part that got hairy. This is what he was ashamed of. "Your mother never worked a day in her life. Where do you think the money came from? Not from him."

"You're lying." Marco said the words but there was no heat behind them. He looked...shell-shocked.

"No." Diego shook his head. "I'm not lying and you know it. He made it impossible for me to care for you and your mother without me losing the ability to care for my mother and the people who depend on me."

Most specifically, those employed by Falco's Jewels, a New York City institution for more than a hundred years. Small and exclusive, it sold exotic jewels to some of the richest people in the world. More importantly, the company kept the magical races of the world supplied with the diamonds, rubies, emeralds and all other jewels needed for their magical rituals. The Falco family had a long history as *gemminex*, jewel workers.

"But I didn't turn my back on you, Marco. Because there were no strictures placed on my mother to stop her from giving you money. Our father thought he'd beaten her into submission. Luckily for you, he'd only taught her to take commands well."

An old and familiar rage began to simmer but he ruthlessly shoved it back down. He couldn't deal with that on top of this.

Marco just stared at him, confusion starting to show on his face. "Why the hell should I believe you?"

Diego forced himself to shrug, as if it didn't matter. "I can show you the will if you want. Or I can tell you what you got for your eighteenth birthday."

He didn't wait for Marco to reply. Diego stepped closer and reached out to pull the chain around Marco's neck from beneath his shirt. A gold medallion hung there. "He specified in his will that he should be buried with this. It's an exact copy of the ring I took off his hand at the funeral. It belonged to our Uncle Francis.

"I bet you never knew our grandfather had this made for Francis as a charm, protection against our father. No one trusted Gilbert Falco, not even his own father." Diego dropped the medal but didn't step away. "And the damn thing didn't work because, when he was sixteen, Uncle Francis had a mysterious accident and died. *That*," he pointed to the medal now lying on Marco's shirt, "is our family coat of arms and *you* are a member of this family. I took it off our father's neck when I took the ring."

His brother's eyes were wide and dazed as he stared up at him. "Why would you do that?"

"Oh, for *fuck's* sake, Marco!" Diego threw his hands in the air. "You're my brother! How the hell do you think your mother paid for your flying lessons? Where do you think you got the money to buy your plane?"

He wouldn't add the rest—his first clients, the loan for his business, the money for his mother's cancer treatments. Marco didn't look like he could take any more. He sometimes forgot his brother was seven years younger and a lot less worldly. He'd been pampered , spoiled, protected.

Marco took a step back, shaking his head. "No—"

"Yes," Diego practically hissed the word. "I wasn't about to let you or your mother starve just because our father wanted to prove a point about me."

With a rough growl, Marco turned away and stormed off toward the edge of the wooded area. Diego started after him but a small, warm hand caught his arm.

"Let him go." Amy Jo's voice grazed his ear. "I think...he could probably use a few minutes."

Damn it, he knew she was right. Still...the pain in his brother's eyes stabbed straight into his gut.

"Gee," Amy Jo continued, "and here I thought my family was dysfunctional."

He actually laughed, just a short exhalation of air, at the dry humor in her tone. But he couldn't look at her. "Yeah, we're definitely the poster children for fucked-up families." He closed his eyes against the memories that tried to creep in. Memories he'd thought long buried. "Sorry you're caught in the middle of all this. You certainly don't need our shit on top of everything else."

Opening his eyes, he watched Marco stop at one of the draping trees, grab an overhanging branch in both hands and let the limb take his weight, stretching like a cat in the sun.

"Actually, it's kind of taking my mind off everything else." Her hand started a slow caress along his arm, soothing and erotic at the same time.

He tore his gaze away from Marco and got caught in her blue eyes, filled with so much compassion he had his hand on her cheek before he realized he was going to do it.

"I won't let anything happen to you," he vowed. Just as he would always take care of Marco. "No matter what."

Her flash of a smile was bittersweet but her voice held conviction. "I truly do believe that."

Her complete and utter trust dumbfounded him.

Just a few days ago, she'd been unwilling to accept her fate, distraught because she wasn't going to be able to reverse the curse and would remain a monster. Last night, she'd slept with him, gave him her body for the first time since she'd been raped and today she was looking at him with a boatload of trust in her eyes.

Christ, didn't she have any sense at all? Yes, he wanted her. Yes, he'd protect her to the best of his ability, but did she have to trust him on top of that? Didn't she know she shouldn't trust anyone, least of all him?

He didn't deserve her trust. He was a bastard. Maybe not by birth, but he'd been brain-fucked by his father for years. His only family hated him and he didn't have a clue how to fix that. He was good at one thing—killing.

He'd been born *grigorio*, a rare honor that he made sure never to take for granted. Yet, even among that elite group, he was an anomaly. His mother was the great-granddaughter of Amalia, one of the cursed *streghe* who'd disappeared a couple of centuries ago. His birth as a *grigorio* had been unexpected and, surprisingly, a great source of pride for his prick of a father. Diego had never been able to figure that one out.

Just as he couldn't figure out why this woman trusted him. He scowled at her and her smile faded.

Immediately, he wanted it back.

Gods damn it. She was screwing with his head and he couldn't deal with that. Not now.

"We'd better get going," he said. "I want to get to New Orleans before tomorrow."

She nodded slowly and withdrew her hand from his arm. "Sure. I'll just...um... I guess I'll—"

"Get back to the car." His voice held more than a hint of his frustration and she blinked and stepped back. "*Shit*. Amy Jo, look—"

"No." She slashed a hand in front of her as she shook her head, her mouth drawing into a straight line. "Just...don't. I'll wait in the car."

He sighed as she spun on her heel and walked away, her perfect ass a perfect torment in those tight denim shorts.

How the hell could he fuck this up even worse?

His gaze fell on Marco, still contemplating trees.

Well, hell. There was a good start.

# THIRTEEN

Steven sat in the lobby, watching the *lucani* go out of their way to avoid him.

It shouldn't matter. He'd been an outcast for so long, the opinions of these people shouldn't matter.

They didn't matter.

Only Bella and Cole mattered. And they were nowhere to be found.

Before he'd come down, he'd knocked on their doors but got no answer. Not seeing anyone he cared to talk to in the lobby, he'd asked at the front desk and been told, by a female desk clerk who let her gaze wander just over his shoulder, that Cole and Bella were in a meeting and couldn't be disturbed.

So he sat in the lobby and waited. And watched.

And wondered.

Who were they meeting? Why? And why hadn't they told him?

He tried not to let that last one bother him too much. Bella and Cole were the sole remaining royalty of the *lucani*. Cole was *legio* not to mention king. Logically Steven knew Cole had responsibilities that didn't—couldn't—include him.

Still, it sucked to be an outsider. Which was mostly his fault. And he couldn't see a way to fix it.

He was what he was.

Out of the corner of his eye, he saw movement.

Quinn Kennett approached. The few men in the lobby saluted him with their right fist to left chest, and he acknowledged them with a nod before sliding into the chair facing Steven, his expression calm. He watched Steven with steady eyes and no smile, something the guy was barely ever without.

"It sucks, doesn't it?" Quinn's voice held no emotion, a perfectly modulated tone that held the slightest hint of a drawl.

He didn't have a clue what he was asking. "What?"

"Being on the outside."

His back went stiff and straight. Quinn didn't like him. Never had and he'd made no bones about it.

Damn it, he didn't need this shit. He made a move to stand but Quinn held up one hand to stop his motion.

"I'm not yanking your chain, Steven. Don't run." He paused, watching him. "Cole missed you."

His mouth opened and closed. Quinn had shocked the shit out of him, even as his words eased something tight inside his chest. But he didn't have a clue what the hell to say. His face must have been easy to read because now Quinn smiled.

"He hasn't been the same since you left. He'll never admit it but, for some reason, he needs you. They both do." He shrugged. "I don't have the faintest idea why. I won't lie to you, Steven. You're not my favorite person but then, I don't know you that well. I *do* know you're dangerous."

Quinn shifted forward in his seat, getting closer, as if he could see into Steven's mind. "Cole and Bella are about to get hit with a lot of shit. They don't have time to worry about you. About whether you're going to leave them again."

His gut twisted into painful knots but he refused to give

Quinn the satisfaction of showing it. His chin lifted. "Are you telling me to leave now to spare them later?"

Quinn shook his head and his expression firmed. "I'm telling you to get your shit together. Cole believes you can conquer the *Mal* influence and come back to the fold."

Steven cocked his head to the side, trying to determine what Quinn thought. "But you're not convinced."

Quinn didn't answer right away and Steven knew it shouldn't matter what he thought. Last week, it wouldn't have mattered. Today...

Quinn leaned back, settling into the chair. "You don't know me that well either, so... You're wrong. Cole believes you can and I believe in Cole."

"And does Cole ever tell you how I'm supposed to pull off this miraculous feat? 'Cause I gotta tell ya, I don't have a fucking clue."

The bitterness that ate at his gut gave his words a sharp edge that wasn't directed at Quinn. His mother, his father, Cole, Bella. They'd all told him at some time that he could overcome the *Mal* influence. That he could rise above it.

They just couldn't tell him how.

Quinn didn't say anything right away. He seemed to be thinking. "I have a few thoughts, yes."

His eyebrows rose in shock. "You're kidding."

"No, I'm not." Quinn leaned forward, looking him straight in the eyes. "Look, you've been fighting a huge part of yourself for years and it hasn't mattered a damn, right? You're miserable. You're worried about losing control. And I know you have a good reason to worry about that. But...have you ever considered just letting the magic have you? Surrendering to it and learning how to work with it instead of against it? Making it work for you instead of the other way around?"

*No.* It went against everything he'd been taught, against everything he'd learned from his mom's death. He couldn't handle his magic, couldn't control it. It controlled him. And his magic was tainted.

He shook his head, ready to dismiss Quinn's suggestion but Quinn spoke before Steven could.

"Don't," Quinn said. "Don't dismiss it out of hand. You're older and smarter than you were when your mom died but you've repressed that part of you for so long I think...maybe you need a release. Like a pressure valve. Vent some of it and maybe it'll take the pressure off."

Damn Quinn. He sounded so rational.

But...it couldn't be that easy. Nothing in his life ever had.

*You managed to control the storm.*

Quinn continued to stare at him, gaze steady, no condemnation.

Could he risk it?

Should he even try?

———

BY THE TIME they reached New Orleans, Amy Jo would've cheerfully clawed her way out of the car.

The last miles had been deadly silent. And the only thing that saved Diego and Marco from one of her full-fledged hormone attacks was the beauty of the city.

She'd never been here before and the architecture astounded her. Some areas of the city still showed effects of the devastating flooding after Hurricane Katrina, but everywhere she looked, something caught her eye. Buildings, gardens, even the cemetery was cool.

At some point during the mostly silent trip, Amy Jo had

asked where they were going to stay in the city. Marco had told her the *lucani* had rented the entire Hotel *Nuit sans Lune* in the Garden District.

Diego hadn't said a word. And when they pulled up to the curb outside the hotel, he slammed the car into park and almost ripped off the door handle getting out of the car. He disappeared around the back and seconds later the trunk door opened.

She heard Marco sigh in the back seat then his hand settled on her shoulder. Warm, comforting.

"Hey, you okay?"

She took a deep breath before answering. "I'll live. Is he always this intense?"

Marco's snort was answer enough. "Unfortunately yes. It's a bad habit he picked up from our father."

She turned to look into his dark eyes, so much like Diego's. "Do you think you two will ever have a normal relationship?"

Marco laughed out loud, his mouth not as rounded as Diego's but just as beautiful when he smiled. She yanked her gaze back up to his eyes before she decided to let her gaze go even lower.

"Define normal, babe," he said. "Did you forget where you are and who you're with?"

How could she forget when the two most gorgeous men she'd ever met had the same beautiful eyes and completely different, panty-dropping smiles? Damn, she needed to get a grip.

Blinking, she dropped her gaze but still felt Marco's on her. "Amy Jo." He paused. "Shit. The calvary's arrived."

The passenger door opened, making her jump in her seat.

"Oh, thank the gods. I was afraid you guys would *never* get here."

Bella stood there, hands on her hips, exasperation all over her face. Amy Jo couldn't help but grin. She nearly fell in her haste to get out of the car but Bella caught her before she could and hugged her.

"I am *so* freaking happy to see you," Bella gushed. "Is everything okay? How was the trip? Are you tired? Hungry? Want to get something to eat?" Her smile popped up, wicked and a little rueful. "Please come in and save me from my brother and Steven. I *so* need someone to talk to who isn't male or 500 years old."

Amy Jo smiled. "It's nice to see you, too."

Bella started pulling her toward the entrance, turning to give her another smile. "You have *no* idea."

Bella waved a hand at the young, dark-haired man standing at the door, watching her like a hawk. "We're going back to my room, Luca. We don't want to be disturbed. If Steven, Cole, Diego or Marco even think about knocking on my door, you have my authority to shoot them. I'm not kidding. No one."

Then they ran through the hotel's small foyer like teenagers. Bella made for the stairs instead of the elevators, which didn't matter to Amy Jo. Since her transformation, she didn't tire as easily as she used to.

They reached the fourth floor in minutes and Bella had her hotel room door open in seconds. They fell into plush chairs fronting a working fireplace.

Amy Jo let her gaze travel the room. "Nice digs." Then she took a deep breath and let herself relax. "You don't know how happy I am to be out of that car."

"Yeah, I can tell. You looked like you were at the end of your rope when you pulled up. Wanna talk about it?"

It'd been so long since she'd had a confidante that Amy Jo wasn't quite how to start. So she just blurted out everything.

Sex with Diego, the car ride, Diego and Marco's discussion. She talked until Bella went to the minibar to get her a soda, which she gulped down while Bella stared at her with a bemused expression.

"And here I thought my day was screwed up."

"So what happened with you?"

Bella paused, as if considering what to say, and Amy Jo knew something major had taken place. Something that made Bella think twice about confiding in her.

Well, sure, they'd only known each other a few days and Amy Jo *had* tried to kill her—

"I've been asked to join the *boschetta*."

Amy Jo's eyebrows lifted. "Okay, that's sounds painful."

Bella laughed, so natural and unguarded that it lifted Amy Jo's flagging spirits.

Until Bella proceeded to tell her what it meant. And Amy Jo figured she'd finally slipped into the twilight zone.

"They want you to be a priestess to an Etruscan goddess?"

"The Goddess Menrva, yes. It's one of the greatest honors an Etruscan woman can receive. It's also one that's never been offered to a *lucani* before. All of the former priestesses have been *streghe*."

"And that means witch, right?"

Bella nodded, her expression slightly dazed.

"That sounds like a major deal," Amy Jo said.

"It is. It's almost...too big." Bella's mouth twisted. "I mean, besides my ability to shift, I don't have a Goddess Gift, a special magical ability like divination—" Bella paused, her expression going thoughtful. "Well, maybe that's not true. Maybe I do have a Gift. Maybe healing is my gift and I just never—" She shook her head. "Anyway, I don't know why they chose me. What if I can't do it? What if I screw it up? This is a lifetime commitment. I can't just give it up if I don't—if I can't handle it."

"What's to handle?"

"There are certain responsibilities that go along with being a priestess. Together, they perform the rituals that fuel the Great Goddess's power. I mean, I know she's been gone for thousands of years—"

"Wait. What do you mean, she's been gone?" Amy Jo's brain stuttered to a stop at the implication in Bella's tone. "Gone? Where?"

Bella blinked. "Yeah, I really do forget that you haven't been part of my world for very long."

"Are you... Do you really..." Amy Jo huffed. "Are you honestly going to tell me that your gods and goddesses are real?"

Bella looked her straight in the eyes. "Yes, I am. You might actually get to meet Tivr, the Moon God. He's the favored god of the *lucani* and I wouldn't be surprised if he shows up sometime this week."

Amy Jo's mouth fell open. "Moon God. And Menrva is...?"

Bella waved a hand in front of her, as if they weren't talking about real live deities. "I'll make sure you get a book. It'll be easier than trying to explain everything. And according to Cole —that's my brother—the *strega* who's going to, ah, read your mind, will be here first thing in the morning."

Yeah, reminding her about what was coming tomorrow was a great way to take her mind off of living, breathing gods. "Read my mind, huh? Now there's a comforting thought."

"Don't worry. She's very discreet." Bella's smile turned wicked. "Of course, if I'd had Diego in my bed, I'd be bragging to anyone who'd listen."

Amy Jo felt her cheeks heat. Curiously, though, she didn't take offense. She knew Bella would never betray her confidence. Not about this.

"I'm still not sure it wasn't the stupidest thing I could have done. Yeah, it was great, and yeah, I wish it was going to happen again. But, he seemed even *more* tense afterward. For me, it was stress relief. And a little... I don't know... I just needed to know I could still enjoy sex. But Diego's wound so tight now, I'm afraid he's going to crack under the strain."

Bella shook her head. "Won't happen. I've never seen that man flustered. Then again, I've never met a woman who's actually been in his bed. I mean, I'm sure there have been other women, but he never talks about his private life. Not ever."

"Oh, he definitely has experience." Amy Jo felt her temperature rise just thinking about him. "And it's not like I'm in love with the guy." She definitely was not. "I'm just...worried about him."

Actually, she was worried about Diego and Marco. Yes, she'd slept with Diego but she cared about both brothers. She felt a connection with them, one she couldn't put into words. Not even to Bella. Not now, anyway.

Bella's eyes narrowed, as if she knew Amy Jo wasn't telling her everything. But the other woman didn't push. "I'm sure Diego's just as worried about you."

She snorted. "Yeah, as a job. Anyway," she'd had enough of this line of questioning, "what's on the agenda until the mind reader gets here?"

Bella waved her hand around the gorgeous room. "Girl's night in. Food, drink, movies. And no guys."

"Sounds like heaven."

———

"WHAT THE HELL do you mean they don't want to be disturbed?"

Steven just shook his head, knowing exactly what that meant. Bella had had enough—of him, of Cole, of secret meetings and headaches. Basically, she'd had enough of everything.

Because the siblings were so different, Cole had never understood Bella's need for space, especially when she was thinking things through. Cole loved to talk. Steven wondered who Cole had talked to for the three years he'd been gone.

After his conversation with Quinn, he'd sat in the lobby, thinking. Trying to make sense of or, at least, *try* to sort through what they'd talked about. He hadn't been making much headway when Cole and Bella had entered the lobby from a door marked employees only. Her expression was thoughtful and he could tell she wasn't paying attention to Cole, who was talking to her.

Then she'd stopped, looked straight at him and sighed. Hell, he heard it from across the room. Cole looked up as well and they veered toward him but Quinn reached them first, saying something to Cole. Then Dorian had come up behind Bella and pointed toward the front door.

Bella had made a beeline for the entrance. Steven hadn't even crossed the lobby by the time Bella had returned with Amy Jo in tow, Luca close on their heels, as they headed for the stairs.

A few seconds after that, Diego and Marco had entered, their faces set in identical expressions of grim determination. They had all trooped up the stairs because Cole had insisted he needed to talk to Bella, but obviously she had a different opinion.

"Cole." Steven placed a hand on his friend's shoulder. "Give it up. You're not going to win this one. Let's go to the bar. I need a drink."

Diego sighed, and Steven thought he heard relief in the sound.

"I could use a bottle of alcohol." Diego slid a look at Marco, who stared back. "Maybe a couple."

Something had happened on their way down here. Something to do with Amy Jo. Something between the brothers, as well. Diego looked...rattled. Which was surprising. Diego didn't do rattled. Pissed off was more his general speed.

"Fine." Cole turned away from Bella's door with a disgusted look on his face. "We need to talk anyway and it'll be easier without them."

Luca's sudden cough sounded suspiciously like a laugh.

Cole glared at him but the kid stared right back. Luca might be young, but Steven had spoken to him earlier. He knew what he was doing and he knew the consequences should he fail. He took his duties seriously. That didn't mean Steven wasn't any less worried. But here, in this hotel, he didn't think any harm would come to her.

The hotel was owned by two *streghe*, members of the cursed thirteen that his father had been sworn by sacred birthright to protect. Madrona and Furia had made this hotel a safe haven in a world that was becoming more dangerous every day.

As they made their way to the darkest corner of the surprisingly large bar on the first floor, Steven watched Cole nod to people as they passed. A few of the women gave him sexy grins that offered more than a greeting. He didn't acknowledge them any differently than he did the men.

"Still haven't taken *tribuni* advice and found a wife, huh?" Steven asked Cole as he pulled out a padded leather chair at a table in the far corner and sat down.

Cole shook his head. "No time."

"And you don't like being a piece of meat any more than I do," Diego added as he sat. "Sometimes, this life sucks."

A thirty-something waitress in a short black skirt and a fitted white t-shirt stopped at their table, giving them smiles all around. "*Legio*, gentleman. What can I get you tonight?"

Steven had the urge to laugh. He knew exactly what he wanted. And exactly what he wasn't going to get if Bella's locked and guarded door meant anything. He looked over to find the same expression on Diego's face. And surprisingly, Marco's face.

And Cole...well, Cole looked ready to hit something.

"Whiskey." Cole said finally. "And tequila. Just bring us a couple of bottles and four glasses."

"Absolutely, your highness." Her southern accent was smooth as silk, but not one man at the table looked interested. "I'll bring you some munchies, too. You're gonna need food to soak up at least some of that alcohol."

When she'd gone, Cole took a deep breath and released it, like he was trying to release something he'd bottled inside.

"Alright." Cole's expression turned determined. "We know we've got a few different problems, so let's line them up and try to knock them out one at a time. Steven, let's deal with you first. What do you know about Charles Jones?"

His hands curled into fists before he could stop them. "Not enough, obviously." He held up one hand before Cole could cut in. "Don't. Just...don't. I checked him out before I went to work for him and nothing, not one goddamn thing sent up a warning flag. The firm's legit. I know he has some clients who are connected to hereditary families. But hell, every major firm in the states has got to have at least one client with blood ties. Maybe that should have been a flag—"

"Steven. Stop." Cole's voice dropped a few decibels. "I'm not coming down on you for this. Jones is *Mal*. He wouldn't have let anything slip unless he'd wanted you to know. That wasn't what I was going to ask."

Yeah, right. "So?"

Cole rolled his eyes. "So...who's he working for? What have we got on him that we can use against him? He has a daughter, right?"

"Yes, Tiffani. She started at the firm around the same time I did. She'd just returned from a year in Europe. She's a bitch, for the most part. A pampered princess whose only goal in life seems to be to land a husband. Namely, me."

"And I'm guessing it wasn't for your looks," Diego drawled.

Steven flipped him the bird. "Hey, Pretty Boy, don't piss me off."

Marco snorted at Amy Jo's nickname then said, "What exactly do they want with you?"

No one answered as the waitress returned with their order. No one spoke, even when she left.

Steven had enough trouble dealing with his own shit without actually talking about it.

Cole finally filled the silence. "Steven has powers the *Mal* want. He has the ability to control the weather, in addition to some other...specialized talents."

Diego knocked back a shot.

Marco's eyebrows flew up. "They want him because he's *Mal*?"

Cole didn't answer, neither did Diego. Both stared at him. Steven grabbed for the tequila bottle.

Fuck this. He was damn sick and tired of apologizing for something he couldn't change.

"Yeah. I was born *Mal*, but I won't..." He took a deep breath and blew it out again. "I don't use my powers."

"Which is another problem in itself." Cole slid a glance his way. "But that's not on the table now. We need to have a plan of attack because the *Mal* sure as shit do. You said Jones was talking to someone on the phone."

"Yeah, but I don't know who."

Cole nodded. "I'll get someone working on phone records though I don't figure we'll get lucky there."

"So we need defensive strategy," Diego said. "Make sure they don't catch us with our pants down."

Cole grabbed the tequila out of Steven's hand and poured

himself a shot. "Which means we need to lure them here. And we already have the bait." Cole pointed at Steven. "If they don't know where you are, we need to make sure Jones finds out. And we need to get Bella and Amy Jo out of here before Jones gets here."

"Maybe tomorrow we'll know more about who's behind this," Diego said. "If Andrea can pull any information out of Amy Jo. But...she's pretty damn traumatized. And I'm not sure Andrea screwing about in her memories won't do more damage."

"Are you saying we shouldn't have Andrea try?" Cole asked.

Diego shook his head. "No, it's just... I can't imagine..." Then he sighed. "I don't *want* to imagine what went on the night Amy Jo was bitten. But whatever happened, it left mental and physical scars that haven't healed. I don't want to create any more permanent damage."

Cole didn't answer right away and Steven knew he was trying to figure out what Diego had going with Amy Jo. Marco was no help. He had his head turned, letting his gaze roam over the rest of the bar, seemingly ignoring their conversation.

"Can you suggest another method of getting the information from her?" Cole asked.

Diego grimaced as he shook his head.

"Then we'll have to go ahead with Andrea." Cole leaned over the table, forcing Diego to meet his gaze head on. "I trust you'll be there to make sure nothing happens to her."

Marco sliced a glance at Diego and the brothers stared at each other for a few seconds.

"We'll be there," Diego said.

"Fine." Cole nodded and leaned back into the chair before standing. "I'll be right back."

Then he walked away.

Steven tracked Cole as far as the door, where he disappeared into the lobby. An awkward silence settled around the table. Diego contemplated the empty glass in front of him while Marco continued to gaze around the room.

"Hey, Marco. What's—"

The sound of a gunshot rang through the bar.

## FOURTEEN

The gunman sat in a first-floor room more than a block up the street from the Hotel *Nuit san Lune*.

Waiting for his targets to leave the security of the building.

The client had provided him with several pictures, which he'd studied until he knew each and every mole on their faces. Yesterday, he'd scouted the location and found this room.

The woman who'd rented it to him had barely registered his presence. He had one of those unremarkable faces. It served him well in his line of work.

A flash of movement at hotel entrance caught his eye and he sighted through the scope of his Parker Hale M85.

Damn, he was a lucky guy.

One of his five targets had exited the building and now leaned against the wall to the right of the front door, under the red and white awning. Probably thought he was hidden under there.

The man squeezed the trigger.

And watched the target fall.

*Let's see who else shows up before I need to get out of here.*

---

BELLA AND AMY JO decided to skip dinner and go straight to the best part.

They ordered one of every dessert the hotel had to offer and added a few plates of appetizers for good measure.

An hour later, Bella looked at the decimated food cart then at Amy Jo and knew she'd found a kindred spirit.

"Good thing our metabolism burns through calories like a wildfire." Bella leaned into the comfy chair in the lounge area of her room. Something bluesy and mellow throbbed in the background from the stereo system.

Amy Jo nodded and wiped her fingers on a napkin after licking off left-over chocolate icing. "That's one good thing." She paused and bit her bottom lip so hard Bella was afraid she'd draw blood. "So...what are some of the others?"

*Finally*. Bella had been waiting for Amy Jo to start asking questions. It signaled a return to normal for the other woman.

"Well, there are lots, actually. Like enhanced hearing and smell. Our eyesight's only a little better than normal, but I guess I should be glad we're not colorblind, like real wolves. We're physically stronger than regular humans and we tend to live longer."

*If we make it past thirty, considering we have more than our fair share of predators.*

But she didn't say that. Amy Jo didn't need to hear about that. Not yet.

"What about people like me?" Amy Jo asked softly.

Bella frowned. "What do you mean?"

"People who aren't born...what do you call it?"

"*Versipellis*. It's Latin for 'skin shifter.'"

"You don't call yourselves werewolves?"

Bella smiled. "No. I'm Etruscan *lucani* and because you

were bitten by a *lucani*, you are, too. Wolves are the largest *versipelli* group in the world. Then there are Norse *berserkirs*. They're bears. And Chinese foxes. I never could pronounce what they call themselves. There are a few other groups, too. Diego and his brother are Iberian lynx. They're only a hundred or so of them left, though I didn't even know Diego had a brother until I met Marco. However, we're *not* ravening fiends and we don't eat babies and we're not cursed by God. Most of us have been raised to the old ways."

Amy Jo's head cocked to the side. "What does that mean?"

"We're not Christian."

Her eyes narrowed as Amy Jo frowned. "You're *Jewish*? I mean, not that there's anything wrong—"

Bella laughed at the complete confusion on Amy Jo's face. She laughed until she had to gasp for air and felt tears flood her eyes.

Poor Amy Jo. The world she'd known no longer existed for her. That narrow, relatively safe little world had been destroyed by what she'd become.

How screwed up was that?

And how strong she was to come through it relatively intact.

Bella admired the other woman more than Amy Jo might ever understand. Yes, Bella had suffered the horrible loss of her parents and brother and, later, she'd lost the man who'd loved her like a daughter. But she'd been pampered and spoiled her entire life, given anything she asked for.

And then what did she do? She turned her back on her family. She became a veterinarian but she didn't use her skills in any positive way for her community, for the people who depended on Cole and, to some degree, her to at least take an interest in their lives.

When her laughter finally calmed, Bella saw Amy Jo sitting with her arms crossed over her chest, eyebrows raised.

"Oh, sure, laugh at the new girl."

Bella sighed. "I'm sorry. I just realized something about myself that... Anyway, no, we're not... Well, I'm sure there are Jewish *versipelli* and Protestant and Muslim and so on. But the Etruscans have an ancient belief system. We worship the Etruscan pantheon."

Amy Jo's brows lowered as she mulled that over. "You actually worship gods and goddesses? I mean, I know you said about becoming a priestess but I didn't think... Well, hell, I don't know now what I thought."

"Yes, we worship gods and goddesses."

"Should I be worshiping them, too?"

Bella shook her head. "Not if you don't believe. They tend to be vengeful."

Amy Jo's eyebrows flew up. "But you believe?"

"Yes," Bella smiled. "I do. I know how weird it must seem to someone who wasn't raised the way I was. But there are deities who walk the earth, who shape fate and meddle in our affairs."

Amy Jo shook her head, her expression shell-shocked. "I never thought there were people around who still worshiped Zeus and—"

"He's Greek."

"Jupiter?"

"Roman. There's also an Egyptian pantheon and Celtic and Norse and—"

Amy Jo threw her hands in the air. "Wait, I surrender. Maybe someday we can go down the list, but not now. Just tell me...about people like me. Are there a lot?"

Bella sobered and shook her head. "Not really, no. Most don't survive the bite."

Shrugging, Amy Jo looked away. "Okay, then. I seem to keep bringing down the mood."

"Then let's forget about that for a while. So are you in the mood to cry, laugh or both."

Amy Jo's smile returned, just a little less than bright. "Definitely both."

"Alright, let's see what sickeningly sweet movie we can find." Bella turned on the TV and began flipping through the pay-per-view movies. "Ugh. Do they show nothing but porn and action film? Why—"

The pop of gun fire cut her off mid-sentence. It caught her off guard because it sounded so close. She froze and gasped as she heard another.

Then the commotion started and she heard a name that made her heart freeze.

"Oh, Goddess, no."

"Bella? Bella, what's wrong?" Amy Jo asked.

She didn't stop to answer. Instead she ran for the door, only to find it locked.

Banging on it, she tried to rip it off the hinges but her *praetorian* had spelled it from the outside. "Luca, goddamn it, let me out!"

"No way." His voice sounded clearly from the other side. "Stay put! They're going to bring him up."

"Bella, what's happening?" Amy Jo again, her voice calm, controlled.

She felt terror creep like silver through her veins. "This can't happen again. I don't think I could stand it again."

"Bella, come sit down. Tell me what's going on."

But she couldn't sit down. She paced by the door, frustration building, fear eating at her insides. She heard men shouting downstairs, so many voices. So much confusion. That confusion fed her fear until it felt like a snake had coiled in her stomach and now gnawed at her to get out.

"I can't lose him, too. I can't."

She didn't realize she was speaking aloud until Amy Jo said, "Oh no. Your brother."

Yes, her brother. Like their parents and older brother. Shot.

A buzzing started in her ears, getting louder until it drowned out everything, as if she were in a vacuum.

She nearly jumped out of her skin when Amy Jo put an arm around her. "Breathe, Bella. You're not going to do your brother any good if you faint."

Amy Jo was right. She had to pull herself together before—

The door flew open and a mass of people rushed in, all of them talking at once.

She only had eyes for Cole. And the blood.

Bright red and running from the hole in Cole's chest, dripping from the exit wound in the back.

Two men carried Cole between them, Dorian holding his head, snapping orders as they placed him on the bed.

"Bella, get over here," Dorian snapped over her shoulder as she stood frozen to the floor. "Dr. Kent's coming but it's going to take him about ten minutes to get here. You have to take care of Cole until then."

Her jaw dropped as she rushed to Cole's side, her hand reaching for his. She heard his breathing, slow and shallow.

"What?" Her gaze snapped to Dorian as her words sunk in. "I'm a vet, not a doctor."

Dorian turned and ordered everyone else to leave the room. "The principle's the same." Dorian grabbed her shoulder and shook her. "Snap out of if, Bella. Come on. You're all he's got right now. You've got to stop the bleeding. The bullet went straight through. I don't think it nicked any major arteries but I'm not sure and it looks like he's lost a lot of blood."

So much blood. All over him.

"Arabella!"

She looked into Dorian's eyes and saw steady confidence. In her.

She took a deep breath. "I need whatever med supplies Dr. Kent has in the hotel. Amy Jo, I need the towels out of the bathroom."

She grabbed hold of Cole's shirt and ripped.

———

STEVEN WOKE WITH A POUNDING HEADACHE.

*Vaffanculo.* What the hell did he drink last night?

Swinging his legs off the bed, he rubbed at his temples—

And didn't recognize the rough-hewn wooden walls or the single bed in the center of the room.

*What the fuck?*

Where was he? The last thing he remembered was sitting in the hotel bar, talking. Then shouting, a commotion—

Cole. *Shit*, Cole had been shot. Adrenaline pumped through his veins as he jumped to his feet. He had to get out of here.

His gaze roamed the room. No windows, no doors. No way out.

Christ, this was bad. Really fucking bad.

He walked to the wall across from the bed and put his hand against it. Magic hummed through the rough boards. But not like any magic he'd ever come up against before. Not *Malandante*. Not *strega*. Not *lucani*.

No, this was something...purer.

He had to get out of here. But first he had to figure out where here was.

"Hey! Where am I? What the hell's going on?"

His voice echoed in the room as he trailed his hands across

the walls, looking for a seam in the boards that would indicate a door. He covered the entire room. Nothing.

"What's going on? Let me out."

He pressed his ear to the wall. Nothing.

He looked up. There. A trap door in the middle of the ceiling. Out of reach, even if he stood on the bed.

Panic he couldn't afford clogged his throat. He had to get out. He needed to get back. Cole was hurt, could be dying. Bella would be terrified.

He wasn't too steady himself. Fear burned in his gut, compounding his headache. He needed a plan of action.

Pulling the bed away from the wall, he positioned it under the trap door and climbed on.

Shit, still out of reach.

He started to yell again, screaming until his throat felt like he'd swallowed glass. He continued for as long as he could. He had no concept of the passing of time. The room's only illumination came from two circular fixtures embedded in the ceiling.

By the time he was ready to throw himself at the walls in pure frustration, screaming every curse he knew, he heard footsteps above him.

The trap door opened and a human figure stepped into the light.

A woman's voice—young, maybe no older than a teenager—called down, "Alright already. Jeez, you've got a foul mouth on you. You kiss your girlfriend with that mouth?"

He stared at the woman for several seconds before he found his voice again. "Where the hell am I? Get me the fuck out of here!"

"Oh wow." The woman shook her head and saw long hair spill down. "She said you were gonna be pissed. Guess she wasn't wrong. Hey, you want something to eat? Some water?"

"Just get me the hell out of here." Damn, his throat hurt like a bitch. "What's going on? Where the hell am I?"

"Hang tight a minute. I'll get you a water bottle. Your voice sounds a little scratchy."

"No, wait—"

The girl disappeared only to return a few seconds later. "Here you go. Catch."

The bottle dropped straight into his hands. He thought about tossing it back, maybe knocking her out, but that still wouldn't get him out of this hole. He was going to have to talk himself out.

So he swallowed all the profanities that wanted to spew out of his mouth and said, "Thanks."

"No problem. You ready to talk?"

What the hell? He shook his head, trying to recall anything that might help him figure out what was going on. "Since I don't know where I am or what I'm doing here, maybe you could talk to me."

"Okay."

And she jumped through the hole.

---

TIME HELD no meaning for Bella.

Once she got past her fear and could think of Cole not as her brother but as a patient, she was able to work.

She knew she needed to stop the bleeding first and she couldn't stitch him up because it could trap infection. So she packed the wounds, front and back, with clean towels and applied pressure.

But there was so much blood. Cole's face was pale and his skin clammy to the touch. He was in shock but she couldn't deal with that yet. With the heel of her left palm jammed against the chest wound and the heel of her right on his back, she pressed, until she couldn't feel her own arms anymore.

She didn't know how long she stood there, holding her brother together, praying he'd be okay. When she finally took a deep breath and pulled back the towels, she nearly fainted in relief. The bleeding had stopped.

Now she packed the wounds with gauze and wrapped it as tightly as she dared. She stared at the wounds for several seconds, but only a tiny bit of blood seeped through. With a sigh, she turned for the bathroom, closing the door just before she lost the contents of her stomach into the toilet.

After flushing, she sat on the floor between the tub and the toilet, waiting for the adrenaline to work its way out of her bloodstream. Her muscles snapped, tiny little explosions under her skin. She moved her jaw, trying to work out the stiffness that had set in from clenching her teeth as she worked on her brother.

It was blessedly quiet in here but she heard voices in the other room—Amy Jo, Dorian. That must mean Dorian had found Dr. Kent.

She should get out there. She needed to talk to Dr. Kent.

She wanted to talk to Steven.

Her brow furrowed. Was Steven out there? She didn't remember seeing him but then everything had been one big blur when they'd brought Cole in.

Where the hell was Steven?

"Bella?" Amy Jo's soft voice came through the door. "Are you okay? Can I come in?"

Was she? Hell if she knew.

"Sure. Come in, Amy Jo."

The door opened only long enough to let Amy Jo slip through. Then she closed the door behind her and sat with her back against the tub wall, staring at Bella. "How are you?"

She didn't know how to answer that question. "Is Cole okay?"

Amy Jo nodded. "He appears to be sleeping fine at the moment. His breathing is pretty steady. Dorian said the doctor will be here in a few minutes."

Relief washed through her, relaxing more tense muscles. "Thank the Goddess. He'll need blood. I'll have to give up some of mine." Though it wouldn't be enough. "We'll have to find another donor, though how—"

Amy grabbed her hand and squeezed. "The other woman, Dorian? She said not to worry. She has the same blood type, too."

That was...interesting. She and Cole shared the same, rare AB-negative. For Dorian to have the same type...that was almost too much of a coincidence. Which didn't mean a damn thing right now.

"Where's Steven?"

Amy Jo's blink gave her away and fear grabbed hold of Bella's lungs and squeezed the air from them.

"No, no ..."

Amy Jo's hand tightened on hers. "No one can find him. He just seems to have...disappeared."

Her breath started to come fast and shallow. Hyperventilation wasn't far behind. "What do you mean he disappeared? Was he shot? Was he taken? Did he just vanish? No one saw anything?"

Amy Jo shook her head. "Diego and Marco just got back from looking for him. They said Steven was the first one out the door. But when Diego got to your brother, Steven wasn't there."

"Maybe he ran after the shooter. Maybe he was shot, too." She stood, wiping her clammy hands on her pants. She had to get outside, find Steven. He could be lying in a gutter somewhere, hurt, bleeding.

Amy Jo stood, putting her hand on Bella's shoulder. "Some of the men are already out looking. You can't go out there, Bella. What if the person who shot your brother is just waiting for you to show yourself?"

"There's no way I'm going to sit on my hands. You have to get me out of here, Amy Jo. I can't just sit here. Would you be willing to be left behind if someone you loved was out there?"

Amy Jo dropped her gaze and shook her head. "Bella, there's something else."

"What?" How could this get any worse?

"Some of the other men...they think Steven was involved in Cole's shooting."

---

SHOCK HELD Steven in place as the girl dropped to the floor.

It had to be at least a twelve-foot drop but she landed on her feet like a cat then drew herself up to her full height—maybe five feet. She wore ripped-at-the-knee jeans and a red halter top and her feet were bare.

He could have been wrong, though, because he was distracted by her pale pink wings.

He actually felt his mouth drop open as she grinned at him.

"Pretty cool, huh?" She turned to the side so he could see those wings more clearly. "They're good for flying, in addition to silencing the natives."

They appeared to be extensions of her shoulder blades, maybe two-feet long and a little shy of that across. Without thinking, he reached out to stroke the closest wing—and she slapped his hand with the tip.

He retracted his hand with a snap. Then awe started to creep in.

"You're *folletti*."

The girl clapped her hands together like an excited two-year-old and squealed. "Very *good*. I told Rainey you would figure it out right away. Rainey wasn't too sure of your intelligence but I knew you'd be smart. You've managed to keep yourself out of trouble this long. You have to have some brains to do that."

Steven heard her talking but couldn't make sense of what she was saying. He couldn't think about anything other than those wings. They were beautiful. And so unusual.

Yes, the woman he loved changed from human to wolf, and he could manipulate aspects of the weather, but this girl had *wings*.

Shaking his head, he forced his gaze to focus on her face. And had to rethink his age estimate. He'd thought teenager but, on second thought, she looked at least as old as Bella.

"I didn't think there were any *folletti* left in North America," he said.

The woman rolled her eyes. "Well, sure you didn't. It's not like we go out and announce our presence to the world. Wouldn't be very smart. Most humans aren't ready to face the fact that they can't pay their monthly credit card bills much less acknowledge *versipelli*, *streghe* and *folletti*. Don'cha think?"

Yeah, he did think. Still... "What do you want with me?"

Her expression said he'd just asked a stupid question. "You're needed."

"What?" He shook his head. "What are you talking about? Needed for what?"

Hands on her hips, she huffed, as if disgusted he didn't know what she was talking about. "Well, to keep the balance, of course."

"BELLA, COLE'S CONSCIOUS," Diego called through the door. "He wants to talk to you."

Everything was happening too fast. Bella felt like she couldn't keep up. But she did know one thing.

She looked Amy Jo straight in the eyes. "Steven had nothing to do with this and, if he's missing, he's in trouble."

She didn't wait for Amy Jo's response. Pushing to her feet, she opened the door to find Diego, ready to knock again. Instead, he grabbed her hand and pulled her forward. "He's really weak, but he's getting agitated. Keep him calm, whatever you do. The doctor's only a minute away."

She moved to the bed where her brother rested, skin pale, eyes shadowed and barely open. But when he saw her, he smiled.

"Hey, brat. Heard you fixed me up."

She nearly fell into the chair someone dragged up to the side of the bed and took his cold hand. The fog in her head kept the tears she felt in the corners of her eyes from falling. "You're lucky I remembered a thing or two from anatomy in college, big brother. How are you feeling?"

"Like I was shot." His weak attempt at a joke made those tears begin to leak down her cheeks. "Hey, don't fall apart on me now, babe. We've got problems. Problems you're going to have to take care of until I'm better."

His eyelids fluttered and she held her breath, wanting him to fall back to sleep yet afraid he was losing unconsciousness. Afraid of what he was going to say.

"Shh, Cole, just get some sleep. You need to rest."

His eyes flew open. "No, not yet. We need to talk. Dori." He turned his head, as if he knew exactly where to find his *praetorian*. "Everyone out. Now."

Bella hadn't even realized Dorian was standing on the other side of the bed until she moved. When only the two of them remained, Steven spoke in a voice so low, she knew no one besides her would be able to hear.

"Someone took Steven." Cole's gaze burned into hers. "One minute he was there, the next he was gone. He just disappeared. Get Diego on it. Find him."

Fear iced her blood. "What are you talking about? I don't—"

"And you're going to have to take my place at *congress* tomorrow morning."

Her mouth dropped open in shock. "*What?* No. I can't do that."

Cole's eyes blazed so brightly, she was afraid he might be feverish. "Yes, you can. The *tribuni* needs to know what's going on as soon as possible. The army started to crack when Dad was murdered. Now they'll hear about me and think all is lost. It's what the *Mal* has wanted all along. And now... You heard what Serena said today. There's a fight coming and we're the front line. We're going to need the army. A strong army. You're Lupo-reale, just like me, Bella. Dad worked so damn hard to keep the *lucani* from splintering. It'll all fall apart if we're not there to guide it. You show them how strong you are tomorrow morning. Don't let this—"

The door flew open, bumping into the wall as Dr. Xavier Kent burst through.

Relief overcame the shock and fear and Bella nearly crumbled in the chair as the man hustled toward the bed, followed by Dorian, Luca, Diego, Marco and Amy Jo.

"Well, Cole. I see you managed to get yourself shot while I was unavailable. Lucky for you, your sister loves you. Fill me in, Princess."

For as long as she could remember, Dr. Kent had been the Luporeale family doctor. If it was something that couldn't be cured with chicken soup, cold compresses or a bandage, Dr. Kent had shown up at the door, whether it was her parents' home or Michael Castiglione's. As Cole had gotten older, Dr. Kent had become a permanent fixture in Cole's entourage.

Bella swore he hadn't aged a day in the twenty-five years she'd known him.

She released Cole only to throw her arms around the short, round man with the bald head and gray goatee, almost embarrassing herself when she couldn't speak for fear she'd sob.

"Come now. It's okay, sweetheart." Dr. Kent's large hand patted her back and petted her hair. "Everything's going to be okay."

Yes, she believed Cole would be fine. If Dr. Kent said so, it was true.

But there was more, so much more, on the line now.

---

STEVEN SHOOK HIS HEAD, feeling like he'd fallen through Alice's rabbit hole into Wonderland.

And knocked his head on a few rocks on the way down.

He should take a few minutes, think about all of this before he opened his mouth and said something really stupid. But he couldn't help himself.

"What the *hell* are you talking about?"

When the woman's eyes narrowed and her wings flapped angrily, he figured he should've kept his mouth shut. But the mythical being was explaining something that sounded like political theory in Valley Girl speak and there was only so much he could take in one day.

"Alright, listen up, Castiglione, 'cause I'm only going to say this once." Hands on her hips, she cocked her head to the side. "There's a balance between right and wrong, you see. Or anyway, there had been." She tossed her head and fluttered her wings. "Anyway, today, most people see black and white. Especially in this country. You're either with them or against them, right? Religion, skin color, hair style, sexual orientation. Bad, good. Many people no longer see a middle ground. There's this line and you're either on one side or the other. Now, you... You were born straddling that line."

Finally, something he could respond to. "I was born *Mal*."

The girl's nose wrinkled and she bit down hard on her bottom lip. "Not exactly."

*What?* He shook his head as if that would help her words make sense. "What the hell does that mean?"

"Well, it means, yes, you were born *Mal*. Except, no, not really. See, it's like this—"

"Tinia's teat, Alpena, you're making a mess of this."

The disembodied voice sounded as if it came from all around him. He spun in a quick circle before putting his back against the wall.

The *folletta* huffed and pouted, crossing her arms over her chest as she spoke to the air.

"Well then, you get out here and do this yourself. I told you I wasn't good at this kind of thing."

A long-suffering sigh echoed before, with a barely audible pop, a woman appeared out of nowhere in front of Steven. No wings this time. Tall, curved, age indiscriminate. But her hair was the most amazing colors he'd ever seen. Black, white, blue and silver.

The newcomer turned to the *folletta* and shook her head. "No, you certainly are *not* good at this. You've scared the poor man into silence. And that's a bad sign from a lawyer."

That hair couldn't be natural. Which was a really stupid thing to focus on right now.

He opened his mouth to speak...and couldn't think of a damn thing to say.

The woman with the wild hair turned back to him and

smiled like you would at the paperboy with diminished mental capacity.

"Hello, Steven." She stuck out her hand and he automatically took it. She shook, firm and sure, then released him. But not before he'd felt the incredible rush of *arus* in her body. "Please don't be alarmed. We mean you no harm."

The *folletta*—what had this woman called her? Alpena?—snorted. "Have you been watching 'Mystery Science Theater 3000' again? I knew I shouldn't have gotten those discs for your festival day."

Rainey—who really didn't look like someone you should nickname Rainey—gave the merest hint of a smile but didn't acknowledge the other woman. "My name is Turan."

It said something about his state of mind that it took his brain several seconds to process the name. But even though his parents had raised him on the outskirts of the Etruscan community, he knew to show the proper respect.

He bowed low and held it, wondering if he was going to live through this. "Goddess Turan, Mistress of the Swans. How can I be of service to you?"

# FIFTEEN

"We'll make a dual out of you yet, Arabella. This is nice work."

A warm glow suffused Bella at Dr. Kent's words even as she shook her head. "Thanks. But you know that's not going to happen."

Dr. Kent continued his examination of Cole's wounds, poking and prodding. "Never say never, honey. Those words always come back to bite you."

Yes, she knew that. But this was an old fight. "I enjoy what I'm doing. I'm good at what I do."

That earned her a brief glance from beneath Dr. Kent's bushy white eyebrows. "Never said you weren't. But, if your work here is any indication, you'd make a great trauma specialist. Goddess knows we don't have enough of them, not in our little circle of the world."

Yes, that was true. The *lucani* had only three doctors who specialized in both human and animal physiology. Dr. Kent was one. The army doctor, Giorgio Marone, was another but he was older than Dr. Kent. And Dr. Dane Dimitriou had only just finished his veterinary courses at the University of Pennsylvania in Philadelphia, Bella's alma mater. Dane had already passed his human medical boards.

She knew Cole had hoped she'd continue her studies and become a dual. But again, she'd shirked her calling and turned her back on her community. Dr. Kent glanced at her, eyebrows raised, when she didn't immediately go into her typical bratty response about how she wanted to choose her own path, live her own life, blah, blah, blah...

"I know that. And I'll consider it."

Everyone in the room stopped what they were doing to stare at her with varying degrees of raised eyebrows. Except for Amy Jo, who just looked confused at everyone else's interest.

"Well, now, I'm glad to hear that, sweetheart." Dr. Kent was the first to recover. And smart enough to know not to push her. "Why don't you go get cleaned up. Then we'll talk."

"It'll have to be much later. I'm going to look for Steven."

There was a two second lull before four of the seven people in the room started to speak over each other. They all had the same thing to say even if they didn't use the same words.

"Arabella, you can't go." Dorian.

"Princess, it's too dangerous." Luca.

"You don't know what's waiting out there." Diego.

"Jesus, are you crazy?" Marco, of course.

Her chest tightened and she felt tears threaten again as they continued to tell her why she couldn't do it. Mostly because of the danger. But she heard what they weren't saying.

They didn't think she could handle herself. Didn't trust her. And a small part didn't trust herself either. Still, she wasn't going to stand by any more and let others handle things for her.

She faced the crowd behind her. "I'm going to take a shower then I'm going out to look. If anyone wants to come with me, fine, but don't presume to tell me I can't go."

That got a moment of silence. Then they started in again.

Only one voice had a different answer.

"I'll go with you, Bella."

Amy Jo smiled at her as she leaned against the door to the room. Bella smiled back.

"Oh no, you will *fucking* not." Diego turned on Amy Jo to continue his rant. In Spanish. Bella was pretty sure he hadn't realized Amy Jo couldn't understand him. But his expression barely hid his fear.

Marco rolled his eyes and threw his hands into the air as he, too, turned on Amy Jo. At least he spoke in English.

And Dorian and Luca continued to rationally explain why there was no way they would allow either of them to leave the room.

Only Dr. Kent and Cole were silent.

After nodding once at Amy Jo, she turned to Cole, who grabbed her hand.

"Take Dorian, Diego, Marco and Luca. No," he shook his head before she could protest, "that's an order. Find Steven. I'll keep Johnny, Bill and Karl. I promise they won't leave my side."

"I can assure you they won't." Dr. Kent gave her an encouraging smile. "Go. But come back."

"You *must* be back before dawn," Cole continued. "Even if you don't find him, Bella. You have to be at *congress* at nine a.m. Someone doesn't want this meeting to go forward. Don't do anything foolish."

Foolish was thinking she could handle the *lucani* army leadership on her own. Foolish was thinking she could find Steven without Cole or any clues to where he'd been taken.

"Arabella, stop it." Cole shook her hand and stared straight into her eyes. "Get cleaned up. Get moving. The longer you wait, the less chance you have of picking up his scent. You know that better than anyone."

She did. That was something she needed to hold on to now.

"I'll find him," she promised. "And I'll be back."

———

"YOU DON'T HAVE to do this," Diego said as he removed his shirt. "I don't— you don't need to be here."

Amy Jo nodded, hearing the tension in Diego's voice. And the words he hadn't spoken aloud. He didn't want her here. He couldn't make it any more obvious if he'd flat-out said it.

But he wouldn't do that. At least not in front of everyone else.

Dorian, Luca, Marco and Bella were also here, in a meeting room on the first floor of the hotel. In the front of the room, Bella and Luca also removed their clothes and handed them to Dorian to put in a backpack. Marco leaned against the door near Bella, staring at the floor.

She and Diego were on the opposite side of the room, as far from everyone else as they could get.

He'd crooked his finger at her when they'd entered the room, his mouth a flat straight line. And she'd followed like a puppy. God, she was pathetic.

Especially considering she was staring at his chest like she wanted to toss him on the table and have her way with him.

The man had a great chest. If she closed her eyes, she could remember exactly what his skin felt like. She drew in a deep breath, trying to steady herself and only made things worse because all she could smell was him.

She shook her head and stared at the wall over his left shoulder. "I said I'd help. I'm not backing out. And if I'm going to—" She took a deep breath. She wasn't ready to go there. Not yet. "Anyway, I should get used to this, right? So, how's this going to work?"

Diego cursed under his breath, something vicious and Spanish. She didn't have a clue what he'd said but she was pretty sure it was directed at her.

"Amy Jo, we don't—" He bit off the rest of the sentence but she knew what he wouldn't say.

They didn't need her. And why would they? Up until this point, she'd been nothing but a liability. Hell, what if she got out there tonight and froze during a crucial moment? Or more importantly, freaked out?

She stared blindly at the wall in front of her as fear swept through her, chilling her to her core.

"*Shit.*" Diego's growl sounded positively feral, drawing her gaze to his as he grabbed her hands. "Look at me. Amy Jo."

"No, you're right. This is a mistake. I shouldn't be here. I should go—"

"*Hell* no. Damn it, woman, shut up."

His tone made her breath catch in her throat. He was pissed and his expression made her heart stutter.

"I don't want to leave you here." His voice was pitched low and harsh. "I don't want you out of my sight and that pisses me off. But I don't want to traumatize you any more than you already are. And, damn it, I'm going to shift in a few minutes and it infuriates me to know that a part of me is abhorrent to you."

Her eyes widened. "What? No—"

"*Don't.*" He slashed a hand through the air. "Just go back to your room and wait for me to get back. And don't make me put a guard on your door. When I get back, we'll talk—"

"Diego, nothing about you is abhorrent to me." She couldn't believe he thought that. Framing his face with her hands, she drew him closer, staring into his eyes. She couldn't care less that the four other people in the room were making it *too* obvious they were trying not to listen. "Just the opposite. But I gave my word and I'm going. With all y'all," she added. "So, how *will* this work?"

Diego didn't look any happier but she felt some of her fear recede. The emotion underlying his words hit her with more power than the words themselves.

It took him a few moments to respond but finally, he cupped her head and drew her close for a short, hard kiss.

Then he stalked over to Marco, leaving her to wonder if she really understood what she'd agreed to.

---

DIEGO KNEW he was in deep shit even before he kissed Amy Jo.

That kiss only confirmed that he'd finally lost his mind.

He was falling for a biter.

He'd never liked that term. It was derogatory and not at all how he felt about her. Hell, he wasn't sure *how* he felt about Amy Jo. He only knew that if something happened to her, he wouldn't be able to live with himself.

But Bella needed him right now and duty demanded he help.

That left only one other person he trusted to make sure nothing happened to Amy Jo.

"Marco."

His brother lifted his eyebrows as he leaned against the wall farthest from Amy Jo, who'd moved next to Bella. "You're toast, man. You know that, right?"

Yeah, he knew it. But that didn't mean he had to admit it. "Don't let her out of your sight."

Marco shook his head, the grin ghosting around his lips pissing off Diego. "Never figured you'd let yourself fall, especially not for someone like her."

Diego felt a growl start low in his chest. "Watch what you say, brother. Or I'll take your head off."

"Yeah, that's what I thought." Marco nodded like he'd just discovered something he'd known but wasn't happy about. Then he leaned in close to Diego, his gaze holding strong. "You hurt her, I'll maim you."

Diego felt white-hot fury consume him for the five seconds it took him to realize Marco was truly worried about Amy Jo. Then he released it on a heavy sigh.

"I don't want to hurt her."

"I know that." Marco shook his head. "Then don't."

What the hell could he say to that? "Don't let her out of your sight. You guard her exclusively. Let me and Dorian and the kid worry about Bella."

Marco's laugh sounded more like a grunt. "Don't worry. I won't let anything happen to your mate, brother."

Diego's mouth dropped open a split second before he caught it. A mess of emotions he couldn't—and didn't want to—put a name to landed in his stomach and twisted it into knots.

*Mate.*

Marco was messing with him, trying to get a rise out him. He opened his mouth to deny it...and caught the words back. Because Marco was dead serious.

*Mate.*

Marco's brows rose and a sarcastic smile curved his lips. "What? You didn't know? How clueless are you, brother? Good thing dear old Dad's already dead. This would've put him in the ground for sure."

True, their father would've had a brain aneurysm if he'd even suspected Diego was thinking about mating a woman who wasn't descended from *versipelli* royalty. But Amy Jo wasn't—couldn't be his mate. She wasn't...

Wasn't what?

Hereditary? True. And if she were, would he be having as much trouble believing Marco's claim?

Hell, three months ago, she hadn't known about *versipelli* or the magical races. Then she'd been brutalized and left for dead and somehow miraculously lived through it and found her way to Bella.

To him.

No, Marco was wrong.

And even if he wasn't, that didn't mean Diego had to make her his mate. He'd never planned to take a woman, hadn't wanted to subject anyone to the constant threat of the *grigori* life.

He stared at Marco and saw one more reason why a relationship with Amy Jo could prove detrimental to everyone's health.

Marco wanted her, too.

If Amy Jo truly was Diego's mate, he'd want to rip his brother to pieces for looking at her.

Instead, he felt strangely relieved that Marco would also be there to protect her.

Damn, this was fucked up.

Shaking his head, Diego practically ripped the pants off his legs.

"Just...don't let anything happen to her."

---

"NOW, ALPENA, YOU SHOULD TAKE NOTES," Turan said. "The boy has impeccable manners."

Still holding the bow, Steven saw Alpena lift one wing in what looked like a vaguely obscene gesture but her amused snort left him with no doubt as to what she thought.

"Oh please. You've been gone for so long—"

"Alpena." Turan's voice held a sharp edge. "Let's not go there just yet. We have a lot to talk about and very little time."

And that's about the time Steven realized what information his brain had been trying to work through.

If this *was* Turan, then something truly amazing had happened.

All Etruscans knew that around the second century AD, the *Involuti*, the founding deities of the Etruscans—Uni, Tinia, Menrva, Turan and Veltune—had retreated from this world to Invol, their home plane of existence.

No one knew why they'd disappeared, why they'd deserted their people and the rest of the pantheon. No one had heard from them or seen them for two millennia.

And now Turan had returned and chosen to talk to *him*?

Or had he finally lost his mind?

As a kid, he'd been taught to worship the gods and goddesses. The Christians called his people pagans. Steven had long believed them all—Christians and pagans—to be fools, allowing their lives to be dictated by the whims of deities who demanded obedience and gave nothing in return.

Who refused to help a little boy who only wanted to be accepted by his community. But who was forced into exile with his parents because he was different. Dangerous.

"Steven." Turan's voice broke through his thoughts and he straightened from his bow when she wiggled a finger at him. Their gazes caught and held, Steven mesmerized by the vivid blue of hers.

"Yes, we have much to answer for," she said. "We've been gone too long. And not yet fully returned. There's been damage we will never be able to repair, losses we can't overcome."

Steven heard a wealth of sorrow in her voice and pure fear shot through him. What could make a goddess that sad? It had to be something horrendous—

"Listen closely, Steven. We don't have much time. They'll come looking for you soon and I've already bent a few too many rules. You're going to have to make choices soon, choices that will affect a great many things. It's not by chance that you became a lawyer. But justice is not righting wrongs. Justice is balancing the scales."

Looking straight into her eyes, Steven now saw streaks of color that matched her hair swirl through her eyes.

He took an involuntary step backward and swallowed, hoping like hell that his voice didn't break when he spoke. "Where am I?"

"In the basement of a home in the Garden District," Turan said. "It took many months to clean up after Katrina. Alpena insisted on hiring local laborers. Took longer than I would have liked but Alpena insisted they needed the work. Would you like to see the rest of the house?"

Turan snapped her fingers and Steven blinked to find himself in another room. Bookshelves lined three walls while the fourth held a lifetime worth of photos.

He moved to examine the wall more closely, drawn by the familiar faces. The photos spanned most of his life. There were pictures of him as a toddler, as a child, a teenager, an adult. The most recent appeared to be from the plane trip with Bella today.

"What is this?" His voice emerged as a whisper.

"Each of these pictures represents a choice," Turan said. "Not every choice is the right one but sometimes there *is* more than one right choice. You're going to have to choose, Steven. A choice only you can make. But one that will affect those you love. Arabella—"

"Leave her out of this." He heard menace in his voice and didn't try to hide it.

Turan smiled. "That was never a choice. Your lives are bound, whether you accept that or not."

He couldn't and wouldn't. He refused to put her in danger. "What choice are you talking about?"

"Now, that *would* be cheating." Turan smiled. "Don't worry, you'll know it when you have to make it."

"I won't use my magic."

Turan's smile widened. "Yes, that is a choice you've already made. Will it be the right choice? Time will tell."

"Of course it will." He sighed and let his head drop back on his shoulders—and stared at the cathedral ceiling. "Look, if you're a goddess, why can't you just zip forward in time and fix whatever imbalance there is?"

Alpena slapped him on the back of his head with her wing. "Because it doesn't work like that, silly. Jeez, for such a smart guy, you're surprisingly stupid."

"Alpena, really," Turan gave the *folletta* a wry grin, "Although her delivery may be a little rough, she's correct. I do not control the power I once commanded."

Shit. That really didn't sound good. In fact, it sounded downright terrifying. Because when the deities didn't have power, the world didn't work correctly.

This situation was getting more surreal by the moment. He surreptitiously grabbed the flesh of his inner arm and twisted until it throbbed with pain. Damn, he wasn't asleep. At least that would explain a lot of this.

"Why did you snatch me off the street?" And then he remembered why he'd been in the street. Fear dropped into his stomach like acid. "Cole? Christ, is Cole okay?"

"Cole will be fine," Turan said. "He's lucky Arabella is so very smart. We took you at that time because you were alone. You've been difficult to catch alone."

"It's been kind of a strange week." And wasn't that an understatement.

"Yes." Turan nodded. "Strange. And it's about to get even more so."

---

AMY JO STOOD next to Marco, determined not to freak.

She wanted to watch, wanted to see what happened, examine it rationally and maybe, just maybe, it would make sense.

"It's considered impolite to stare."

Marco's voice rasped in her ear, startling her with his nearness. She turned to see him standing behind her.

"I'm sorry. I didn't know. Should we leave?"

He shrugged. "No, just don't watch. Talk to me."

Right, talk. "There's so much I don't know."

"Yeah, you didn't have the best introduction to our world, did you?"

Marco's wry grin, so similar to Diego's but with a lot less sarcasm, made her hormones sit up and dance. Which was just not good. She's slept with his brother. She had feelings for his brother. But there was something about Marco—

God, she was *so* screwed up.

She dropped her gaze and shook her head.

"Hey, Amy Jo." His voice lowered even further, soothing and sexy as hell. "Talk to me."

"Does it ever stop hu—"

She broke off as she heard the first sounds of transformation behind her. Bone ground against bone and cartilage stretched and popped. Her breath stuck in her chest and she couldn't catch her breath. Her muscles shook with the urge to run.

"Hey, babe. Look here. Look at me."

With an effort, she lifted her gaze to tangle with Marco's. His eyes, so similar to Diego's, caught and held hers. "When they're done, they're going to pick up their leashes and give them to whoever they want to lead them out. Never pick up someone's leash unless they hand it to you. It's rude and sometimes it's considered aggressive. It's a good way to have your hand bitten off."

Why didn't she hear any screaming? She screamed a lot when she changed. The process of reforming your entire body into another shape was painful. And completely insane. She—

"Hey, Amy Jo." Marco grabbed both of her hands and squeezed. His hands, huge and warm, calmed her heart rate just a tiny bit. "Did you hear me?"

She took a deep breath and focused on Marco. "Yeah, yeah. Never put a leash on a...a *versipellis* unless they give you permission. Otherwise you might be missing a few fingers."

Marco smiled again and her heart rate spiked for a completely different reason. "That's right. And allowing you to hold a leash is a sign of trust. We don't trust easily. Don't hold the leash too tight. They're designed to break apart with a specific amount of pressure."

The noises behind her were starting to fade but she didn't want to release Marco's hands. "So then why have the leash?"

"For appearances. We're not exactly dogs and people realize that. But because we've got leashes, people think we're civilized."

Something nudged her leg. Or rather, someone.

Amy Jo turned to find a gray wolf with Bella's dark eyes standing by her side, purple leash in her mouth. She knelt to be on a level with the animal's eyes, finally breaking Marco's hold on her hands.

She reached out to stroke Bella's gorgeous gray fur but stopped. "Whoa, so not fair. You're even pretty as a wolf."

If a wolf could smile, Bella did, her mouth filled with sharp teeth curving up on the sides. Then the wolf shook her head and the leash rattled.

"Go ahead," Marco said. "Take it."

Amy Jo did, feeling like she should curtsy as she attached the jeweled collar and leash. "Jeez, I hope I don't pinch you or something. Are those really diamonds? Can I pet her?"

She directed the question at Marco but Bella gave her a short nod.

"Guess that answers your..."

Amy Jo glanced at Marco, whose gaze was fixed on the gorgeous creature in front of him. She'd never seen a lynx before but she guessed that's exactly what stood before him.

That cat was Diego, who looked like an exotic housecat with spotted fur and tufted ears. The biggest freaking housecat she'd ever seen. It was surreal, to say the least and she shook her head and blinked a few times, just to make sure she wasn't really dreaming.

Diego stared at Marco with his human eyes and a leash in his mouth. Marco didn't take it right away and Diego just kept staring at him.

Suddenly realizing she was probably interrupting some sort of brother-bonding moment she looked back at Bella to give the boys some room.

"I gotta say, Princess," she whispered in Bella's ear, "I love the diamonds. They make the whole ensemble."

Bella snorted, as close to a laugh as she could get, Amy Jo figured. And Bella did look regal, even if she was a wolf, complete with fluffy tail and sleek coat.

But her eyes were pure human. It was slightly weird but it helped. Oh hell, it was *really* weird, but she was learning. She could deal. She had to if...

Out of the corner of her eye, she saw Marco kneel to take

the leash from his brother's mouth, his expression still shocked. She realized just how much Diego's action meant to Marco.

From the little she'd overheard and from what Diego had told her, the brothers had a lot of family issues to work through. But she could tell Diego was determined to be close to his brother.

And here she was, lusting after both of them.

*Yeah, that was really a good way to mend fences between brothers, idiot.*

Marco didn't pet Diego, merely took the leash and snapped the collar around his neck. Then Diego's mouth moved in that way cats had. To her, it looked like pure feline satisfaction. Marco just shook his head and stood, leash in hand.

"Alright, people." Dorian stood by the door, Luca's collar in hand and a pack carrying the shifters' clothes on her back. "We don't have all night. Let's get this fucked-up parade on the road."

# SIXTEEN

Under the cover of a glamour spell wrought by Serena before they left the hotel, Bella stalked up and down the street in front of the building.

She'd known immediately when they got to the place where Steven had disappeared that something strange had happened.

And not just strange in the fact that he'd disappeared.

Strange in the *way* he'd disappeared.

She sniffed the air, trying to block out the smell of Cole's blood, metallic and thick and terrifying, while keeping Steven's scent at the forefront. She sniffed up and down the street but couldn't catch Steven's scent anywhere but in front of the hotel. It just disappeared.

Not like he'd been shoved in a car and driven away.

Like he'd been sucked out of existence.

Fear made her heart pound furiously but she gave her entire body a shake and forced it to settle down.

Maybe the stench of garbage from the alley around back had clouded her senses. Maybe she just needed to concentrate. She had to be able to pick up his scent, no matter how faint, and use it to track him. It should have been a snap in her wolf form, where her sense of smell was so much more sensitive.

Of course, it couldn't be that easy.

Just to make sure she hadn't missed anything, she stalked the street from end to end, Amy Jo keeping a light grip on the leash.

Nothing.

Sitting on her haunches under the awning, she gazed at the street in front of her. Which way? If she chose wrong— No, she couldn't think like that.

What was she missing?

Something warm and furry sat beside her, causing her wolf to growl and consider grabbing the throat next to her and biting. After all, she was canine and the feline next to her was prey. But she knew Diego would smack her down with one swipe of his paw. He was larger than a real lynx and much stronger.

And he was waiting for her lead.

*Think, think, think. What are you missing?*

Okay. She didn't smell Steven. So what else did she detect that might lead her to him?

Closing her eyes, she drew in all the smells she could. Familiar ones like gasoline and diesel fumes from the street materials and cars, rotting garbage and the overwhelming scent of human flesh that wasn't Steven...those she could block out.

But there was something else, something she couldn't put a label on right away.

Something magic. But not like any magic she'd ever come across. Something...pure.

She turned west and walked to the end of the block. Nothing.

She walked to the other end of the alley, away from the hotel.

*Bingo.*

She barked to Diego to follow then shot off down the alley, breaking the leash, chasing that almost-elusive tingle in the back of her nose. She heard Amy Jo shout behind her and felt Diego and finally Luca catch up to her as she ran.

Even though they were in the Garden District and it was close to three in the morning, she passed a couple of people on the streets. She ignored the startled and fearful looks and ran flat out, pulling ahead of Amy Jo and Marco in seconds. Only Dorian, Diego and Luca kept pace with her.

She didn't bother to look for landmarks or street signs. It didn't matter where they were going just as long as they got there soon. She had to be right.

The blocks became longer and less densely packed with buildings the further into the Garden District they ran. The houses grew bigger, the yards more spacious and the trees larger and older. The streetlamps shed little illumination, making for gloomy conditions. That didn't matter. She was using her nose more than her eyes anyway.

She didn't know how long she ran. All she knew was that she was going to find Steven.

Here. The scent was strongest here.

She stopped in front of an ornate black fence surrounding a lush garden. She couldn't see a house but she knew there had to be one. Closing her eyes, she took a deep breath...

*Yes!* Steven was in there.

Diego hissed at her, wanting her to wait for the others. Luca was still at least a block away and Dorian nearly two. She growled back and slipped through the iron bars, designed more for show than protection. Diego followed after a decidedly feline snit.

The dense vegetation swallowed her almost immediately but she focused on Steven's scent. Keeping to the protection of the overgrown garden, Bella pushed forward until she saw a quaint, one-and-a-half story cottage through the thick foliage.

There, that's where Steven was. And only Steven.

She sensed no one else.

Shifting back into human skin, she ran for the door, barely noticing the branches whipping at her bare body or the rough, uneven ground under her now-tender feet.

She had to get to Steven, had to save him from...whatever.

Up the three brick stairs to the front door, and without hesitation, she twisted the doorknob, startled into stopping her forward motion when it opened.

Diego, still in his lynx body, hissed at her to stop, actually butting his head at her legs as he pushed in front of her. But there was no way she was going to stay behind now.

Fuck caution. She wanted Steven. She could smell him. He was here.

"Steven!"

Her voice echoed down the long center hall, doors set at random intervals down either side. So many doors. Too many doors. Diego shifted while she stared down that seemingly endless hall.

"Arabella, get back outside," Diego's voice held a commanding edge she ignored. Instead, she began pushing open doors.

The first one to the left held a sitting room—chairs, sofas, a fireplace. To the right, an identical room. Completely, weirdly identical.

Same with the next two. And why didn't it seem like they were making progress down the hall?

"Arabella, stop." Diego's tone caught her attention this time and she did. "Something's not right."

She sighed, frustration giving an edge to her words. "Yeah, I kind of figured that out on my own. What the hell's going on?"

"Damn. This place, it's charmed pretty heavily," Luca said behind them. "Can't you tell?"

Well, no, she hadn't been able to tell because all she could concentrate on was Steven. Now she stopped and let the *arus* in her blood connect with the magic in the house.

*Whoa.* The power, the amount of it, nearly rocked her back on her feet. Charms were kind of like wards, protective spells used to protect buildings or open areas from deliberate acts of harm. But where a ward had to be maintained and recharged, a charm never did. It took an immense amount of power to make a charm.

Shit. Now what?

She looked at Diego, who was shaking his head. "Someone really doesn't want us to find—"

"Steven!" She called again, hearing the tension in her voice, the tremor that let Diego know she was about to lose it. Charm or no charm, he was here and she would find him.

"Bella, I think we should wait—"

"Bella. I'm here. I'm okay."

Steven's voice came from somewhere down the hall and the relief nearly took her to her knees. Swallowing a sob, she called to him again. "Where are you? Steven, please..."

When he stepped from a door halfway down the hall and opened his arms, she ran and leaped into his arms, knowing he would catch her.

---

STEVEN CAUGHT Bella out of the air, wrapped his arms around her and let her wind her naked body around his. When her head burrowed into the curve of his neck, he felt the warmth of her tears and held her tighter.

He held up one hand to stop Diego and Luca. "It's alright.

I'm alright. Just let me calm her down. I assume Dorian's coming?"

Diego nodded. "Yeah, but they won't be able to get through the gate."

"It'll open. Just...give us a minute."

Without waiting for an answer, he walked back into the library with Bella.

"Shh, stop crying. Come on, Bella, pull it together. Tell me how Cole's doing. Is he all right?"

He rubbed her naked back, feeling like a pig because the warmth of her skin was turning him on, even as she shook. Christ, didn't he have enough to deal with at the moment?

It took her a minute to gain some control, until she drew in a deep, shuddering breath and lifted her head. With her eyes on his, she clasped his face between her hands and kissed him. And not a gentle peck, either. No, her kiss threatened to make him forget everything else, daring him to tear his clothes off and sink himself into her right here and now.

Then she pulled back and smacked him on the back of the head.

"What the hell happened to you?"

The next smack was on his shoulder.

"What are you doing here?"

Smack on his chest.

"How did you get here?"

A kiss this time, hard and fast.

"Who—"

He clapped a hand over her mouth before she could speak finish that thought. "Bella, sweetheart. Shut up. How's Cole?"

She took a deep breath and the tears that had stopped with her tirade returned. Blinking until they receded again, she sniffed. "He's okay. Dr. Kent's with him now. There was so much blood, Steven. I didn't think I'd be able to stop it in time. Did you see who shot Cole?"

He should've been there for her. He would've been there if only... He shook his head, replaying her words so he could answer her. "I only got a glimpse of Cole before—"

Damn, what should he tell her? The truth? It would be a hell of a lot easier and Turan hadn't told him *not* to tell anyone, but he was still trying to figure out what exactly she *had* told him. How the hell did he explain something he didn't yet understand? Or even trust?

Bella stared at him, waiting, so much love in her eyes it nearly made him dizzy. "We need to get back to the hotel and talk. Include Cole."

"But who took you, Steven?"

"It'll be easier to do this all at once with Cole. I'm fine. The...person who took me only wanted to talk."

Bella opened her mouth to speak again but Dorian called out from the hallway.

"Steven? Bella? Where are you?"

Dorian was on her way, whether they were ready or not.

"We'll talk, I promise." Steven punctuated his words with another kiss then set Bella on her feet. "Once we get back to the hotel. Let's just get back there without any problems."

---

"YOU'RE SURE IT WAS COLE?"

The *eteri* sniper nodded, his eyes cool and unwavering.

The human had shown no emotion whatsoever since he'd walked into Remo's French Quarter hotel room. The sniper was a sociopath, capable of cold-blooded murder yet able to function in society without revealing the fact that he felt nothing. A fascinating subject.

"I'm sure it was Cole Luporeale," he said. "The wound wasn't lethal, just as you asked."

"Good." He didn't want Cole dead. Not yet, anyway. He might still be useful if he needed to deal with Veive again.

Remo held out an envelope filled with cash. The man took it, not bothering to check the amount.

Nodding once, the *eteri* said, "Thank you for your business."

He turned to go but hesitated at the door before turning to face Remo again.

"A second man exited the building only seconds after Luporeale went down." A flicker of something Remo interpreted as interest flickered through his eyes. "He wasn't one of the other targets you had given me so I didn't mark him. However...as I was watching, the man disappeared."

Remo let his eyebrows lift in disbelief. "I'm not sure I know what you mean."

The man's expression didn't change. "I mean, one minute he was there, the next he was gone. Vanished. I found that...interesting."

Then the assassin turned and left. As if he hadn't just told a stranger he'd seen a man disappear. Like magic.

Coincidence? Trick of the eye?

Or was something else going on?

Remo had started this chain of events and he would see it through to the end. He'd promised Veive he would show the wolves just how vulnerable they were. That the murders of the Luporeale king, queen and heir had not been a lucky strike.

By striking at Cole away from his base of power, Remo had put the wolves on notice.

Their king wasn't safe.

WHEN THEY GOT BACK to the hotel, Dr. Kent refused to allow anyone but Dorian in Cole's room.

"Are either of you hurt?" he asked, staring hard at Steven. When they all shook their heads, the doctor crossed his arms over his chest. "Then I order everyone to get some sleep. Whatever you need to talk about can wait until morning. Cole needs rest and, from the looks of you, you could all do with the same."

Then he went back into Cole's room and shut the door behind him.

Steven sighed, knowing this was probably for the best. Besides, he wouldn't win a battle with Dr. Kent. The guy was a lion in wolf's clothes.

It was nearly three o'clock in the morning and Bella had told him she had to be at the meeting table at nine. His eyes hurt he was so tired, his stomach ached from adrenaline overload and his temples pounded with a tension headache.

He wanted to go back to Bella's room, tumble her into bed and get inside her as fast as he could. Then he wanted to stay there until she had to leave for *congress*.

The meeting he needed to be at. Where he knew he wouldn't be welcome.

"Steven?"

Bella's voice drew his gaze away from the wall. He'd been staring at a speck of dirt, didn't know for how long.

Concern was written all over her beautiful face and he raised a hand to cup her cheek. He was about to crash. Emotionally, physically. He was suffocating under the weight of his worry for Cole and Bella and the information Turan had told him. Tinia's teat, had he really talked to Turan? He needed to tell Bella—

"Steven. Come with me."

Bella took his hand from her cheek and pulled him along after her to her room down the hall. She didn't bother to turn on the light, just shut the door behind him and guided him to the bed.

She stripped him down to his boxers but didn't take them off. Then she pushed him into bed with a light hand and took off her clothes before she joined him.

Curling against his side, her hand on his chest, she kissed the side of his neck and whispered "Good night" into his ear.

He closed his eyes and fell asleep.

---

AMY JO WATCHED the door shut down the hall and took a deep breath.

The tension between Bella and Steven had been as thick as her mother's pound cake. It made her twitchy.

But not near as twitchy as being left alone with Marco and Diego.

The brothers stared at each other...stared each other down, if she had to guess. And her tension level ratcheted up to full throttle.

She didn't want to spend the night alone.

She wanted Diego. She wanted to take him by the hand just like Bella had done with Steven and lead him to her room. Actually, she guessed she'd have to go to Diego's room because she hadn't actually been given a room. Bella had taken her right to hers and Cole was in there now.

So, the whole taking-Diego-by-the-hand thing wasn't going to work. But still...

She sighed and both men looked at her. She caught Marco's gaze first and the heat in his eyes seared her before he blinked and it was gone.

*Oh, God.*

It took an effort to tear her gaze from his and when she did, she got caught in the desire in Diego's expression.

Hyperventilation became a distinct possibility.

And that wasn't nearly the worst part.

The worst part was she wanted them both. And that was a Shakespearean tragedy just waiting to explode.

She drew in a deep breath in an attempt to calm her racing heart and heard Marco say "Good night." Something in his softly spoken words broke through the haze of heat Diego threw off and shifted her attention back to him. He smiled, just a twist of his lips, then turned and walked away.

"Amy Jo."

The sound of Diego's voice ran through her like an electric current.

*Get a grip, girl, or you're going to lose it again.*

And she didn't want that. No, she wanted the man standing ten feet away from her.

Diego stared at her, no emotion on his handsome face, but she was beginning to realize just how much he hid behind that blank expression.

So she said the first thing that popped into her head. "You make a beautiful cat."

At first, he didn't do anything. Then slowly, a grin kicked up the corners of his mouth and he bowed.

Her mouth dropped open as he performed the salute without an ounce of hesitation or awkwardness. As if it was a natural function for him.

Well, hell. The guy *was* a freakin' king. Of people who could turn into big exotic kitty cats, but still. The closest she'd ever gotten to royalty before now was dating a guy who worked at Burger King.

He began to close the distance between them but she shook her head and he stopped in his tracks, still a few feet away, his expression showing the first hint of confusion. And hurt?

"Would you like me to show you to your room?" he asked.

He thought she was rejecting him? Man, he really didn't know how to read women, did he?

"I've never had a man bow to me before."

His head tipped back as if she'd insulted him and she held up her hand to stop the response she saw forming in his eyes.

"I've also never met a man who turned into a huge cat before. It takes a little getting used to."

He took another few steps forward then paused, now only inches away. His masculine scent, something she'd never really paid attention to before she'd been attacked, drenched her senses and made her heart stutter.

"And are you?" he asked.

Her stomach fluttered. "Am I what?"

"Getting used to?"

She knew what he was asking, even if he didn't come out and say it. Staring into his eyes, she nodded. And smiled. She hadn't had much to smile about recently. And with tomorrow's hypnotism or whatever session with the witch-woman looming on the horizon, Diego could be classified as the best thing that had happened to her in at least the past year. Maybe ever.

His eyes narrowed, as if he were trying to figure out exactly what that smile meant.

Good. Let him guess. But that didn't mean she couldn't help him along.

When she held out her hand, he took it without hesitation.

"So, no one told me where I should sleep tonight."

His fingers intertwined with hers. "Do you want to sleep alone?" His expression never wavered. "If you do, take the room next to mine and keep the connecting door unlocked. I don't want anything to happen—"

"And if I don't want to sleep alone?"

He drew in a deep breath. "Then I want you in my bed."

The sheer carnality of emotion in his words made her cheeks flush and her entire body burn. And she knew this time wouldn't be like the first.

She could explain away their first night together as stress relief. Tonight... Tonight, she wanted what she wanted the way she wanted it.

Diego seemed to understand that. What she didn't know was how he felt about it.

He stared at her, his hand holding firm on hers. Earlier tonight, he'd nearly taken her head off when she'd said she was going with Bella. His anger had been palpable. And she was only beginning to realize that most of it had been directed at himself.

Voices from the stairwell made her glance over her shoulder, and the next thing she knew Diego had opened the door to his room and pulled her through.

He didn't bother with the light switch, as the shades were up and a pale silver hue bathed the room.

Now, instead of staring at each other in the hall, they stared at each other in the confines of his room.

And suddenly it was awkward.

Until he reached for her shirt.

"What are you doing?" she asked.

"What does it look like I'm doing?"

She glanced down and found herself entranced by the sight of his long fingers making short work of the buttons.

"It looks like you're taking off my shirt."

"Then you'd be right. We seem to get along better when we're naked in bed. I thought it might help if you were naked again."

"Only if you are."

"Then give me a hand."

Diego wore a black cotton t-shirt that molded to his chest like it was wet and a pair of grey pants that looked custom made.

Slipping her hands under the t-shirt, she drew it over his head and slipped the button on his pants at the same time he pushed her denim capris down her legs.

In just a few seconds, they had each other naked and Amy Jo felt something inside her settle.

Diego kissed her, placed one hand on her rear and pulled her against his mighty fine erection.

She made him like that and she loved the effect she had on him, loved the way that, when she was with him, she felt in control.

Moaning into his mouth, she tilted her hips into that hard ridge.

He must have misinterpreted her response because he released her immediately.

"Are you okay?"

In answer, she wrapped her hands around his thick cock and squeezed, loving his swiftly indrawn breath. "I'm fine. More than fine now."

She ringed the base with the thumb and forefinger of one hand and, with the other, pumped him from root to tip.

He jerked in her grasp, groaning as his hands moved to her shoulders. She felt the tension in him as he fought not to exert any kind of pressure on her. But she knew what he wanted. And she wanted the same. On her terms.

Turning her head into his neck, she rubbed her nose against his skin and breathed in. God, he smelled good. What would happen if she slid down his body and took him in her mouth? Would she faint from sensory overload or would she be thrown back into that horrific night?

She tensed and Diego froze.

"Amy Jo. Are you okay?"

When she heard him speak, her name, she knew, without a doubt, that he would never hurt her like those other men had.

"I'm fine." She resumed the slow, caress of her hand over his rock-hard erection. "So very fine."

"I won't do anything you don't want me to. You know that, right?"

She licked his neck and he shuddered against her. "Yes. And I'll return the favor."

"Then tell me what you want."

She wanted it rough. Before her attack, she'd liked it a little rough—hair-pulling, nail-scratching, bouncing-off-the-walls rough. She wanted to tie him to the bed and tease him until he exploded and then work him up again. She used to get off on that. Hell, she'd *enjoyed* it. And those bastards had taken that away from her.

Now, she wondered just how trusting Diego really was.

She lifted her head and stared into his dark eyes. She didn't say anything, just stared, until finally he said, "What's wrong?"

"We really don't know each other that well, do we?"

Diego's breath caught in his throat. He wasn't sure how he was supposed to answer that question. Especially since she still held a very vulnerable part of him in her hands.

What he did know was that he wanted to keep her. No, they hadn't known each other long. That didn't matter. He knew all he needed to know about her to know they were meant to be together.

But was she ready to hear it?

Running his hands from her shoulders to her elbows and back again, he kept the pressure sure and steady, just as she did on his cock. "I know enough to know I don't want to be anywhere else."

Her expression softened. Apparently, that had been the correct answer.

"I want to tie you to the bed over there," she said, "and make you scream."

His mouth dropped open a second before he could stop it as lust surged through his body. "You what?"

Her top teeth lodged in her bottom lip and her hand stopped pumping him. "I'm sorry, just forget—"

"Oh, *hell* no. I will not forget what you just said. I nearly came at the image in my head."

She blinked twice, fast. And the corners of her mouth kicked up slightly. "Really? I mean, I'm not really that kinky, no whips and chains and stuff, but a little bondage, blindfolds, some spanking... I liked that stuff before... I just don't want to freak out if—"

Jesus, how much more perfect could this woman be for him? And how perfectly awful if those sons of bitches who'd assaulted her took away something she'd enjoyed.

Moving his hands to her waist, he lifted her until her feet were off the ground and her eyes were level with his. She had to release her hold on his cock but he hoped it wouldn't be for long. "Leather restraints. Bottom of my suitcase. Never leave home without them."

As her eyes widened and her pupils dilated, he decided not to tell her he'd only ever used the restraints on bad guys in the course of his *grigori* duties. He'd never used them during sex.

He'd buy a new set, just for her. If she wanted. If she stayed with him.

She swallowed and drew in a deep breath. "Where's your suitcase?"

Those three words lit a firestorm of desire in his blood, pulsing through him like an electrical charge. But it was the look on her beautiful face that nearly sent him to his knees.

Desire, excitement, lust. Not one hint of fear.

He set her on her feet, but not before sliding her body against his, until the tip of his cock brushed the hair on her mound.

Then he had to set her away or risk disgracing himself.

"By the bed."

She turned and looked then looked back at him and smiled. "Convenient. Get on the bed."

Diego had never thought of himself as a submissive person. Quite the opposite, in fact. But when the tiny—he didn't realize how tiny until just now—naked blonde walked over to his suitcase and started rummaging through it, he pretty much figured he'd submit to anything she wanted.

He watched her pick her way to the bottom, knowing she had to have questions about some of the things she found in there. He didn't own a traditional gun, but there were knives and other, specialized *grigorio* equipment in there.

Sure enough, when she turned, now on the other side of the bed, she said, "We're gonna have a talk about the contents of that case a little later, but right now..." She dangled the leather straps from her fingers. "You're not on the bed."

He waited a second before he knelt on the mattress and held out his arms. Watching her lips part to draw in a breath before she reached for him made his cock throb. Her gaze dropped then moved back up his body before landing on his outstretched wrists.

She reached for him then stopped. "Do you need a safe word or is 'no' enough? I don't want to hurt you."

His laugh was short and full of burning lust. "Honey, you can't hurt me. So no, I don't need a safe word."

Caressing the underside of his bicep with the leather straps, she cocked her head to the side and stared at him. "What do you mean?"

"It means, you can tie me as tightly as you can and it won't hurt because my body can take a hell of a lot of wear and tear."

Expertly tying slip knots in the leather, she slid one loop over his right wrist and pulled it taut. The motion brought him an inch closer.

"On your back, Diego."

Dear Goddess, he loved hearing her say his name in that sexy tone. And when she punctuated her command with a tug on the strap, his breath stopped in his chest.

He did what she asked, so turned on he could barely breath. Hyperventilation became a very real threat when she tied his wrist to the thick post on the right side of the headboard. Then she climbed onto the bed and straddled his chest, and the warm, moist heat of her sex brushed against his skin.

He must have made an involuntary motion with his free hand because she immediately had another loop around it then leaned forward to fasten it to the headboard.

When she had him bound, she sat back to look at her handiwork and now she did sit flush against him, showing him just how wet she was.

"Are you okay?" she asked.

He nodded, swallowing hard when she smiled, her expression filled with pleasure. Deliberately lifting her hand, she traced her index finger in a straight line from his lips to his chest, where she twirled it through his chest hair.

"Good, because I'm done playing nice."

Dragging her wet lower lips down his body, she conveniently shifted just enough to miss his aching cock. He thrust up —and found her mouth there waiting to take him in.

Warm, moist suction sealed over his flesh, causing his body to arch in pleasure. Because she was sitting on his thighs, the only motion he made caused him to force himself deeper into her mouth. She took him without complaint but released him after only a few seconds. His groan rang through the room.

He raised his head and found her smiling at him. "I don't want you to come yet, Diego. I'm not nearly finished."

That's exactly what he was hoping.

"And now it's my turn."

With deliberate motions, she crawled back up his body, stopping to rub her breasts against his chest, tight nipples scraping across his aching ones. She sighed, her hot breath caressing his sensitized skin. Grabbing hold of the headboard, she continued to slide up his body until the lips of her sex were directly over his mouth.

He didn't know if she gave him permission or if she simply lowered herself to him, but he finally had her exactly where he wanted her.

Caught in the leather thongs, he couldn't pull her tight against him so he licked at her with broad strokes, taking care to swipe her clit when he could. But her body had a rhythm of its own, and it took him a few seconds to align himself. And when he did, he caught her delicate flesh between his teeth and nibbled.

She moaned and let him have his way until she cried out his name as her body convulsed.

When she slid down and collapsed against his chest, he tried to put his arms around her and nearly broke the headboard.

Shit, he'd have to watch that. He was strong enough to break the restraints with little effort but he didn't want to frighten her.

Cock throbbing, close to release, he forced his body to relax. He turned and kissed the top of her head, inhaling her scent along with the smell of sex in the air.

It was enough to make him seriously consider popping the restraints anyway and rolling her under him. Instead, he felt her rouse until she propped herself on an elbow to look down at him.

He didn't see an ounce of embarrassment or regret. Just a sweet, sexy heat.

"You okay?" She lifted a lazy hand and trailed one finger in the line of hair from his groin to his belly button. "You look a little tense."

What could he say to that? Hell, yes, he was tense. She'd teased him to the brink of release twice. His jaw ached, he had it clenched so tight.

"I've got a hard-on you could hammer nails with. I'm so fucking turned on from being tied to the bed that if you look at me the right way, I'll come. And if you don't fuck me soon, I may have a heart attack."

Her eyes went so widen he thought he might've finally pushed her over that fine edge away from him. When she didn't move after a few seconds, he knew he had and he mentally prepared himself for her to get up and walk away.

Then she straddled his hips and pulled his cock straight into the air. Slowly, her gaze rose from his groin to his eyes.

The throbbing in his cock intensified until he swore it beat in time with the pulsing vein in her throat.

Lifting her hips, she positioned herself directly over his tip then hung there, her heat close enough to feel but not close enough to touch. Then with one smooth movement, a testament to how wet she was, she took him into her body. Slid down until he felt her clit press against his groin.

Her moan and the way her eyes fluttered closed assured him she was okay. But she didn't move.

He tried to wait for her. Hell, he even counted to twenty. Then he thrust because he couldn't help himself.

Her eyes snapped open and her hands landed on his chest, nails digging into his skin like a cat kneading a blanket.

"I didn't tell you to move." The tightening of her inner muscles around him belied the rebuke in her words.

"Then do it, babe. Take me. Come on, I'm dying for you to ride me."

Her mouth parted on a moan and her sheath contracted around him as she slid up and down, so fast she got him off in seconds as she came again.

When she collapsed against him, still holding him in her body, she untied his wrists then made it clear she wanted him to wrap his arms around her by snuggling against him.

He did, figuring she'd better get used to it, because he wasn't letting her go.

# SEVENTEEN

Bella caught small pieces of sleep all night but couldn't shut her brain off long enough to slip into complete oblivion like she'd hoped.

When she and Steven had gotten back to her room, she'd taken one look into his exhausted eyes, stripped him and pushed him toward the bed. She thought he might've been asleep before his head hit the pillow.

He needed the sleep more than she needed to know what had happened last night.

At least, that's what she'd told herself as she lay there, staring at the wall across from her. Steven curled around her back, an arm around her waist, dead to the world.

She needed sleep so she'd be alert for the morning meeting. Just thinking about it wreaked havoc on her nerves so she couldn't fall asleep.

Cole was depending on her to convince the *lucani* army leadership that they had to prepare for war against the *Mal*. Something it had taken her father years to convince them *not* to do.

A war that could uncover Etruscan society to the rest of the world. And possibly destroy it.

Uni's ass, could this situation get any more screwed up?

Her new best friend faced an excruciating ordeal today. Her brother had been shot. Her lover had been kidnapped and she still didn't know—

"Bella, you're thinking so hard I swear I can hear you."

Steven's breath whispered across her ear, firing a heat deep in her body, one that never cooled around him.

"Can't sleep."

"Yeah, I can tell. Sorry I fell asleep."

She couldn't tell from the tone of his voice if he regretted that or not. Of course, the erection nestled against her backside told a story of its own.

Resisting the urge to rub herself against him, she took a deep breath. "Do you want to talk?"

He didn't answer right away. Instead, his hand slid down a few inches from the sedate position on her stomach. "Do *you* want to talk?"

Her breath caught in her throat at the inflection in his tone and the caress of his fingers bare centimeters above her mound.

For as long as she could remember, he'd never made the first move. It had always been up to her to reach for him, to kiss him. He'd never disappointed her after she'd made the initial contact but in the back of her mind, she'd always known he was holding back.

And intellectually, she'd known why.

He was afraid of letting go completely, afraid of what might happen if he did. She didn't sense that fear in him now as his fingers brushed the hair on her mound.

"Steven?"

She didn't have to ask the rest of the question.

"It's okay, Bella. I'm okay."

Then he pushed her flat on her back and kissed her, stealing her breath.

Her arms wound around his neck and she tried to pull him closer but he'd already decided he wanted that himself. Burrowing one hand under her hip, he palmed her ass, lifting her into him as he slipped between her legs. Her knees fell apart to make room.

He'd always been welcome here, in her arms, in her bed, in her life. Tonight, he kissed her with the steady deliberation of a man who had all the time in the world. He'd already licked his way into her mouth, his tongue insinuating itself around hers, sliding, arousing.

He couldn't seem to get enough of her mouth and she loved to kiss him. He tasted hot and dark, and she couldn't breathe without the scent of him burrowing deeper into her soul. When she moaned and opened her mouth further, he slid his free hand beneath her head and angled her so he could delve even deeper.

When he finally lifted his head, he trailed a string of kisses from her jaw to her neck, biting the sensitive flesh where her neck became shoulder. A shudder ran through her body, making the muscles of her thighs shake and her stomach clench.

His five-o'clock shadow scraped along her flesh as he kissed his way across her upper chest, carefully missing her breasts, to her other shoulder, where he bit her again, hard enough to leave a mark. If he did that enough, he'd make her come. She was more than halfway there already.

Breathing hard, she lifted her hands to tangle them in his hair, sifting the longer-than-normal strands through her fingers as his mouth continued its torment to her breasts.

But just as she was getting ready to grab his shoulders, he sucked her left nipple into his mouth and pulled it taut, almost to the point of pain.

She gasped and her hands fell off to the side to twist in the sheets.

"Steven, what—"

He stuck his finger in her mouth and she sucked on it instinctively. His breathing, already tortured, deepened even more and the hand on her ass moved to splay across her stomach before sliding straight into the wet channel between her legs.

He found her clit without a moment's hesitation and she was so turned on it only took one flick of one finger to give her a short, sharp orgasm that left her body begging for more.

But he seemed in no hurry to give her more. Instead, he moved to caress her inner thighs as he trailed kisses down her stomach. He blew across the skin above her belly button, causing her legs to draw together.

"Keep 'em open for me, sweetheart."

He spoke the words directly above her mound, ruffling the fine hair and nearly setting her off again.

"Steven, please..."

She didn't know what else to say. They'd never made love like this. Before, he'd always seemed to hold back, let her take the lead, set the pace. They'd both been virgins the first time and they'd learned everything together.

She'd often wondered if he'd had other lovers in the years they'd been apart. She'd never wanted anyone but Steven, but he was a man. He'd probably had other women in his bed.

And Blessed Goddess, why was she thinking about this now?

"There's never been anyone else for me, Bella. Don't you know that?"

Her eyes flew open and she found him staring down at her. He'd moved, laying his body over hers, his erection, hot and hard, nestled at the aching entrance to her body. When had he gotten rid of his boxers?

"How did you know…?"

His mouth twisted in a smile as he eased an inch into her body. "Because I know you, even better than I know myself." He withdrew the tiniest bit then flexed forward again, seating more of himself this time.

His deliberate pace made her groan and lift her hips trying to make him go faster. He pulled away with a smile.

"Because I love you so much my chest hurts when I think about you."

He flexed again, this time going deeper, teasing delicate inner tissues until she wanted to cry in frustration. Her eyes began to close but he stopped his forward motion.

"No. Look at me, Bella."

Her eye flashed open and she stared straight at him. Even though it was dark, the only light coming from the nightlight in the bathroom, she swore she saw deep into his soul. He was letting her in, closer than she'd ever been.

And all she could think about was making him go farther, deeper.

"Put your hands on me." His voice was little more than a husky rasp as he forced himself deeper, centimeter by centimeter. "I need you to touch me. I don't think I'll ever get enough of you."

How long had she dreamed of him saying just that? She couldn't get enough of him.

Raising her hands to his shoulders, she tilted her pelvis and he slid a few more centimeters. His skin was warm, almost overheated, and a light sheen of sweat made her hands glide over his skin.

Lowering his forehead to hers, he thrust and seated himself fully, wrapping his arms around her. "God, Bella. Don't move. Just let me stay here."

Working her arms between them, she linked them around

his waist and rubbed her breasts against his chest. "I'll never let you go."

She felt his release start in the shudder of his shoulders and his sharply indrawn breath. Sealing his mouth over hers, he began to move, setting a deliberate rhythm. He was fighting off the inevitable, but it was a battle neither of them would lose.

She met him thrust for thrust, clenching her inner muscles on his inward glide, wringing a groan from him.

Her love for him rose up in a suffocating wave of emotion and she clutched him tighter, their skin stuck together with sweat, breathing through their noses so they didn't have to break the kiss.

And then her body convulsed in a sharp orgasm, blindsiding her, dragging him with her.

He ripped his mouth from hers and threw his head back, pressing his hips forward.

When his cock finally stopped pulsing, he fell to her side, his uneven breathing brushing her neck, sending goosebumps along her skin.

Several minutes later, as his breathing regulated, she wondered if he'd fallen asleep again. But he rolled to his back and pulled her with him until her head rested on his chest. His hands rubbed up and down her back.

His heart pounding under her ear, she knew she'd be able to sleep now, even though it was almost time to get up.

She loved this man. And even though her brother was counting on her to handle the meeting this morning, she'd blow it off in a heartbeat if Steven asked her to run away with him. She'd go anywhere he wanted, do anything he wanted. He had to know that.

"What happened last night, Steven?"

His hands stopped and he drew in deep breath. He was silent for so long she thought he wasn't going to answer.

"I ran out of the hotel," he started, "after I heard the gunshot. One second I saw Cole lying on the ground, and the next I woke up in a room. I had no idea where I was. And then ..."

She felt him shake his head.

"And then a *folletta* dropped out of the trap door in the ceiling."

It took her a few seconds to process what he'd said. Then she rolled to the side to switch on the bedside lamp and propped herself on one elbow. He wore the closed expression he got when he knew she wasn't going to like what he said. She'd always assumed it was stubbornness. Now she knew it for what it was. Uncertainty.

"Are you sure you weren't drugged?"

He nodded.

"And you really met a *folletta*?"

She watched his mouth turn up at the corners at the awe in her voice. Her father had told the most amazing bedtime stories about the legendary creatures.

"Yeah. And..." He sighed, his expression turning dark. "And a woman who said she was the goddess Turan."

Her mouth literally dropped open. "You met someone who said she was Turan? Goddess Turan of the *Involuti*, who disappeared two *millennia* ago?"

He nodded. "And the strange part is, I believe her."

―――――

HALF AN HOUR LATER, they'd each given a rundown of the night's events.

Bella, so comfortable in her nudity, sat naked on the bed. She was a constant temptation so Steven moved to the chair in front of the window. Early morning light seeped under the curtains, signaling the encroaching return to reality.

"Are you going to join the *boschetta*?"

Bella's head cocked to the side, her chin propped on her bent knee. "Do you think I should? I wasn't raised *streghe*. I barely remember the most basic spells because I don't use them and I'd have to learn the rituals from scratch. I know they said they wanted new blood but ..."

"But what?"

She sighed. "But what if I screw it up?"

"You're stronger than that, Bella. You won't screw up."

He knew that down to his bones. She'd make a phenomenal priestess, though he wasn't quite sure what the position entailed. He didn't think Bella knew all the details either.

Still, he knew Bella. She'd be great at whatever she put her mind to.

Shaking her head, she let her gaze drop for a second. "So, the...goddess said you're not really *Mal*?"

It was the second time she'd asked this questions but he still didn't know exactly what to say. He'd ducked it the first time around but he knew she wasn't going to let him get away with it a second time.

He shook his head. "Not exactly, no. Her exact words were I was 'born straddling the line.' I don't have a clue what line she means."

"But she was talking about choices, that you would have to make a choice. Does that mean you can choose *not* to be *Mal*?"

Hope sucked.

Steven knew that for a fact. Because sooner or later, you were going to lose it and be crushed. "I don't know. I don't think so." That would be too damn easy and nothing was easy when dealing with deities.

Bella bit her top lip. "Does she know who shot Cole?"

"She wouldn't say."

She threw her hands in the air in exasperation. "So what good is she?"

Steven laughed, short and sharp. "I wouldn't ask her that if you ever meet her."

Bella frowned harder, the little lines between her eyes now furrows. "Yeah, I'm not that stupid. So now what?"

"Honestly, I don't have a clue." And didn't that just suck? "I think we just have to continue forward, see what happens."

He took a deep breath and stopped at the window, pulling back the curtains to let in the still-weak morning sun.

Seconds later, Bella pressed her naked body against his back. Her strong arms encircled his waist and squeezed tight.

"We'll figure it out." She spoke the words against his skin, the heat of her breath and her lips branding his skin. "I need you, Steven. Don't leave me again. Not now."

Turning in her embrace, he stared down at her, lacing his fingers through her hair. "I like it like this. Bares your neck."

She smiled, taken off guard by his words. "Cole says it makes me look like a teenager."

"You were the hottest teenager I'd ever seen. But if I'd touched you before you turned eighteen, my dad would've strung me up by my toenails. I'm still not sure he approved of us."

"It wouldn't have mattered. As much as I loved your dad, I would have done anything to have you. There's never been anyone else for me. There never will."

His heart contracted until he swore the ache would take up permanent residence there. He'd lived like a monk without her. He hadn't wanted anyone else. Had only ever wanted this woman.

Maybe...

Her smiled turned bittersweet. "Let's just get through today, Steven."

He sighed. It was going to be a long day.

---

"SO, how's this going to work again?"

Amy Jo forced herself to draw in a deep breath through her nose and release it through her mouth. Diego stood to her left, Marco on her right in their— Well, in Diego's bedroom. She had to admit their presence was making this a little easier. At least, she wasn't freaking out. Yet.

And considering it was only eight in the morning, the fact that she was coherent was somewhat of a miracle. Lately, she'd become a night owl and last night she hadn't gotten much sleep.

The woman in front of her smiled. "It's not much different than taking a nap. Really, it'll be painless."

Andrea Guiliani was a short, curvy woman with straight dark hair hanging to her waist, rounded features and wide sherry-brown eyes. She looked like a hippie in her gypsy skirt and peasant blouse, and she smiled a lot, as if the motion was second nature. But Amy Jo saw sorrow in her eyes. It comforted her, made her feel she wasn't the only one who felt lost.

"And I won't remember anything?"

That terrified her. She remembered enough. She didn't need to know what else, if anything, had happened that night.

Andrea—she'd pronounced it Ahn-dray-ah, with a hint of an Italian accent—shook her head. "Not if you don't want to."

"And you promise not to ask too many..." she struggled for a word to say what she meant without having to spell it out, "invasive questions?"

Diego stiffened behind her but stayed silent. As much as she wanted him here, she didn't want him to know anymore than he already did about that night.

Andrea nodded, her expression sobering. "I promise to keep the questions specifically targeted."

Okay, that was probably as good as it was gonna get. Amy Jo nodded and took a deep breath. "Alright, let's get it over with."

She lay on the bed and prayed Andrea could dig something useful out of her memories.

---

"WHOA, brat. If I didn't know you better, I'd say you were trying a little *too* hard."

Stepping through the bedroom door, Bella covered a wince at the weakness of Cole's voice. But she made a good show of it, looking down at her outfit and frowning.

"What are you talking about, you idiot? I look amazing."

Following her into the room, Steven shut the door behind him, so it was just the three of them and the ever-present Dorian.

Cole smiled, so Cole-like that she breathed a little easier as she stopped at his bedside to take his hand. If it made him smile like that, she'd play this to the hilt.

"I've never seen you in a suit, especially not one that's so..."

"Hot?" Steven supplied.

Cole shot him a look. "Don't even go there go. She's still my sister." Then he returned his sharp gaze to her. "You ready?"

She nodded, though she felt anything but ready. "Yes."

Cole shook his head. "You know, you'd be a little more convincing if you didn't look like you're going to puke."

"Screw you, Cole. I'll be fine." If she could just make five older, stronger and wiser men believe her.

*Yeah, good luck with that, Princess.*

"Nice mouth. Hey." Cole tugged on her hand. "I know you can do this, Bella, or I would've pushed off the meeting. And if you can't, well, then they weren't going to listen to me, either."

That was complete bullshit and everyone in the room knew it. Cole was the royal *legio*. Even as children, he'd been the one to take charge of everything, from who got to go first in hide and seek to how many minutes she should brush her teeth at night. As a teenager growing up in a house of men, without her mother, it'd driven her nuts. Now she realized he was just a natural born leader.

"Cole—"

"Bella," he cut her off, staring into her eyes, his still shadowed with so much pain. "You can do this. You're Luporeale, just like me. You know what needs to be done. You know what's at stake. The *lucani* have to get behind us on this or everyone will suffer.

"Watch out for Angelone, he'll try to do an end run. He's been a pain in my ass since I took the sceptre. Quinn will back you one hundred percent. Patrick and Levanti will need to be convinced. Trust Weichelt to steer you if you need help. Barrasso is solid to the core but the legion comes first with him."

She knew all of this. At least, she tried to tell herself she did. She hadn't completely stuck her head in the ground the past few years. She listened when Cole talked about what he did. She'd just never considered having to deal with this stuff. The army had always been Cole's job. She couldn't be bothered.

*Stupid girl.*

Now she had to go into that room and convince five formidable, hardened veterans who had more than thirty years on her, to listen to a twenty-five-year-old female whose only claims to fame were a degree in veterinary medicine and the shared genes of two men they highly regarded.

"Bella, breathe."

She drew air into her starved lungs and stared at Cole. His smile, though weak, had returned.

"Sweetheart, *you* are our stealth weapon. They all love you. They still talk about the day you were born like it was a national holiday. The first girl born to a royal family in nearly a century. They treasure you. If you ask me, they're just going soft in their old age because I know what a brat you really are. But they *will* listen to you, even if they think they're only placating you."

His teasing eased her fears a little. But, he was right, to a degree.

Those grizzled veterans *had* always had a soft spot for her. And if they gave out degrees for wrapping men around fingers, she'd have a doctorate.

She'd use it to her advantage. She didn't have to do exactly what Cole would do. She could do it her way.

"Okay." She nodded. "I'm ready."

## EIGHTEEN

Steven watched Bella walk into the meeting room like she owned it.

In a previous life, Cole must have been a motivational speaker. Or emperor, which probably wasn't far off the mark.

Just as Cole had predicted, the council fell all over themselves to welcome Bella.

They weren't too pleased to see him, though.

David Angelone, especially.

"Arabella, we all understand the need for bodyguards, but I can't abide a *Mal* presence at our council table."

Steven forced himself to meet Angelone's cold gaze. He didn't want to leave Bella alone, not even with these men. Not after last night.

However, if she asked him to wait outside, he'd do it. He watched for some subtle hint on her part that she wanted him to leave.

Bella never let her gaze flicker his way. She spoke directly to Angelone. "Steven has never posed a threat to Cole or me. He's a loyal friend and advisor and Cole and I trust him completely. He stays."

Well, hell. The little wolf had sharpened her claws.

Swallowing his smile, Steven checked the other men's reactions to Bella's jab.

*Praefect* James Patrick didn't bother to hide his smile. Neither did Quinn. Respect crossed the expressions of *tribuni* Daniel Levanti and Garth Weichelt. Only *primus pilus* Michael Barrasso seemed unaffected by her stand. Steven would keep an eye on him. Barrasso was the oldest of the council members, one of the most respected men in the legion. He'd served two tours in Vietnam as a Marine before taking a position with the *lucani*. Cole's father had wanted to promote him to *Praefect* but he'd refused the post. He wanted to serve with the men, not above them.

After what seemed like forever, Barrasso turned his gaze to Steven, who braced himself for a fight.

Damn, he didn't want to fight anymore. He'd been fighting his love for Bella, his love for Cole, his very nature, for so long and he was fucking tired.

And now, when not only his life but his entire society hung in the balance, people still wanted to fight with him.

Shock ran through Steven when Barrasso waved to the seat next to Bella. "Well, sit down, son. Apparently we've got a lot of ground to cover."

Steven didn't bother to look at the other men. He nodded to Barrasso and sat.

Bella took her seat last. "As you all know, Cole was shot last night and Steven was abducted. We don't know who shot my brother or why. The *praetorian* guard are working on that as we speak. I have no doubt Dorian will find whoever's responsible. We do know that Steven's kidnapping was unrelated and we know who took him."

"And that would be..." Angelone said, sarcasm thick in his tone.

"The Goddess Turan."

Silence fell for all of three seconds. Then the men began to talk over one another.

Bella let them go for at least a minute until Barrasso said, "Princess, how can you be sure this isn't a hoax. Isn't it possible Steven was drugged or the victim of a spell?"

"No." She said it with such conviction, Steven knew she believed completely. "You can question Dorian. She was there when we found him. She can attest to the fact that he was under no spell nor was he drugged. She can also tell you about the unusual nature of the *arus* permeating the house. It certainly wasn't *Mal*, or *lucani* or *streghe*. It was...different. Pure."

"This is bullshit," Angelone sneered, pushing away from the table as if he were going to walk away. Which he didn't do. The bastard didn't dare. "Princess, there's absolutely no—"

Bella's fist slammed on the table as she stood, startling everyone into silence. The action was at odds with the placid expression on her face, one he'd seen Cole adopt many times. Steven had called it Cole's King Face. He'd ragged Cole about it before... Hell, that seemed a lifetime ago.

"I didn't tell you this information so you could debate it, gentlemen," she said. "I'm only informing you of what happened. And there's more. So you need to be quiet and listen, because this you *will* want to hear."

Angelone looked stunned and furious, but the man was smart enough not to contradict Bella in front of the other men, who also looked stunned. Except for Barrasso. Now he had a smile.

"I believe Steven's meet-and-greet with Turan has some-thing to do with the reason Cole called for *congress* in the first place." Straightening her back, Bella stared at each man in turn, pausing to smile briefly at Quinn. "The Priestesses of Menrva are returned to the Etruscan people. And the *lucani* legion is about to become the first line of defense."

---

"NO. Absolutely not. I won't allow it."

"Gods damn you, Diego. I happen to agree with you, but it's not your decision to make."

"There's no way in hell I'm going to allow her to do it. I don't care if the fate of the world hangs in the balance. She's been through enough."

Amy Jo heard the men arguing but couldn't quite wrap her brain around what they were saying. Her head felt heavy, like she was coming out of a deep sleep.

"Gentlemen, keep your voices down. She's waking."

Andrea's calm tone soothed, helping her rise through the fog.

Someone took her hand. Diego. Funny how she could tell just by his touch. Or maybe not so funny. She wrapped her fingers around his as she opened her eyes.

And looked straight into his fierce scowl.

She shook her head, trying to loosen the last of the fog. "What's wrong?"

Diego's hand squeezed around hers. "Nothing. You're fine."

She looked at Andrea, who also smiled. "There were no adverse side affects."

Amy Jo raised an eyebrow at the other woman. "But...?"

"But nothing." Diego shot Andrea a look meant to cut out her tongue.

"Diego." Amy Jo sat up, even as Marco appeared on her other side to put his hand on her shoulder to keep her down. "Guys, please. Stop."

The brothers released her and stood so fast it would have been funny if it weren't so frustrating.

"Andrea, what's going on?" She turned to the other woman. "Were you able to get anything helpful out of me?"

The other woman shook her head. "Unfortunately, no. Your thoughts are too jumbled, your memories too deeply buried to be of much use."

Amy Jo's spirits plummeted straight to the ground. "Well, shit. That's not good, is it?" Then she remembered that the guys had been arguing. She looked at Diego.

"What aren't you telling me?"

Diego shook his head, his mouth a sharp line.

Which just pissed her off. "I am not a child, Diego, so *back* off. Andrea, what's going on?"

The other woman sat on the chair next to the bed. "I believe I may be able to discover more if you allow me to help you bring the memories to the forefront."

Buzzing filled her ears, and the room darkened at the edge of her peripheral vision.

"Amy Jo." Diego's arms wrapped around her, encasing her in warmth, warmth she desperately needed because the air had turned frigid. Or maybe that was her.

"You don't have to do this." He whispered the words into her ear, his warm breath not nearly warm enough. "We'll figure out what's going on without putting you through hell. I won't allow it."

She laughed at that. "It's not really up to you, though, is it?"

"Amy Jo, listen—"

"No. You listen." She took a deep breath and made a decision that could very well make him turn away from her forever. "I'll do this. This is my world now, too. I want to get the bastards who made me—" she had to bite back the words. She was going to call herself a monster but then she'd be calling Diego and

Marco the same. And she knew better. "I want to get the bastards who hurt Cole. And I want to make them pay for hurting me."

She turned to Andrea, watching her with dark, steady eyes. "Let's do this. Now, before I lose my nerve." She squeezed Diego's hand then disengaged. "But you and Marco have to leave."

---

"PRINCESS, forgive me for being a little skeptical," Angelone sneered, "but you want us to believe the Goddess Turan, one of the blessed *Involuti* who've been MIA for more than two thousand years, approached your *Mal* boyfriend to tell him he's needed in an upcoming war and that the legendary Priestesses of Menrva have returned to lead our people's spiritual rebirth so we can fight a battle against some unknown foe."

Bella nodded. "Basically, yes."

Angelone began to laugh, shaking his head and turning with an expression of "What the fuck" to the other men. "Are you seriously going to believe this shit? How do we know for sure this is what Cole wants? Is he even coherent enough to speak? He must be pretty damn far gone—"

"Cole will return to the council table later today," Dorian spoke up for the first time. "He has full faith in Arabella or she wouldn't be here. You all know that."

*Thank you, Dorian.*

Bella acknowledged the *praetorian* with a slight nod and had to restrain a smile when the other woman winked at her. Dorian's support bolstered her waning trust in herself to convince these men that what had happened was true.

Angelone snorted in disgust and Bella forced herself to meet this gaze. He was the only man at this table, excluding Quinn, who hadn't served in his position under her father. He'd inherited the position from his own father, who'd retired shortly after her dad had been killed.

As one of Cole's highest advisors, Angelone held a position of power that he wouldn't continue to hold if Cole didn't think him worthy.

But he treated her like a bubblehead who knew her way around the mall but didn't know jack shit about a council table.

Which was where Angelone was wrong. Not about the mall. She knew every centimeter of the Court at King of Prussia. But she'd also spent years sitting alongside Cole as her dad and her brother Cal had met with the council.

Time to show these men she was her father's daughter.

"Cole wanted you all briefed as soon as possible about what was going on," she said. "This afternoon, you will meet members of the *boschetta*. Cole trusts your opinions and—"

Someone knocked on the door a second before it opened and Luca popped his head through. "Marco's here."

She nodded as the room fell silent and Marco walked through the door, which Luca shut tightly behind him.

The *lucani* sized him up as he walked around the table to get to her, his gaze locked with hers.

Her blood froze at the carefully blank expression on his face.

*Shit.* Something had happened to Amy Jo.

"What the hell's going on now?" Angelone asked, anger and exasperation in his voice. But no fear. "Who's this?"

"Marco, what's wrong?"

He shook his head. "I need to speak with you in private."

"Oh, for fuck's sake." Angelone threw his hands in the air. "Who the hell is this guy and why does he need to see you in private?"

She tore her gaze from Marco's to stare down Angelone. "This is Diego Falco's brother, Marco."

"Does this have something to do with Cole's shooting?" Barrasso asked.

Marco waited for Bella to nod then turned to address Cole's advisors. "We've just received information that the *Mal* were involved with Cole's shooting. Three months ago, a group of men was overheard discussing this *congress* and exactly where it was being held. They talked about harming Cole and Bella and throwing the *lucani* into turmoil. That they had a mole in the legion who'd told them everything."

The men erupted in a furious chorus. Names flew around the table as long-held grudges, suspicions and outright anger made the air in the room heavy and hard to breathe.

Bella looked into Marco's eyes. She saw pain and fear. For Amy Jo. Her heart ached with the need to go to her new friend.

She also saw anger.

"Marco. Did she..."

How he heard her over all the yelling, she didn't know. Maybe he read her lips. He turned to her and looked her straight in the eyes. "Levanti."

Though she heard him plain as day, his mouth never moved. He somehow whispered it into her mind. She gaped at him for all of two seconds before the enormity of the situation hit her.

*Shit.* Oh shit. They'd been betrayed by one of their own.

Daniel Levanti.

The knowledge cut into her chest like open-heart surgery without anesthesia. Cole would be devastated.

Drawing in a deep breath, she tried to calm her now-racing heart. What should she do? Confront him? Denounce him in front of the rest of Cole's advisors? Was he working with anyone else? What the hell should she do?

Steven clasped her shoulder, the warmth of his hand

seeping into her through the casual touch before drawing away. Then she glanced around the table, making sure not to single out any one person.

When she got to Barrasso, she found him staring at her, eyebrows raised.

With a nod, she again smashed her hand on the wood table, this time so hard, she cracked the wood.

Silence descended as everyone turned to her.

Then she looked straight at Levanti. His expression showed absolutely no hint of fear, no surprise, just curiosity. The snake.

"You will burn for this," she said. "I'll make sure of it."

Levanti's eyebrows rose as his mouth quirked up in a bemused smile. But his eyes... Now she saw a flare of fear spark in the depths of his eyes.

*That's right, you bastard. You better fucking squirm.*

It'd been three centuries since a *lucani* had been charged with the attempted assassination of a king. The stories of what the *praetorian* guard had done to the man should have been enough to discourage anyone else. Her brothers had told her the tale by the light of a campfire, a horror story meant to deter anyone else from betraying the legion.

That had been long before her great-grandfather had taken control of the American *lucani*, those Etruscans who had emigrated to America in the early 1800s, drawn by the promise of fertile soil and dense forests and an escape from the oppressive Catholic Church.

America had turned out to have a little too much space for the *lucani*. Too much freedom, too little order. For a hundred years, they'd run feral until a small group banded together after they'd come close to being exposed. They'd approached her great-grandfather, who still bore the title King of the *lucani*. They'd begged him to give up his comfortable life in Sicily and wrangle the American *lucani* into some semblance of order. His reputation for fairness made him the most likely candidate for the job.

He'd done better than the *lucani* could have hoped.

And his blood ran in her veins.

Without moving her gaze from Levanti's, she said, "You plotted with the *Mal* to kill Cole."

Levanti shook his head, his expression a perfect mask of derision. "You don't know what you're talking about, Princess Arabella." He made her name sound like a verbal pat on the head. "I'd never hurt Cole and every man at this table knows it. You're barking up the wrong tree. If anyone's working for the *Mal*, we know where we should be looking."

Beside her, she heard Steven draw in a hard breath. Reaching for him, she laid her hand on his shoulder to keep him in his chair, even as she forced her own fury back.

"Trying to shift focus is a well-worn tactical defense for someone who's got something to hide," she said. "How long have you been working for the *Mal*?"

"Now, wait just a minute," Angelone blustered. "You can't mean to tell me—"

He cut off as Barrasso stood, five feet and eleven inches of pure solid muscle honed to warrior perfection. The man might be in his 6os, but he could still fight like a twenty year old. And he commanded the respect of everyone in the room, much more so than Bella ever would.

"You have proof to back up your claims?" he asked.

She nodded. "The testimony of an eyewitness."

Barrasso turned to Levanti. "May the Blessed Goddess protect you—"

Levanti shifted so fast, she almost missed it between one blink and the next.

Barrasso and Weichelt weren't far behind but Levanti had

the element of surprise on his side as he leaped across the table straight for Bella.

She braced for impact—and gasped in horror as Steven pushed her behind him and met Levanti's attack head on.

Levanti's paws hit Steven dead in the center of his chest and the wolf's weight and the force of his attack took Steven to the ground.

Stunned, Bella scrambled up to help Steven but found herself caught in Dorian's arms.

"No, Bella. You can't risk getting hurt. Let them help Steven."

Fear made her struggle against Dorian, even as she watched Barrasso and Weichelt latch onto Levanti's haunches with their powerful jaws and attempt to get Levanti away from Steven.

Steven had managed to keep the *lucani* traitor from biting him by getting his hands around the animal's neck but the beast's mouth was getting closer and closer to Steven's neck. Steven struggled to throw the wolf away from him but the wolf was heavy and had his paws planted on Steven's chest.

Levanti had desperation on his side. He'd basically admitted his guilt by going after her. He had to know the only outcome of this situation was his death. But she planned to make sure he lived long enough for Andrea to dig into his mind and expose his secrets.

And for harming Steven... She'd make damn sure he suffered.

Grinding her teeth, she watched Steven struggle as Barrasso released Levanti's leg and lunged for his midsection while Angelone, also shifted into his wolf, made a play for Levanti's throat. Even outnumbered, Levanti made no effort to protect himself. Instead, he growled, low and deep, a millisecond before he managed to loosen Steven's hold and went at his neck.

Screaming, Bella struggled against Dorian's hold, helpless

and horrified as Levanti scrambled up Steven's body, managing to drag Barrasso and Weichelt the precious few inches he needed to reach the most vulnerable part of Steven's body. His jaws opened and—

Levanti flew across the room on a gust of wind so powerful, it scattered everything in its path, furniture and bodies. Weichelt, Barrasso and Angelone hit the wall as hard as Levanti.

Quinn and Patrick had flanked Bella, Marco and Dorian as the wolves fought, which was the only reason they'd remained standing.

The room fell silent except for the sound of labored breathing.

Bella looked at Steven, still on the floor. She watched sweat drip down his face and made a motion toward him. But Dorian refused to release her.

"No, Arabella. Not now."

Thunder cracked. Inside the room. Wind whipped through the space as if they were outside in a storm, all of it circling Steven. Static electricity charged the air.

Bella knew lightning wouldn't be far behind.

And the wild look in Steven's eyes didn't bode well.

"Let me go, Dorian, or none of us are safe."

It took a few seconds but finally the *praetorian* released her and Bella dropped to her knees by Steven's side. He didn't see her though he was looking right at her. His entire focus was inward.

His hands shook and his eyes were glazed. He looked ready to collapse as the wind continued to blow and the thunder crackled.

"Steven." She reached for him—

And found herself on the other side of the room. Her back and head hit the wall with an audible crack and she swore she smelled burning hair. Looking down at her arms, she saw the hair on her arms looked singed.

Low, angry growls from the other side of the room told her Barrasso and Weichelt had recovered. They would take care of Levanti.

But all of them were in more immediate danger from Steven.

Staying on her butt on the ground, she slid back across the floor, but didn't make the mistake of touching Steven this time.

"Steven, come on, love. Pull it back. I know you can do it. *You* know you can do it."

"Bella." Her name was a groan, ripped out through his clenched teeth. "Get out. Everybody."

"No. You have to—"

A tiny bolt of lightning cracked above Steven, the scent of ozone wafting through the room.

She knew where the next one was headed. "Steven! *No!*"

She watched as he turned his hand palm up just as another bolt began to crackle. It sparked and sizzled and arced directly into Steven's outstretched hand. Awestruck, Bella watched him grab the bolt as if it were a solid object.

Then, between one second and the next, the lightning absorbed into his body, like water into a sponge. Gone.

He sat so still, Bella would have thought he was dead if not for his shaking hand and the rapid rise and fall of his chest.

"Steven?"

From the other side of the room, Bella heard renewed growling and the sound of claws scrabbling against the floor. She didn't bother to see what was going on. Barrasso and Weichelt could handle Levanti.

"Steven?" She reached for him.

"No, don't touch me."

His voice sounded strange. Lower, with a hint of something dark. Something *not* the Steven she knew.

Cold fear curdled her stomach as she slid closer until she was sitting next to him. His eyes were shut tight, his mouth clenched. They barely moved when he said, "Just...give me a minute, Bella."

In her peripheral vision, she saw Quinn and James Patrick move toward Levanti, snarling but pinned in a corner by Weichelt and Barrasso.

Steven sat there, breathing, staring straight ahead. Finally, after a minute or so, he shook his head, blinked and turned to face her. She waited for him to make a move and when he reached for her, she threw her arms around his neck and held on.

# NINETEEN

"How is she?" Bella asked.

"She won't open the fucking door."

Diego's voice held a violence that was directed inward and Bella sighed, knowing exactly how he felt.

Steven hadn't said anything other than "I'm fine, Bella" for the past half hour.

He wasn't. He smelled worried, confused. And nauseous, if the constant hand he rubbed across his stomach was any indication.

She didn't think he was reacting to what they'd done to Levanti. His screams still rang in her ears but it was the images in her head as Barrasso had forced him to change against his will that kept her own stomach in turmoil.

She'd walked out of the meeting room intending to force Steven to go with her to talk to Cole but Diego had grabbed her the second she'd stepped out the door and dragged her upstairs.

"She locked the door and I don't want to break it down but I will," Diego said.

From inside the room, Amy Jo yelled, "No, you w-will not, Diego. I'm f-fine. I just need a l-little time."

Even through the door, Bella could hear the pain in her voice. Maybe the price to get Levanti had been too high. "Amy Jo, can I come in? Just for a few minutes?"

Silence. For at least half a minute. Then finally the lock on the door flipped.

Diego sucked in a sharp breath as the door cracked open a bare inch.

Bella peered in but couldn't see Amy Jo. She could only hear the other woman's voice. "Just you, B-Bella."

Diego looked ready to argue but Steven said, "Diego, come on, man. I could use a drink. I've got a few bottles in my room."

The last thing Bella heard before she slid through the door was Diego's heavy sigh.

Then she saw Amy Jo, curled in a shivering ball on the bed. Her mouth quivered, her skin was pasty white and her pupils were dilated.

Bella ran for the bed and put her arms around her. "Oh Gods, Amy Jo. Let me get Dr. Kent. Where's Andrea?"

"Sh-she went to get s-something from her room."

"You're freezing." Bella grabbed the blanket at the bottom of the bed and wrapped it around her, then went to the closet for more. "Let me send Diego for Dr. Kent, please. He'll know what to do."

"No. I don't want to s-see anyone. D-did you get the guy? At least, tell me this wasn't for nothing."

"Yeah, we got him. Don't worry about that now. Please, let me get Diego. He's going crazy—"

"I d-don't want him to s-see me like this."

Diego had told her what Amy Jo had done to get them the information they'd needed. It made Bella sick to her stomach to think about what Amy Jo had endured.

"He doesn't care what you look like. He just wants to be with you."

Amy Jo's eyes, already red and puffy, welled with tears. "If he k-knew what happened, he wouldn't be able to look at me."

Bella sat on the bed, her arms going about the other woman's shoulders. "No, Amy Jo. If you let him in, you'll see he just wants to comfort you. None of what happened to you is your fault. You have to know that."

"But how can he want me after... after..."

The door opened and Andrea walked in with a glass of something in her hand. "Alright, Amy Jo. I want you to drink this. All of it. Then I'm going to insist you get some sleep."

Amy Jo's eyes held hope and despair. "I don't think I'll be able to sleep."

Andrea nodded. "You will after you drink that."

"I'm afraid to sleep."

Andrea's smile was a little strained. "There will be no dreams, believe me."

Amy Jo drew in a breath. "Okay, good. That's good."

Stomach roiling, Bella took her hand. "Let me get Diego. You'll sleep better if he's here."

Amy Jo took a deep breath, dropped her gaze to the glass then nodded. "Alright. You're right. I'm b-being silly."

"No, you're not," Bella said. "You're entitled to feel however you want, but he cares about you. Let him take care of you. I think we all could use a little TLC right now."

---

DIEGO LEANED against the wall in Steven's room, a gnawing fear eating at him from the inside out.

To his right, Marco watched Steven with wary eyes as Steven pulled a liter of Mezzaluna vodka out of the mini-fridge.

Marco was freaked, possibly in shock. From what Diego had heard from Dorian, Marco had good reason after what'd he'd seen in that room—not only Levanti's punishment but Steven's display of power.

Diego had never seen the guy throw so much as a sleep spell at anyone. According to Cole, Steven's power rivaled the strongest of the *grigori*. Possibly the gods. He could've wiped out the whole room in a few seconds.

And Marco's death would have been Diego's fault. Because he'd sent Marco.

Diego should have gone himself but he hadn't wanted to leave Amy Jo. Even though she refused to allow him in the room while Andrea screwed with her mind.

He hadn't been able to hear a sound from the room and realized Andrea must have erected a sound barrier spell. His cat wanted him to shift so he could rake at the door with his claws.

Then one of Cole's *lucani* had told him he should get downstairs, that Marco needed him...

If anything had happened to either of them—

A glass appeared in front of his face, the liquid waving back and forth like a rough sea.

Steven wasn't too steady either.

Diego took a good look at the guy. Hell, Steven wasn't even trying to hide the fact he was holding himself together by a string.

Diego took the glass and swallowed a quarter of it.

The warmth of the alcohol spread through his blood, calming some of the nerves. He watched to make sure Marco drank then focused again on Steven.

"You okay?"

Diego admired the guy for not lying when he said, "Not sure yet. Ask me after we kick this bottle. Maybe a couple more."

"Marco."

Marco grunted.

"How are you?"

Marco considered the question for a few seconds before he nodded toward Steven. "Did you know he can create lightning and then catch it in his hands?"

Diego's eyebrows rose at Marco's expressionless tone and he again wondered if his brother was in shock. "Yeah, I knew. But I've never seen him do it."

Marco shook his head, took another drink then looked Diego right in the eye. And smiled. No hint of snark or smart-ass to be seen.

*Holy shit.* Diego felt his lips curve into an answering smile.

"Coolest fucking thing I ever saw," Marco said, shaking his head.

Steven snorted and nearly choked on his drink. "Glad you enjoyed the show."

Now, Steven's voice...that held a whole roomful of smart-ass but Diego also heard worry.

Diego hadn't been too keen on Steven, though he'd only met him once or twice before the airport incident. Everything he'd heard about the guy had been bad. Hell, the fact that he'd been born *Mal* damned him in Etruscan society.

But Steven had proven himself loyal to Cole and Bella, loyal to a fault, maybe. He'd sworn not to use his powers but, with this threat to Cole and Bella looming over their heads, he'd be forced to make more of the same choices he'd had to make today. Use his power to save his loved ones and risk becoming the evil most people already believed him to be. Or stand by and possibly watch his mate and best friend be killed.

"Can I do anything to help?" Diego asked.

Steven's gaze shot to his. His shock at Diego's sincere question would have been laughable at any other time. As it was, Steven didn't answer right away, as if waiting for the hidden backslap to come.

But Diego wasn't kidding. As much as Diego trusted anyone, he trusted Steven.

Steven nodded his head, just once. "Thanks, but I just need a little time to decompress."

Silence fell for a few seconds before someone knocked on the door.

"Come in, Bella," Steven called before Diego had even caught her scent.

Bella opened the door, her gaze running over Steven before seeking out Diego. "Amy Jo needs you."

*Finally.* Damn it, Diego felt like a weight had lifted off his chest. As he headed for the door, he saw Marco bow his head over his drink, hands clenched around the glass.

And realized he was about to do something he couldn't turn back from.

"Marco, let's go."

His brother's head whipped up, his gaze startled. "What—"

"Just come, brother."

***

AMY JO DRANK the sweet-tasting liquid Andrea had brought her and knew there had been more than herbs and fruit juice in the glass.

Not alcohol but something... else.

*Well, you're not in South Carolina anymore, are you?*

Not by a long shot.

"So, the, uh, drink is...uh, magic?"

Andrea smiled that sphinx smile again and nodded, sitting on the bed and tucking the covers around her like she was her mother. The woman didn't look more than thirty, but there was something about her, something in her eyes that seemed much older.

"Yes, it is. A spell to calm you. Are you sure you don't want me to erase your memories, Amy Jo?"

Gosh, how easy would that be?

Too easy, really.

She'd never been a coward. She'd gotten through her life to this point, survived a brutal attack, became...something else, found a man who might actually want her even though she had probable mental problems.

And here she was huddled in a ball on a bed.

Well, fuck that.

She shook her head, swallowing the rest of the potion. "No. No, I don't. I want to do this on my own. I need to know I'm strong enough—"

"Not on your own."

She turned toward the door to see Diego and Marco walk through.

An emotion she refused to dissect hit her square in the chest. At least it displaced some of the fear.

Andrea rose from the bed. "Drink all of that and I'll check back with you later. I'll just go...do something somewhere else."

Jeez, that door should revolve.

"How do you feel?" Diego walked to the end of the bed, gripping the footboard so tightly his knuckles turned white. Marco leaned back against the door, arms crossed over his chest, his expression as set as Diego's.

Okay, how weird was it that she was glad they were both here? Shouldn't it be just a *little* weird, considering she'd spent the night tying Diego to this bed? Did Marco know? Why was he here?

Maybe it was better not to think about that. Instead, she asked, "Did you get the bastard?"

Diego nodded. "He won't harm anyone ever again. He gave us some leads, other names, before he was...disposed of. You'll never have to worry about him. We'll hunt the others down. They won't get away."

Another one of those weights lifted from her shoulders and she took a deep breath. Her eyelids dropped, closing out the room and the brothers.

"We won't let anyone ever harm you again," Diego said. "Don't. Don't shut us out, Amy Jo."

Funny, that "us" and "we" did strange things to her nerves and had nothing whatsoever to do with her memories of that horrible night.

"I'm not. It's just...for so many months, I've dreamed of making those men pay for what they did to me, of what I'd do to them." She opened her eyes and looked at Diego then Marco and back to Diego. "But if not for them, we wouldn't have met. And I'm glad we met."

Diego smile was blinding and Marco's actually mirrored his brother's. "Then I guess it's a good thing we want to keep you around."

---

"STEVEN?"

"Yeah?"

Bella cocked her head to the side, unable to get a read on him as he stood in the middle of the room, studying the empty glass in his hand. Avoiding her.

"Are you okay?"

As soon as she said the words, she cringed. It was a really fucking *stupid* question. Of course, he wasn't okay.

"Damn it, I'm sorry—"

"Bella. Stop." Finally, he looked at her and she was shocked to see he was clear-eyed and steady. She'd expected to find him shaken. Maybe a little scared.

As Barrasso and Weichelt started to work on Levanti, Steven had practically shoved her and Marco out of the room and up the stairs to Amy Jo.

Now, alone again, she didn't know what to say.

Steven set the glass on the closest table and closed the distance between them. Without hesitation, he wrapped his arms around her and pulled her against him.

Immediately, the *arus* in her blood rushed to meld with his. And surprisingly, he allowed it.

Before, he'd always been so careful to keep his magic from coming close to hers. As if he were afraid he'd contaminate her.

But the essence of her that was magical wanted more. She yearned for it. She wanted to be blood bound. Wanted to tie their souls together for all eternity through the exchange of blood during sex.

That dream had faded until she'd forced herself not to think about it in the past year.

Today, that dream made her heart pound and her *arus* sizzle and burn.

With a sigh, he tightened his arms around her and rested his forehead against hers. "Are *you* okay, Bella? Do you want to talk about it?"

Was he talking about him using his power or what had happened to Levanti? Did she want to talk about either?

She shook her head. "Not now." Later, she knew they'd have to, but not now.

Steven sighed. "Then we should go talk to Cole. He's probably making everyone crazy wondering where we are."

He was right. A week ago, she would've blown Cole off until she was damn good and ready to talk to him. Today she knew she couldn't do that.

Guess she'd grown up some.

"I know. Just—"

Fisting his hand in her hair, he pulled her head back and sealed his mouth over hers, sinking his tongue between her lips and sliding it around hers.

A wave of pure lust rose until she melted, arms tightening around him as he crushed her against his body. He hardened against her immediately, his erection pressing low on her stomach and setting her on fire.

She moaned, hands searching for the edge of his shirt so she could get under it to his bare skin.

Steven held her steady and kissed her. Hard and uncompromising. She felt only his desire for her in his kiss. No hesitation, no fear, no worry.

He kissed her like she'd dreamed he would.

And when he released her with an audible groan, she actually smiled.

"Later," she said. A promise. "Cole first."

———

"COLE LUPOREALE IS SAID to be up and about in the hotel. Daniel Levanti hasn't been seen since this late this morning."

Remo looked at Charles Jones, sitting across the meeting table. The lawyer hadn't looked happy when Remo had walked into Case and Jones' office, though Charles had put on a good show.

Charles liked to think he was autonomous down here, a thousand miles from Remo's home in New York City. Maybe Remo had given the man too much leash.

"Levanti served his purpose."

From the look on Charles' pale face, he'd caught Remo's unspoken meaning.

Charles wasn't a stupid man. His family had been loyal *Mal* for centuries but Charles had begun to show signs of independent thinking. Never a good thing in lawyers, Remo thought. Especially not one he controlled.

But he really should cut the man some slack. Jones was about to lose something very precious to him.

"And our target was not injured?"

Jones shook his head. "No."

Remo waited for Jones to continue but the man showed no indication that he knew of Castiglione's still-unexplained disappearance. Remo couldn't abide mysteries. And he'd solve this one just as soon as he obtained Castiglione.

Remo turned to the other person at the table. "Tiffani, my dear. Are you prepared for your role in the festivities?"

The blond beauty looked like every red-blooded male's version of the American Dream. The perfect accessory to hang on your arm and declare you'd reached the heights of power to afford someone like Tiffani.

Her personality... Well, that left something to be desired. Frankly speaking, she was a bitch, spoiled rotten and willful.

But Remo had a cure for that.

Even pouting, Tiffani managed to look like Sex Incarnate. "I've been ready, Mr. Paganelli." Then she smiled. "You know I'll assist you in any way I can."

Remo knew what she was up to. Bagging the leader of the *Mal* as her mate would be a coup not only for Tiffani but for her father. Unfortunately, the Joneses were about to find out their loyalty came with a high price.

Standing, Remo held out his hand to Tiffani and pulled her to her feet. "I'm glad to hear you say that."

Tightening his hand on hers, Remo made sure he had a firm grip before he began to chant the spell he'd created for this moment.

"Paganelli, what—" Jones cut off as Remo held up one hand to freeze the man in place with another, easier spell.

You didn't live for five hundred years and not pick up a few tricks.

"What the hell do you think you're doing?" Tiffani screeched, trying to twist away from Remo but having no luck. And when Remo pulled the small *pugio* from his suit pocket, she began to scream and struggle in earnest.

Good thing the conference room had been sound-proofed.

Lifting the small dagger, Remo slashed it across Tiffani's wrist. Releasing her, he smiled as she turned to run. He let her get as far as the door before he used another spell to pin her to the wall, immobile.

With her hands pinned at her sides, blood dripped to the floor in a steady crimson flow. She wouldn't bleed out, at least not yet. And he'd be done before that happened.

---

"I'M GOING to take a shower and check in with Amy Jo."

Steven watched Bella kiss her brother on the forehead then turn and walk to him.

Her dark eyes were serious and still a little worried as she put her arms around his shoulders and kissed him on the lips.

"You two be good. I'll be back in a little while."

With one more look at her brother, she walked out the door.

Steven stared after her for several seconds before Cole said, "Wanna tell me what you plan to do about my sister?"

Steven met Cole's surprisingly sharp gaze. No trace of pain.

"You look a lot better," Steven said. "How're you feeling?"

Cole's brows lifted. "I'm fine. Don't change the subject. What are you going to do about Bella?"

Steven didn't give himself time to think, which he was beginning to think was overrated. "I'm going to keep her. I never want to live through the hell of being without her again. Or without you."

Cole nodded, as if that was exactly what he'd expected to hear. "You know I wanted to take back the words the minute they left my mouth. We were standing by her bed and I kept hearing that damn heart monitor. Each time it beeped, it was like someone raking their nails over a chalk board. I got more and more angry. And then you said something. I don't even know what the hell you said anymore. But it was the last straw. I heard myself tell you to leave and never come back. I knew you felt responsible. I knew what I'd said would push you over the edge and you'd go. But my heart felt like someone had sliced it open. I wanted you to hurt as badly as I did. And I fucked us all over royally."

Steven leaned closer to the bed to grip Cole's shoulder. "I think there's enough blame to go around. Let's just agree to a private fight until we're bloody and can't stand when this is over."

"After we get through this."

Steven nodded. "After we get through this."

---

"MS. LUPOREALE, WE NEED TO TALK."

"Who is this?"

"We have a...shared interest."

The female's voice was unfamiliar and set Bella on her guard immediately. She was in her hotel room to change clothes. Steven was still with Cole. It seemed too much of a coincidence that this caller would be lucky enough to find her alone.

"And that would be...?"

"Steven Castiglione."

And weren't those the magic words to get her attention? "And you are?"

"Tiffani Jones."

Now the woman had her full and undivided attention as her laughter grated across the phone line. "I'm assuming from your silence that you know who I am."

Bella couldn't help her soft snort. "And *what* you are."

The bitch laughed, a twitty, high-pitched giggle that grated on Bella's nerves like sandpaper on rough wood. "Oh really? Honey, you have no idea."

Bella felt the hair on her neck lift and her *arus* began to bubble under her skin like lava. She wanted to snap her teeth and claw the woman's face to shreds. "What do you want, bitch?"

"Now, we all know who the real bitch is, don't we, little wolf." Tiffani sighed, the sound so false Bella had to catch back a growl. "Anyway, I guess I just called to gloat."

Bella's blood began to boil even as a cold pit opened in her stomach. She should hang up. She knew it, but she couldn't help thinking she might learn something about how the *Mal* planned to steal Steven away.

"I wouldn't start gloating just yet. Steven will never go to you willingly."

"He doesn't have to. Haven't you figured that out yet? Well, I'm sure I'll be seeing you soon, Arabella. Goodbye for now."

The phone fell silent and the only sound she could hear was her own too-fast breathing.

Anger, fear, jealousy. They all roiled in her stomach until she had to run for the bathroom, trying hard not to lose her lunch. She hated to be sick, hated the weakness that came with it. She didn't want to be weak.

When she finally had her stomach under control, she sat on the closed toilet, head in her hands.

Her first instinct was to go to Cole and Steven. But neither of them needed this added worry. Besides, she was pretty sure Tiffani Jones was merely trying to psych her out.

But what did the woman hope to gain from warning Bella? Just the thrill of taunting her?

The woman wouldn't be able to get into the hotel, not with so many *grigori* here. They'd sense her coming a mile away. And Bella wasn't foolish enough to leave the hotel without a guard.

Although...she was no coward. She was a gods-be-damned royal princess who shouldn't cower in her hotel room because that bitch had made her think too much.

*Well, shit.*

She looked at the clock on the bedside table. Three o'clock in the afternoon. Definitely time for happy hour.

And she was sick to death of this damn suit. She stripped it off and left it on the floor. Digging through her duffle, she grabbed a pair of denim shorts that barely covered her ass, a tight t-shirt with the words "Spoiled Rotten" in glittered script across the chest and a pair of well-worn Birkenstock flipflops.

*So* much better.

Pulling a pink Braves ball cap over her hair, she grabbed her room key and headed out into the hall.

"Hey, Luca."

Her *praetorian* took one look at her and raised his eyebrows. "Uh, hey, Bella."

She couldn't help it. She laughed. His expression was classic "Oh shit, what's she up to now?"

"Don't worry, Luca. I'm just going down to the bar. Is Steven still in with Cole?"

Luca actually sighed. "Yeah, Dori came out a few minutes ago then went back in. Said they were working on something."

They could keep their secrets for now. "Come on, Luca. I think we deserve a drink."

THE BAR WAS SURPRISINGLY EMPTY.

She and Luca took a booth in the back, away from the few other people sitting near the door. Bella nodded at the few familiar faces but didn't stop to talk. She was done with politics for the day. She didn't want to think about traitors or punishment or magic or the invitation to join the *boschetta* still hanging over her head.

She wanted a couple of margaritas, a never-ending plate of hot wings and a little peace.

A waitress took their order—soda for Luca—and then they sat there.

Luca was the first to break the silence. "Long day, Princess?"

She laughed, though there was no amusement in the sound. "You could say that. I don't think I'm cut out to be a politician."

"I think you did just fine."

She smiled at the handsome young man she really didn't know all that well. He was a year younger than she was but he'd worked his way through the ranks to *praetorian* already. As such, he was held in high esteem. "Thank you, Luca. But I certainly hope I never have to do that again."

Neither the meeting nor what had come after. She could still hear Levanti screaming in her head.

Closing her eyes, she took a deep breath and tried to release all the tension in her body on the exhale.

"Arabella Luporeale?"

She caught back a sigh and opened her eyes to find a beautiful blonde standing next to their table. The smiling woman held out her hand and Bella took it without thinking. "May I help you?"

"It's nice to finally meet you," the stranger said.

Bella frowned. Why did that voice sound so familiar? "Do we know each other?"

The other woman smiled but there was something funny about her face. Something about her eyes—

"No," the woman said, "and unfortunately for you, we won't be getting to know each other. But you can call me Tiffani."

*Oh shit.*

The air stilled then got heavy. And hot. So damn hot Bella felt like she was suffocating.

Reality shifted before her eyes. She heard Luca shouting, but he sounded so far away. She tried to release the other woman's hand, but Tiffani dug her nails in her skin and held on.

And then there was nothing but black.

# TWENTY

"What do you mean, she's gone?"

Steven tried to keep his voice down. He didn't want to upset Cole, still resting in the room behind him. But Luca wasn't making any sense.

When Luca had come to the door and asked to speak to him, Steven knew something was wrong from the man's expression. So he'd hustled him back into the hall.

"She just...disappeared." Luca's voice didn't exactly shake but Steven could tell the guy was shook up. "This woman... She just walked up to the table, shook Bella's hand and then they were gone. Just blinked away."

Steven felt fear zip through his blood stream like acid. "What did the woman look like?"

"Blond, pretty, mid-twenties. Blue eyes, about five-eight."

Steven felt that fear ratchet up a notch. Shit, it couldn't be. "Did she say her name?"

Luca nodded, his eyes still a little wild. "Her exact words were, 'We won't be spending much time together. But you can call me Tiffani.'"

Acid tore through Steven's veins, making his *arus* boil. He forced it down, forced back the fear, the fury, the raging desire to hit something. Those emotions were destructive. They wouldn't help him. He needed to be icy cold. Logical. He needed to think like a *Mal*. "And they both just disappeared?"

Luca nodded, his hands shaking as he ran them through his already disheveled hair. "*Vaffanculo*, it happened so damn fast I didn't have time to react. One second she was there, the next she was gone."

Could Tiffani truly have that much power and have hidden it so well for so long? The Tiffani he knew had been selfish and arrogant. And, he'd thought, harmless.

Had Luca seen Tiffani or was it more *Mal* trickery, a ploy to make Steven think...what? Did the *Mal* think they could discredit him with the *lucani*, with Cole?

And how the hell had she gotten into the hotel? After the shooting, Dorian had locked the building down as tight as a prison. No one went in or out without checking with the guards stationed on every door.

The only thing he knew for sure was that Tiffani had taken Bella to lure him out.

Fine, consider him lured. He'd make an even trade for her.

"Let's go, Luca. There's someone we need to see."

---

BELLA WOKE with the sense of falling.

Probably because she was.

She landed with a breath-stealing thud on a hard surface. She couldn't have dropped far, but still, it was a jolt.

Glancing around, she saw bare white walls, a mattress and a chair. She didn't see a door, not on the walls or the ceiling, which was at least fifteen feet above her.

She considered screaming for help, then figured why bother.

Besides, it was beneath her. And she refused to give the blond bitch the satisfaction of hearing her scream.

As if Bella had conjured her just by thinking about her, the blonde materialized in the corner, leaning back against the wall and smiling at her as if they were best friends.

"Hello again, Arabella. Feeling okay?"

Bella straightened her spine and willed herself to breathe normally. "Who the hell are you?"

The other woman smiled. "Just call me Tiffani. But I already told you that. The fall must have knocked you for a loop. So sorry."

Yeah, the bitch really looked sorry. Actually, she looked smug. And so damn confident it made Bella's heart stutter in her chest.

Didn't the woman know it wasn't smart to taunt a wolf? If Bella shifted, she could rip her throat out in seconds. But she'd have to shift first and those precious first moments of her change left her vulnerable. Of course, this woman would know that. Therefore the smug smile. *Fucking ugly cow.*

Bella rose to her full height and adopted the same lazy pose against the opposite wall, staring straight at the other woman. "So you're Tiffani Jones. I was expecting someone a little...thinner."

The woman's eyes narrowed the slightest bit but her smile widened, and not in a good way. "Ooh, you get a gold star. Very good, Arabella. Except, I'm not really Tiffani. Tiffani's been... replaced by a better model, so to speak."

Bella tried not to show her confusion but the woman wasn't making any sense. "What the hell are you talking about?"

The woman's expression got even more nasty. "How well do you know your mythology, little girl?"

*What the fuck?* "Well enough."

The other woman stood a little taller, throwing her

gorgeous blond hair over her shoulders, looking like a life-size Barbie doll. "I am *Impusa della Morte*, feared by all and rightly so."

Struck dumb, Bella could only stare at the woman. She'd been truthful when she'd said she knew her mythology well enough to know *Impusa della Morte* was an evil sorceress who the *Mal* worshipped like a goddess, though she wasn't a true deity.

According to legend, she was a *Mal strega,* a witch who'd been born *Mal.* She'd died more than a millennia ago, an avaricious soul who had rejected Aitás to stay on this plane of existence to guard her supposed treasure. Her services could be bought and apparently had been bought by the *Mal.*

Bella couldn't help the laughter that bubbled up at the woman's over-the-top performance. It helped to clear her mind of the fear and Bella crossed her arms over her chest and leaned back against the wall. "Wow. You sound like a bad Universal horror movie, lady. Who writes your script? John Waters? And what the hell do you want with me?"

Impusa, if it really was her, looked dumb-struck before her sneer returned. "Your only use to me is as bait."

Yeah, that's what Bella had been afraid of. "Steven's not stupid enough to fall for your tricks. And my brother will hunt you down and tear you apart."

Impusa's face twisted in a mockery of sympathy. "Poor little Arabella. Still relying on men to run your life? I would've thought you'd grown up by now. But at least your men do seem to love you. They'll come after you. And when they do...well, that's when the fun will start."

Bella refused to be afraid as Impusa stepped away from the wall. She would not cower, although anyone who could transport a person through the fabric of reality could probably stop Bella's heart just by looking at her.

"Steven is the one with true power," Impusa continued. "He's the one who will bring about change. You're nothing."

*Bullshit.* Bella had been asked to join Menrva's priestesses, an honor only thirteen women could boast about at a time. But this woman didn't know that. And she never would if Bella had anything to do about it. "Well, if I'm nothing, then you won't be able to turn Steven just because you threaten me."

Impusa snorted. "The man foolishly assumes he's in love with you. After the *Mal* kills you and turns him, he'll see how wrong he is."

Over her dead body. Which was a distinct possibility. "You'll never turn him. I'm not a defenseless child," Bella said, more for herself than Impusa. Then she smiled. "And you're not a goddess."

Ah, she'd hit a nerve. The bitch scowled and Bella tensed for an attack, which never came. Instead Impusa, or whoever the hell she was, turned her expression into a sneer. "Don't piss me off, child. You won't like the results. "

"You hurt me and you'll just piss Steven off."

A sly smile crossed Impusa's face. "That's what I'm hoping."

---

"I DON'T THINK she's home," Luca said. "We should go back, wait for Andrea and Serena to scrye for Arabella."

"I don't think they'll be able to find her and they can reach me on my cell if they do. Trust me, Luca. This is our best shot at finding Bella." Steven pounded on the door of the garden district house. "Alpena, open the door!"

He knew eventually she'd answer because he wasn't leaving until she did.

And, after three minutes, Alpena opened the door, a sour look on her face. "Hey, Steven. What's up?"

"Someone took Arabella."

Alpena's brows raised. "And...?"

"And I need you to help me find her."

She crossed her arms over her chest and leaned against the door frame. "Why would you think I'd help?"

Steven didn't let her indifference faze him. "Because I need you."

"And that matter's why...?"

"Because apparently you need me, too, and if anything happens to her, I'll be of no use to you because I'll get myself killed avenging her death."

Alpena smiled now. "Whoa, drama queen, slow down. Come on in." She gave Luca the once-over then waved him in with one tip of the wings she'd kept hidden behind her back, smiling when Luca gasped. "Both of you. I'll see what I can see."

---

BELLA DIDN'T KNOW how long she sat in the room. Since there were no windows, she couldn't gauge the time passing. The light—far enough overhead that she wouldn't be able to reach it—never flickered and no one reentered.

After sitting on the bed for a while and trying to think her way out, she decided that even though she couldn't see a door in the walls, that didn't mean there wasn't one.

Starting at the nearest corner, she used her hands to cover every inch of wall she could reach, searching for a seam. After she'd worked her way around to where she'd started, she admitted defeat.

Of course, this had to happen just when she'd decided to take charge of her life. And now she had to wait for someone to come rescue her.

Didn't that just suck?

---

"SO THE WOMAN who took your Bella, you think it was Charles Jones' daughter, Tiffani."

Steven nodded, watching Alpena settle onto the floor in front of a shallow pool set directly into the floor in one of the rooms off the seemingly endless main hallway.

Luca stood by the door, gaping at the *folletta*.

"From the description Luca provided, yes. But the power, I never got a hint of power from either Charles or Tiffani when I worked there." He grimaced and shook his head. "Obviously I missed it."

Alpena rolled her eyes as she hit a button next to the bowl, which began to fill with water. "Don't sweat it, big guy. You kept yourself from cracking all this time, that's what's important. But it may be that the Joneses don't have much power to begin with."

"Then how would Tiffani manage to get Bella out of there?"

"I don't think Tiffani's in her right mind at the moment."

"What the hell does that mean?"

Alpena huffed as she turned off the water. "Geez, you ask a lot of questions. What I mean is, I think the *Mal* may have called in *Impusa della Morte*."

Steven was too worried about Bella to dig through his own memories. "Who's that?"

"She's a fairy tale," Luca said. "The spirit of a *Mal strega* who refused to enter Aitás on her death and now walks the earth. She can inhabit the body of a living person at the moment of their death and keep the body for however long she wants."

Alpena threw a bright smile at Luca, making the poor kid blush like a teenager. "Ooh, I like smart guys. Very good, cutie.

You go to the front of the class. What you might not know is that she's worked for the *Mal* for centuries."

"Fine, it all makes senses," Steven said. "But I don't care. I just want Bella back."

"She won't harm your little wolf. Not her style." Alpena bent over the water and Steven felt the spell she was working brush against his *arus*. The water in the pool became cloudy, murky. "She's more of a manipulator. She took Tiffani's body because she knows you would go easier on a female than you would a man. And she won't hurt Bella until it will do the maximum damage to you. So you have a window of opportunity to get your wolf out alive."

Alpena closed her eyes and the level of power in the room increased a hundredfold, crawling along Steven's skin like thousands of tiny bugs. He rubbed his hands along his arms as the water cleared and Alpena opened her eyes.

"Damn, I hate being right."

"Where is she?" Steven demanded.

Alpena shook her head. "Not far. Impusa wants you to come for her. She wants *you*, Steven."

"Can you tell where she is?" Luca asked.

"Good question." Alpena stood and crooked a finger at Luca. "Come here, kid. I've got a use for you."

Alpena pushed open a section of the wall behind her and led them into a small room filled with maps.

A detailed map of New Orleans covered much of the floor.

Alpena gestured at the floor. "Do a seek spell. I guarantee Impusa won't make it that hard to find her."

Then the *folletta* crooked a wing tip at Steven. "You and I need to have a little talk."

BELLA HEARD a slight hissing pop and watched Impusa materialize out of thin air.

The look on the woman's face was hard to decipher. "Well, your so-called boyfriend seems to be uninterested in your disappearance. He's nowhere to be found."

Bella noted the pissed-off look on the other woman's face and decided against a smart remark as Impusa started to wear a path on the floor. "Where did he go?"

Sue her. She couldn't help herself. "Aren't you supposed to be the all-powerful one? Find out yourself."

With the flick of one finger, Impusa threw her off the bed and across the room, smashing into the wall and landing on the floor on her hip. She hadn't been ready for it and her body hit with a force strong enough to make her see stars.

"Sure you don't have an answer for me, little dog?"

*Bitch.* With the taste of her own blood on her tongue, Bella's wolf wanted to be let loose to rip out Impusa's heart with her teeth, a few of which now felt loose.

"You can toss me around all you want, but you won't get anything out of me."

Impusa snorted. "Except blood. You can lose an awful lot of that without dying. Something your brother knows a little about, hmm?"

Bella restrained herself from taking the bait. The bitch wanted her to come after her, but Bella wasn't going to give her the satisfaction. So she bit her tongue and rose to her feet.

Impusa's sneer ruined her beautiful face, which wasn't really her face, come to think of it. It was Charles Jones's daughter's. "Not going to play anymore?"

"Playtime is for children," Bella said. "Why don't you just tell me what the hell your deal is?"

"I want Steven," Impusa said. "He'll be a great asset to the *Mal* in the coming battle."

"What battle?"

"Foolish little Arabella. Haven't you noticed the world's changing around you? Why does it seem to be a scarier place all of a sudden? Maybe because it is." Impusa moved closer until she stood only inches away, an ugly sneer on her lips. "There's a war coming. Good, evil. Light, dark. It's going to be nasty and the players are already taking sides. You're on the losing side, dear. Because in the real world, the dark always wins."

Bella rolled her eyes. "Who writes your scripts? J.J. Abrams? Your kind no longer rules the world."

Impusa shrugged though her eyes narrowed to slits. "That doesn't matter. We only need a few persuasive men to further our cause. And when we're ready, we will rule the world."

Okay, even as "SyFy Channel" as that sounded, it *was* a little scary. The woman had a plan. And she wasn't working alone. She was working with the *Mal.*

Bella needed to keep the crazy woman talking, get more information. If she lived through this, her people needed to know as much as they could.

"Oh please." Bella's tone dripped with skepticism. "Now you're beginning to sound like a bad George Lucas sequel. So the *Mal* have a little power? That doesn't add up to revolution and overthrow of the free world."

Impusa merely shrugged. "Not from where you sit, no. But take my word...or don't. It doesn't really matter. There's a battle coming, one you and yours are going to lose because you play by the rules. Too bad not all of your trusted advisors play by the same rules."

Bella refused to let this creature get to her. "Did you shoot my brother?"

Impusa shook her head. "Guns have no class. But consider it a warning. A demonstration of how...vulnerable you really are."

Fury moved like liquid silver through Bella's veins but she

reined it in. She took a deep breath and tried to think. She needed to be smart, needed to have a plan for when Steven showed up. And he would.

Bella shook her head. "So, now what? We hang out and talk clothes until Steven gets here? 'Cause I gotta tell you, that shade of pink washes you out."

Impusa's gaze narrowed. "I've had more than enough of your mouth, Arabella. Time to show you just how much you really don't want to fuck with me."

Impusa crooked her index finger in Bella's direction and pain washed through her body like acid.

She barely realized Impusa was forcing her change until her skin erupted with fur.

Gods, no. This wasn't right. This change wasn't natural. Her body fought against Impusa's control and the battle tore her body in different directions.

Looking down, she realized her legs had changed into her wolf form but not her arms or her chest. Her face had elongated into the snout and her ears were pointed but nothing had finished.

She was caught between human and animal and she had the terrifying thought that Impusa was going to force her to stay like this forever.

She fought harder, struggled to make her body complete the change.

Her throat raw from screaming, she dug deep for one final burst of energy...

And everything went black.

———

LUCA'S SPELL gave them Bella's exact location.

Alpena had been right. Impusa hadn't made it difficult to find her.

He and Luca walked the few blocks from Alpena's to the location indicated by Luca's spell.

"I don't think this is a good idea." Luca stared at the unassuming house before them. "Help will be here soon. I'd rather wait a few minutes—"

"No time." And Steven already had a plan. "The *Mal* want me so I'm going to give them exactly what they want. The first chance you get, you take Arabella out of there."

The younger man looked at him, working out his meaning. "And leave you."

Steven nodded. "Yeah. If you have to knock her out to get her away, do it."

Luca continued to stare at him with cool, assessing gray eyes. "What are you planning?"

He shook his head, not wanting to give away his plan just yet. "Something I don't want Bella anywhere near. It could get...messy."

"Messy how?"

"How much do you know about what I can do?"

Luca's gaze narrowed. "I know you're a strong *fulminifex.* Other than that, not a lot."

"Ever seen the first 'X-Men' movie?"

Luca's eyebrows lifted. "Yeah?"

"You remember that scene near the end, at the Statue of Liberty, where Storm calls down the lightning and starts zapping the bad guys?"

The other man nodded.

"That's what I'm going for. Only, my control's not so good and the last time I attempted anything like this, I lost it and my mother died to save my life."

Luca's mouth dropped open. "Shit. *Shit*. That's not a plan, that's suicide."

He hoped not. Hell, he really hoped not but...

Steven walked to front door and read the runes carved into the lintel. They were disguised as decoration, but anyone with any shred of magic could see the dark power they held.

"Your only priority is Arabella, Luca. Don't worry about me."

Steven didn't bother to add, "I can take care of myself," because he wasn't sure it was true.

But he was fucking sick of running.

It was time to show the bitch who took Bella and the *Mal* she worked for what they wanted to see.

"So," Luca said, "you wanna knock or should I?"

The door opened before he could answer to reveal Tiffani Jones, smiling at him.

"Hello, Steven. So nice to see you again."

Gooseflesh covered his skin at the sound of her voice. It sounded like Tiffani but there was an undertone he'd never heard before. And her eyes... Her eyes were no longer human. They glowed red beneath the blue.

"Hello, Tiffani. Though I guess we really should stop the subterfuge and use your real name."

Impusa mock-shivered. "Ooh, subterfuge. Such a great lawerly word. And you are such a very good lawyer, aren't you, Steven? Too bad we're not in court because if we were, you'd be intimidate the hell out of a jury. But there's no jury here. You need to bargain with me to get your little bitch back."

He refused to let her digs get to him. "Bring her out. Let her leave with Luca."

"And what do I get in return?"

"Me."

The woman's eyes narrowed to slits. "Seems way too easy. What's the catch?"

Steven shook his head. "No catch. You let Arabella go and I'll stay. Then we'll see if you can keep me."

Impusa smiled. "Ah, I get it. A battle to the death. How romantic. Alright, big boy. Come on in while I gather your baggage."

Without hesitation, Steven walked into the house where the spirit of an ancient witch might just kill him.

Never a dull moment.

# TWENTY-ONE

Impusa would've dropped Bella's wolf at Steven's feet like dirty laundry if he hadn't been fast enough to catch her.

And now he *really* wanted to kill the bitch because Bella was out cold, her body slack and her breathing shallow and pained.

It took a hell of a blow to knock out a *versipellis*. He swallowed bitter anger as he gathered her close to his chest, his fingers stroking her soft pelt. But he refused to show that anger. He wouldn't give Impusa the satisfaction.

Trying to keep in check the emotion boiling in his blood, he turned to Luca and handed Bella to the younger man, dropping a quick kiss on her furry head before releasing her completely.

"Take her back to the hotel. Lock her in her room. If she wakes up before you get there, she's going to fight you. Knock her out before she realizes what's going on. Worry about how pissed off she's going to be later."

Luca looked him straight in the eyes. "Are you *sure*?"

Steven nodded. It was the only way. "Get out of here now, Luca. Just take her and go."

"Yes, take the little bitch and get out of my sight before I decide I'm not going to let either of you leave," Impusa added, drawing Steven's gaze back to her.

The vicious hate in her eyes chilled him to the bone. Behind him, he heard Luca back through the door. Taking Bella to safety.

"Why don't you have a seat, Steven?" She waved a hand at the beautifully furnished living room, a mocking grin on her face. "We're not animals, are we?"

With Bella out of the crossfire, he held Impusa's gaze without flinching and stood his ground. Letting the rage he'd been holding back for decades begin to filter through his system.

His nerve endings sizzled with the power. In the distance, he heard the rumble of thunder.

Impusa heard it too. She turned to the nearest window, a smile on her lips.

"Alright, little man. You want to play. Let's play. In the end, I'm sure you'll see things my way."

He was halfway across the room before he realized she'd thrown a blast of energy at him that flung him toward the wall. He hit with an audible crack, chunks of plaster falling around him.

Wincing at the ringing in his ears, he shook his head and stood, letting his own energy reverberate under his skin like an engine in a hot rod.

"I don't think it's going to be that easy," he replied. "Hope your homeowners' insurance is paid up because it was about to get messy."

Then he drew down the elements that called to him, beckoning him. Always.

And he let them have free rein.

BELLA WOKE to warm rain beating on her aching head. It felt good.

"Tinia's teat, Bella. I was afraid I was going to have to take you back to the hotel."

Luca's voice came from above her as he held her on his lap.

She stood, shaking herself, testing her bones for weakness or breaks.

She didn't seem to have any injuries.

But fear had crept in. Would she be able to change forms?

Closing her eyes, she focused inward, focused on her human form. At first, it seemed as if she couldn't find the power to make the change and the fear became an almost raging terror.

But she stomped it down with determination and tried again.

And nearly wept with joy when her body reverted to its true form.

Kneeling on the grassy earth, she stopped for a second to just breath. Then she took the shirt Luca had pulled over his head and was handing to her.

Looking around, she realized they were in a cemetery, one of the amazingly creepy, aboveground cemeteries New Orleans was known for.

Thunder rumbled overhead, lightning cracked... And she knew.

Fear cramped her stomach. "Gods, Luca, please don't tell me you left him alone?"

Luca's strong hands settled on her shoulders, holding her in place and she knew she wouldn't be able to get away unless she hurt him.

"He made me promise to get you out of there." Luca had to raise his voice to be heard over the storm, a fierce one by the sound of it. "But I knew you'd want to stay close. I already called Diego and he's on his way."

"We have to go back, Luca."

Luca shook his head. "He doesn't want you there, Bella. You'll distract him and he needs to concentrate—"

"Do you know what he's planning? Do you know what it could do to him?"

Luca glanced up at the angry gray sky then back to her, sympathy in his eyes. "Yeah, I know. It's his choice, Bella. I gave him my word I would keep you safe and out of it. Your safety is my only concern."

Gods, how could she make him understand?

She began to struggle against his hold, trying to find a weak spot without hurting him. She had to get back to Steven. But where the hell was he?

A lightning bolt struck a house down the street, showering sparks .

Showing her exactly where she needed to be.

---

STEVEN KNEW why his mother had trained him so relentlessly to control the darker emotions of rage and hunger.

They were so damn seductive.

The storm had rolled in almost immediately when he'd called it. The power in knowing he controlled the storm ran through his veins like supercharged adrenaline.

His body buzzed with electricity, blood pounding in time to the thunder outside. He knew he'd shocked Impusa with his frontal assault. The surprise on her face when the force of his magic hit her had made him smile. He'd laughed out loud when she hit the wall.

But when she rose and dusted herself off, he knew it wasn't going to be easy to best her. And he had to if he was going to end this once and for all.

"Did you think it would be that easy?" she sneered. "Nothing is ever as easy as it seems, boy. Especially when you're dealing with me."

She shoved a wall of air at him that lifted him off his feet and flung him twice as hard in the opposite direction. His head hit the wall again, making spots swim in front of his eyes. He got to his feet, but she immediately threw him like a rag doll up to the ceiling, bouncing him against the plaster and letting him drop to the floor.

His body, unused to this physical punishment, wanted to give up the battle right there. His knees buckled as he tried to stand and he decided to stay on his knees, play this up. His stomach rolled, threatening to toss its contents at the pain in his head and he didn't know if he could raise his left arm because that had taken the brunt of the fall to the floor.

Impusa came closer but still out of physical reach. "Does it hurt, Steven?" she cooed, as if talking to a child. "Your body wasn't made for physical pain. You've spent too much time behind a desk. Your father... Now, your father was a fine specimen."

She was baiting him. He knew it, yet couldn't stop himself. "You know nothing about him. Don't bother telling me your lies—"

Impusa tsked. "Such a tragedy, his death. Trying to save that young girl. Pity there really was no young girl to save. What you might not realize is that we've been planning this quite a long time, Steven."

He tried to shut out her words and prepare to take this fight to the next level. Now that he'd called the storm, he had to harness its power so he could knock this bitch into the last century. And if that failed... Well, maybe he'd get lucky and damage her enough that she'd have to kill him before he could kill her.

"Your poor mother, such a burden she carried all those years. And her family, so closely involved with the *Mal*. Makes you wonder, doesn't it?"

No, it didn't. Anything she said was suspect. His parents were dead. Killed because the *Mal* was evil.

What mattered now was that Bella was alive. He wanted to stay alive to love her but if he couldn't, well, he was taking this bitch with him.

The electricity in the air began to build, a huge static charge that made his hair stand on end.

Impusa didn't look impressed. In fact, she laughed. "I've done my homework, Steven. You don't have the training to harness the type of power you're playing with. And even if you did, you wouldn't be able to control it. If you try to strike at me, you might hit yourself. And you have something to live for, don't you?"

Yeah, he did. But he also had something to die for.

To a creature that didn't have to worry about mortality, she wouldn't know what that meant.

"I may not have the training." He continued to draw the electricity out of the air, to gather a charge. "But then I don't need training to channel the lightning. I just need to draw it to me."

And he did.

The bolt split through the roof and struck him in the shoulder. The shock to his system nearly knocked him out.

Vaguely, he felt chunks of plaster and wood fall around him, as did the rain through the gaping hole in the ceiling.

The electricity fought to get to the ground but he wrestled enough of it through his body to be able to direct it out at Impusa.

She hadn't been expecting it, hadn't thought he'd be able to pull it off, and took the shot of redirected energy directly in the chest.

He heard her scream and, through a nearly blinding sheet of pain, he watched her fly into the wall behind her, her body actually making a hole straight through.

Lightning trailed after her, coursing through her until her skin sizzled with energy.

He tried to hold steady, but the lightning decided it'd had enough of being directed and shot through him to the ground.

And then the pain started.

So much pain, the hair all over his body ached with it. His bones felt like they'd been set on fire and his skin felt as if it were stretched

And then everything went dark.

---

"HOLY SHIT," Luca said.

Bella struggled in his arms, trying to break his binding spell. "Release me, Luca. Now. Steven needs me."

She knew it with every particle of her being. He was in pain. She felt it as surely as she felt the binding spell locking her in place.

"Luca, please, let me go."

Her *praetorian* looked into her eyes and released her. She scrambled to her feet and bolted for the house.

The smell of ozone and charred wood burned her nose. She ran faster at the smell of smoke.

She heard Luca call for her, felt his presence behind her but she couldn't stop. She had a very real sense of déjà vu as she ran. She remembered the day her parents had been murdered. She'd run through the forest, knowing she needed to get to her parents, feeling an urgency she couldn't explain.

Today, she knew well what could be waiting for her at that house.

She couldn't lose Steven.

The house was on fire when she got there but she hit the door at a flat run and bounced back when it bowed but didn't break.

She threw herself against it again, frustration and fear beginning to gnaw at her. She didn't even realize she was screaming Steven's name until strong arms wrapped around her from behind.

"Bella, you're going to hurt yourself," Luca said. "Let me."

He moved her aside and smashed through the door with one well-placed kick near the lock.

"Steven!"

She ran into the house and into chaos. The front room had collapsed in on itself and flames licked at the walls even as rain fell through the hole in the ceiling. Bits of wood and paper and fabric floated in the air and the foul stench of burned things nearly made her retch.

"Steven!"

The framework of the house groaned around her and she heard Luca tell her to be careful.

She barely heard him. She had to get to Steven. He was in here and he needed her.

She called to him again and heard a faint groan from somewhere in the back of the room. Heading for the sound, she started throwing debris out of her way. Luca moved ahead of her, seemingly oblivious to the heat and the flames flaring around him.

They found him pinned beneath a beam, unmoving.

"No, no, no."

She heard the despair in her voice and had to force the fear away.

Blood ran from a gash on his head, so much it had stained most of the front of his shirt. But it was the blood running from his ears and the corners of his mouth that terrified her.

She dropped to her knees beside him but Luca was there before her. Before she could tell him not to, he lifted the beam off Steven so she could pull him out. Then Luca picked Steven off the floor as if he weighed nothing and turned to leave.

They were almost to the door when the building began to shake.

"Run, Bella, it's coming down!"

They ran, making it outside just as the house collapsed behind them.

Bella heard sirens getting closer, surprised the police and fire engines weren't here already. Luca didn't stop. He took off, away from the sirens.

"Bella, here. Quick." Luca stopped at a car on the street. "Open the door. Hurry."

Without checking to see if it was locked, she smashed her hand through the passenger-side window and opened the door. Climbing in the backseat, she helped Luca slide Steven's unmoving body into the car.

Luca practically ripped open the driver's side door to get in and placed his hand on steering wheel. With a muttered spell, the car started.

The first cop pulled around the corner as Luca floored it. Sirens blaring, he came after them. She didn't care. She ripped at Steven's clothing, a hand on his wrist. He'd gone so still.

And now she couldn't find a pulse.

"Bella, we'll be there in five minutes."

Someone screamed, a continuous wail. After a few seconds, she realized it was in her head. She couldn't think, could barely function. Steven was dying. She had to do something but she didn't know what, didn't know how.

No. She *did* know how. She *could* do this. She *had* to do this.

Houses whizzed by as Luca tried to lose the cop, still close enough that she could hear the squeal of tires behind them. She drew in a deep breath and shut it out. Shut everything out except Steven.

She couldn't lose him like this.

She wouldn't.

## TWENTY-TWO

Steven woke in a haze of pain so severe, he couldn't even cry out.

It was all he could do to keep conscious.

"Shh, Steven. Go back to sleep." Bella whispered in his ear, her voice soothing. "You need to rest."

He tried to shake his head, tried to make her understand. Wanted to tell her he loved her, in case he didn't wake again, but he couldn't form the words. All he could do was stare at her beautiful face and try to ride out the pain before it went dark again.

The next time he surfaced, the pain had receded to the point that he could speak.

"Bella."

"Hey, bro. Take it easy." Cole's voice this time, his hand almost too heavy on Steven's shoulder.

Steven turned his head toward the voice, groaning at the pain in that simple movement. "Bella?"

"Asleep. Right here." Cole pointed behind him but Steven couldn't bring himself to see that far. "Don't be an ass and wake her. She hasn't slept much the past two days."

"Two days?"

"Yeah, you did it up right." Cole's hand tightened on his shoulder for a few brief seconds, but Steven still felt the tremor running through him. "Don't fucking do it again. You scared the shit out of us, man. Your heart stopped twice after they got you back to the hotel." Cole turned his head to speak to someone behind him. "Go get Dr. Kent." Then Cole leveled his dark gaze back on him. "How do you feel?"

"Like...maybe dying would've been easier."

Cole's expression hardened. "If you weren't in such bad shape, I'd punch you for that. Don't *even* say that around Bella. She *will* hit you. That was a fucking stupid stunt, you idiot." He paused. "Did it work?"

Shit, he should have known Cole would figure it out. Still, he wasn't sure he wanted to own up to it yet. "Don't understand."

Cole shook his head. "Bullshit. I know what you tried to do. I'm not sure Bella realizes it yet, but when she does, you might wish you *had* died."

"I think...I think I'm still in shock. I'm not sure if I...drained all the power or not."

A yawn caught him by surprise and suddenly it was a struggle to keep his eyes open. But he had to know.

"What happened to Impusa?"

Cole expression went blank. Not good. "We're not sure."

*Shit.* "What does that mean?"

"It means when the firefighters made it into the house, they didn't find any bodies."

His eyelids felt like they had lead weights on them but he had to warn Cole, had to make sure he knew what was going on. "She'll be back, Cole. She's working with the *Mal*, using them for her own purposes. She'll try..." Damn, it was almost painful to keep his eyes open. "She'll..."

Cole's hand tightened on his shoulder again. "Go back to sleep, *ceffo*. We'll talk later."

---

"DIEGO, could I speak to you a moment?"

Sitting at a table in the hotel dining room, Diego pulled his attention away from Marco and Amy Jo, debating the merits of bacon over coffee as a morning essential, and lifted his gaze to Serena's.

He rose to greet her and saw Marco do the same.

"No, please, sit." Serena included Marco and Amy Jo in her smile. "I don't mean to interrupt your breakfast. I just need to talk to Diego for a few minutes."

"Of course." Diego rose, turning to look at Marco. His brother nodded, just once. Marco wouldn't leave Amy Jo's side. "I'll be back in a few."

When his gaze caught Amy Jo's, she smiled. It wasn't her normal, sunny smile but, considering this was the first time he and Marco had been able to coax her out of the bedroom, it was enough. For now.

He hoped to see it again soon. Then again, he might not be around to.

Following Serena to one of the conference rooms behind the reception desk, he shut the door then pulled out a chair for her to sit.

She smiled at him and waved him into a chair opposite her across the table. "Amy Jo seems to be doing well."

Diego nodded. "She's resilient." And so damn beautiful. "I believe she'll be fine."

"I am glad to hear that." Serena sighed. "I'm sure you've already figured out what I'm about to ask of you, Diego, and I understand why you might be anxious at this time to fulfill—"

"Serena." He held up one hand to stop her. "I understand where my duties lie."

Her smile flashed bittersweet then disappeared. "I know that, Diego. But I know how duty and honor and family obligation can sometimes screw up your life. So I have a plan that may suit all of us."

"I'm fully prepared to become Furia's *grigorio*."

For the past several years, the twins had been assigned a single *grigorio*. Maddie and Furia had lived here in New Orleans with Donal for years. For reasons only the twins and Serena knew, the girls couldn't or wouldn't be separated. Since Donal had been strong enough to protect them both, Diego's services as *grigorio* hadn't been needed.

Now that the curse was broken, he'd known eventually the twins would separate and Furia would need her own guardian since Maddie and Donal were practically mated.

Serena smiled. "I'm so glad to hear that. And I hope you'll be glad to hear that Furia will be moving back to Reading with me for the foreseeable future."

Now, that he hadn't expected. Reading wasn't far from Marco's home in Allentown and the *grigori* were based in Reading.

"As you know," Serena continued, "my home is huge. It has numerous bedrooms and two full suites that are unoccupied at the moment. Gabriel, Shea and Leo spend a lot of time there as well but there would be more than enough room for you and Amy Jo."

Gabriel was Serena's son and a *grigorio* who'd fallen for the woman who'd broken the curse on the *boschetta*. Diego had always gotten along well with Gabriel. Shea and Leo had been through their own personal hell and would be able to relate to Amy Jo.

"I believe the safety of my home would be an asset for Amy

Jo's continued recovery," Serena continued. "The acreage would allow her space to run and become more comfortable with her newly acquired abilities. And she would be close to the *lucani* and Arabella, as well."

Serena paused, as if trying to gauge his response to her proposal. "Or if you'd like, I'm sure we could find you—"

"I know this is a lot to ask but...would you mind if Marco moved in, as well?"

Serena's smile made a weight lift from his shoulders. "I would be pleased to have Marco. My home has been so lonely for so long. Having it filled again is wonderful."

"The Brady Bunch" theme began to run through Diego's head and he gave a short, sharp laugh.

He sincerely hoped Serena still had that sunny outlook once they all moved in.

***

WHEN STEVEN WOKE the next time, he saw sunlight lining the edges of the window drapes.

Experimentally, he shifted his jaw back and forth, relieved to find it didn't hurt. Actually, as far as he could tell, nothing hurt.

He sat up, taking it slow, the sheet sliding over his naked body. The pain was gone but he felt like he had a huge black hole in the center of his body. A dead, empty space.

He heard a faint movement to his right and turned to see Bella asleep in the bed next to his. In the pale light seeping beneath the curtains, he could tell she was deeply asleep, her face relaxed in utter exhaustion.

Swinging his legs over the side, he let his feet touch the carpet, testing his balance before he stood. It was only a couple of feet but he didn't want to embarrass himself by needing someone to lift him off the floor.

Cool air brushed his naked skin and raised goosebumps. The air conditioning was way too damn high.

Carefully, he crossed to her bed and slid between the sheets, turning her on her side, so he could mold his cool skin to her warm body.

He pulled her into him, her back to his front. He needed to hold her. Arms tight around her, he knew instinctively only she could fill the hole in his chest.

Sighing, she burrowed back against him, rubbing her perfect ass against his stirring cock. He couldn't believe he could get a hard-on after everything his body had been through. At least it still worked.

"How are you feeling?" Her voice sounded husky with sleep as she ran her fingernails along his arm, bringing his body to full arousal.

His arms tightened around her, emotion surging. "Surprisingly better."

He could practically hear her smile, though her body was still tense against him. "Yeah, I can feel that for myself. But really, Steven, how do you feel?"

He thought about her question, knowing exactly what she was asking. "I feel...empty inside. Like there's a part of me missing."

She went still. "Is your magic gone?"

Ah, the sixty-four-thousand-dollar question. Frankly, he was a little afraid to dig around in there and find out.

When he didn't answer, she turned in his arms, trapping his erection between their bodies. He wondered what she'd do if he shifted her up just a little...

She looked into his eyes, hers filled with questions and tears. "That was a really stupid thing to do, Steven. And don't think I won't make you pay for it later. You nearly killed yourself. How could you do that to me?"

Now, there was his spoiled beauty. He wouldn't have her any other way. He pulled her up so he could look straight into her eyes. Just good fortune that his erection now nestled between her legs.

"I didn't want to die, Bella. I don't want to leave you." He pulled her even closer. "Hell, I won't, not ever again. Remember that choice Turan talked about? I thought it meant I'd have to choose between you and my life. But that wasn't it. The choice was choosing you over death."

Her mouth dropped open before she said anything, shock evident on her pretty face. "What does that mean?"

"It means I'm not leaving you. Not again. If the job's still open, I'll take Cole up on his offer to join the inner sanctum. He's going to need help. I'm a damn good lawyer, babe. I can make a grown man cry in less than five minutes on the stand. And I know you're planning to join the *boschetta* so you're going to need protection."

Her eyes widened. "You know that, do you?"

"I know *you*, Bella. I know how very much you want to be useful."

She nodded, eyes welling with tears. "I want to make a difference."

"And you will make a damn fine priestess. And I'll be right there with you. You get into too damn much trouble when I'm not around."

Her lips tilted in a small smile. She was starting to relax, her face losing that pinched look. "*I* get into too much trouble? You're the one being hounded by an ancient evil spirit." She frowned again. "Who's nowhere to be found, by the way. Steven—"

"Shh, Bella." He smoothed the hair from her face then let

his fingers sink into the curls and cup her head. "We'll find her. She won't be able to stay hidden forever."

That just made her frown deepen. "And what happens when she comes for you again?"

He shook his head. "I don't think she will. Without my magic, I'm of no use to the *Mal*. But my father was a *grigorio* and I will protect you to the ends of the earth."

It took a few seconds but finally her smile emerged as she linked her arms around his neck, stretching her body against his and sliding her smooth calf along his thigh. It wouldn't take much to thrust into her. His erection strained toward her, brushing the short, soft curls on her mound, making his breath catch in his chest. "Well, I'm sure I can find a few uses for you."

Damn, he really wished she would.

Then she sighed and removed her leg. "We should probably get up and get ready—"

"Honey, I am up. And more than ready."

Flipping her onto her back, he spread her legs with his knees, lifted her hips and sank into her with one smooth push.

Her tight sheath surrounded him, sending sharp blades of heat from his head to his toes.

Groaning, he rested his forehead against hers and stilled, letting the warmth of her body surround him, the heat of emotion making his blood heat and his cock throb.

"I love you, *Bella mia*."

Her arms and legs wrapped around his body and held him close, her skin smooth against his.

When she placed her lips just beneath his ear and kissed him—sharp, stinging little kisses that made sweat slicken his skin —he started to sweat. And when she ran her tongue along his jaw, his restraint broke.

His hips thrust and retreat in an ever-quickening motion as his mouth fastened over hers. Their tongues dueled as their bodies moved together in a rhythm they'd perfected so many years ago and had never lost.

Unable and unwilling to slow, he let his body dictate the pace, feeling her climax build in the tightening of her arms and legs around him and her short, sharp gasps. And when she came, her sex clasping around him, her hips pressed into his, he felt the wash of her *arus* flow over and into him, settling into his soul, filling that empty space and pushing him into his own orgasm.

"You know I love you, Bella," he whispered when he had enough breath. "That I can't live without you and I don't want to."

"You don't have to, love." She tightened her arms around him. "Not ever."

# EPILOGUE

"You have no idea what happened to Impusa?"

"No, sir. She's disappeared."

Remo sighed. "And Steven?"

Peter hesitated and Remo knew he wasn't going to like this answer either. "We're not sure. There were reports that he was taken out of the building and died later but we can't confirm."

Well, shit. Remo hated losing.

Time to regroup.

And to break a promise.

---

BUT WAIT! There's more to discover in the Etruscan Magic world.

Check out the Magical Seduction and Lucani Lovers series.

And be sure to sign up for Stephanie Julian's newsletter at her website at www.stephaniejulian.com.

# GLOSSARY

Aitás – Underworld

*Arus* – magical power inherent in the races of Etruscan descent

Attonitum – looks like a cross between a revolver and an inoculation gun and would be useless in the hand of an *eteri*, a regular human. The iron grip warms to the touch, while the quartz crystal concentration chamber pulses with a pale pink light. The solid copper barrel focuses the magic.

Blood Bound – An ancient tradition tying two souls and their fates together for all eternity by mingling blood during sex.

*Boschetta* – a group of thirteen *streghe*

*Enu* – humans of magical Etruscan descent

*Eteri* – Etruscan for foreigner, used to describe regular humans

*Fata* – mythical beings of magical Etruscan descent such as *folletti* (fairies) and *linchetti* (night elves)

Goddess Gift – magical abilities including but not restricted to scrying, healing, far-seeing, affinities to herbs and crystals

*Grigorio* – a male born with enhanced senses and strength and an affinity to metal; in ancient times, the *grigori* were warrior priests and guardians of the Etruscan race; they were thought to have died out

*Involuti* – Founding gods of the Etruscans, those from whom all other Etruscan deities are descended

*Lucani* – Etruscan werewolves; they form the Etruscan army, based on the ancient Roman Legion

Priestesses of Menrva's – originally a group of thirteen unmarried women who pledged their lives to the Etruscan Menrva, Goddess of Wisdom, and kept safe her most sacred gift to the Etruscans, the twelve Nails of the Ages; through the centuries, they handed down their duties to their nearest living female relatives

*Strega* – (plural *streghe*) Female of Etruscan descent endowed with Goddess Gifts

*Stregone* – Male of Etruscan descent endowed with Goddess Gifts

*Salvanelli* – one of the races of the Etruscan Fata, thought to be extinct

*Versipellis* – literally "skin shifter," shapeshifters including Etruscan *lucani*, Norse *berkserkir* (bears) and French *loup garou* (wolves)

# ALSO BY STEPHANIE JULIAN

## DARKLY ENCHANTED

Spell Bound

Moon Bound

## REDTAILS HOCKEY

The Brick Wall

The Grinder

The Enforcer

The Instigator

The Playboy

The D-Man

The Machine

## FAST ICE

Bylines & Blue Lines

## INDECENT

An Indecent Proposition

An Indecent Affair

An Indecent Arrangement

An Indecent Longing

An Indecent Desire

## SALON GAMES

Invite Me In

Reserve My Nights

Expose My Desire

Keep My Secrets

Rock My Heart

LOVERS UNDERCOVER

Lovers & Lies

Sinners & Secrets

Beauty & Brains

Thieves & Thrills

# ABOUT THE AUTHOR

Stephanie Julian is a USA Today and New York Times best-selling author of contemporary and paranormal romance.
Stay in touch for all new releases and sales. Sign up here.